Praise for Jillian Hart
and her novels

"This poignant family story will restore
your hope during the cold winter months."
—*RT Book Reviews* on *Holiday Homecoming*

"Jillian Hart's *A Soldier for Christmas*
is a finely written romance."
—*RT Book Reviews*

"It's a pleasure to read
this achingly tender story."
—*RT Book Reviews* on *Her Wedding Wish*

"A heartwarming story
with likable characters."
—*RT Book Reviews* on *His Country Girl*

JILLIAN HART
Holiday Homecoming

❦

A Soldier for Christmas

Love Inspired

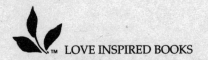 LOVE INSPIRED BOOKS

ISBN-13: 978-0-373-65149-8

HOLIDAY HOMECOMING AND A SOLDIER FOR CHRISTMAS

CONTENTS

Books by Jillian Hart

JILLIAN HART

grew up on her family's homestead, where she helped raise cattle, rode horses and scribbled stories in her spare time. After earning her English degree from Whitman College, she worked in travel and advertising before selling her first novel. When Jillian isn't working on her next story, she can be found puttering in her rose garden, curled up with a good book or spending quiet evenings at home with her family.

HOLIDAY HOMECOMING

These are the things that will endure—faith, hope,
and love—and the greatest of these is love.
—1 *Corinthians* 13:13

Chapter One

November 23

Disaster.

Kristin McKaslin took one look at the snow-caked airplane window and groaned. She was doomed. That window had been only a little bit icy less than twenty minutes ago, when she'd looked up from her work. Now she couldn't see through it, not that there was anything to see at this altitude and with the plane swinging in the turbulence.

At least it gave her something to think about other than heading home to Montana. Thanksgiving was tomorrow, and that was both good and bad. She loved her sisters. She loved her parents. She loved going home to visit.

What she wasn't looking forward to was facing her mother's disappointments. She lived too far away. She didn't come home to visit enough. She wasn't married. *And* she wasn't married. Mom was doubly unhappy about that one.

Just because she wasn't married, it didn't mean she was a failure, right?

Right. So, why did it feel that way? And why was it such a big deal? A marriage certificate came with no guarantees, and as far as she could tell, it didn't protect a person against heartbreak, disappointment and loneliness.

It wasn't as if Mom and Dad were ecstatic in their nearly forty years of marriage. But it wasn't as if she could say that to Mom. She hated pretending, as if nothing had changed in their family, when everything had.

That was the real reason she didn't want to walk through the front door of her childhood home. It was too painful to think about.

"Kristin McKaslin, is that you?"

She studied the well-dressed man who sank into the empty seat across the aisle. He was good-looking with disheveled black hair and eyes a sharp aquamarine blue. He had a straight blade of a nose, high cheekbones and dimples cut into his cheeks. He was dressed in a casual outfit that shouted, "Money!"

Nope, she didn't know him, but wait, there *was* something familiar about him. But what?

She didn't know him from work, the gym or church—either in Seattle or in Montana. Still, there was *something* distinctive about that devastating smile, those dimples…and that strong jaw.

Of course! She saw a flash of a boyish face with longer black hair standing before the podium at a high-school assembly. The image of a leaner, younger star running back whipping off his helmet after the final touchdown for the state championship. The caustic face of her mom's best friend's son, who wanted to be anywhere but stuck waiting in the car while their mothers talked on the sidewalk in town.

"Ryan Sanders?" She couldn't believe it. She blinked, and the remembered youthful image of his face blended with the older, wiser one staring back at her across the aisle. "It *is* you."

"The one and only. I look different, I know, everybody says so. I went and got respectable."

"You were always respectable."

"Nope, I wasn't. You're just being nice." His cute lopsided grin had matured into a slow curve of a smile. "You look better, but the same. Still have your nose in a book."

"Guilty. I confess."

Those blue eyes, which could have been cold, sparkled. "That's how I recognized you."

"I'm surprised you could see me over the seats. I'm still short."

"The word is 'petite.' I was bored and people-watching and I could see your profile from way back there. I got the last seat on the plane I think."

"Waited until the last minute?"

"I didn't think I'd be flying out of Seattle. Hey, you cut your hair. It was always long. Hiding your face. It still does, even short." He reached across the aisle to touch the curled end of her chin-length hair.

She felt a jolt, like the snap of static shock, as the lock of hair rebounded against her jaw. What was that? And should she act as if she *hadn't* felt it? "Your hair's shorter, too."

"It goes with my more reputable image." He shrugged one dependable shoulder.

Yeah, he looked reputable, all right, decked out in a loose-knit black sweater that hugged the lean curves of his muscled shoulders and chest. Black trousers, crisply pleated, completed the image.

He could be a corporate heavyweight, with a stuffy MBA and an impressive portfolio. Except for the black boots, scuffed and rugged, showing there was still a part of the Montana boy in the polished, educated man.

He raked his hand through his short, unruly black locks and leaned into the corner of the seat. A big powerful man, sprawled out like a kid, his large feet crossed at the ankles in the aisle.

"So, what's a pretty girl like you doing with a laptop and a book at—" he glanced at the gold flash of his Rolex "—9:07 at night?"

"Working."

"Yeah? I remembered you were studious in high school. What did the valedictorian of Valley High grow up to be?"

"An advertising executive."

"Well done. You live in Seattle?"

"I do. Not a hard guess, since the flight originated there. You, too?"

"Nope, just up checking out a job offer." Less comfortable talking about that, he hauled his feet in from the aisle and sat up straight. Too late to change the subject. It wasn't pretty Kristin McKaslin's fault his life was messed up.

Okay, it wasn't a mess *yet,* but it wasn't the fit he wanted, either. He'd become a successful doctor. It just didn't feel right to him. And after the breakup with Francine—

"Wow, a job offer." Kristin was even prettier when she smiled. "Who in their right mind would hire you?"

"Right. I'm suspicious of their offer right up front." They'd been good people, that's what. Professional, smart, with a good, positive focus. Not at all like the profit-oriented outfit he was stuck with in Scottsdale. "What kind of dudes are they, if they want me to join up with 'em?"

"Smart ones. Are you gonna go for it?"

A loaded question, but his problems weren't Kristin's, so he'd leave out the personal stuff. "Not sure about what I'm gonna do. I'm looking for a change. I have a great practice, but Phoenix is a little hot for me in the summers. Still, I suppose that's why air-conditioning was invented."

"Your practice? Oh, wait. I remember something about you getting into medical school long ago. Knowing you, that *couldn't* be true."

"Hard to believe they actually took a no-account like me."

"For a jock, you weren't *too* dumb. Guess how hard I had to study to beat your GPA?"

"Hard? Good, cuz I worked my toes off and I couldn't get half as many one hundred percents as you did."

She sparkled, but not in the way of women who realized he was a single man *and* a doctor. No, she was quiet class, all the way from her polished brown loafers to the carefully folded neck of her sort-of-brown turtleneck. Warm, though, not stuffy.

Her voice was soft elegance. "What kind of doctor are you?"

"An orthopedic surgeon."

"Sure, you have the ego for it."

"Hey, I don't deserve that. Okay, maybe I do. But I like helping people. Fixing their blown-out knees and torn ankles. What about you? An advertising exec, huh? Does that mean you're a big shot in the advertising world?"

"Yeah, right. I make sure the agency runs without a hitch. It's a good job but not very glamorous."

"I can see you, diligent and kind and handling everything just right."

"Same old Ryan, charming and full of it. Some things never change."

"Don't they? Back in school you were too high and mighty for me."

"High and mighty?"

"One of the perfect McKaslin girls."

"Perfect, my foot! Good grief, I'm a mess. A walking disaster."

"Yeah, uh-huh. You sure look like it." He rolled his eyes to emphasize his point. Ryan didn't think there could be a nicer family of women on the planet.

Part of the McKaslin genes, he figured. With Kristin, there was no mistaking her girl-next-door freshness, even in her power suit.

What kind of executive did she make? One who said please and thank-you, was his guess, and it clashed with the ice-princess high-end designer jacket, sweater and slacks she wore.

Maybe he'd lived in a big city for too long. Whoa—that thought was something his mom would say. Not for the first time tonight he wished he'd paid for his mom to come down for Thanksgiving. Montana came with too many lessons learned. Lessons that haunted him to this day.

"It's weird seeing you like this. On the same plane heading home." It blew his mind, that's what, because he didn't believe in coincidences. All things happened for a reason.

"I haven't seen you since, what, high school?"

"When I left for college, I left for good. I keep trying to lure Mom to Phoenix, but she won't do it. She calls every Sunday afternoon, after church. To make sure I've gone to worship like a good son."

"Good. You need someone to keep you in line. I've lost track of nearly everyone. It's weird how in school we had all the time in the world, our future ahead of us, and now that we're in the middle of those futures, there's no time at all."

"Exactly. Now I put in long hours. I've got no time."

"What? You're a doctor. Why are you working long days? Don't you people golf on Tuesdays and Fridays?"

"Some do. I have school loans to make good on, and the balance is higher than most people's mortgages."

"Ouch. I'm glad I worked my way through school."

He crooked a doubtful eyebrow. "Worked? Didn't you get the only four-year scholarship in our graduating class?"

"Yeah, but that was for tuition. I had a part-time job in the university library on the weekends, and I worked during the summers."

"I was volunteering in clinics and did a year in the Peace Corps so I had a better shot at med school."

"I've heard medical school isn't all that competitive."

That made him laugh. "Yeah. I spent a year in the Dominican Republic assisting a physician. That year did more to make a man of me than anything. I hope it made me a much better doctor."

"I can't imagine you're a bad one. Arrogant, maybe."

"Hey!" He laughed with her. He liked her, he

couldn't help it. But seeing her reminded him of a time in his life that was complicated. "It's good to see you. I'm glad you're doing well."

"You, too." Kristin closed the laptop and focused her full attention on Ryan Sanders. Dr. Ryan Sanders. That was going to take some getting used to. She could still see the spirited young boy inside the responsible man.

Not that she was interested. So she'd noticed that his left hand was suntanned and ringless. He'd made the effort of renewing their acquaintance. He'd been so complimentary and friendly. Why was she even thinking in this direction?

Doom. Disaster. She'd never wanted a relationship. She would never lean on a man. She was fine all by herself, even if that got lonely sometimes.

"Here comes the beverage cart. I'd better get back to my seat now or I'll be trapped here." He rose, all six feet plus of him, filling the aisle. "Maybe I'll see you around town?"

"Maybe. If I see you on the sidewalk, I won't run in the opposite direction."

"Deal. I'll try not to run into a store and hide from ya."

And he was gone, ambling down the aisle.

Ryan Sanders. He filled her thoughts as she opened the three-ring binder and flipped up the laptop's screen. Imagine that, running into him. Had she even heard much about Ryan over the years?

No, just comments from Mom now and then on

how Mary's son had straightened out his life. Finally. And how Mary was lonely for him.

Wasn't loneliness an integral part of life? Troubled, Kristin tried to concentrate on the Myers budget and couldn't. The numbers on the screen fuzzed, and she rubbed her tired eyes.

Father, I don't want to go home. Guilt warred with the other emotions coiling up in her stomach. *What do I do?*

She couldn't disappoint her mom. Mom had been pressuring her since Labor Day, to make sure Kristin would come home. What did you do when home was no longer a refuge? A place that hurt instead of sheltered?

A sharp pain slashed like a razor in her stomach and had her digging through her bag for the roll of antacids she ate like candy. She loved her parents. She loved her sisters.

But all her girlhood illusions of family had died along with Allison. Time had not mended the broken places in her heart or in her family.

How could she go home and pretend nothing was wrong?

She *wanted* to see her sisters. Hold her newest niece, Anna, who'd been born in late summer. Gramma would be there. She wanted to see her parents.

If only there was a way to come home without the pain and sadness...

The plane dipped sharply to the left, and fear

shattered her thoughts. She gripped the armrest. Was her heart really beating that fast? She took a deep breath, her chest pounding. What was wrong? She *hated* flying. Absolutely hated it.

What if it was engine trouble? Ice had crusted over the little window next to her. What if there was a problem with ice or something? She tried not to think of horror stories of air disasters. *This* was how Allison had died, in a plane crash in bad weather.

"Attention, passengers, this is your captain speaking."

Kristin's ears popped. Were they losing altitude? Before she could unscramble her thoughts to pray, the pilot continued speaking. "There's a blizzard in Missoula so we're diverting to Boise International."

A blizzard? That was all? They weren't going to crash? Relief slid through her like ice water. *Thank you, Lord.* She clutched the small cross at her neck. That was the good news, but a blizzard? What blizzard?

Sure, it was snowing, but the weatherpeople had promised the snow would be light. Okay, so it wouldn't be the first time a weatherman was wrong, and this *was* Montana. Extreme weather happened. But Boise?

Going home might not be the easiest thing, but she missed her sisters. She didn't want to spend Thanksgiving alone.

See? She would have been better off driving, with snow forecasted or not! There was that Murphy's

Law in effect again. Whatever would turn out worse, she had a habit of picking it.

This will work out for the best. She took a deep breath, willed her tensed muscles to unclench just a little. *Right, Lord?*

Right. Everything happened as it was meant to be. So this was simply a safer route than if she'd driven over the pass and right into the blizzard. By going to Boise, they were going around the storm. It made sense.

She'd just catch a flight when she got to Boise. Surely there would be a few vacant seats somewhere on a late-night flight to Bozeman.

And if not, she'd just rent a car and drive. The blizzard was in the other direction, right?

Thanksgiving

Wrong. The flights had been canceled. The Boise airport was closing down due to the rapidly approaching surprise storm. The blizzard was bringing dangerous conditions to half the cities in northern Idaho and to all of midwestern Montana.

Great. And if that wasn't bad enough, there wasn't a car left to rent in all of Boise. Kristin ought to know. She'd called every place that would answer their phone at 12:06 on Thanksgiving morning.

There were no hotel vacancies, no motel vacancies and the local bed-and-breakfasts weren't picking up.

Definitely a problem. Kristin buttoned her coat

and stared at her reflection in the black windows of the airport terminal. What was she going to do? Fat chunks of snow floated to the white ground on the other side of the glass where a single taxi waited along a vacant curb.

No passengers rushed from baggage claim or hurried to make that last-minute flight. She was practically alone and the security guards were eyeing her suspiciously. The swish of a janitor's wide mop seemed loud in the echoing silence.

It looked as if she would miss Thanksgiving at home.

No sisters. No baby niece to hug close. No roasted turkey with Gramma's special stuffing.

On the other hand, she wouldn't have to face Allison's empty place at the table.

But not seeing *any* of her sisters... Her chest ached with sadness. How could she be sad at completely opposite things at once?

So, she'd spend this holiday alone. She lived alone. She spent lots of weekends alone. She was used to it.

Still, loneliness grabbed hard and squeezed. For as much as she dreaded some things, she missed others very much. The way Mom always greeted her at the door, wearing her apron and opening her arms wide for a hug.

The big country kitchen would be warm with the delicious fragrances of roasting turkey and baking bread and desserts set out to cool on the counter.

Her sisters laughing and quibbling while her nieces and nephew toddled around the living room, and everyone turning to shout, "It's Kristin. Kristin's here!"

Exhausted from starting work at six o'clock this morning so she could leave early for the airport, she was too tired even to pray. Aching with despair, she buried her face in her hands.

Chapter Two

If that wasn't a sign from above, Ryan didn't know what was. He'd stood in line at one car-rental place after another. No rental cars. The passengers had dispersed; he detoured to baggage claim and was stunned to see his suitcase circling. He had the worst luck *ever* when it came to airport baggage.

Yup, it was a sign. This attempted trip home wasn't over yet. Okay, he was going to give the rental counters one more try. If there were no cars, then he'd done all he could. It looked as if he *wouldn't* be going home for Thanksgiving.

But he couldn't be that lucky. He was probably the only human being on the continent who was hoping to head *away* from home.

Of course, there was a last-minute cancellation and an SUV with four-wheel drive just happened to be available—the only car left for rent in the entire city. Providence had spoken. Ryan Sanders was going to spend Thanksgiving with his family. No excuses, no exceptions. He might as well accept it and make the best of it.

It would mean a lot to Mom. That's what mattered, at least telling himself that gave him enough grit to accept his fate. He loved his mom, he loved his sister, but he didn't miss Montana. He wanted to put that part of his life away and lock the door tight. Throw the key in a deep well and cover it up. For good. There were some places too painful to go, like the past.

That's why he believed in going full steam ahead. Why he never looked back. Why he wasn't thrilled as he loaded up the Jeep and flipped the defroster on high. The Good Lord was making His will pretty clear in spite of the weather. The snowstorm was working up into a blizzard on the other side of the snowy windshield. The wipers couldn't keep up.

Great, how was he going to see where he was going? Ryan squinted into the dizzying downfall but it didn't help. He couldn't read the directional signs through the whiteout conditions. Should he go left or right?

Clueless, he went left. He barely touched the brake and the tires did a little skid on the ice. Talk about dangerous conditions. He was a decent driver, but there was no sense in putting himself or anyone else at risk. A fair amount of his practice was comprised of car-accident victims. He'd done enough rotation time in the E.R. to know what could happen.

Maybe the wisest thing to do was hunt down a

hotel room *somewhere*. Boise was crammed full of stranded travelers who'd booked every available room for the holiday weekend. He knew because he'd spent forty straight minutes on the phone. But maybe there was something available farther down the road, in one of the little towns a few miles north. He'd drive until he found a motel room—he wasn't picky. He was too tired to drive on icy highways until dawn.

Okay, where had the road gone? It had to be somewhere in front of him. There was a metal post, good thing he didn't hit it. Wait—a soft glow of light broke through the blizzard.

Perfect. He was headed the wrong way. The snow thinned on the lee side of the terminal as he crept through the empty passenger-loading zone. There was only a lonely taxi waiting alongside the curb with lights blinking. It was quickly being covered by snowfall.

Light from the terminal broke through the downfall to sheen on the road ahead of him and that's when he saw her in his peripheral vision. Kristin McKaslin in her chic tan coat and designer clothes, sitting with her head in her hands, alone behind the long wall of windows.

She was stranded, too. And all by herself. That just wasn't right. He eased the vehicle to the curb with a bump. No way was he going to let her sit there. Not when Providence had handed him a four-wheel drive and, like it or not, he was still heading home.

Through the glass, backlit by fluorescent light, he could see her perfectly, with that short golden bob of her hair falling forward as she sat. He could feel her misery.

Yet although she looked every bit the stranded traveler, Kristin McKaslin was still the picture of perfection in her upscale clothes and her every-hair-in-place do.

It must be nice to have a life like hers. He tried not to hold it against her, and the old envy surprised him. It wasn't exactly envy, but it was close. As a boy growing up, he'd gotten an eyeful of the McKaslins' storybook life via his mom. He saw the Thomas Kinkade-like coziness of the house she'd grown up in, heard endlessly from Mom how the McKaslin girls never gave their mother any grief the way he did. As a kid, his own inadequacies hurt and he was ashamed of them, so he did his best to cover them up with bravado and stupid recklessness.

He'd grown up, tried hard to be a good man. But some things didn't change—like the truth in a man's heart. He'd wanted *that* life. To live in a warm and roomy house with a whole family, instead of in a cramped, tumbling down house with a widowed mom who worked three jobs to keep food on the table. He'd never been able to come to terms with his father's death. Or the simple fact that Mom's life would have been without hardship and he would have grown up differently if his dad had been there.

Maybe—just maybe—his heart would be whole if tragedy hadn't struck.

Let the past go, man. Sometimes it was the only thing he could do. Instead of reexamining a past he couldn't fix, it was better just to do the best he could now, in the moment. And that meant helping Kristin. The way he figured it, anyone who looked so broken over the thought of missing her family, didn't deserve to be stranded and alone on Thanksgiving. Maybe that was another reason the Lord had made sure a vehicle was available. So that he could offer her a ride.

Ryan liked it when the Father gave him a purpose. It was easier to forget his own troubles and to not think about what awaited him in Montana. He'd worked so hard to stay away since he left for college.

He tapped the horn, hoping she could hear over the wind and through the terminal's walls. Her head popped up and her hands fell away to reveal her heart-shaped face twisted with melancholy. No tears, just emotion so raw it made his chest squeeze with pain.

I'll make sure you get home. He watched her squint through the windows and storm, trying to figure out who was honking. She frowned and looked away. All she probably saw was a strange vehicle lurking outside from where she sat. Okay, she couldn't see through the vehicle's tinted windows. He hit the window lever and the tinted glass slid down, bringing in the storm.

He shivered, but being cold was nothing compared to the look of relief on Kristin's face. The sadness faded like night to dawn and an astonished look replaced it. He gestured for her to come join him.

She lifted one eyebrow, as if making sure of his offer.

He waved her over again. Her beaming smile was the prettiest thing he'd seen in some time. She bounded to her feet, slipped her computer-case strap over one slim shoulder and her garment bag over the other. She marched toward him with a buoyant grace that showed how happy she was.

Yeah, it was a good thing he made the wrong turn and wound up in the right place to help her. Icy wind seared like razor blades through his thin Phoenix-bought coat, but he didn't mind. There was something in the way she hurried toward him that warmed him on the inside. Like a lightbulb's steady glow.

It must be nice to have the kind of home she wanted to get to so badly. He fought a twist in his chest as he climbed out into the snowfall—whatever emotion that was, he refused to deal with it. He was a world-class ignorer of emotions.

Kristin slid to a stop on the icy sidewalk and he steadied her with a hand to her elbow.

"Careful there. I don't want to have to splint a broken leg for you."

"Whew. No, but at least you would be handy to have around if I did fall." She found her balance and eased away from his steadying grip. "I can't believe it's really you. How did you happen to be lucky enough to get a rental car?"

"The angels smiled down on me, I guess." He took her bag off her shoulder and stowed it. "You wouldn't happen to want a lift to Montana, would you?"

"What? Are you kidding me? I thought I'd be stuck in that terminal. I couldn't believe my eyes when I saw you waving at me from behind your steering wheel. For a second there, I thought I was dreaming. This is too good to be true."

"I guess it's your lucky day. Want me to take the computer case, too?"

"What?" She swiped the snow out of her face. And what a pretty face she had, all lit up with joy and happiness. One of the golden McKaslin girls, who had grown up to be a fine woman. It was easy to see her good heart and her sincerity. He'd forgotten there were still women like her in the world.

"Oh, the computer." She rolled her eyes before shrugging the strap off her shoulder. "I'm getting ditzy. Well, ditzier than usual. Too many hours without sleep."

"That makes two of us." He stowed the computer safely between the seat and a suitcase, so it wouldn't slide around. "Don't stand there freezing. Get in the car."

Kristin felt the blush flame from her throat to her hairline. Was she really gawking at the big handsome doctor who looked about as fit as an NFL quarterback? Yeah! She ripped her gaze away from him and hopped into the passenger seat. The slam of the door meant she was safely inside away from him and she could gather her wits.

Why was she acting as though she'd never seen him before? He was Ryan. Mom's friend's kid. The one who drove his family car into the ditch when he was eight.

It was hard to see that bothersome kid in the broad-shouldered, competent man who settled behind the steering wheel. He smelled of snow and winter nights and spicy aftershave. Just right.

And why was she noticing? She was a self-avowed, independent single woman. She was too smart to fall in love with any man. Let alone someone who lived half the country away.

Ryan clicked his belt into place. Grim lines carved deep into the corners around his mouth. "Buckle up. It's gonna be a tough drive."

Kristin hadn't realized the windshield was a solid white sheet until the wipers snapped to life and beat the accumulation away. "The snow is really coming down. Do you think we can get very far?"

"I'm gonna try. We may have to overnight it somewhere, *if* we can find a vacancy."

"Sounds sensible. We want to get home safe and sound."

"That's the idea." He winked, put the Jeep in gear and eased down the accelerator. The tires slid, dug in and propelled them forward. "I've got a cell phone if you want to call home. Your folks are probably up worrying."

Was that nice or what? Ryan definitely had done a lot of changing. "Thanks, but I tried with mine. I couldn't get through. The storm."

"Ah." He concentrated on navigating through the whiteout conditions.

She didn't say anything more. If she couldn't make out the road in front of him, how could he? But he was somehow, driving with a steady confidence that made her take a closer look at the man Ryan Sanders had grown up to be.

A volunteer in the Peace Corps. A doctor. He was a man of contradictions. He still had that "I'm trouble" grin and the stubble on his jaw made him look rugged and outdoorsy. Mom was always mentioning Mary's son on her weekly calls, but Kristin had dismissed him along with all the other eligible men Mom talked about.

Poor Mom, who was never going to give up hope for another wedding to plan. What was it Mom had said about Ryan? Kristin couldn't remember. She automatically deleted any talk of men and marriage and how Mr. Right would come along one day.

There was no such thing as Mr. Right! How could Mom be in an unhappy marriage and be so blind to the truth?

Maybe it was how she made it through the day. Troubled, Kristin tried to turn her thoughts away from painful things. Stuff she tried not to think about, but going home only made it impossible to ignore. The hole in her family that remained—Allison. The missing face no one mentioned. The place at the table where a chair used to sit. The oldest sister who'd been alive and beautiful, and whom Kristin had loved with all her heart.

The years passed, her parents had slipped into a resigned distant marriage, her sisters had gone on to make homes and marriages of their own, but some things would never be the same. If there was something Allison's death had taught her, it was that nothing lasted. Nothing. Not family, not love, not life.

Ryan broke the silence that had fallen between them. "Hey, are you hungry? There's a drive-through that's open. It's the only one I've seen so far. If we don't stop, it might be our last chance to eat until daybreak."

"I'm starving. I definitely want to stop."

"Looks like only the drive-through is open." He braked in the parking lot to study the front doors. "Hope you don't mind eating in here."

"I'm not picky."

"Me, either." He slid to the order board, where the whiteout had blocked out half the menu. "I have no idea if you can see to order anything."

"It's no problem. There's one of these near my town house. I know the menu by heart."

"Me, too." Why that surprised him, Ryan didn't know. It made perfect sense she would eat at restaurants. He just didn't picture her as the fast-food kind of girl.

A mumbling teenager who sounded unenthusiastic about his job took their orders. After waiting at the window while the winds kicked up, blowing the snow sideways, they were handed two sacks of piping-hot food. Ryan crept through the blizzard to park safely beneath the glow of a streetlight.

"Not that any of the light is reaching us," Kristin commented with a wink as she unpacked the first bag.

Ryan flicked on the overhead lamp. "It's weird. I haven't *seen* snow since I went skiing winter vacation of my senior year in college. And it was on the slopes, not falling."

"I bet it never snows in Phoenix."

"Once, but it was just a skiff. The entire city shut down. It was incredible. Had that same amount fallen back home, no one would have blinked twice. I've sure missed real winters."

Wind buffeted the driver's side of the vehicle, and the gust of snow cloaked them entirely from the nighttime world. Kristin shivered with excitement. She loved a good winter storm. "It looks like you're getting your wish. A full-fledged blizzard in the making!"

"Yeah, I'm one lucky guy."

His crooked grin could devastate a less stalwart

woman. Kristin gave thanks that she was a dedi-
cated and sworn single gal who had full immunity
to a man's hundred-watt charisma. Because if she
wasn't, she'd be caught hook, line and sinker.

He probably charmed all the women in the Southwest with that grin, she thought as she clasped her
hands together in prayer. She didn't dare glance in
Ryan's direction to see if he'd bowed his head. She
had grace to say, and she was going to say it.

But Ryan's melted-chocolate baritone broke in
before she could begin. "Dear Father, thank you
for watching over us. For bringing us together on
this night when we had hoped to be with family but
found ourselves alone. Please watch over us on our
journey north. In your name."

"Amen," they said together.

The whir of the heater and the fury of the storm
filled the silence between them. Kristin unclasped
her hands and didn't dare to look at the man beside
her. Paper crackled as Ryan dug through the closest sack. The crisp scent of hot greasy Tater Tots
filled the air. The overhead dome lamp spotlighted
the center console where Ryan was popping the tops
off the little plastic salsa containers.

Why was her heart beating as if she'd just finished a ten-kilometer run? Kristin grabbed a straw,
ripped off the paper wrapping, stabbed it into her
soda and sipped hard. She'd never seen this side of
Ryan Sanders before. She could remember him at
church through their growing-up years, slumped on

the pew next to his mother, staring off into space with the supremely bored look he'd perfected.

That boy had turned into a sincere man of faith? She never would have guessed the troublesome boy she remembered would have become so serious. Where had the real Ryan gone? Not that there was anything wrong with the man he'd turned out to be—not on the surface, anyway.

But what about deep inside? The parts of a person that were harder to discover? That was the real question. And it was why Kristin refused to date. Why she would never marry anyone.

Because you never knew what a person was really like, until it was too late.

"I think this is yours. Extra sour cream." He held out the wrapped taco in his big, capable hands.

Healing hands, Kristin realized, and they looked it. Powerful but circumspect. "Th-thanks."

The food was piping hot, but she hardly noticed as she unwrapped the chicken taco. Ryan was consuming his beef taco with great gusto. He stopped to nudge the container of hot sauce her way.

"No, too much for me."

"I say, the hotter the better. I can have all of this?"

"Go for it."

"Awesome." He dumped an extreme amount of blistering sauce on his giant soft-shell taco and gave a moan of satisfaction after he took a bite and chewed. "Not nearly hot enough. I like melt-the-lid-off-the-jar hot."

"*There's* the Ryan I remember."

"Hey, I grew up. But I really haven't changed all that much. Down deep. I'm still a country boy at heart."

A country boy? There was nothing obviously country in the polished, well-dressed man seated beside her. He looked as if he'd walked straight off the pages of a magazine. "You've been away from home for what, more than a dozen years?"

"Thirteen, nearly fourteen. What I can't picture is you living in a big city. Why didn't you marry your high-school sweetheart and buy a house near your folks?"

"Because I didn't have a high-school sweetheart." His innocent question took her back to places best left forgotten.

"Why not?"

His question was an innocent one—he didn't know what he was doing to her by asking. The steel around her heart snapped tight into place, blocking out all the painful memories of that time in her life. When her older beloved sister had left home packed for a church retreat and bubbling with excitement, never to return again.

Kristin's entire world changed that day. Nothing had ever been the same.

But Ryan had left the valley for greater things by then. With a football scholarship in hand and a free ride to an out-of-state university, he'd probably only heard about the small-plane crash that had taken several lives at the time. His mom had probably mentioned it to him on the phone when it happened, but it had only been a newsworthy item to him.

That day years ago had tipped her world on its side and showed her the truth. You could surround yourself with family and friends, make a marriage, a home and a family, go to church and pray faithfully, but it couldn't protect a person. Not even God seemed to be able to do that.

The truth was too personal. She'd tried to talk about it before, but no one seemed to understand. Pastor Bill from her hometown church had been wonderful and understanding, but his well-meant advice had been useless. Why did God want to take Allison from them? She'd been beloved by everyone who knew her, and as an older sister, she'd been awesome. She was beautiful and kind, generous and selfless and smart. Anytime Kristin had needed her, her oldest sister had been there, no questions asked.

It wasn't only her sister that she'd lost that day. She'd seen the world for what it truly was, and she couldn't surround herself with people and things and pretend that if she was faithful enough, nothing could hurt her or those she loved.

Loss was inevitable. It was a part of life she didn't care for, thank you very much. Kristin grabbed a Tater Tot and bit into the crispy, greasy goodness. Ryan was still waiting for an answer as he watched her, unwrapping his third taco.

"I'm just not into the whole marriage and kids

thing." She shrugged. It was a cop-out, she knew it, but there was no way this handsome man who probably had left a string of hopeful women pining away in Phoenix would understand.

"You're a career woman. I get it." Ryan chomped into his taco and chewed while he studied her thoughtfully, as if he were assessing her. Seeing something new in her. "Being a doc is great. I love what I do. It's real satisfaction, gives your life meaning, when you love your work."

"Yeah. That's me. I love my job." She did. So, why did her chest feel hollow as she took another bite of her chicken taco?

"I bet you're good at what you do. I can see it." He grabbed two Tater Tots and dragged them through the hot salsa. "You're organized, smart, likable. Efficient, I bet."

"Yeah, and a devoted workaholic."

"Me, too. That's the reason why I'm headed home to Montana after about a billion years of staying away."

"Because you're a workaholic?"

"Yeah. I've always had to stay wherever I was living. First it was because I was in college and I'd stay to get extra hours at whatever part-time job I had. I needed the money, and Mom understood that. But then it was med school and I needed to study. I was an intern and then a resident and there was no way I could get time off. I worked holidays."

"And now you're a doctor with your own practice. You make your own hours, right?"

"I wish." He rolled his eyes. "I'm in control of my schedule more than I have been. But I'm low man on the totem pole. I'm in a practice with some of the top orthopedic surgeons in the Southwest, and they pull rank. Plus, it's that student-loan thing again."

"The one the size of a house?"

"Exactly. Sometimes on Saturdays when I've got paperwork piled as high as my computer monitor, I get this urge to run off and windsurf the day away on Lake Powell."

"You windsurf?"

"I used to. Then I did something really inane. I decided to get engaged."

"You're getting married?"

"I'm not the type, I know. It took me about three months to figure that out after being dragged to a wedding planner to see about seven thousand different kinds of napkins we could get monogrammed, and my life flashed before my eyes. A life with no windsurfing. It didn't work out." He shrugged, as if it didn't bother him a bit. "It was for the best."

Kristin didn't miss the shadows in his eyes. His tone might be light, but there was pain there. She could feel it as tangibly as the cold seeping in from outside. Whatever happened had been complicated and deeply painful.

She tried to think of something comforting to say, but drew a blank. No simple words of comfort or empathy could begin to ease the hurt from wounds in a person's heart. She knew.

"Well, we better get a move on." Ryan cleared his throat as if dismissing his loss or wiping away his sorrow. He crinkled up the paper wrappers, and the sound was as jarring and abrupt as his movements.

Kristin took the last bite of her taco as Ryan switched on the wipers. A few swipes of the blades and the accumulated snow was gone. The twin beams of the headlights reflected back to them in the whiteout conditions.

"Don't worry. I'll keep us safe." He tossed her a roguishly charming wink, before putting the Jeep into gear.

"I wasn't worried." Kristin balled up the wrapper, pretending to be busy and unaffected by the man beside her.

He's unhappy, she realized. Lonely. She knew what that was like. It was like the storm blocking out the glow from the town's lights until there was only the cold darkness and the howl of the worsening storm. As if there could be no light to warm the long drive ahead.

Chapter Three

Ryan swore it felt as if they'd been driving for an eternity, but when he glanced at the clock in the dash, the green numbers showed less than two hours had passed. For one hundred and twenty long minutes they'd been creeping in a vast darkness, closed off from the world, the tenacious storm allowing him to see only a few feet in front of him.

Twice, he'd spotted the faint sudden pinpoint of oncoming headlights. Each vehicle had been traveling as slowly as he was, fighting to stay on the road. He hadn't seen another driver in the past fifty-three minutes in front of him, behind him or on the other side of the double yellow.

Exhaustion made every nerve ending burn. Three times they'd stopped in the small towns off the highway to look for vacancies. No luck. Every other traveler had the same idea. They had no other option than to keep driving.

"How are you doing?" Kristin's soothing alto

broke the long silence between them. "Want to trade off driving?"

"Maybe. I figured we'd switch once we got to the next town."

"Sounds good. If we don't lose track of the road."

"Pray this storm doesn't get any worse." Grim, Ryan recalled all the cases he'd read about in med school where innocent drivers had gotten caught in harsh winter storms and gone off the road. He saw how easily that could happen.

The blizzard closed in with a vengeance. The falling snow began to spin, washing over the windshield with a dizzying speed. The twin beams of the headlights glared on the downpour, reflecting back at him until he lost complete sight of the highway.

"Thank God for the tracks." Kristin leaned forward, straining against her shoulder harness as if to help him watch for signs of danger. As if they were about to plunge off the road and down a ravine.

"Just what I was thinking." Some brave soul was ahead of them. The lone set of tire tracks was rapidly filling with snow, but it was enough to keep him headed in the right direction. His vision blurred and he blinked hard.

Just stay alert, man. He fidgeted in his seat, fighting the belt. He could use the rest of his soda, both the sugar and caffeine would help, but he didn't want to take his hand off the wheel or his attention from the road. There was no way he was going to let anything happen. He had Kristin to keep safe. Mom was waiting for him.

Thank you, Lord, for the help. The tire tracks in the snow unspooled ahead of them like a sign from above guiding them toward home.

Home. If his head wasn't pounding from exhaustion and the effort of concentrating so hard, he could try to get his mind in the right place. He didn't want Mom to see him like this, undecided and unhappy to be walking straight back to his past.

Luckily, driving took all his energy. He didn't have to think about anything other than this moment and keeping the car on the road. It was like driving in a dark tunnel. He glued his attention to the tire tracks barely visible in the sheen of the headlights.

The road beneath them seemed to heave, tossing the SUV around. Fear hit him and he swung the wheel left, but it was too late. A tree bough swiped across the roof. The passenger-side tires dipped low into the pitch of the shoulder.

He saw it all in a flash, the sharp drop, the void of a forest. Already he was picturing what it would be like to crash through those thick limbs and plunge into the darkness, out of control. Flashes of car-accident victims he'd treated in the E.R. haunted him and he fought to stop the inevitable as the top-heavy SUV began to tip.

Please, Lord, he prayed as, teeth gritted, he fought the jolting steering wheel. *A little help, please.* Crashing into old-growth trees was going to be a very bad thing. Time slowed down. He saw the minute detail of the pine needles on the limb swinging toward them. Beside him Kristin gasped, grabbed the dash, expecting the worst, too.

Then, miraculously, the tires dug in. The vehicle swung left toward the level road, and he eased it to a shaking stop. *Thank you, Father.*

Adrenaline pumping, he tried not to think of everything that could have happened, how hurt they could have been and what those tire tracks meant. "That was a close one. Are you okay?"

Sheet white, Kristin studied him with wide eyes. She nodded. "But whoever is in that car isn't."

He didn't answer. He flicked on the overhead dome light to see as he searched the dash for the hazard lights and hit them on. "Check around and see if there's a first-aid kit. Then button up and come with me."

Gone was the hint of the boy he'd been. He was all man, mature and focused. Reaching beneath the seat, Kristin's fingers tapped over the nubby carpet and bumped into a plastic edge. She got down on all fours to extricate the small box and realized that Ryan was already climbing outside. The brutal sub-zero winds cut through the warm passenger compartment as he slammed the door shut. The night and storm stole him from her sight.

The box came loose. It *was* a first-aid kit, as she'd hoped it would be. Relieved, Kristin twisted back onto the seat, dug her mittens out of her coat. Her door swung open. Ryan stood just outside the light, shadow and substance as she held up the kit for him to see.

He took it from her. "Do you know how close we are to the next town?"

"I'm guessing maybe twelve, thirteen miles." Kristin sank to midcalf in drifting snow. "It might be quicker heading back. We went, what, ten miles?"

It all added up to potential disaster. He ignored the bitter wind and the sting of flakes needling his face. All that mattered was helping the people in that car.

If he could. If it wasn't too late.

He yanked his cell out of his pocket. *Lord, please let this thing work out here.* He hit auto dial and prayed for a signal.

There were no other sounds but the rapid-fire beat of his heart, the tap, tap, tap of snow and the howl of the wind through the trees. He shook his phone, not that it would do a lick of good. *C'mon. Connect.*

He heard the squeak of leather shoes in the compact snow behind him. One glance told him Kristin was managing. He kept in front of her, taking the brunt of the blizzard hiking along the tire tracks as they rolled through a jagged hole in the guardrail and into the darkness.

His phone beeped. He froze in place. He had a signal! There was a ring, and an emergency operator answered. It sounded like a small county station; he could hear the buzz of activity in the background.

It was a busy night for the sheriff's department, and about to get busier.

"I have a single-car accident on highway 84." He squinted at the milepost marker hanging from a jagged arm of the guard post and reported the number to the operator.

What was he going to find? His guts twisted as he swept the miniflashlight on his key ring through the darkness. Nothing. Only horizontal snow in a black void.

Please, Lord, be with whoever is in that vehicle. Or was. Ryan steeled his spine. Prepared for what he might find, he took a step and skidded down a nearly vertical slope.

Not a good sign, either. He dug his heels in before he crashed into a tree. With pine needles cold against his face, he flashed the small light through the underbrush. Nothing. No, wait. There was a faint something. Squinting, Ryan swept the area again. Sure enough, there it was. The edge of a broken taillight reflecting some of the light back at him despite the heavy downpour and thick foliage.

It was enough of a miracle on this brutal night, that Ryan gave thanks as he crashed through limbs and over dormant blackberry bushes, following the ragged trail of tracks that led to a small sedan. The vehicle was dark and still. A very bad sign.

Help me, Father, he prayed as he snapped limbs and tore branches out of his way, sidling along the quiet car.

Too quiet. That couldn't be good. Between shock, trauma and the freezing cold, he didn't expect to find anyone alive.

"Hello?" Calm, focused, he broke the icy layer of snow off the driver's window with the side of his hand. The glow of his flashlight showed a lone driver with a mass of dark curls slumped behind the wheel.

He tried the door and the handle gave. The passenger compartment was cool, but not yet cold. He began talking, calm and steady, in case the young woman could hear him. So she wouldn't be afraid.

He wasn't aware of Kristin crowding close to see if she could help or the snow slicing between his neck and his coat collar or the wind as he worked.

Wow, he's sure something. Kristin's heart hitched as she watched him work, methodical and skilled. He pressed two fingers to the woman's jugular and some of the tension in his shoulders eased. She was alive.

Kristin leaned against the car. She'd never felt so helpless in her life. If a rental car had been available, then she may well have been here alone to help the injured driver. What good could she have done? Ryan was a blessing. He checked the young woman's pupils while talking to her, low and soothing.

I bet he's a great doctor. Admiration for him filled her up. She loved medical dramas on television, but this was something greater. This was real. Somber lines dug deep in Ryan's face as he turned to her in the faint glow from his flashlight. How badly was the woman hurt?

"What can I do to help?"

"Go through the trunk. I'll pull the latch. See if there's anything to wrap her in. Blankets. Sheets. Something. We've got to get her warm."

At least she was alive. That was something. Praying, Kristin scrambled to the back of the car, lifting the trunk after it popped up. How could he be calm and steady? Okay, he was a doctor, he was used to this, but she wasn't. Fear jittered through her veins, leaving her quaking and her fingers clumsy as she began to push through the crowded trunk. Full laundry bags, textbooks, a laptop case… She spied a flashlight and tested it; it worked. She tucked that under her arm.

As she kept digging, Ryan's voice pulled at her like a fish on a line. She was hooked and unable to turn away. Had she ever heard a man sound like that? A deep gravelly baritone that was both hard-edged man and infinitely caring. Powerful and dependable. A man who could make anything right.

Please, Father, help guide his hands tonight. Kristin moved aside a University of Idaho book bag, realizing the young driver was a college student, probably heading home for Thanksgiving, too. Would she be all right?

She wasn't moving. She was unconscious. At least Ryan was here. He knew what to do. Clutching the stadium blanket she'd found beneath the book bag,

Kristin carefully picked her way through the knee-deep snow.

Ryan must have heard her coming. Crouched in the open door, he twisted toward her. Worry lines furrowed deep in his forehead, but he managed a strained nod as his gaze pinned on the folded blanket. "Good. That will do just fine."

"How is she?"

"She's trying to stay awake for me." Solemn, he took the blanket in exchange for his cell phone. "I've got dispatch to make this a priority."

Kristin didn't need to ask. She could see the truth in his eyes. The young college girl could be seriously injured. "What do you need me to do?"

"The car is stable. I'm not worried about it rolling any farther down the ravine. The trees here are pretty sturdy. How do you feel about climbing in the back seat?"

"Sure." Kristin slipped the cell into her coat pocket, struggling with the stubborn door. Ice cracked around the handle and she slipped into the rapidly cooling interior of the compact sedan.

The beam of the flashlight danced eerily around the silent passenger compartment, as Ryan wedged it into place on the dashboard. The golden stream illuminated a beaded cross hanging from the rear-view mirror, a small stuffed puppy tucked into the middle console next to an insulated coffee cup with the name *Samantha* and the Greek symbols of a sorority printed on it. And then she saw the college girl's thick and beautiful brown wavy hair matted with blood.

Kristin shivered all the way to her bone marrow. The only time she'd seen anyone seriously hurt was after the private plane went down, when Allison had died. Her sister Kirby had also been in the plane, but had survived.

Kristin had been a freshman in high school, and with all the time that had passed since, it felt so long ago. But the images returned as crisp and clear as if they'd happened an hour ago. The fear for her critically injured sister, the beep of machines, the frightening reality of death as they all waited for Kirby to regain consciousness, terrified that she'd slip away into an irreversible coma and death.

Kirby had survived.

Please, Lord, help this young woman. She was too young to die.

"I need your help," Ryan said, fracturing her thoughts, working quickly as he dug through the first-aid kit with one free hand. "Hold her head and neck steady from behind while I try to stop this bleeding."

"Steady, huh?" That's the last thing she was. Kristin stared at her quivering hands. She took a deep breath. Willed the fear to stop.

"Like this." He guided her hands. "Cradle her as still as you can. She could have a neck injury, and this will minimize any further damage while I work. All right?"

Kristin knew he meant how important this was. The difference between paralysis and movement, between life and death. Her hands had to be rock steady. She made sure of it.

Ryan was unbreakable steel. Checking vitals, applying pressure and bandages, assessing for further injuries. As he worked, he talked low and reassuring.

"Can you hear me, Samantha? I'm a doctor, if you can believe that. And that's Kristin, in the seat behind you. Say hi, Kristin."

"Hi, Samantha."

The injured woman murmured, but nothing more. Kristin felt the slightest of movements beneath her fingertips, the drum of a very slow pulse and the flex of muscles, as if the girl was trying to awaken.

"Hold her steady." Ryan's grave gaze said everything.

Samantha was seriously injured. Without mercy, the storm raged, the snow pounding like rain. Could help even make it through the blizzard in time? There was so little Ryan could do here, with few supplies. She didn't dare say the words aloud. She'd never felt so helpless.

But Ryan looked confident. In charge. He was amazing. Hope seeped into Kristin's heart as she watched his skilled hands working to stanch the flow of blood from several gashes along the girl's hairline. Blood seemed to be everywhere, but he worked on,

composed and sure. She saw on his face the dedica-
tion she expected a doctor to have. The seriousness.

And something more rare. Compassion.

When he was done, he seemed to give a sigh of
relief. He checked his patient's pulse using his wrist-
watch, frowned and asked for his cell. Shivering and
seeming to be unaware of it, he made another call to
the county dispatch.

"They're almost here." Ryan handed her the flashlight. "Or so the operator says. It's hard going for
them, and with this poor visibility, they could drive
right past the Jeep and miss us. Would you mind
going up to flag them down?"

"Sure."

His fingers moved into place between hers, sup-
porting Samantha's head and neck with extreme
care. She read the fear he held for the young college
woman in his shadowed eyes. She remembered when
her sister Kirby had been in intensive care. She knew
exactly what hung in the balance. A life. She knew
all that meant, truly meant, unlike so many people
who went around living lives they took for granted.

All it took was a split second for everything to
change. For life to never be the same again. Would
Samantha live? Would she be in a wheelchair or on
crutches for the years to come?

Holding on to hope for the best outcome, Kristin
scrambled up the slope, fighting the wind and snow
driving at her back and the brambles grabbing at
her feet. The shadows she saw in Ryan's eyes stayed

with her as she fought to the top. Shadows of grief that broke her heart as she burst onto the lonely expanse of country road, where no other soul stirred on this cruel night. And so she waited, shivering and alone, for help that felt as if it would never come.

The rumble of the fire truck's engines, muffled by the snow, faded into the distance. Although the taillights had long faded, Kristin watched. She couldn't get the injured college student out of her mind.

Ryan marched toward her, swiping snow out of his eyes as he crossed in front of the SUV's headlights. Burnished by light, surrounded by darkness, he looked more myth than man as he yanked open the passenger door for her.

Woodenly she eased into the seat, stiff with cold, but not feeling anything but a horrible void. Tepid air breezed out of the vents in the dash and she couldn't feel it. The clock glowed the time—not thirty minutes had passed since they'd nearly followed Samantha Fields off the road.

Snow drifted inside with Ryan as he collapsed in the seat and slammed the door. He filled the seat, slumping with his head rolling back against the headrest. His presence made the passenger compartment shrink. "I was able to get through to Tim, a friend I used to work with. He's one of the best surgeons in this area, and he's agreed to meet Samantha at the hospital. He'll take excellent care of her."

"You took the time to do that?"

"Sure. Helping people is what I do. It's why I studied all those years. Why I'm in debt for a few hundred grand." Although exhaustion lined his face and bruised the skin beneath his eyes, his wink was saucy.

She had watched while he worked tirelessly alongside the medics stabilizing Samantha's neck and spine so that she had the best possible outcome, in case of a spinal cord injury. All in a day's work for him, maybe, but she'd never seen anyone like him.

She pulled off her mittens, now that the heater was kicking out a decent hot breeze. "Let's trade places. I'll drive and let you sit here and warm your hands. You've got to be half frozen."

"The cold never used to bother me. I've been away from Montana too long. It's the Phoenix weather. It's thinned my blood. Now I turn into an icicle the second it snows. It's not manly. It's embarrassing."

"I'm embarrassed for you." She'd never met a better example of what a man should be, but he seemed unaware that he was that and more. "Move. Go on. I can't drive from over here."

As if too exhausted to lift his head from the seat back, Ryan swiveled his eyes to focus on her with a disbelieving look. One eyebrow crooked with obvious skepticism. "You'd really drive? You're not just saying that, right?"

"Right."

"You're not afraid to drive in this stuff?"

"Do I look as if I'm shaking in my boots? No."

"But you're a *girl*. Girls don't drive in lots of snow. At least not in my experience."

"You *have* lived in Arizona too long!" Kristin took one look at the man slouching beside her, dappled with big flakes of melting snow, his face chapped from the bitter temperatures outside. "Don't let the designer clothes fool you. You can take the girl out of Montana, but not Montana out of the girl. Let me behind the wheel and I'll show you."

"Yeah? I'd be grateful if I could just close my eyes for about ten minutes."

"How about all the way until the next town?"

"Deal." Ryan opened the door and shouldered out into the dark. "No, you climb over and stay inside. I'll brave the storm. I'm still frozen anyway."

With a lopsided grin, he was gone, leaving the scent of wind, a hint of expensive cologne and man. A pleasant combination. Kristin climbed over the console and into the seat that was pushed too far back for her feet to reach the pedals. She adjusted the seat, snapped the shoulder harness into place and checked out the controls.

Ryan cut through the headlights with that confident, jaunty walk of his. He was like a hero out of an old black-and-white movie, tough and strong and compassionate. She didn't know they made men like that anymore.

He collapsed beside her, bringing with him the frigid wind and a blast of snow. He swiped icy flakes off his eyebrows. "Believe it or not, the blizzard's winding down some."

"Some. Not a lot." Kristin switched off the hazard lights, staring into the impenetrable conditions. No cars had passed, except for the emergency vehicles, since they'd arrived. The road ahead lay like a pristine ribbon of white rolling out of the reach of the headlights. Dangerous driving ahead. Kristin released the hand brake and shifted into low gear.

Ryan unzipped his coat, settling in. "Just tell me if you get too white-knuckled."

"Don't worry. I can handle it. Belt up and hold on." Was he a skeptic or what? It had been a long time since she'd driven anything with more power than her sensible sedan, but she was used to this weather. She hadn't always flown home. She'd driven more often than not over the treacherous mountain passes and she was still in one piece. "This is nothing compared to commuting in Seattle traffic twice a day for more years than I care to count."

"That's what I can't picture. You living in a city. I don't know why. It just doesn't go with the McKaslin image."

"I won't say it wasn't a big adjustment when I first moved there. When I went to college, I thought Bozeman was a big city."

"Bozeman?" he asked.

"Yeah, I know. It's a tiny city compared to someplace like Seattle. I felt lost. Every time I left my apartment I got turned around. I'd never seen so many streets and roads and freeways in my life."

"I know how you felt—moving away from a place with one main street through town, where you know all the roads and shortcuts by heart, to a huge city where the checkers at the grocery store ask for ID because they don't know you, your family, your grandparents and all your cousins by name."

"See, that's where we differ. I didn't mind living someplace folks didn't know me."

Ryan leaned the seat all the way back and stretched out his legs as far as he could. Not comfortable, but an acceptable snoozing position. Except thinking about his past made him antsy. As tired as he was, his nerve endings felt as though they were twitching and his muscles felt heavy as lead. His emotions were going every which way. Regret, guilt, grief.

Nothing Kristin would understand. Some people, like her, could go home again. They would always know the warmth of their childhood awaited them, that the ghosts of memories from holidays past were happy ones. Not haunted by what should have been, and more failures than the young boy he'd been could cope with.

Or the man he'd become.

He liked to think he wasn't a coward. He faced challenges head-on. Sucked it up and did what needed to be done. He wasn't afraid of hardship or hard work. But some things were best left unexamined. Some memories best left buried. He had a good life, he made a good living, and he loved his work and his practice. What good was having to pick apart a past that only brought pain? That exposed wounds that could never be healed?

No, Kristin didn't look as though she'd rather be running away instead of heading home. Her delicate profile was brushed by the glow of the dash lights, burnishing her creamy porcelain-fine skin, the feminine line of her nose and the dainty cut of her chin. He supposed her parents would welcome her with open arms, and tomorrow there would be only happiness in her home where her sisters and their families gathered to make new memories for the holidays to come.

He closed his eyes, wondering, just wondering. If he would have turned out the same if his dad had lived instead of withered away in a coma. If the logging truck hadn't crossed the double yellow on the road to town. If, instead of being struck and pinned to the ground beneath a load of logs, Dad had returned home with the ice cream he'd gone to fetch.

God made all things for a reason. But what about tonight? Why had Samantha Fields been hurt tonight? How would her life be changed?

Only God knew.

Still, it troubled him deeply. He closed his eyes, too troubled to fall right asleep. Listening to the swipe of the wiper blades on the windshield, he felt the blast of heat from the vents. The vehicle fishtailed now and then, and Kristin handled it skillfully, keeping them safe as they journeyed through the dark and snow. He couldn't remember feeling more lonely as the hours dragged on and sleep claimed him, blessedly deep.

Chapter Four

Something was hurting his eyes. Something shiny. Bright like sunlight.

Consciousness returned in a nanosecond—the ache in his back from the seat, the binding restriction of the seat belt, the hum of the engine and low murmur of music on the radio. And Kristin, with her golden hair tangled and windblown, and fatigue bruising the fragile skin beneath her eyes. She smiled, and he swore he could see heaven.

"Good morning." Her gentle alto was the single most beautiful sound he'd ever heard. A *good* way to start a new day. Thanksgiving Day.

Rational thought pierced through his sleep-fogged mind. Kristin had let him sleep through until daybreak. Sitting upright, he swiped a hand over his face and looked around. Sure enough there was that celebratory shine of the rising sun cresting the granite peaks to the east.

Even though he hadn't seen those particular

mountains in more than a decade, he recognized the rugged snow-blanketed peaks thrusting into the silky wisps of clouds and sun.

The Bridger Range. Mountains he'd climbed in, biked in, hiked in and skied on. Where he would take off just to get away. Where he retreated just to play. Every morning he'd sat at the breakfast table shoveling in bowl after bowl of cereal while he stared through the old warped glass windows and there they were, those mountains jagged and snowcapped and close enough to touch.

Mountains he hadn't seen since he was a restless eighteen-year-old who couldn't wait to leave the prison of his small town. Who'd never looked over his shoulder as he drove away.

Looking at those proud summits and those breathtaking slopes made it real. He was home. For better or worse. "I only meant to catch a few z's. Not sleep through three mountain passes and two states. You should have kicked me in the shin to wake me up."

"It was tempting, but I didn't mind driving. It was the least I could do, considering you were so valiant saving Samantha's life."

"Valiant? Me? No way. I just tried to get her stable. That reminds me, I meant to check on her before this." He dug around in his pockets for his cell, but he only got Tim's voice mail. He left a message, there was nothing else he could do for now. "What about you? You drove through a blizzard for hours."

"They had just plowed, so it wasn't too bad."

"You had to stop for gas. Why didn't you wake me up so I could take the next shift?"

"Oh, I tried. I shook you and you didn't even move. You were so out of it you slept right through the ding when I left the keys in the ignition and the banging when I filled the tank. A truck at the next fuel pump accidentally hit his horn and nothing. Not even the slightest hitch in your snoring."

"I don't snore."

"That you know."

He didn't snore, but Kristin couldn't resist teasing him. He looked adorable, all rumpled and sleep-soft. He'd sprawled all over his side of the vehicle, and he drew his legs up and yawned widely.

As much as she was *so* not interested romantically, the woman in her couldn't help appreciating a fine, good-hearted man. If she wasn't careful, she'd be crazy enough to start developing a crush on him. He was a doctor, he made a difference with his life, he was handsome and kind and funny and smart.

He's probably commitment shy and has a list of typical male faults a mile long, she thought to intentionally counterbalance the admiration glowing in her chest like the rising sun.

He rubbed his eyes and his nose. Scrunching up his mouth like a little kid, he looked ten times more handsome as he did. He blinked, as if his eyes were still trying to focus on the rolling mountain valley and the dazzling peaks rimming it. "Look, the snow's stopped."

"Yeah. About an hour ago. There's nothing like a Montana morning." Her eyes hurt with the beauty of it. She was home. Rose-hued sunlight shimmered on miles of quiet, pristine snow, like thousands of tiny faceted jewels flung across the land. A land so big and untamed, it still felt wild over a century after it was settled.

Wooden fence posts draped in snow marched along meadows and over undulating hills, not unlike the fences the pioneers had sunk into this land. Up ahead an elk, a light milk-chocolate tan against the dazzling snow, ambled onto the two-lane highway. He swiveled his elegant head to look at her, his polished antlers gleaming like ivory in the light.

She slowed on the recently plowed roadway. Ice had her fishtailing but she steered into it, shifted into neutral and eased to a stop. With no traffic so early in this desolate place, she waited instead of going around.

"I haven't seen that in a while." Ryan breathed, sitting up straight. "We used to have a whole herd of them that would graze in the fields next to our house."

"We did, too. They'd come and eat the grain set out for the horses."

"Is he awesome or what?"

Pure, elegant power, the male elk lifted his head to scent the wind. Muscles rippled beneath his tan coat as he stretched. As if sensing danger, the great animal gathered up into a breathtaking leap. Agile and lithe, the bull galloped across the ruby-hued landscape, a streak of brown against the wonder of the dawn. A ray of sunlight haloed him and he vanished.

"Awesome," Kristin agreed into the silence.

As the SUV crept forward on the ribbon of road, Ryan fought the memories crowding up from the deep well in his heart he'd boarded shut decades ago. Memories of the crisp winter air searing his face. His boots sinking deep in the snow as he tried to walk in his dad's tracks, though the footprints were too far apart. The crackle of the dried marsh reeds as they rustled when Dad knelt down. The black stock of his hunting rifle resting on his thigh.

"What made these tracks, son?" Dad had asked in that hushed voice he used, not as harsh as a whisper but so quiet Ryan had to scoot up closer to hear. "Look carefully."

His eight-year-old body had been thrumming with excitement. He hitched up the woolen hat that had slung too low and into his eyes, and frowned at the tracks. They looked just like the deer tracks they saw on the north side of the marsh. But he didn't want to blurt out the wrong answer without thinking long and hard on it first. He didn't want to disappoint his dad.

"Here's a hint. First figure about how long they are."

"I shoulda known that right off, Dad!" Ryan remembered to keep his voice down even if he wanted to shout with excitement. "It's an elk. Elks' tracks are bigger than deer. And, uh, it's a bull elk. He'd been polishin' up his antlers on that cottonwood. The bark's all gone in spots."

"That's my smart boy. My guess is if we move along nice and quiet, we just might be lucky enough to get a good look at him."

The rasping hum of a diesel engine tore Ryan from the past and from his father's side. He sat with the morning sun stinging his eyes in the passenger seat as Kristin merged onto the wide-open lanes of I-90. The three-trailer semi barreling along in the lane beside them pulled ahead, the driver in an obvious hurry to get home.

Home. How was he going to make it through the next twenty-four hours when he hadn't even reached his mom's house and he was already dragging up the past? And feeling torn apart by it. He didn't know. He didn't have any answers. He flipped down the visor and winced at his reflection in the mirror. He took one look at his red-rimmed eyes, dark spikes of hair that looked like a twister tore through them and a day's growth shadowing his jaw.

Yeah, Mom's gonna take one look at me and start right in. Ryan could hear it already. She'd want to know if he was sleeping enough, eating right, et cetera, et cetera, and there was no way he could tell her the truth. No way he could drag up the past that would only devastate them both. For her sake, he had to be tough.

Troubled, he stared out his side of the windshield and blinked. It was the marsh. Buried in snow, the surface rough and choppy due to a few of the hardier, taller reeds and cattails poking through the snow. The marsh where Dad would take him to learn what a man needed to know.

It wasn't the hunting. It wasn't the tracking. It was the self-reliance. *The world's a harsh place, son.* He could hear Dad's mellow baritone as clear and true as the day he'd said it. *A smart man adapts and perseveres and learns to take care of himself. Look, there's the elk.*

Ryan saw it perfectly in memory—the proud bull poised at the frozen shore, antlered head lifted to scent the wind on a morning lit by gold and rose, in a world layered with white.

Yeah, Dad, you sure taught me that lesson well. Ryan swallowed past the knot in his throat, turning his head to watch as the marsh whizzed by and fell behind them. Lost from sight like the past. Yeah, his dad's death taught him way too much. He'd learned to take care of himself at an early age.

"This is our exit." Kristin's voice sounded thick.

With excitement? Probably. She had her family waiting, her sisters coming home, her grandparents to draw near. Self-reliance wasn't something a McKaslin girl needed to know to survive. He realized what felt like envy was really longing. Longing for what could never be.

You can't change the past, man, he told himself, although he knew that lesson well, too. The past is gone, done, no sense in letting it in. He was changed. A man he hoped his dad would be proud of. Someone who was about as self-reliant as possible in this world of Internet and cell phones, of urban sprawl and shopping malls.

"Look." Kristin gestured ahead as she circled off the icy ramp and onto the two-lane road that nosed them toward town. "A lot has changed. Oh, that restaurant is new. There's Gramma's coffee shop. She has a new awning out front. I'll have to tell her how cute it looks."

Ryan scanned the green-and-white-striped awning giving a decidedly *Country Living* look to the shop that advertised "Espresso" in loopy purple neon. That was the coffee place Mom was always talking about. She'd picked up extra work whenever Kristin's grandmother needed help.

That's when he realized the town, with its old-fashioned main street and neat, sturdy buildings that hadn't changed since the fifties, had grown up, too. A few quaint restaurants, more cafés than the old red Formica-countered diners, brightened up the faded brick buildings marching down the length of several blocks. Corey's Hardware had a new neon sign, fresh paint and a bench out front.

There was a new antique store prettied up with

lace curtains in the wide windows. And the Sunshine Café, where, after he'd saved up change from collecting aluminum, he'd splurge on chocolate milk shakes for him and his little sister before handing over the bulk of the hard-earned dollars to his mom.

"Do your cousins still run that place?"

"Yeah. They make the best chocolate shakes anywhere."

"I was just thinking about that. Thick and sweet and so chocolaty." Ryan's stomach growled. "Wow, I remember you and your sisters would ride your horses into town and tie them up in the parking spots in front of the café."

"And you would ride your bike."

His bike. As Kristin navigated along the snowy street, where previous tracks of chained-up vehicles had broken a clear path, he saw snatches of the boy he'd been. Pedaling on his secondhand mountain bike down the wrong side of the road, a rebel without a cause and a chip on his shoulder. Holding down two jobs, bagging at the grocery on weekends and cleaning barns for Kristin's uncle. Wanting his mother's life to be easier. Hating that it wasn't. Missing his dad so much, it hurt to breathe.

I never should have come back, he thought, his eyes stinging. It was too much. Earlier, he'd vowed to keep his thoughts in the present. But what did a guy do when the past was tangled up with the present?

"The closer we get to home, the sadder you

look." Kristin sounded concerned. Caring, the way a friend was.

He lived such a busy life, he didn't have a lot of friends. And he liked it that way. He shrugged. His problems were his own. "I'm just dog tired. You doin' okay? I could take over. In fact, why don't you let me drive?"

"Because those are my dad's fields. Okay, they're my sister's now. Michelle and her husband took over the farming. I'm almost *home*."

Kristin probably didn't realize how much warmth she placed on that word. Her emotion came through as easily as if she'd opened wide her heart. What a blessing she had, in the family she'd grown up with. In the childhood home that rose into sight nestled on the crest of a low rolling hill. The front windows reflected mauve in the rising sun, and the clouds overhead began spitting out tiny airy flakes of snow, as delicate as spun sugar. Like a blessing on this day of homecoming.

"I get to see how my new baby nieces are growing. Now I'm getting excited! The last time I came home, it was when little Caitlin was born."

"I take it Caitlin belongs to one of your sisters?"

"Yep. I'm a proud aunt many times over." Okay, there were a hundred excellent reasons for coming home. Her sisters were married, and when they all gathered together for holidays, they'd become a sizable group. It was exciting to see how happy her sisters were. Happy with the lives they'd chosen. Her sisters were mothers now, and that meant a whole troop of nieces and nephews she got to spoil.

Both bitter and sweet, her visits home. Very hard on her poor heart.

"That's a pleasure I haven't enjoyed yet, being Uncle Ryan." For the first time on the trip, he smiled, genuine and true, and it was as if his defenses lowered and she could see more deeply into him. See a glimpse of his dreams. "Mia has just finished vet school. She's worked hard to get this far, and she hasn't taken the time to fall in love."

"She's smart, finishing her school first." It's what she did. "A woman has to be able to make a living on her own."

"That's what Mia says, and I agreed. Look at my mom. She married Dad right out of high school. They had a happy marriage until the day he was struck by that truck. It was hard enough facing each day without him there, for all of us, but we struggled financially, too. In a small town with no training whatsoever, Mom cleaned houses and worked at the cannery outside Bozeman. Yet no matter how we all worked, it was never enough to make ends meet. It was hard for her. Mia and me—"

He paused, raked his hand through his dark hair and turned to stare out the window. His throat worked. "We did everything we could to make it easier for her, but it was a hard road to walk."

He fell silent, gazing off into the fields where tender shoots of winter wheat hid beneath the numbing comfort of snow. Like the anguish that Ryan clearly worked so hard to hide. Kristin's heart twisted so hard it hurt to breathe, and she trained her attention where it belonged—on the road and not on a man's silent pain.

She remembered a strong-willed boy who was a little too loud, a tad too reckless. He'd been in the background of her growing-up years, not someone she hung out with. Sure, she'd known he'd lost his dad and that his mom worked a lot. But she'd been a girl herself, and then a teenager too caught up in friends and school and her own family's loss to have given more than a passing thought to a boy who was nothing but trouble.

That boy's pain was in the man, a tangible presence that ached like a festered wound. One that had tried to heal over the years, but could not.

She knew what that was like. Some wounds could never close. Some hurts always ached. Some tragedies changed a person forever.

She drove in stinging silence until her parents' house rose up on the road before them, graced by the soft morning's glow. The ache inside her eased. The familiar sight of the big wraparound porch, the wide old-fashioned windows, the lights from the kitchen where Mom was already hard at work caused emotion to ball in her throat. She was *home*.

Ryan broke the silence. "It's just like I remember it."

"It's always the same. A safe place to come to."

But not an easy place. The tangle of opposing emotions left her feeling conflicted—as always. Mom and Dad's sadness, their strained marriage, Allison's loss that was never spoken of. *Never.*

And the good things, too: the laughter of her sisters over dinner, playing Monopoly after the dishes were done to the sounds of the football game from the living room. Gramma's loving presence. Nephews and nieces to hold close.

She hesitated. A busy day awaited her in the house that loomed over them, casting them in partial shadow. "Will you be all right?"

"Sure." He nodded, but his smile was shallow and didn't light his eyes. He looked faraway, as if his thoughts were troubled and elsewhere. He looked tired as he swiped his palm over his face. "Thanks for driving, Kristin. You didn't have to let me sleep."

"I figured Samantha's savior deserved some rest. If you hear how she's doing, will you let me know?"

"Sure. I should reimburse you for the gas."

"Oh, no. Consider it my contribution. It's the least I can do. If you hadn't come along, then I'd be in Boise right now."

"Look, there's your mom." Ryan saw the woman who'd aged since the last time he saw her long ago. He didn't know why that surprised him, it was completely logical. Time passed and it changed everyone. But to see the woman who used to be so young-looking with gray accenting her golden hair and her face lined from hardship—he felt it down deep.

Everyone had hardship. Life had trials, and it wasn't the bad things that happened but the way a person rose to the challenge that mattered. He had lost a father. Alice McKaslin had lost a daughter. The worry clear on her face turned to relief when she recognized Kristin behind the wheel of the SUV.

"Kristin! There you are! Oh, we were so worried!" Alice, still in her quilted housecoat and matching quilted slippers flew down the snow-covered steps.

"Didn't you get my message?" Kristin asked, hopping into the cold, closing the door behind her as she cut behind the vehicle and out of sight.

In the side-view mirror, Ryan could see Kristin step into her mother's outstretched arms. The love unmistakable on Kristin's face, shining in her eyes, made her glow.

Family. Yeah, it was important, but he wasn't looking forward to the price of it. He loved his mom. He'd do anything for her. But he couldn't look anywhere without seeing the past. Even the fields where he'd worked long and brutal days in hundred-degree heat bringing in hay for Mr. McKaslin brought memories flooding back. He dreaded the drive back to town, where he would see more of the past, more of the boy he'd been. More of the turmoil and pain he'd worked so hard to leave behind.

While mother and daughter were still holding on to each other and exchanging greetings, he climbed out and grabbed her computer case and bag.

"Why, Ryan Sanders, is that you?" Alice Mc-Kaslin noticed him trying to slink past.

He'd wanted to avoid the gooey mess of female emotions if he could, but no such luck. So he faced the teary-eyed females with a man's courage. "It's me. It's good to see you, Mrs. McKaslin. Happy Thanksgiving."

"Why, happy Thanksgiving to you! Your mom has been talking of nothing else for weeks. She's baked every last one of your favorite treats, I hope you know."

"I figured she would." He froze, knowing what was next, but he couldn't do anything to stop it. Mrs. McKaslin released her daughter and came at him next, her arms outstretched, to give him a hug. "What on earth are you two doing together?"

"It's a long story. I'm sure you can get Kristin to tell you. I've got to get home. Mom's probably worried about me. I was supposed to come in last night."

"Come here and let me hug you, young man."

"Oh, I wouldn't do that if I were you. I haven't shaved. Showered. Been deloused."

"Oh, you can still make me laugh." Refusing to back down, Alice came at him and wrapped him into a kindly hug and, being a self-reliant man, he endured it—okay, it was nice. Alice was like a dear aunt to him when he'd been growing up. He brushed her cheek with a brief kiss as he moved out of her embrace.

"You're more handsome up close than in those

pictures your mom shows me. You don't see her enough, young man."

Standing behind her mother, Kristin winked at him. "Go easy on him. He's a busy, important doctor and the only reason I'm here and not snowed in at Boise is because he's a good guy."

"You're not so bad yourself, Miss McKaslin." The way both women were looking at him, as if he'd hung the moon and lit the stars, made him itchy.

He was uncomfortable with looks like that. With anyone getting too close. He'd gotten used to being alone. That was why Francine had returned his ring last September. He didn't need her at all, she'd said.

It was time to go. He let Alice lead the way to the front door, ignoring Kristin when she gestured for her bags. He was a lot of things, but he tried to use his manners when he had them. And what Kristin had done for him, in letting him sleep, he appreciated more than she could ever know. She looked as exhausted as he'd felt before getting some shut-eye, and he didn't mind at all carrying her bags into the house and depositing them at the top of the stairs.

"You didn't have to do that." She looked at him as if she appreciated the gesture. "But thank you."

"No problem." The delicious aroma scenting the house—apple and pumpkin pies, frying bacon and the roasting warmth of a baking turkey made his stomach growl loudly. He blushed. "Sorry about that."

"Would you like to stay? Breakfast is in the

works. Eggs and bacon and pancakes and sausage. Real homemade hash browns."

"I can't tell you how good that sounds, but Mom would box my ears. I'd best get home. She's waiting for me, and I'm late. I'm probably in trouble. Wow, I haven't said that since I was eighteen."

"Some things never change." Kristin breezed down the stairs, aware of her embarrassing grade-school pictures marching along the wall at her elbow. Hopefully, he wouldn't notice.

He didn't say anything as he headed for the door. "Take care of yourself, Miss McKaslin."

"You too, Dr. Sanders."

She didn't know why, but she hated seeing him slip through the door and stride down the steps. Even in the slick conditions, he walked with an athlete's assurance. With the power of a man who had confidence and integrity. Inside she sighed a little, remembering how he'd probably saved a young woman's life.

"Kristin, honey, close the door, would you?"

"What?" She shook her head, realizing she was letting in all the cold air. Shivering, she shut the door but watched through the window as Ryan climbed into the rented vehicle, belted in and drove away, leaving her behind. Adding another ache to the others she was collecting inside her heart.

Chapter Five

Ryan took one look at his childhood home and wanted to keep driving right past the unplowed driveway. *I'm not ready for this.*

He was in his thirties. If he wasn't ready now, when would he be? He'd nearly been away from Montana more years than he'd lived here. How could it be that time looped back upon itself so that as he spun the wheel to the right, slipping and sliding on the fresh snow, he saw the past more clearly than the world in front of him?

The small wooden, open-faced shed that sided the road looked every bit the same. His dad had built it to keep him out of the weather while he waited for the bus as a nervous first grader, with his superhero lunchbox in hand.

The hill, grown over with sturdy young trees now, that Dad had cleared and they'd used as a sled run during the long winters. The sounds of younger Mia's delighted screams as she slid down the slope on an inner tube, the low rumble of Dad's laughter and Mom's gentle chiming voice as she brought out a thermos of hot chocolate to keep them warm as they played.

The past haunted him with every turn of the wheels as he slowed to a stop along a private road where a small ranch house with brand-new siding and vinyl windows waited quietly. It wasn't the same house he remembered. Mom had made improvements over the years. She'd had a front porch built. She always admired the McKaslins' and could never afford the lumber for him to build her one when he was growing up.

Snow carpeted it now and clung like vanilla icing to the rails and steps. The large front window was shadowed, but a generous gray plume of smoke rose from the stovepipe. Homey. He grabbed his overnight bag and loped through the snowfall, snapped open the gate that was new and didn't squeak, and went around to the back door.

A glad brightness shone from the new bay windows—he'd sent Mom the money for the kitchen remodel as last year's Christmas present, and now he could see directly into the small kitchen and eating area. There was Mom, dressed in her usual worn jeans and a sweatshirt, her thick hair caught up in dainty clips, a crisp white apron at her waist as she stirred something at the stove.

Once again, the past and the present merged. Like every day of his childhood, she'd made breakfast at the stove while she hummed her favorite inspirational songs and sipped a cup of coffee laced with hazelnut coffee creamer. Only the two years following Dad's death, she hadn't sung once. Not once. Not even in church.

Slowly, over time, the music had returned to her life. But there had never been another man in this house. Until now.

Knowing the door was unlocked, as it had been all his life, he turned the handle so he could see the look on Mom's face as she turned. Her eyes widened and her mouth opened; tears gleamed in the same instant she dropped the spatula on the counter, the eggs forgotten.

"Ryan!" As if he'd just rescued the world from certain disaster, she ran to him. "You're home! You're here. I can't believe it! Oh, it's so *good* to see you!"

Happiness lit his heart as he dropped his bag, opened wide his arms and hugged his mom to his chest. She was a little thing, wrapping her arms around him, smelling of coffee and shampoo and the lilac lotion she'd always used. Her laughter bubbled through him as she stepped back and studied him with a mother's keen, knowing gaze.

"You're going to be the death of me, young man. I was worried out of my mind, what with this weather and your flight diverted. Yes, I checked with the airport. You could have *called* and let me know you were *alive*."

Okay, so no matter how old a man was, his mom was always his mom. "I know. I should have called and I meant to, but stuff happened. Are you gonna ground me?"

"I have half a mind to do it, too!" But her eyes were laughing and crying at the same time. "Oh, son, you look awful. You're not getting enough sleep. You're working too hard."

"I've just got a lot of stuff going on right now—"

"You stop sending me money, right now. You're not taking care of yourself. Have you eaten?"

"Uh, no. Nothing was exactly open, since we drove up through the middle of nowhere."

"We?"

Boy, did Mom jump on that quick, or what? And how was he going to minimize the fallout? He'd tell her the truth, he wasn't the kind of man to lie to his mother, and then she'd get all excited because he'd spent time with a woman. And not just with any woman, but with her best friend's daughter. Wasn't that just what she'd been hoping for all these years? For him to marry one of the nice McKaslin girls?

Yeah, right. He wasn't the marrying kind. He'd always suspected it, but Francine had been all the proof he needed. The last thing he wanted was to settle down. Not that Mom was going to understand that. Not in the slightest.

Look at the way she was practically vibrating with hope. He knew his mom, and she was secretly praying right now, as she retrieved her spatula and rescued the eggs from the frying pan, that he was going to say he'd driven up from Boise with a woman. A special woman.

And the second he admitted it was Kristin, she'd leap ahead and draw her own conclusions and there was nothing he could do to stop her. It would snowball into this big thing, when the truth was simple. He'd offered her a ride. She'd accepted. That was it. End of story.

"A stranded traveler I picked up at the airport, that's all." He shrugged out of his coat and dropped it on his suitcase. "And before you start getting all crazy, it was one of the McKaslin girls. She was alone and it wasn't safe for her to spend the night in a strange city."

"Oh, I should hope not!" Mom lit up, shining as if she was about to spontaneously emit her own energy field. "Kristin McKaslin. My, my. You know, she's got some fancy job on the coast. Alice was just saying—"

As if on cue, the phone rang. Mom lifted the eggs from the pan with her spatula. He was gentleman enough to hold out the platter for her and carry it to the table as she raced for the phone.

"Oh, Alice! Yes, Ryan told me. Isn't that something? On the same flight from Seattle?"

Yep, some things never changed. Mom was an eternal optimist, and he was an affirmed bachelor. How could he be anything else? There were only three chairs at the table, in the nook that had been

widened to accommodate the same wooden table
Mom had bought after her wedding long ago. It had
been refinished and looked as good as new sitting
on the braided rug on the polished hardwood floor.
Although the room had changed, life went on.

But the little boy who'd lost what mattered most—
his father—and the grown man who watched people
die every day in the emergency room in the hospital he was affiliated with had taught him one thing.
Nothing in life was guaranteed. The only certain
thing was God's grace, that was all, and getting close
to people was a fool's quest. It was bound to end.
People died, and their love went with them, and that
was it.

While his mom chatted with her lifelong best
friend, he rescued the bacon and sausage links from
the oven and set four slices of bread to toasting. Just
as he did when he was a kid. He settled into his chair
at the table, facing the windows that looked out over
the meadows and forested hills to the giant jagged
mountains that were shrouded with clouds.

He couldn't say why his heart felt as if it was shattering all over again, and the pain was blinding. He
blinked hard as he gulped down orange juice, the
past like a ghost standing behind him, and the future
as hard to see through as the clouds at the horizon,
bringing more snow.

Over the sounds of Dad and the brothers-in-law
settling into the football game, Kristin scooped the

newest addition to the family out of the playpen and into her arms. Four-month-old Caitlin with her curls of gold gave a final outcry before settling against Kristin's shoulder with a whimper of relief.

"You just wanted to be held, huh?"

As if in agreement, the infant relaxed in Kristin's arms. So precious. She brushed a hand over Caitlin's soft, soft hair. So fine and downy it was like touching the most heavenly cloud. With the drowsy baby falling back to sleep, Kristin rocked her gently from side to side, beneath the new collection of framed pictures Mom had started on the wall.

Photos of the six grandchildren filled the space between the living room and kitchen, from newborn to christening to every stage along the way. The newest picture of Kirby's son, Michael, dressed up like a fighter pilot for the church's Harvest festival. Karen's two girls, Allie in a ballerina's costume and one-year-old Anna in a bunny suit. Michelle's Emily taking her first steps captured forever with Dad holding out his strong, capable hands for her to toddle to.

It was what was missing that made her eyes burn. If Allison had lived, she would have married, and her children would be on this wall, too. Sadness gathered inside her until she had to turn away.

If Allison had lived, then Kristin's life would have been different, too. Mom and Dad wouldn't have fallen away from one another in their grief.

The family would have remained whole. And Kristin would have been different, too.

She closed her eyes and turned away, willing down the memory of taking a calculus test one moment and the next having her safe world torn to shreds as the principal interrupted to pull her out of class. Her dad was waiting in the office to tell her of her sister's death.

"Oh, did you see the latest addition?" Mom appeared around the corner, her full apron smudged with flour from the rolls she'd been making. Wiping her hands on a dish towel, she gestured toward a golden framed photograph. "Caitlin's christening. It was a shame you missed it."

Kristin knew her mom didn't understand. Over half of the company's business rode on their clients' successes at the trade shows. Her boss had refused her request for a day off flat out. "I'm here now. Do you need more help in the kitchen?"

"Don't change the subject, young lady." Mom gave her sternest look, but it faded away as she studied the pictures. "I expect your little one to be on this wall one day. I understand you like having a career, it must be exciting to live in a big city, but your roots are here, Kristin. Your family is here."

It was an old argument. One that hurt. What did she say to her mother? That marriage and family hadn't made her mother happy? She couldn't say the words. Couldn't stand the distance between her parents and knew there was no way for her to fix it. That it couldn't be fixed.

"Gramma's asking for you, Mom." Kendra came to the rescue, breezing in to sweep her baby daughter from Kristin's arms. "Oh, she likes her auntie Kristin."

"The feeling's mutual." Kristin stroked Caitlin's soft cheek, careful not to wake the drowsing infant. "She's pretty great."

"Cam and I think so, too." Kendra beamed with the quiet glow of happiness, and Kristin wondered about that as she watched her mom and sister retreat to the warm kitchen, where the women in the family gathered.

This was her favorite part of the holidays. In the flurry of activity in preparing the meal, for one moment, the family felt whole. Undiminished. Michelle laughing as she teased Karen about her latest shoe faux pas, Kirby whipping the potatoes and stopping midway through to search through the kitchen for more butter. Karen teasing Michelle back when a carrot coin rolled off the center island and onto her shoe. Kendra, with babe on her hip, digging the condiments out of the back of the fridge. Gramma bemoaning the lumps in her gravy that didn't exist, interspersed with the disorganized discussion of the latest family news.

Dad ambled into the women's domain in his only good red-and-black flannel shirt and brown jeans.

Quiet as always, he searched through the drawers for the carving knife.

"It's right there on the counter." Mom's tight words broke the magic, and the cheer faded.

Dad picked up the knife and went to work slicing the waiting turkey, and Gramma tried to heal the awkward silence by complimenting Mom on the perfect turkey.

Kristin took the covered wrap off the fruit salad and sunk a serving spoon into the sweet froth of whipped cream, sliced apples and bananas and carried it and the serving dish of jellied cranberries to the table. She wondered how Ryan was faring. Better, she hoped.

Images of him whisked through her mind. Was his first Thanksgiving at home since he'd graduated as happy as it should be? Surely this hardworking man with values and integrity, who had undoubtedly saved the accident victim's life, deserved one good day. At the very least.

She set the bottles and bowl on the table. Why was she thinking about Ryan? She liked him. She wished him well. But it wasn't as if she'd see him again. Why would she? Their paths would never cross again.

She couldn't say why that made her so sad, but it did. It felt like another loss that didn't fade but lingered as she returned to the kitchen, where the strain between her mom and dad was as unmistakable as the floor at her feet.

* * *

He was suffocating as sure as if his lungs had collapsed. Ryan took a long pull of the cherry soda Mom had dug out of the back of the refrigerator, from behind her bowls of salad and cranberry jelly and the covered plates of homemade fudge. The bubbly sweetness chased down his throat but didn't help him breathe any better.

Snow was starting to tumble from a peaceful sky, falling in a hush. With the pop of the woodstove and squeak and bang of the open door and Mom's cheerful hum as she checked on the turkey in the oven, he couldn't hear the quiet reverence that came. But it was there just the same. The world quieted, as if just to hear the fragile tap, tap, tap of snowflakes on the earth.

Heaven must be like this, Dad had said once, on their early Sunday-morning forays into the wilderness. Ryan nudged aside the ruffled edge of the frilly curtains to gaze out at the tree line.

If he looked hard enough there was the past, alive within him, as he remembered the cold creeping through the layers of wool Mom had wrapped him up in. Snow crept over the top of his high boots to wet his pant legs tucked inside, and melted as it slid down to his ankle.

There was a cadence to the falling snow, and he, like nature surrounding him, leaned forward, holding his breath to hear it. Feel it. The reverence of the hills, as if relaxing to accept their mantle of snow.

The mountains rising like awed worshipers, their faces lost in the mist and clouds.

Everywhere, the land felt at peace, as if at prayer, and Ryan had felt it, too. The stroke of God's hand in everything, and then Dad's low baritone, rumbling low out of respect for the Maker, as he leaned close.

"I've always thought that heaven would feel like this, solemn and awesome and so beautiful it makes your eyes water to look at it."

Ryan cleared his throat, looking away, setting the half-empty soda can on the edge of the counter. Too many emotions. He'd worked most of his life not to remember. Not to feel. Like ice cracking beneath the snow, pain splintered inside his chest.

"Oh, that was Alice." Mom set down the cordless handset he hadn't noticed she'd even picked up. "She loved my recipe for cranberry jelly. She said it was much better than the recipe she'd used last year. It was the hit of their Thanksgiving dinner."

"We had a bet going. I told her if she didn't just love it, then I'd treat her to lunch. It's a new recipe I found in one of those fancy cooking magazines, and oh, it's a winner." Mom beamed with a steady happiness as she brushed lustrous strands of hair out of her eyes. "Oh, it's so *good* to see you standing in my kitchen."

"It's kinda good to be here, too." Okay, here it came. The mushy part. He braced himself. He wasn't one to let his defenses down. He opened his arms and let her walk into them. Let her squeeze him in a bear hug. Warmth glowed inside him, melting away the pain. But love came with its own pain.

"I love my little mom," he said to make her laugh.

She stepped away to look up at him. "How did my little boy get to be so big?"

"Remember those vitamins you made me eat with breakfast every morning? They worked."

"I see that." Tears gleamed in her eyes, eyes that were wise and kind and a beautiful hazel-green. In them, he saw her pleasure at having him home, and noticed something else. No more shadows. She was finally at peace.

She'd worked so hard for them. For him.

Time looped back on itself, in the fluid way of memories, and he saw the kitchen of his youth. The yellowed linoleum floors and the ancient cabinet doors that wouldn't stay shut but would swing open whenever the mood suited them. The red countertop worn white in places from several decades of wipe downs and dripping dishes drying in a rack beneath the window. Mom, hollow-eyed with exhaustion as she worked, humming away to make their meager Thanksgiving Day meal a feast.

It wasn't the poverty that had ever bothered him. It wasn't the odd jobs he worked for the neighbors to bring in cash to help out, before he'd been old enough to be hired on at the grocery. None of that really mattered. It was the deep yearning for his dad.

If only he could have one more day. Just one more day of wading through the knee-deep snow and listening to the music of snowfall alongside the man who'd always been so tall, seemed so big and strong and everything good in a man. Invincible.

I miss you, Dad.

The ice shards in his chest seemed to splinter into more sharp blades stabbing into his heart. If he let it, it was a pain that could drown him until there was nothing else. He fought it by shutting off his feelings.

"My, it gives me a start to see you standing there." Mom had turned from checking on the progress of something on the stove, one hand clutching the neck of her shirt. "You look so much like him. Like your father. It's takes me back to when he was alive and standing in my kitchen. Right there at the window, like you are now…"

Don't go there, Mom. The thought blared in his mind, but he didn't dare open his mouth to speak. He couldn't take any more memories.

"…with shoulders so broad and strong, I felt as if he could handle anything. That nothing would ever hurt me as long as he was there." Mom's words resounded with true love, like a candlelight hymn, but they bore wounds in his heart as surely as if they'd been bullets blasting into his flesh.

He turned away, thinking of last night's blizzard and how it had shrouded him from the rest of the world. He made himself like that, steeling the walls of his heart.

Mom kept talking, but he wouldn't listen. He just couldn't let her in. He was like a drowning man going down for the last time. Feeling the icy waters welling up from within, he prayed for relief.

As if the angels heard and took pity on him, his cell chirped. His E.R. doc buddy Tim's number flashed on the phone's small screen. You'd better have good news, man, Ryan thought. Because right now he couldn't take any more bad news.

Chapter Six

Kristin entered the post-Thanksgiving dinner calm of the unoccupied dining room, slid the Monopoly box onto the table and sank into a cushioned chair. Yawning from too much turkey, she could put her feet up and sneak in a nap—yeah, as if her sisters were going to let her get away with that.

She could hear their voices throughout the house. Karen and Kirby in the kitchen talking about the family's beloved pony, Honeybear, which they'd all learned to ride on and now was teaching a second generation of McKaslin girls. Their laughter rose higher and fell below the hum of the dishwasher and the clink of pots as they put the last of the hand-washed dishes away.

Kendra, who kept the pony at her riding stable, chimed in with a comment Kristin couldn't quite make out as the roar of the football game in the living room rose into a frenzied crescendo. It wouldn't feel like a holiday without Dad glued to the big-screen TV he'd splurged on and his muttering commentary on the referee's call was a sound she'd heard every game day since she was little.

It was good to know some things would never change. That's what got her through the sadness of sitting at this table where Gramma occupied Allison's chair, which had remained empty for years. With the leaves in the center, the table stretched to nearly fill the entire room. There were so many of them with the additions to their family—her sisters' husbands and kids. It was a good thing she'd decided not to ever get married. Because there would be no room for another man at the table!

Oh, it's good to be home. Kristin breathed deep, and the warm scents of this day soothed her. The spicy goodness of Gramma's pumpkin pie warming in the oven. The vanilla candles she'd gotten Mom last Christmas burning with a cheery brightness in the corner by the window. The steady comfort of brewing coffee seasoning the air.

She rubbed at the tension in the back of her neck. Wow, her muscles were knotted up good. It was always this way. Allison's loss was like a layer of ice over a cold pond of grief. No matter how many layers of snow covered it, no matter how hard her family tried to reach for that contented wholeness that used to exist, the ice was there. The loss. There was no solid place to stand on.

Youngest sister, Michelle, glowing in the second trimester of pregnancy, padded out from the kitchen with a bowl of rippled potato chips and stacked covered bowls of different flavors of homemade dip. She unloaded them on the table. "There's no place like home, is there?"

"Nope. It's good to be back."

"This house used to be so lonely. You know… after Allison." Michelle peeled back the plastic wrap from the first bowl of dip. "But not anymore. Good changes, don't you think?"

It was the same—the house, the sense of family and the feeling of home. But time had changed the details, added texture. Little kids ran around the living room, now scattered with colorful plastic toys. A baby drowsed in her swing, her blond curls glistening.

Kristin leaned just enough to see through the archway into the living room. The back of Dad's head, his hair thinning and graying, was visible over the back of the couch. But he wasn't alone. Gramma's new husband, Willard, had claimed the recliner. Michelle's and Kendra's husbands flanked Dad on either side. Karen's and Kirby's husbands took up the sectional in the corner.

It was weird to think all her sisters had married. Were wives and mothers.

And mothers-to-be.

"You have another good change coming." Kristin nodded toward Michelle's thickening waist.

"I know! Gabe and I weren't planning a second child so soon, but, oops!" Michelle stole a chip from the heaping bowl and crunched on it. "During the ultrasound, we accidentally found out if we're having a boy or a girl. No, I'm not going to tell you. It'll, like, ruin the surprise for everyone else."

"How am I going to know what color stuff to buy for your shower?"

"Ooh, and you buy good stuff, too. You're the only sister I have with any fashion sense at all. If I give you a hint, then it's not like really telling."

"Exactly. I'm a great secret keeper. You know that."

Michelle pushed a lock of hair behind her ear and stole another chip. "Let's just say I'm not going to be able to use Emily's baby things for this little one. I'm going to need all new stuff."

That could only mean one thing. A little nephew was on the way. "Michelle. Lucky you. Congratulations."

"Thanks. I am pretty lucky."

There was no mistaking her happiness. Now. But what about down the road?

Troubled, Kristin grabbed a bowl and flicked off the plastic wrap. "Hmm, French onion. Gramma's secret recipe. I'm glad some things never change."

"The best stuff just keeps getting better, don't you think?"

"Yeah. I know what you mean." For all her sadness, there was gratitude, too, for the blessings surrounding her. Home and family, health and hope.

Everything good in her life was because she'd grown up here, because of the people in this house.

Michelle lifted the tattered lid of their old Monopoly box. "Kirby and Karen are planning on rounding up the kids and bedding them down in my old room. Once everyone's napping, we'll get started. Sound like a plan?"

"A good one. Are the husbands going to join us, or will it be just us girls?"

"Hmm. Let me think." Michelle turned to study the strapping men clustered around the television, leaning forward, attention one hundred percent on the game. The big screen showed the quarterback passing the ball to a wide receiver, and the men leaped to their feet, shouting and cheering.

The baby woke up and sniffled.

"Hmm, I don't think we should let dudes who act like that near us," Michelle decided with a twinkle as she went to rescue her little one in the swing.

"Good decision."

Kristin considered her brothers-in-law. They all seemed like good men. She hardly knew them, having spent bits and pieces of time with them through her visits home. What mattered to her was how those men treated her sisters. As long as her sisters were happy, then she liked her brothers-in-law just fine.

But marriage was marriage—inevitably love faded, problems and hardship broke the best of relationships. Diminished the greatest romance. Men let women down; yeah, she got that. That's why she was way too smart to ever get married. To put that much trust in anyone. Sisters were one thing. They had bonds that would never break.

But romantic love was a whole different story—*that* kind of love was like a fragile bloom on the hard Montana plains. Short-lived and quick to wither in the bitter north winds.

A movement caught her eye. A man's broad-shouldered shadow fell across the snow in front of the picture window. That profile sure looked familiar. The doorbell rang, although it was hard to hear above the noise of the cranked-up TV and the men shouting like the crazed fans they were in the living room. She alone seemed to notice the visitor's silhouette against the etched glass in the door.

Kristin yanked open the door, glad to see Ryan Sanders blocking the porch light, snow glistening in his dark hair. "Hey, what are you doing here? You clean up real nice."

"Right. Oh, I shaved." He ran one hand along his square jaw. "I bring good news and the fudge my mom promised your mom but didn't get a chance to drop by. She said since I was coming over, I'd better not come empty-handed. I need something to bribe my way through the door."

"We don't let your kind in otherwise."

When he laughed, dimples framed his smile. He had a great smile, the kind that lit him up from within. And it made Kristin feel bright inside, too.

She took the offered tin, topped with an amber-and-orange ribbon.

She breathed in the fudgy aroma. "Hmm, my mouth is already watering. Your mom makes the best fudge in three states. Did you want to come in? Or are you just dropping this by? Did you hear about Samantha?"

"I did. God must have heard your prayers because Tim told me they took a bone spur out of her neck, between C2 and C3 vertebrae. The bone didn't penetrate her spinal cord, and except for a little swelling against the nerve roots, she's fine."

"And does that mean she's going to be all right?"

"Yeah. They pinned a broken bone in her lower right leg, turned out to be a fracture, but other than that, she's fine. Considering the cold, it could have been a lot worse. It's a good thing we came along when we did."

It was no coincidence. The certainty of it steadied her. The long events of the last night had happened for a reason. What if Ryan hadn't flown into Seattle for his job interview? Then he would never have been on the flight that was diverted to Boise. And if not for the storm, then he wouldn't have been anywhere near the lonely stretch of road where Samantha Fields had crashed. As the Good Lord would have it, Ryan, a doctor, was there to help when he was needed. He made a true difference in the world.

"Is that football?" Ryan leaned past her to sneak

a look at the game in full-color glory on the wide screen. "Man, look at that TV."

"It's Dad's pride and joy. Don't tell me you like football."

"Like it? It's only like the most important thing in the world." He rolled his eyes, which sparkled with humor. "How could you not know that?"

"My mistake. Sorry. Football ranks right above world peace. I should have known. You're welcome to come inside and watch the game."

"Thanks. Ooh, a fumble!" Ryan's groan matched the series of painful noises rising up in the living room.

"Come in. Stay. There's probably room for you on the floor in the corner. We won't charge you admission *this* time, since you're a friend of the family and all."

"Kristin, you're fabulous. You know that, right? It's been killin' me not being able to see this game. Mom's satellite is out." He took a step forward, enough to see the replay of his team's fumble. "That's killin' me, too."

"Take off your coat before you go gawk at the TV." She held out her hand.

But Ryan, all his attention focused on the game, shrugged out of his black leather jacket and went to snag it on the coat tree all by himself—and missed. He got it on the second try.

Kristin closed the door against the gentle drift of snow. What was it about men and football? "Do you want something to drink? We've got soda, coffee or juice."

"Soda, if it's not too much trouble." He flashed her a wink, friendly and easy, not flirty at all.

Then why did her toes tingle? That was certainly the wrong response. She was not interested in him at all. *Not in the slightest.* So, why wouldn't her toes stop tingling as she sashayed into the kitchen, slid the fudge on the counter and plundered a can of cola from the crowded fridge.

Mom looked up from the corner table where she was sitting with Gramma and doing needlework. She looked far too, well, innocent. As if she was incredibly surprised by the simple tin on the counter. "Goodness! Is that Mary's fudge? Why, was that her at the door?"

"No, her son is in our living room right now." Kristin didn't have to turn around. She already knew what Mom was going to say next. "Yeah, I know he's a doctor and I know he's an eligible bachelor. But I'm not *interested*." She enunciated very clearly so Mom couldn't misunderstand.

Her mother was clearly plotting. There was no way she was going to believe that Ryan just *happened* to come over today, of all days, when the two of them had driven up together in the same car. No, Mom had been on the phone with Mary earlier. "You're not going to fool me, Mother dear. I know Mary sent him over and the two of you are hoping we'll fall madly in love and get married."

"Married? Why, of course not. What ever gave you that idea?"

Kirby looked up from counting out the good dessert plates from the china cabinet. "Gee, I wonder. Maybe I heard you tell Mary it was a sign from above, the two of them bumping into each other at the airport. Then you suggested that Mary send her son over today, so the kids could get better acquainted."

"Why, we were talking about the fudge. Surely you misunderstood." But Mom looked way too pleased with herself. "But since you brought up the subject, then yes. What Kristin needs is to find a nice doctor like Ryan."

"Mom!" Kristin groaned.

"Mom!" Karen protested.

"Mother!" Kirby chimed in a lighthearted reprimand. "Let Kristin find her own man. I have perfect faith she'll find the right one."

"Thanks." How she loved her sisters. There was nothing like solidarity. "Maybe I don't want a nice doctor."

"Yeah, Mom, maybe Kristin wants a mean doctor." Kendra spoke up from slicing pie at the counter.

"Any old doctor will do," Kristin added, kidding.

"Yeah," oldest sister Karen agreed as she uncapped a pitcher of Gramma's lemon-lime punch. "We wouldn't want our dear Kristin to take her time and find a loving and strong man. No, we want her to take any old guy who comes along. So what if he's mean? Or lazy? Or can't keep a job?"

"Yeah, Mom." Michelle tugged out clean forks and knives from the silent dishwasher. "Kristin would be married. *That's* what matters. So what if it's to the wrong guy. It isn't the guy that's important. It's the wedding ring. Right?"

"Oh, you girls!" Mom chuckled as she pulled her embroidery thread tight. "All right, you win. I'll stop."

"Stop?" Kristin wasn't fooled. "No, you'll never stop. You'll just cease to harp on my getting married for about two minutes. *Maybe.*"

"Two minutes?" Karen piled a thick wedge of pie on a dessert plate. "Do you think Mom can hold out that long? I say a minute and a half."

"One minute." Gramma set down her crocheting and held up her wrist to stare at her gold watch.

Mom pretended to look shocked. "You are all exaggerating. I do not harp."

"Yes, you do, Mom." Kirby's gentle ribbing included wrapping their mother in a big hug. "Admit it."

"Yeah, admit it, Mom." Kristin set down the glass and soda can and wrapped her arms around Mom and Kirby. "It's the second thing you talk about every time you call, right after 'hello.' You say, 'have you met anyone yet?'"

"I'm not that bad."

"You're *that* bad." Kendra was next, joining the circle.

Followed by Karen. "We like our Kristin happy and we want her to stay that way, married or not."

Kristin leaned her cheek against Karen's. What would she do without her sisters?

Michelle entered the room with a distressed cry. "Like, leave me out!" She joined the circle with outstretched arms.

Boots knelled on the linoleum and stopped. "All right, break it up. What does a man have to do to get a drink around here?"

Ryan. Kristin took a step back, unaware of her sisters milling around. Mom's warm greeting buzzed like a fly next to her ear. Yep, by the sound of it, Mom was definitely hoping for a match between them.

She knew her mother meant well, but please! She held up the glass. "I wasn't about to let you dehydrate. I know you have to keep your throat well lubricated for all that yelling you men do at the refs and the players."

"And the coaches. Thanks." Ryan took the glass. "I can remember the last time I've been in your kitchen. I think it was the summer I turned eight and Mom made me go everywhere with her."

"Wasn't that the summer you drove the family car into the ditch?"

"Yep. Not one of my better moments. I was just pretending to drive. How was I to know the parking brake wouldn't hold? I popped in the clutch and the car rolled backward down the driveway and into the irrigation ditch."

Her sisters' laughter filled the air. "I remember," Karen began. "Dad drove the tractor over to pull the car out."

"You were the talk of the church picnic the next day," Kirby added. "No one figured you'd wreck the family sedan before you hit your teens."

"Mom grounded me for life after that. She commuted my sentence to three weeks when the same thing happened to her and she dented Mr. Winkler's Buick. Seems the parking brake really *was* faulty so she got it fixed."

Ryan couldn't believe it. The McKaslin girls may have grown up and gotten married, were wives and mothers, but they were still the same—warm, friendly and lighthearted.

It had been a long time since he'd felt this at-home anywhere. Obeying the demands of his rumbling stomach, he flicked off the lid and took a big fat gooey piece of fudge. "Karen, Kendra, Kirby. It's good to see you again. And little Michelle, look at you. When are you due?"

"This spring. This one will be my second. Emily's in the living room with her daddy." Beaming, Michelle stroked her sizable stomach and stopped to listen. "I hear more groans coming from the living room. Bad news?"

"Painful. That's why I'm here. Thought I'd hide

from the grim sight of my lifelong favorite team getting thrashed. Figured the sight of you beautiful ladies would help ease the sting of defeat."

"That compliment earns you a piece of the pie of your choice." Kristin, by far the most beautiful of the sisters, held out two plates. "Apple or pumpkin?"

Was that real whipped cream? Yep, it looked like the real thing. As genuine and rich as the woman in front of him. "Are you kidding? It's Thanksgiving. Pumpkin."

Mrs. McKaslin leaned over the table to say, in that way of matchmaking mothers, "Kristin is an excellent baker. Aren't you, sweetie?"

"I'm the worst baker of the group and you know it." Kristin turned a cute shade of pink. Embarrassed, she jabbed a fork at him, taking the slice of apple pie over to her mom. "You promised to stop."

"Yes, but he's a *doctor.*"

Poor Kristin. She looked so exasperated and embarrassed. He had lots of practice with this subject. "If I had a buck every time I heard a woman's mother say that, I'd have my med-school loans paid off by now. I know. Marrying off your daughters is a mother's duty."

"That it is. I want all of my girls happy."

"*Mom.* I'm happy the way I am." Kristin marched the length of the kitchen, keeping far away from him.

She wasn't even giving him those telling looks,

the ones that said that she was hoping for a doctor to marry and zeroing in on him, since he was single.

After yanking open the freezer, she dropped a gallon of Neapolitan ice cream on the counter with a resounding thud. "Don't take this personally, Ryan. Mom has had so much fun planning everyone's wedding, that she wants to plan mine next."

"Oh, I understand. Believe me. It was my mom who conveniently 'forgot' to bring the fudge by."

"I know your pain." Kristin looked a little less embarrassed. "Ice cream?"

"With my second piece of pie, sure. Let me finish this one first."

"What makes you think that you get seconds?"

"My charming personality?" That made everyone laugh. Okay, so he liked being the center of attention. Who didn't? And it felt good to be accepted so easily into the McKaslins' family circle, when his mom's house offered him no peace.

"All right, Mr. Charming. Make yourself useful and take that with you." Kristin shoved two dessert plates at him. Huge pie wedges topped with scoops of vanilla and chocolate. "The apple's for Dad. The other is for whoever grabs it first."

"Me, useful? You've got the wrong impression of me. I'm never useful."

"Never. *Right*." Sparkling with held-back laughter, Kristin breezed away, taking with her the scent of vanilla and something else. He couldn't name it as he hesitated.

He didn't want to leave just yet. There was something troubling him. Something within him that wanted to stay in the light of her presence. "Anything else I can carry for you, while I'm here?"

"Nope. That's it." Her eyes danced as she studied him from behind the refrigerator door.

An odd sensation tightened deep within his chest. The ice within him cracked, and that hurt, too, although he didn't know why. Maybe because he stood in the kitchen of a real family. One with both parents. He'd always admired the McKaslins. In truth, when he'd been young, been envious of them, too. Not that he was proud of it, but he'd learned since then that the grass is always greener on the other side of the fence.

Although, standing in this kitchen looked pretty great to him. Since that was way too domestic of a thought for a guy like him, Ryan trained his attention on the living room. Exit stage left.

"I'm getting out of here before I eat *all* the pie." He caught Kristin's twinkling gaze as he left the room, leaving the women laughing behind him.

He handed off the pie plates and took the corner of the couch. That TV sure was something. He could see every detail with perfection as his team lined up on the thirty-four, third down and five to go. They were behind, okay, so they were losing, but if they made a good play, they had a good chance to—

"Yeah!" Shouts rose around him, Zach and Sam, two of the brothers-in-law, jumped to their feet, urging the running back on. The twenty-two, the eighteen— "Keep goin', c'mon!"

Down at the fifteen. Ryan was on his feet. Excitement zinged through him. He shoveled down pie, along with the other men in the room during the huddle, which took forever. When he should have been willing his quarterback to pass, his thoughts were not on the game. But on the golden-haired woman, her short hair sweeping against her jaw as she circled around the couch and into the dining room.

The team broke up, warriors hungry for victory.

"Run it," Mr. McKaslin advised.

"A pass, high and long," Sam, Kirby's husband, shouted at the screen.

"No, all they need is a field goal," Zach argued.

The center hiked the ball. Ryan's fork froze in midair as he watched the play unfold. A sack attempt by the defense, but the quarterback feigned right in time, stepped left and arced the ball with the perfect spin to set it in the tailback's hands behind the goal line. Touchdown!

Ryan yelled right along with the others. Yeah! They had a chance of winning this one. Something buzzed at the back of his neck. He slapped his hand there—not a bug or an itch or anything. The tickle remained. When he looked up, Kristin was in his line of sight, unboxing a board game on the dining-room table.

She sure was nice. He'd noticed that before—

but not like this. Never like this. On the plane she'd looked coolly professional in her power suit. On the long drive through Idaho, she'd looked in charge and competent. Everything he'd expect in an urban woman with, as his mom always put it, a highfalutin job. He'd liked that Kristin.

He liked this one more. She was one hundred percent pure Montana girl in worn jeans and a gray U of M sweatshirt. Girl-next-door fresh and warmhearted. Deep in his chest his steel defenses buckled a little, letting in a crack in the armor. Giving way to a hitch of emotion, but he shut that down before the feeling could grow.

His cell chirped from the entryway. Taking the pie with him, he wolfed down the last of the rich spicy pumpkin as he dashed through the room and down the hall. He dug out the phone and flipped it open. "Hey, Mom."

"I hope you're not ruining your appetite."

"How do you always know when I'm misbehaving? Not only do you have eyes in the back of your head but you have X-ray vision, too."

"Of course! Mothers are extraordinary, my boy. Besides, I can tell you're talking with your mouth full. My bet is pie."

"And it's good pie."

"Not one more piece, young man! The turkey comes out of the oven in twenty minutes, and I want you front and center to carve it for me. Oh! Your sister just drove up. I've got to go."

"I'm on my way," he promised, snapping off the phone.

Home. His guts tightened. Tension snaked through his muscles and he realized he was holding his breath.

Time to go home. To face again the house that brought back memories that could make him bleed.

He felt her presence behind him, knew it was Kristin before he turned with his coat over his arm. "My mom said I have to go home now. It's dinner-time. It's funny. I haven't said those words since I was eighteen."

"Ah, that's what you get for coming home. No matter how old you are, you're still your parents' kid."

"Yeah." He felt awkward. He didn't know why.

Maybe it was because he didn't want to face the past, or maybe it was that he didn't want to leave this house full of love and family togetherness. Of easy laughter and unfailing devotion. He simply didn't want to leave just yet and Kristin was the reason. The pretty woman with the shadows in her expressive eyes and the amazing blend of honest country girl and successful career woman.

Haloed in the soft illumination of the wall sconce, she seemed to softly glow. Her hair shimmered with a hundred different shades of gold, and light burnished her shoulders so that when she reached out to take his plate, she was the most beautiful image he'd ever seen.

Her hands were slender and fine-boned with beautifully tapered fingers. Her nails were short and painted a seashell pink. It looked as if hers would be a nice hand to hold in his.

Not that he was looking for wife candidates. He was deeply committed to his bachelor status. Still, she was sure something, as if the light moved through her and he could see her goodness. Her kindness. He swallowed past the sudden tightness in his throat and shrugged into his jacket. "Take good care of yourself, Kristin McKaslin."

"You, too, Dr. Sanders."

The next step he took felt like a momentous one. As if he'd reached a fork in his life path offering two very different choices. It was a weird way to feel, because there was nothing consequential about opening the door and walking into the snow. Nothing life changing about zipping up his zipper and digging the keys out of his jeans pocket.

Then why did it feel wrong, somehow? When his mom was waiting for him, and his sister was probably chatting a hundred miles a minute in the kitchen. In twenty minutes he'd be sitting down for Thanksgiving dinner.

His feelings didn't make sense. Not at all.

He was just troubled about being here in Montana. Maybe that was it. As he crunched down the snowy steps and the winter air radiated through his coat to make him shiver, no other explanation came to mind. Only four more hours, he thought, glancing at his watch. His flight departed at seven-thirty—the airport had recovered from the blizzard and was up and running. He could survive until then.

As he drove off, the day was already changing. Twilight cast a somber mood across the snow-mantled world. Making the shadows a deep blue-gray and the sky a mourning shroud as memories, cold and dark, had a hold on him and didn't let go.

Chapter Seven

December 3

With the temperate heat of the Phoenix sun on his back, Ryan pushed hard for the last quarter mile. Jogging wasn't his favorite thing—it made his shins hurt, his knees ache and it was plain hard work—but for some unexplained reason he looked forward to setting out on his five-mile run every day after work. Even on a perfect Saturday like this one.

Not a cloud in the bright blue sky. The sun a friendly brightness reflecting off the miles of concrete and pavement that comprised the Scottsdale neighborhood he lived in. All different kinds of palm trees, from the short stubby pineapple palms to the tall tropical ones, waved their fronds in the breeze.

His neighbor's cat darted out from beneath the oleander hedges and streaked down the sidewalk and out of sight. Nothing but a blur of gray and white.

Tonight, as usual, he'd terrify the poor animal, without meaning to, by opening his slider door.

The cat napped on Ryan's lounge-chair cushion. Not that he minded, but he would rather befriend the animal instead of always watching it run in the opposite direction.

He understood, though. He and that cat had a lot in common. Keep your distance. Don't trust anyone.

He was so good, he'd perfected it into an art form.

At the end of the hedges, he dropped into a walk. Sweat sluiced off him, but it felt good to have pushed like that. He worked indoors all day. He loved his work; he just hated being confined.

Probably because he'd spent most of his youth outside—playing in the meadows and woods, riding his bike for miles on quiet country roads and, when he was older, working in the fields for extra money. Throughout the long years of his medical training, he'd spent endless hours indoors. He'd never acclimated to it.

It had gotten worse since he'd been back home for Thanksgiving.

Scottsdale had its own strange beauty. Not the rugged granite mountains and lush fertile river valley of his hometown. Still, the eerily human forms of the saguaro cacti, with their arms stretched toward heaven, and the stubborn green of the palm trees and the rocky camelback ridges of the Superstition Mountains were a form of beauty, too.

It just wasn't Montana.

Ryan wasn't sure if it was Montana he missed or the woman he'd reunited with there. Kristin had been on his mind since he'd left the McKaslins' home to carve Mom's turkey. He didn't know why he kept thinking about her. Probably because she was really something, that's why. Just because he planned on being unattached forever didn't mean he couldn't appreciate a fine woman.

It didn't help matters that Mom had done nothing else but talk up Kristin. Through their Thanksgiving meal, Mom kept peppering the conversation with comments about Kristin, even if she had to change the subject back to the pretty Montana girl. She was so successful that she'd bought her own place. She was smart with money. She wasn't dating anyone. She had a lot in common with him. She loved movies and books and she jogged, too.

Poor Mom. He knew it was hard for her to understand why he stayed single. That really perplexed him because she'd lost Dad, too. She'd never dated. She'd never considered getting remarried. So, why did she want him to? Both of them knew there was no sense in going through that kind of pain again. People died. Life ended. As a doctor, he couldn't deny how frail life was.

He wasn't about to get close to anyone again. No. He couldn't take that kind of devastation one more time. He was just fine alone. It hadn't been easy for the eight-year-old he'd been to attend his dad's funeral. To try to pick up the pieces shattering all around him—his mom's grief, his own heartbreak, the gaping hole that Dad had left behind. To live every day without him, to comfort his mom and sister, to worry about money, to know that if he lost one parent, then he could just as easily, just as suddenly, lose the other.

No, he'd lived with enough of that uncertainty. Swiping the sweat from his brow, he stopped in front of the mailboxes and bent down to give his hamstrings a good stretch. He'd missed a few days of running, with the holidays and the long office hours. He was paying for it now.

He looked in his mailbox—the standard stuff. The water bill. Pizza ads. A flyer for free windshield-crack repairs. And a bonus—an envelope from Tim, his buddy in Boise. The E.R. doc. Ryan ripped that one open.

"Hey, Ryan," he read in Tim's typical hurried, doctor's scrawl. "Samantha Fields was discharged last week, and she asked me to pass these notes on to you. I didn't know the woman you were with, but I figure you'll know how to reach her."

Ryan looked in the envelope at the two note cards, one addressed to him and the other simply to Kristin.

There he was, thinking about her again. How there'd been steel in her that night—how she'd worked without complaint in the bitter cold to help him tend to Samantha. And there was light in her, the kind that shone as true as the sun. A kindness that moved even a grouchy old bachelor like him, who was so set in his ways.

The trouble was, he didn't have her address in Seattle. If he called his mom, boy, would she make a big deal about it. She'd think she was making progress on her campaign to match him up with a suitable woman. No, he couldn't call his mom. A call to Kristin's mom was out, too.

One of her sisters. Yeah, he'd give Kirby a call. Kirby was a nurse. She understood about confidentiality. He'd get her number from information. Yep, that was a good idea. This way his mom would never know he wanted to write Kristin.

It wasn't his idea to write her, after all. Nope. It was his duty to forward the note from Samantha Fields. And, being an honorable man, what else could he do?

December 8

Rain smeared the windshield of Kristin's sedan and the wipers couldn't keep up with the downpour. Water rushed in rivulets down the paved city streets and sheened on the blacktop of her complex's parking lot. It was only seven o'clock, but it could have been midnight, for the evening felt bleak and endless.

She hit her garage-door opener, grateful to be home safe. The freeway through the downtown corridor had been a mess. Accidents everywhere, lanes of traffic idling in both directions for miles. She turned off the engine, clicked off the headlights, gathered up her work and hit the garage-door button. With the wind and cold locked safely outside, she hopped up the three steps to her kitchen door and unlocked it.

Two frowning Persian cats were two shadows of fluffy shades of gray in the middle of the kitchen. They studied her with unblinking eyes. *Uh-oh, there was a reprimand coming.*

"I'm late, I know. I'm sorry." She dropped her armload of work on the counter, along with her purse, and shrugged out of her waterproof coat.

The garment was still a little damp from her run from the office building to the parking garage— the economical parking was down the street, of course, she didn't want to pay a premium just to park close—but today she'd regretted her sensible budgeting. She'd been soaked the instant she stepped outside. Lovely. She was still wet through. And cold.

The dripping water was another transgression to the cats that had obvious standards to maintain. They still hadn't entirely forgiven her for leaving them for Thanksgiving.

"I know it's hard being inside in the warm house all day." She knelt to thread her fingers through the warm silk of their fluffy hair. Minnie, who held a grudge the longest, looked away, but Mickey, her brother, leaned into Kristin's touch and gave a gravelly purr.

"I missed you, too." She loved animals. She'd

never been without a pet of one kind or another until she'd left home for college. As soon as she had her own place, she'd bought the pair of kittens, who'd been the best company. A little demanding, but then, cats were very wise and regal creatures.

She refilled their water bowls and Mickey's dish was low on dry food, so she filled that, too. Shivering, she turned up the heat as she hurried through the living room. It was a small place, but cozy, with a wide bay-window seat near the front door and a gas fireplace in the back wall.

Even though she'd lived here for two years, she was still fixing it up, according to her budget. She'd taken a week of vacation in October and had painted the living room a soft butter yellow. On cold dark nights like this one, the walls glowed with soft warmth.

She'd reupholstered the matching couches in amber tweed that matched the walls. When she took a few extra days after Christmas, she was going to refinish the built-in bookcases packed with hundreds of paperbacks that filled three of the four walls from floor to ceiling.

The TV tucked in the corner was tuned to the one that seemed to interest the cats—the Discovery Channel. Kristin grabbed the remote off the coffee table she'd picked out with last year's Christmas money from Gramma and flipped through the cable listings until she found a beloved Doris Day movie.

Minnie flicked her tail and hopped onto the arm of the couch. Daintily picking up her tiny, soft downy paws, she settled on the back of the cushion and made an adorable fluffy ball. The feline eyed Doris Day swimming around in a mermaid's costume with clear disapproval.

Next trip home, Kristin decided, she was definitely taking the cats with her.

Thoughts of Montana naturally led to memories of Thanksgiving and of Ryan Sanders—of how he'd changed into a man to admire.

It was a no-brainer that Mom had turned his visit on Thanksgiving into a major deal. Every time Mom called since, she'd mentioned something she'd heard about him, through Mary. How busy he was, that he'd just bought a new car, how he'd taken a weekend and gone skiing in New Mexico with some of his doctor buddies. "What he really needs," Mom had confided, "is a wife. Mary worries about him."

If there was anyone who could take care of himself, it was Dr. Ryan Sanders. As she unlocked the door and stepped out onto the covered front step to grab her mail from the little white box, she wondered if she'd ever met anyone more competent. She'd never forget how he'd handled the emergency that night—his hands so steady, his actions so controlled, his calm wisdom.

Why did she sigh when she thought of him? It wasn't as if she was interested in him.

She slammed the door shut against the damp night

and stood over the heat register, shivering. A letter from Gramma. She'd save that to read while she ate. A reminder from the state vehicle people that her license tabs needed to be renewed. Oh, and a letter from…she squinted at the strange names of the return address etched in gold. A law office? No, a doctor's office. In Arizona.

Ryan! She ripped the envelope open and she didn't care if she was way too eager. They were, well, sort of friends. It was always good to hear from a friend, right?

Dear Kristin.

It was hard to read his block letters, his hand-writing was more of a scribble. So she sat down on the corner of the couch and switched on the table lamp.

Our patient has made a full recovery and is back at school. I don't know if I ever thanked you for everything that night. You were really something. Thanks. I still owe you for driv-ing through daybreak so I could sleep. Since Mom has twisted my arm and made me prom-ise to come home for Christmas, I've actually got more than the one day off. I get the entire weekend, too, so what do you say I treat you to milk shakes at The Sunshine Café? You name the time and the date, and I'll be there.

Milk shakes? She laughed, amazed that he'd remembered they'd discussed chocolate milk shakes as they'd driven through town Thanksgiving morning.

P.S. Samantha sent this to me.

Inside the envelope was a sealed note card—a note from Samantha Fields.

Dear Kristin, I can't believe how blessed I am to have been rescued by you and Ryan. I just wanted to thank you for helping me. God bless you.

It was signed, Sam.

Wow. Of course, Ryan was the one who'd made the real difference, being the doctor. He'd known just what to do to help minimize Sam's injuries. Yeah, he was definitely one fine man.

She noticed he'd scribbled his e-mail address on the bottom of his letter. Now the question was, how long would it take her to get up enough courage to write him?

December 22

A cold Seattle rain streamed down Kristin's bedroom window. Wind gusted against the eaves and rattled the barren alder branches outside. They moaned in protest, adding to the desolate feeling of the night.

But inside the house, she was warm and cozy. Snug in her favorite yellow flannel pajamas and thick slipper socks, she cuddled beneath her electric blanket and relaxed against the feather pillows piled up behind her. The laptop rested on the covers, the cursor patiently blinking.

It was now or never. She'd procrastinated long enough.

Okay, what should she say?

Her pair of Persians kept a wary eye on her, especially Minnie who did not approve of computers. The feline, curled on the foot of the bed, watched the glowing contraption with great displeasure. In her opinion, computers obviously did not belong on the bed.

Dear Ryan. Two o'clock. Saturday afternoon. I'm looking forward to it.

The phone startled her. Since she hadn't gotten online yet, she grabbed the cordless handset and glanced at the caller ID screen. "Hi, Mom."

"Hi. I know it's late, sweetie, but I wanted to check in with you. You've been on my mind today. I've got all my shopping done except for you."

"I told you. Something for my house. Oh! Better yet, my kitchen."

"I can't think you'd like a mixer for Christmas.

Lord knows when Pete bought me one for my birthday two years ago, I didn't take too kindly to it. It was sure a nice mixer, but Christmas is for something special."

"I know, but there's a lot of stuff I'd love to have."

"Well, I'll have to think about it. It doesn't seem right. Unless…" Excitement flickered across the miles. "You know a woman considering her future might want a well-stocked kitchen."

Oh, here it comes. Trust Mom to see buying a small appliance as a prelude to a trip down the aisle. "I agree, Mom. I should consider a future with a lot of small appliances in my kitchen. Since I'm a single career woman, I'm sure I'll enjoy healthier meals with my own, say, bread maker or one of those rotisserie roasters."

"Well, you just never know when you might be cooking for two."

"Exactly. Two weeks ago I went out to lunch with Cousin Rachel. It sure would have been nice to invite her over for a home-cooked meal."

"Oh, you! You know what I mean. I can't believe you want to be alone. Goodness. I'll rest so much better when I know you have a husband to take care of you in that big city you insist on living in."

"I like it here. I'm staying. Without a husband. Sorry."

"I worry. It's a dangerous world out there."

"I've got a security system."

"Well, I'll feel better knowing my last daughter is settled."

"I am settled, Mom. I have my own home, I have a great job, I'm happy. Why isn't that enough for you?"

"Oh, it is. But think of all that you're missing. A husband and children of your own. Kirby had a doctor's appointment—you know how they've had trouble trying for a second child—and I kept Michael so Sam could go with her to Bozeman for those tests she needs."

"I was just about to get online and check my messages. Kirby said she'd e-mail me if she felt up to it tonight and tell me what happened. How was Michael?"

"A handful! It took me back to when you girls were small. So much energy! It seemed as if I never could have a moment's rest, and now look at me. You're all grown and gone and I have all this time on my hands."

Kristin ached for her mom. For the child she'd had to bury, for the depression that troubled her for years after. Mom's life had crumbled into irrevocable pieces. It was sad, because Kristin had found a way to go on. She'd built a life that she could count on. Mom hadn't been as lucky.

"What's Dad up to now that he has so much time on his hands?"

"He's planted himself right in front of that expensive television he insisted on buying and doesn't move off the couch. Retirement is fine for him, but he's underfoot all day long."

Her parents had their problems. Kristin's stomach squeezed. Marriage. She didn't understand it. How her parents could have been so in love once—they'd been deeply bonded in the years when Kristin was small. But their marriage, as strong as it was, had suffered from their daughter's death. Now they were like two strangers living in the same house.

If love was something that could break, she didn't want any part of it, thank you very much!

"I had lunch with Mary again today. We had our own Christmas, just the two of us, a little early. We met at her house. I brought the eggnog and dessert, and she whipped up the best meal. Cornish game hens that were perfection. Anyway, she happened to mention that Ryan is coming home tomorrow. Isn't that something? He's finally got enough seniority in that doctor's office to get Friday and Saturday off. He'll be here, in Montana."

"I knew you were going to mention that. I already know, Mom."

"You do? You've spoken to him?"

"You sound as proud as if I'd won the Nobel Peace Prize. Mom!" Was her mother predictable or what? "He's not my type, and I'm not his. So stop. If you don't, I'm going to call each of my sisters and tell them that you're pressuring me. When you promised to stop."

"I just can't help myself. He's a *doctor*."

"Yeah. That's been established. Good night, Mom."

"Before you go, what time should I be looking for you tomorrow?"

"I'll be home sometime in the evening. Snow's forecasted through the mountain passes, so it'll be slow going. Don't wait supper on me."

"All right. You drive safe. I can't wait to see you. I love you, honey."

"I love you, too."

She hung up, aching. She loved her mother so much, but that only made Mom's comments about marriage hurt more. Mom's heart was in the right place, but she didn't understand. She couldn't. Her life was different. They were different women, different choices. That's what it came down to.

Wind moaned beneath the eaves, spattering rain against the windowpanes. The furnace kicked on, blowing at the closed curtains, ruffling them gently.

It was a lovely room. The big picture window, during the day, looked out over the grass lawn and through the treetops for a seasonal view of Green Lake. Gramma's old bedroom set, refinished in a honeyed oak, gleamed as if it were new. The reading chair tucked in the corner by the window, the oak bookcases stuffed with inspirational romances—this was home. Her home. Safe and snug and welcoming. Everything she'd ever wanted.

She'd never set her sights high on being rich or successful or renowned. She'd never wanted to base her future on unstable ground or on someone she could lose. But this place was nice and sensible at once, and it was her center. Her sanctuary. Her life. She was happy here. Content. Blessed.

The screen saver had clicked on and she tapped the keyboard to bring the e-mail program to the front. The letter sat, just as she'd left it.

She reread the e-mail, pondering. The mattress dipped slightly as the second cat hopped onto the bed and padded across the quilt to inspect the screen. "What do you think, Mickey?"

The gray longhair sneered, lifted one paw and washed his face.

"You're right—I shouldn't meet him. It was a nice offer, to treat me to a milkshake. But with our matchmaking moms and all their hopes, it's a bad idea."

Ryan Sanders lived like two thousand miles away. Too far away to be friends. So what was the point? She didn't want another e-mail pen pal. She couldn't keep up with the messages she got from her sisters!

She hit Delete and clicked the command for the modem to start dialing. She read Kirby's letter first—a report on the state of her sister's fallopian tubes—and sent a sympathetic response. Then she moved on to Michelle's note about their joint gift for Mom. She laughed reading her last note from Kendra—who was getting her sleigh ready for the Christmas-tree expedition Christmas Eve morning.

She signed off without contacting Ryan.

Their lives had crossed paths once, for a higher purpose, perhaps only to save Samantha Fields. Kristin believed God worked that way, all things for His purpose and His good. That meant there was no reason she would see Ryan Sanders again. She wasn't about to manufacture one—not with the way her mom was frothing with excitement in hopes of a final marriage in the McKaslin family.

She tucked the computer onto the nightstand shelf, eased into her feather pillows, soft and comfy, and switched off the lamp by her bed. In the dark, she drew the snuggly electric blanket to her chin.

Sure, she was alone, but she liked the peace of it. Rain hammered with a new fury on the roof above. Wind thrashed against the siding, making the fir boughs dance, their shadows from the faint porch light hovered on the wall.

This was her life—safe, predictable, independent, unshakable. She remembered to thank God for it before her heavy eyelids drifted shut and sleep claimed her.

December 23

Three minutes past midnight. Ryan yanked loose the tie that had been trying to throttle him for six hours. Way too long for a party, in his opinion. Their office Christmas party had taken place in one of Scottsdale's finest restaurants. The food had been amazing. The gifts generous. His heart hadn't been in the festivities. As usual.

He respected the people he worked with. He liked them as people. Talk about lucky. Not everyone could say that about the folks they worked with. He could make small talk, but he was beginning to think his former fiancée had been right. He was horrible when it came to getting really close to people.

He didn't want to get too close. That was the problem.

He tossed his tie on the bed. Francine had been right about a lot of things. He wasn't controlling, but he did control how much—or how little—he let people in.

He buried his emotions. He didn't express his feelings very well when he did allow them to surface. His career was demanding and left little time for any personal relationships. He pretty much kept to himself, other than the quick e-mail a few times a month, and superficial friendships with other busy doctors that were based mostly on talking about the job and sports.

Yeah, Francine was right on target.

The house echoed around him. Dark and shadowed. He rented it—it was easier than committing to a mortgage and taking on the added responsibility of being a homeowner. He'd worked hard to become a good surgeon. That took a great amount of devotion and responsibility.

Well, he wasn't a shrink. He didn't know a thing about psychology, not in the practical application. He only knew that for some reason the lonely shadows in his house felt as suffocating as the ones in his past. In his life.

He flicked on the hall light to chase away the darkness. That was enough introspection for one night. He was flying out tomorrow, that's why all this was troubling him.

Maybe he'd volunteer to work through the holidays next year. He loved his mom, but he couldn't take the memories. It had taken three weeks for him to stop waking up in the middle of the night in a sweat. The nightmares from his youth had returned. Dreams where he lost his mom, his sister, his home, everything that mattered. And his dad, over and over again.

He couldn't take going home, but he had to. How many times had he picked up the phone to dial his mom and cancel the trip? To try to explain to her? But how could he bring up his grief? Talking about Dad's death had always hurt her terribly. Over time she'd begun to mention him now and then in conversation, but to really talk, to go back in time—no, he couldn't do that to her.

He was going home tomorrow, whether he liked it or not.

In the bedroom he kicked off his shoes and shrugged out of his shirt. A paperback book was facedown, spine open on the crate he used as a bedside table. He usually read before he went to bed, but he didn't feel like it tonight.

What he needed to do was pack. He'd put it off,

and since he had an early-morning flight, he'd run out of time. It was now or never.

The suitcase was buried on the floor of the closet where he'd left it after his last ski trip. He'd pack for cold weather. Maybe he'd be able to get some cross-country in while he was home. Mom wouldn't have any skis. Maybe he could borrow a pair somewhere, since there was no place in town that was likely to sell them. Kristin—he bet her family would have a few extra pairs of skis somewhere. Not that she'd taken him up on his offer of a milk shake.

She had a full life, too. She was probably busy, and it wasn't as if they had much in common.

It was just as well.

He tossed underwear, socks, jeans, a thin sweat-shirt and a bunch of T-shirts. All warm-weather stuff, basically. He'd gotten rid of his winter clothes when he'd come here after his residency, and in the years that had followed, he'd bought only clothes suitable for Phoenix temperatures. As if, subconsciously, he was making a choice. In truth, he'd never intended to go home again.

He didn't want to go now.

He'd go to Montana this last time, but no more. Phoenix was home. This house was home. It was where his future was and where the past didn't crop up every time he looked out the window. The sparse brown and jagged rocks of the Southwest were as different from Montana as a man could get. He'd invite his mom and sister to visit him here instead for holiday gatherings.

He'd forgotten to pull the blinds, and as he grabbed his razor bag and headed for the bathroom, the flash of light caught his attention. The merry Christmas lights of the houses down the street— the Carlsons with the white icicle lights dangling from their tile roof, the Millers with multicolored bulbs cheerfully outlining their stucco home and the Cooks with their front yard saguaro cactus draped in solemn blue flashing lights.

There were no icicles dripping from his roofline. No lighted angels in his front window. No flashing strings of bulbs adorning the cactus in his front yard.

The shadows of the night felt cold. Hollow, he finished his packing and left the suitcase at the front door for easy grabbing on his way out the door at 5:00 a.m. He set his alarm, climbed in bed and left the tableside lamp on. The darkness felt as if it were closing in on him.

When sleep came, it was fitful. He could not find peace.

Chapter Eight

December 24

Kristin tugged her favorite cable-knit sweater over the white turtleneck she wore. The soft wool was deliciously warm. It would definitely keep her toasty on the sleigh ride into the hills. With a pair of long johns under her sturdiest pair of jeans and wool socks on her feet, she was ready for a McKaslin family tradition. Christmas-tree gathering, the same way her great-great-grandparents did when they homesteaded the ranch in the 1860s.

"Kristin! Hurry!" Mom's call echoed up the stairwell.

"I'm coming!" she answered just as there was a rattle at the back door. It was amazing she could hear it over the racket downstairs.

New greetings rose over the excited voices in the kitchen below. It sounded as if Mary was here.

Mary. Kristin froze in the hallway. If Mom had invited her best friend, then did that mean she'd invited Ryan, too?

No. There was no way a man like him would be interested in a sleigh ride into the hills. Relief sluiced through her. She couldn't imagine it—

"Merry Christmas, Mrs. McKaslin." A familiar male voice. *Ryan's* voice.

He was here. Her knuckles gripped the banister but she couldn't make her feet carry her forward. She hadn't answered his letter. Hadn't taken him up on his offer of a milkshake. And why? Because Mom would make such a big deal about it if she found out. Because she was under enough pressure. She'd disappointed her parents enough.

"Nice kitty." Allie, dainty and precious in her pink sweater that said Grandma's Little Princess and the cutest little pair of jeans, collapsed on the landing. Her arms wrapped around Minnie's middle and squeezed. "Soft kitty."

Kristin wasn't fooled by the disgruntled frown on the feline's face. She could hear the contented purr from six steps up. She stopped to give her three-year-old niece a kiss on the cheek.

"Kristin!" Mom sounded impatient. "We're leaving without you."

It was tempting, but she wasn't about to miss one of her favorite holiday customs. She'd have to talk to Mom about this later.

As for Ryan, she'd be polite to him. She liked

him. But she didn't *like* him. Mom would just have to accept that her and Mary's matchmaking was an abysmal failure.

As Kristin hurried to the kitchen, the merry ring of dozens of jingle bells filled the air with their sweet music. Two matched pairs of Clydesdales flashed past the dining-room window. In the next room, she could hear Mom ordering everyone outside and giving Karen last-minute instructions.

"I know, Mom, don't worry, just go," Karen said laughingly as she scooped up daughter number two and held the squiggling toddler captive on her hip. "Have a great time. Remember, I want something small. Not ten feet tall. Where's Dad? I'll tell him myself. Last Christmas you got us a tree that didn't fit in our house. Hi, Kris."

"Hey, big sister." Kristin gave Karen a hug and baby Anna a raspberry kiss that made the toddler giggle. "Yeah, where's Dad?"

"He headed into town to have breakfast." Mom's words were tight, but her smile was firmly in place.

Her fake smile. The one she used when she didn't want to acknowledge something was wrong.

Kristin saw the question on Karen's face, too. Dad leaving for town on a day like this? Getting the family Christmas trees was something he looked forward to every year. Kristin opened her mouth to ask if they should wait, but Karen shook her head.

That could only mean one thing—there had been serious discord between Mom and Dad. Perhaps they'd had an argument or a heated fight. Maybe this was the one that would tear them apart for good.

Kristin's stomach twisted. *Please, Lord. Not now.* Since the birth of their first grandchild, her parents had been on speaking terms and had been creeping incrementally closer to one another. And now, who knew? She just wanted them to love each other the way they used to.

"I'll join Mary outside. Kristin, you'll close the door behind you?" Mom handed her a thick parka and a pair of gloves. She looked frail and tired.

Why hadn't she noticed that last night when she'd arrived? Because she'd been tired herself after about fifteen hours on the road. She was still tired.

"Sure." She waited until Mom was out of hearing range to whisper to Karen. "What about their gift?"

"Yeah. I know." Karen looked troubled, too, as she set Anna down on her pink tennis shoes. The toddler took off on a flat-footed gait after Mickey, who was hiding beneath the table. "Pray."

"Yeah. Big-time."

Snow drifted on the wind, tiny spun-sugar flakes, as delicate as air. They caught on her lashes and tickled her cheek as she zipped up her old winter coat. She tugged the back door shut behind her, lost. What were they going to do about their parents?

"I say we don't fight it." A man's melted-butter baritone had her turning around. Ryan, chain saw in hand, waded through the knee-deep snow from the direction of the detached garage.

"Fight what? And why do you have Dad's chain saw? Oh, I get it. That's what you're doing here."

"Yep. Believe me, I'm freezing and it's early and I'd rather be reading the morning paper in front of the woodstove. But my mom and yours pleaded with me. Since Pete isn't going to work the chain saw, they needed a man, they said. I couldn't turn them down."

"Our moms have way too much time on their hands. I know how to work a chain saw. I helped Dad every year bring in wood for the winter. So did Karen and Kendra."

"So basically I'm here under false pretenses?" Ryan watched her nod and it didn't surprise him— not one bit. Yeah, Mom was up to no good. Just as he'd suspected. "Our moms have worked so hard plotting how to put us together. Like I said, why fight it? It will only make them try harder."

"I'm sorry about this." Fiery pink crept across Kristin's fine-boned face.

Ryan doubted it was from the cold wind alone. He understood, and he hated seeing the reserved way she was keeping distance between them. Normally that kind of thing didn't bother him, but he liked Kristin. She was into her career, that was her focus. He sure understood that, and he figured they had to stick to-gether against the marriage-minded. "Don't be sorry. We'll ignore them. What's the saying around these parts—you can lead a horse to water but you can't make him drink?"

"You can't make *her* drink," she corrected, and some of that fiery sparkle returned to her eyes.

Yeah, she was a girl with spunk. Ryan held out his hand. "Let's make them pay for manipulating us. C'mon, friend."

He loved her smile. Big, bold, genuine. When she smiled, it was like sunshine on a snow that lit up the entire world.

She slid her delicate hand into his. "You're on, friend. Do you know how to use that chain saw?"

"How can you ask that? I'm a Montana boy at heart."

"Yeah, but you're a city man now."

"No more than you're an urban woman. Cutting down a tree is something every real man knows. My dad used to take me up into the woods when I was a kid. Don't worry. I know how to use this thing." He hiked the dangling chain saw for emphasis.

Kristin bit her bottom lip to keep quiet. Testosterone!

"Hurry up, you two!" Kendra popped up beside the giant horses, tugged on the harness, patted one of the gentle giants on the neck and took up the reins. "Ryan, have you ever been on a horse-drawn sleigh?"

"No, ma'am. Looks like I'm in for a treat. Aren't the little ones coming along?"

"It's too dangerous," Kristin answered, stole the chain saw from him and stowed it safely beneath the front board seat. She talked to her sister in a low whisper, heads together, in the way that women do, before leaving Kendra to settle the dual set of thick leather reins between her gloved fingers. "Karen's staying behind with the kids. Allie might be old enough next year."

That made sense. The chilly temperature alone was enough to give a guy hypothermia. Of course, maybe that had more to do with the thin summer-weight sweatshirt he had on beneath Dad's old coat. The goose-down parka cut a lot of the wind's bite, but not enough. And it only covered him so much. His legs and feet were bone cold.

His mom had taken up position on the board seat next to Kendra, and she looked proud of herself. "You two find a place and sit down."

"Sure, Mom." Yeah, he was going to have to have a talk with her. Set it out straight and tell her how it was. And not just about Kristin. About Dad, coming here—*everything*. But now wasn't the time.

Kristin climbed aboard the sleigh, which was more of a sled for hauling than riding. A layer of local hay, sweet smelling and soft, lined the back in a fluffy bed. She snuggled in, sitting so her feet dangled off the back.

He climbed in beside her. "So, you people do this every year?"

"Sure. It never occurred to me that other people didn't cut their own trees every year, until I was away at college and saw a Christmas-tree lot. I laughed so hard, I cried."

"There aren't a lot of fir trees in Phoenix. They have to truck them in. It costs a bundle for a real tree. So I bought a plastic one. It stays in a box for pretty much a whole year and I let Mom take it out when she comes down."

"Plastic trees. Yeah, that's what I put up in my house. I have one of those little ones. My cats hate it, but it's simpler, since I always come here for Christmas."

"Yeah." Christmas. Ryan hated to think about the lights he didn't put up and the tree still in its box in the garage. "It doesn't seem right without my dad."

He heard the words coming out of his mouth. Too honest. Too private. He stared down at the coat he wore, the navy-blue nylon flecked with snowflakes, and willed the pain to stay down. Didn't quite succeed at it.

The sleigh jerked forward, the skids squeaking on the fresh snow. Ryan's bones rattled. His teeth clacked together. His spine snapped. The jarring start smoothed out into a sensation of gliding. The tiny bells on the harnesses made a sweet sound. "Not too bad."

"Wait until the horses pick up speed. Then it's like flying. Oh! Here we go! Hold on!" Her gloved hands curled around the ends of the floorboards as the sleigh pitched again, accentuated by the jingling bells, and eased into an eye-watering cruising speed.

It was too cold to talk, with the wind whipping by. Silence was the best way to enjoy the ride as she got caught up in the rhythmic chink of the horses' hooves on the compacted snow, the caroling bells and the lilting rhythm of the women's voices in the seat up front. Somehow, Ryan's melancholy seemed out of sync with the pleasant grassy scent of the hay, and the snowflakes falling in a lazy waltz from a white-gray sky that went on forever.

Despite his soul-deep pain, Ryan savored the sheer exhilaration of the snow-mantled earth flying out from under him, the solemn stance of wooden fence posts wearing snowlike hats, their wooden rails outstretched like arms. Nothing moved, not bird or deer or rabbit except for the crystal flakes everywhere descending.

Kristin leaned close, bringing with her the scent of fabric softener and vanilla. Her scarf felt like a kitten's fur against his cheek. Something sharp as a pin's prick jabbed him deep inside, turning him inward again. His chest ached and he felt...

He didn't know what he felt.

The earth felt solemn, as if sleeping. The morning was calm as the valley fields rolled away and the horses started to climb. Random trees appeared, then more and more, until it was a forest draped in white, silent with grace. It felt as if something were speaking to him, not with words, but to his heart. A tug that pulled at his very sturdy defenses.

He watched her as she breathed deep the cold air and lifted her face to the sky.

"This ride blows me away every year." She

blinked at the snowflakes caught on her eyelashes. "I've done nothing for the last three weeks but shop and stress and worry and rush here and there. Wait through traffic without moving. Circle parking garages for over half an hour looking for any old spot to park in. Push my way through crowded malls and wait in long lines. On top of work, feeling like there's never enough time and so much to do."

"I did all my shopping late. Made a list, made one stop at the mall. Caught a bunch of sales, wasn't too bad at all. Okay, I only have Mom and Mia to buy for, except for the office girls at work and my nurse, so it's not bad. We don't have a big family, the way you do."

"Yeah. But when I'm here, feeling the snow on my face and seeing it grace the trees, it hits me every time. All the stress melts away. Nothing has changed, not in two thousand years. All the hustle and hurry-up and decorating and gift buying is all done because of a single child born long ago. That the heart of Christmas is the same and always will be."

"I hear it wasn't easy for the Wise Men, either. Sure, they didn't have mall traffic to deal with, but they rode forever on a camel's back. Think of it. No air-conditioning. No roadside convenience stores. No motels or fast food along the way. No Global Positioning System. No triple A."

"I hadn't quite thought of it like that before."

When she laughed, the sound was as dulcet as the bells ringing.

Whatever was hurting within him lifted through him like a bird in flight, filling his eyes so he turned away. It was the cold making his eyes tear.

Nothing more.

The sleigh slowed to a stop on snow so pure, it looked like clouds. The sun poked out between a break in the clouds to smile on the wintry forest, and a billion glimmers shone everywhere making the world so bright, it hurt to look at it.

"Notice how they sent us out to scout for trees." Ryan's stride was bigger than hers, and the knee-deep snow hardly troubled him.

"I noticed." Kristin trekked beside him, working harder to keep up with him. The snow was deep and dangerous. While they weren't in the mountains, snow pack avalanching off the ridge nearby had them sticking to the thicker woods, where the trees offered protection.

Though it made it tougher to hike. She pushed aside a branch, and snow cascaded down on her, slipping between her collar and the back of her neck. Talk about freezing. She shivered. "I don't know if they're trying to pair us up or give us hypothermia."

"Yeah, notice how they didn't offer us one of those thermoses your sister brought with her. Hot chocolate?"

"And coffee." Kristin knew from experience.

"When we were kids, Mom would bundle all of us up and Granddad would come by on his sled. Gramma was the one who brought the hot drinks then, and a bag of homemade Christmas cookies, too, and we'd sing carols all the way up and all the way back. But things change."

"People leave you."

"Yep. First Granddad. Then Allison. You said it doesn't seem right without your dad. That's the way it is with me, too. I don't know how my sisters do it. They go on, they get married, have kids. I don't know. I guess they've coped with it in their own ways, but I can't pretend Allison didn't die. It's like saying she didn't exist, that she didn't matter."

"Yeah." Ryan sounded choked. "Yeah."

Because it hurt, she said nothing more. Let the cold chap her face and burn down her throat when she breathed. "What about that one?"

"I think it would be just the right size for Mom's living room. Here, let me get this contraption started." Pointing the tip downward, safely away from their feet, he yanked on the starter. The small motor coughed before it started on the second pull. The earsplitting whine shattered the serenity.

Kristin held the shoulder-high cedar by the trunk, as Ryan knelt to dig the saw into the bark at the snow line. The vibration rocketed through her arm until the tree came loose. The roar died, and Ryan set the saw aside as she kept the young tree from falling on its perfect branches.

Yep, he was a Montana boy at heart, just as he'd said. He handled the chain saw with the same competence that he did everything.

When he helped her lay the tree gently on its side in the snow, the solid length of his arm bumped hers. He was one hundred percent substantial man. Dependable. Amazing.

Was it her imagination, or was her pulse skyrocketing?

He hiked the chain saw up by the handle. Snow clung to him everywhere—hair, jaw, shoulders and thighs. "Your family wouldn't happen to have an extra pair of cross-country skis, would they?"

It took a few seconds for her brain to register his question. "Uh, in the garage. I'll check when we get back."

"Thanks. I appreciate it. Mom sold my old pair at a garage sale, like ten years ago." He trudged toward a huddle of firs. "These trees are about eight feet. Think your sisters would like them?"

Kristin squinted at the threesome of evergreens. It was easy to imagine each proudly bearing twinkle lights on their tender branches.

By the time they'd cut all three trees, she and Ryan were working together as a team. She held the tree, he used the saw, and they stacked the trees carefully to keep the limbs and needles from being damaged.

"Can I ask you something pretty personal?" Beneath the arching pines and reaching cedar, he looked more dream than man as the sunlight faded, leaving him in shadow.

She felt rooted in place as snow began to pummel down, tapping on her coat, catching in her hair. It was as if a veil shrouded them, and although their mothers and Kendra were just on the other side of the rise, maybe ten yards away, the curtain closed around just the two of them.

It felt as if they were the only two people anywhere.

Did Ryan feel this, too? She swallowed. "What do you want to know?"

He leaned so close all that separated them was the snow-filled air. "You lost your sister years ago. How can you do it? Come back here and go on. How did you make everything okay?"

"It's not. It will never be fine again."

"Then how can you come home year after year? How do you get past it? I—" Pain lined his face, shadowed his eyes, tensed his jaw.

He was talking about his father. Sympathy tugged in her chest and she reached out. His arm was iron solid beneath her fingertips. The image of him that night when he'd helped the car-accident victim arrowed into her mind. He'd been awesome. She'd never have guessed he had wounds of his own that would never heal.

She knew exactly what that felt like. "I—"

"Ryan? Kristin?" Mom's voice carried on the rising wind. "Where did you two get off to?"

Kristin withdrew her hand as her mother trudged into sight, but it was too late. Mom was already grinning from earmuff to earmuff. "Interrupted you, I see. Ryan, be a dear and come with me. We've found the perfect tree for my living room."

Mary joined them, and there was Kendra leading the double team of horses. Kristin stayed behind, insisting on helping load the trees, while Ryan stepped through the mist and disappeared. She and Kendra loaded the cut trees with care, while Mary broke out the thermoses.

Although Ryan was no longer beside her, Kristin could feel the echoes of his pain. Of his grief. Or maybe it was simply her own.

Mary talked of her daughter Mia who was expected home today, and of the candlelight service at the church tonight. Hopefully the storm wouldn't make the roads treacherous.

When Ryan returned, breaking through the curtain of snowfall with the tree hefted on his wide shoulder, she looked away. Willing her pulse to slow to normal, she quieted the beat of sympathy for him in her heart.

She didn't want to talk about the past or her family's loss. The storm blew hard from the north, the arctic winds chasing them down the hillside and through the fields to the ranch house on McKaslin land.

She couldn't endure the hope on her mom's face as she watched them so carefully for the tiniest signal that a romance was about to blossom between them. Ryan seemed quiet and he didn't meet her gaze as he unloaded the tree meant for the living room. He carried it inside, and she took the chance to dash to the garage. Finding an old pair of Dad's skis, which he never used anymore, she secured them on the sleigh.

By the time Ryan stepped out of the house, she was heading back to the garage for the big storage bins of ornaments. He drove off in the sleigh alone on the bed, his big feet dangling off the back as the whiteout conditions stole him away.

While she untangled tree lights, hung delicate glass balls, or even when she'd plugged in the star atop the tree, he never left her thoughts.

Nor did the ache within her. It felt as if he'd put another one there, deep into her heart where she could take no more. As Bing Crosby sang of a white Christmas, the daylight waned. The blizzard struck hard against the northwest walls of the house, cutting off the outside world. She wondered if he was thinking of her.

"Oh, now it feels like Christmas." Mary Sanders stepped back to study her workmanship. The multicolored lights twinkled on boughs of evergreen. Little toy soldiers and jolly Santas and heavenly angels hung from the tips of every branch. At the top, the same angel his father had bought the year before he died glowed with a bright assurance.

Christmas has never been the same without you, Dad. Ryan rested his face in his hands. The feelings rising within him were too much. He tried to shut down, but couldn't. They were too powerful. A train of images chugging through his brain. Dad, young and tall and alive, kneeling down before a Christmas tree in the same corner of the same living room, his voice a low baritone and warm with affection. "Let's see what else Santa brought. Here's a present for you, Ryan. And look, Mia, this one's for you." His little sister, preschool age with brown ringlet curls, took the package with her eager hands.

Another Christmas. Another image. Of Dad seated on the floor beside him, the fire roaring in the stone fireplace, puzzling out the deluxe train set Santa had brought. So much track, so many crossings and bridges. By the time Mom had the Christmas ham out of the oven for the noon meal, a train tooted as it raced on the track lapping the living room and winding around the huge dollhouse, where Mia was busily setting up furniture.

The last Christmas with Dad. He'd been laid off, and they'd done without a lot of gifts, but Santa had come through. Ryan hadn't thought of it at the time, but he realized now how tight his father had to scrimp and save, and how much he'd had to sacrifice to make sure there were gifts beneath the tree. Ryan had been speechless with joy when he saw his dream gift—a sleek black bike with the knobby tires and shiny chrome. And his elation intensified listening to Mia squeal with delight over the array of Barbie stuff she'd gotten.

That was the year he'd learned there was no Santa Claus. When he'd asked Dad, his father had said gently, "There is if you believe."

He'd always resented that his dad had lied about it. He knew there was no jolly man in a red suit that came down the chimney. Dad had died a month later and taken the last of Ryan's illusions.

"Tired?" Mom ruffled his hair, running her fingers round the cowlick in the center of his head as she'd done all his life.

Tired? Hardly. His soul felt weary.

"Here, have a candy cane." She held out a red-and-green-and-white-striped candy. "Spearmint. Your favorite."

"Thanks." He took the treat and tore off the wrapper while his mom sat down beside him.

"I don't see you in my living room nearly often enough." Mom sounded serious, the way she did when she was about to give one of her wise-mother lectures.

He didn't think he could take it. Everywhere he looked were memories of Dad. Wearing his coat today had been too much. He felt as if he were ready to explode like a keg of old dynamite. "Don't start, Mom. You know I have a hard time around the holidays."

"I know you were close to your father. So was I, you know." Her love was patient and warm, like a candle glowing in the dark, like hope in the midst of despair.

Lord knew how she'd been that light for him, as a boy, broken to the soul over his dad's death. He'd been too young to understand it well. Only that his father was gone. That there would be no more early-morning treks into the marshes, no more tracking the white-tailed deer.

No more magic winter mornings as calm as heaven's grace.

No more family.

They'd scrambled and fought to survive for so long, to keep hold of the house and food on the table, that there had been no time for grief.

He'd lived his adult life the same way. Little time for play, less time for living. He remained, deep inside, that same little boy trying to survive. To do his best to help provide for his mom and sister. Even now after the crisis had long passed.

"Your father watches over us, I know he does." Mom rubbed away the tears from her eyes. "Heaven knows if anyone deserves to be an angel, it was that man. The best husband a woman could ask for."

"The best dad."

"I know this stubbornness of yours, of not finding a nice girl and settling down—"

"No, please." Pain clawed through his chest with sharp talons, leaving him ragged and bleeding. "I tried that. I wasn't any good at it. Francine wasn't at fault. She was a great person. I just—" *Can't get close to anyone.*

He couldn't let his mom any closer, either. Panic had him launching out of the recliner and across the room. The tree lights blinked in a merry rhythm, sending enough light to guide him through the dark room and into the kitchen. Where a plate of Mia's favorite iced Christmas cookies waited, a treat for when she finally arrived.

"Ryan." Mom followed him. Love was in her voice—and concern. "Where are you going?"

"Mia's here." At least he figured the twin beams slicing through the whiteout were his sister's. She was home safe, finally, and Mom could devote all her motherly energies to Mia. Good. Because he was going out.

He grabbed the coat and elbowed open the door. Bitter wind needled through him as he struggled into the parka. He didn't care about the worsening storm or the dangerous temperatures. As Mia's old Toyota skidded to a stop in the driveway, he knocked on the back-quarter panel.

The trunk lid popped with a tired groan. He grabbed the heavy suitcases and book bag and hauled them into the back door. He ignored his mom's distress over him and kissed her on the cheek.

"Take care of Mia," he said as he grabbed gloves from the hooks over the furnace register. "She's had a long hard drive. I'll be fine."

He steeled his heart against the sadness on Mom's face and the confusion on his sister's as he strode away into the snowy night.

Chapter Nine

"What are we gonna do about Mom and Dad's present?" Michelle whispered when Dad disappeared into the kitchen to answer the knock at the back door. "Karen, Kirby and Kendra kept calling me, like I'm supposed to know. I've got, like, no clue what to do."

"Me, either."

Kristin managed to breathe around the knot in her throat. The one that came from watching her parents all evening. How they ignored each other. How they spoke to one another, when at all, tersely. How much distance they kept—Mom in the kitchen or in her chair by the fire, Dad on the couch. Finally Mom had retired upstairs to read in bed, and hadn't bothered to glance in her husband's direction as she left the room.

"Tell me again why you got married?" Kristin asked her baby sister.

"I was forced at gunpoint." Pretending to be totally serious, Michelle stole another macaroon from the plate of cookies on the coffee table in front of her. "Hmm. I love these and, lucky for me, I'm eating for two." She smiled. It was not a superficial grin, but one that came from deep within.

True happiness. Okay, so her sisters were happy with their lives and marriages. Fine. She understood that. But what about down the road? Romantic love didn't last. It was a bright fire that quickly burned out, and then, from what she could see, there was only darkness and ashes. Silences that felt razor sharp.

No, she wanted a life built on a more solid foundation than that.

"I hear you and Ryan are getting pretty tight." Michelle waggled her eyebrows. "It was all Mom could talk about on the way to church."

"And on the way back." Kristin leaned forward on the couch, studied the colorful choices on the cookie plate and chose a red-sprinkled Santa. "What happened between Mom and Dad? I thought they were doing better."

In the kitchen, Dad's voice rose in greeting, his words indistinguishable over the noise of the TV.

"I don't know. They were doing better. Having grandchildren was starting to really bring them together, or so I *thought*. Anyway, who knows? Dad is closed up tight. And Mom refuses to talk about it. Believe me, I tried. *You* should go talk to her."

"Okay."

"Good. That's probably my husband. I'm going to take my daughter and another one of these—" She stole a macaroon from the plate. "I'm outta here. Merry Christmas. We'll be over after Emily unwraps all her loot from Santa."

"Merry Christmas."

Michelle lifted Emily's carrier from the floor, where she slept peaceful and warm in her pink flannel sleeper. Her golden curls were mussed, corkscrewing around her cherub's face, making her look angelic.

Brody poked his head around the corner to wish her a Merry Christmas and to take his sleeping daughter from his wife. His strong arm wrapped around Michelle's slim shoulders, drawing her close, and they walked away together into the brightness of the kitchen and out of sight, blessed by the halo of twinkle lights spanning the arched doorway.

They looked like a team. Like a unit. Together and happy.

But hadn't Mom and Dad been the same way once?

Voices rose from the kitchen—probably Karen's husband, Zach, come by to fetch the present Mom and Dad had been hiding for them. Not in the mood for network television, Kristin grabbed the remote and clicked off the power.

Silence settled into the room like the snow outside. The white lights on the fragrant fir tree glowed pure and true. The glass balls reflecting a thousand pinpricks of light. The star topping the tree shone in memory of the star burning brightly centuries ago on this very night.

Minnie hopped soundlessly onto the cushion and curled into a ball on Kristin's lap. She threaded her fingers through the cat's silky fur and was rewarded with a contented purr.

How can you come home year after year? How do you get past it? Ryan's question troubled her in the quiet moments. She'd been able to put it aside as she and Mom decorated the tree and then hurried to put supper on the table on time. Michelle and Brody had joined them, with little Emily, who kept them entertained as she banged in rhythm on her high-chair tray to the Christmas songs Michelle had been teaching her.

It had been a busy night. First, there were the dishes, and a quick change of clothes and the journey to church in the near blizzard conditions. Then, the service and the traditional gathering of the entire clan, cousins and all, at the cousin's restaurant. And finally, dessert, gift exchange and then the drive home.

She'd hardly had a moment to herself, but now that she did, Ryan's question troubled her. She missed her sister. She missed the family she used to have. The closeness. The happiness. Was that why her sisters had all married? In the attempt to find that time again?

And if so, then how long would it last? Didn't

they know you couldn't trust someone else to build your life around? That standing on your own two feet was the best bet?

"Wow. You look deep in thought." A man's broad silhouette ambled from the bright kitchen. Ryan. "I'm interrupting."

"No. Come in. Have a cookie. I didn't hear you drive up."

"That's because I skied."

"You know there's a blizzard out there, right? They closed down, like, half the county roads."

"I *am* a little cold. Oh good, a fire." He crouched down in front of the hearth—all six feet plus of him. Orange light danced across him and he held out his hands. "Wow, that feels good. I saw you with your family at church tonight. I tried to catch up to you, but there were too many people."

Kristin gently scooted Minnie into the crook of her arm and made her way over. She snagged the cookie plate as she passed by. "I didn't see you or your mom."

"We came late. Sat in the back. We didn't want to leave home until we heard from Mia."

"Was she driving home from school?"

"Oh, I love these." He grabbed a gingerbread man decorated in colorful icing. After his first bite, he moaned. "Anyway, yeah, she's home safe and sound. I was pretty worried about her."

"Sisters are pretty precious."

"That they are."

And here she was trying not to think about Allison. She slid the plate on the corner of the hearth. "You've got to be freezing. I can feel the cold radiate off you."

"Yeah, I stopped feeling my toes halfway here."

"And why didn't you turn around and head home?"

"It's complicated. I guess I just needed a friend."

"Then you're in luck. First, we'd better warm you up. We have tea, coffee or cocoa."

"You said the magic word. Do you have marshmallows?"

"What's cocoa without them? Just a cup of chocolate. Sit down." She curved around the hearth, laid the cat on the nearby recliner and swept from the room, leaving him alone in the shadows.

But not in the dark. White twinkle lights draped from the window valences to circle the room. Bigger bulbs decorated the ten-foot fir that he'd cut for Mrs. McKaslin. Elegance was the word he'd use to describe the tree. Fragile white glass balls and handblown glass angels.

When he got up to take a closer look, he realized there were words etched into the glass. "In memory of our own angel, Allison, Christmas 2000." Another bore the current year. Another nearly eight years in the past. Mrs. McKaslin must have hired a local artist to make an ornament every year for a daughter she still loved.

Yeah, that was the problem, wasn't it? Love died

with the loved one, and then where did that leave you? Cold through to his soul, he retreated to the fire where it seemed the heat couldn't touch him. Where the light couldn't find him.

Kristin returned. She set a tray on the coffee table, kneeling to unload it. Two steaming oversize mugs. Spoons. A plastic bag of marshmallows. Her movements caught his eye. A Polaroid picture was propped against a crystal candlestick holder.

He leaned closer to get a good look. A preschool blond-haired little girl with the bluest eyes. McKaslin eyes. She was dressed in red velvet and white lace. Her baby sister—a year-old identical replica—stood beside her, ringlet curls bobbing. Next to them, frozen in the act of stomping his foot hard on the floor, was a dark-haired boy.

Two other smaller girls completed the photograph. Michelle's year-old daughter, who looked exactly like her mama. And a small infant lay cradled in a car seat carrier—the newest addition to the family. A new generation of McKaslins.

"Little Caitlin. She belongs to Kendra and Cameron, but I stole her as much as I could today."

"A little fond of your sisters' kids?"

"You could say that. They're all so precious." Kristin sank to the floor beside him, the soft fuzz of her sweater's sleeve an intimate brush against his wrist as she leaned in to study the picture.

A gold cross on a chain fell out from the neckline of her sweater and swayed back and forth, drawing his gaze. He admired her heart-shaped face, the fire-light in her hair, the delicate cut of her neck, shoulders and arms.

Vanilla tickled his nose and a roar filled his ears. A strange, bittersweet yearning broke through the ice around his heart and punched him. Left him without breath. Awareness zinged through him, surging through nerves and veins, warming him from his chest outward. What was wrong with him? Maybe he was more hypothermic than he thought.

Kristin scooted the plastic bag across the table. "Add more marshmallows. You don't have enough melted fluff in that cocoa. True cocoa enjoyment is all about proportion. Tons of chocolate. Tons of melty marshmallows. There are scientific studies proving the healing benefits of it."

"I think I read one just last week in one of my medical journals."

"See? Cocoa makes everything better." Kristin swirled the spoon through her brimming mug, mixing melted fluff with the rich milky chocolate.

It was his senses mixing, too. He couldn't tear his attention away from the dazzling highlights glinting in her hair, shining a hundred different shades of gold in the glow of the fireplace and the faint shine of the lights from the Christmas tree behind her.

It had been a bitter-cold journey through the dark, that was all, that was why he was feeling this way. The warm room, the steaming cocoa and Kristin's brightness combined against the cold that ached in his bone marrow had him hurting.

A mild case of frostbite. His blood was warming his extremities, that explained his physiological symptoms. He'd be lucky if he didn't come down with pneumonia. He wasn't a greenhorn; he was a Montanan, born and bred. But it had been oblivion he'd been seeking when he ran out into the storm. The cold had frozen him down to the soul.

He'd skied with all his might, skidding down gullies and kicking up hills by memory. The years he'd been away had seemed to fall away, and he'd known where the fences were that separated fields and marked property lines. He'd known the deep irrigation ditch siding the country road he'd used for the last quarter-mile stretch. He'd found his way, succeeding in losing his pain.

For a while.

But he was thawing. So was his pain, which coursed through him like the blood in his veins. His fingertips seared and throbbed. Nothing serious, so he ignored it and wrapped his hands around the big stoneware mug with hollyberries rimming a Christmas scene.

He'd been wrong to come here. He'd tried to get away from the holiday memories in his mom's house, but this was no better.

Did the McKaslins know how to do anything halfway? Christmas was everywhere, from the ten-foot tree decorated like an interior designer had gotten hold of it, piled with gifts beneath, to the wreaths on the walls. Twinkle bulbs raced along the ceiling and cast light like stardust onto a snowy Christmas village on the mantel. Peppermint-striped candles sat in snowflake-shaped holders, and the scents of pine and wood smoke grabbed him by the throat and squeezed.

Voices rose from the kitchen. Gruff male voices followed by the *clink* of metal hitting the floor. Before the past could jerk him backward in time, the fire popped like a gunshot and Kristin leaped up to sweep the burning spark off the carpet and onto the stone hearth. The ember glowed brightly, pulsing with light and dark.

With the present and the past. Ryan realized he'd been holding the cup in midair, so he took a big gulp. Chocolaty and sweetly frothy, it burned him from his tongue to his stomach lining.

Kristin settled back to her spot on the floor, cringing from the sounds from the kitchen. Dad had offered to help Zach put Allie's new tricycle together. Judging by the sound of things, there were a few problems.

A horrible clash of metal reverberated through the house followed by the angry sounds of displeasure coming from her dad. She heard Zach's frustrated comment on the inadequacy of the directions and a missing screw. There was a bang of the back door, the eerie howl of the wind.

Dad was probably going to search through the

garage to see if he had something in his toolbox that would work. She hoped he bundled up first. She took her mug with her as she crossed to the window. There was nothing—only night reflected back to her in the shine of the glass and the glow from the tree lights. Ice clung in filmy streaks along the edges of the panes.

"The storm's getting worse." Ryan spoke behind her. He'd come without a sound. The light from the tree and the fire lapped around him, stroking the long neat lines of him, of his breadth, his height. A substantial man, even in shadow. "Maybe I'd better get home before—"

The wind punched the house with a fury that rattled the windows. That seemed to move the entire structure an inch off the foundation. Black pellets scoured the glass and the sudden chill penetrating the window had her shivering.

"Maybe I won't be heading home just yet." Ryan's hand settled on her shoulder.

Comfort. That's what his touch gave her. Not a friendly kind of comfort, or a brotherly kind of steadiness. The weight of his palm on the curve of her neck, the heat of him, the might. He felt powerful enough to protect her from the wind and darkness, the cold and the night. Her entire being sparkled in the silence that seemed to fall between them.

There was only him, the sound of his breathing, the rustle of his socks on the carpet as he shifted his weight to draw her away from the cold. The winter-and-man scent of him and the faint hint of fabric softener on his shirt. The shadows in her heart seemed to fade, and the ache vanished.

Dad, raking snow out of his hair, stepped into the archway. The wind was too loud to have heard him come in, but there he was, safe and sound, his dear face chapped red from his trek outside. "Ryan, you'd best stay here for a bit. And whatever you do, don't go skiing back. I'll leave my keys on the counter. You take my truck, you hear? It's four-wheel drive. It'll get you home safe."

"Thanks, Mr. McKaslin. I appreciate it."

"You wouldn't happen to know anything about tricycles, would ya? I've worked on farm machinery all my life, and Zach's a mechanic. You'd think between the two of us, we could put a kid's trike together." Dad shook his head, managing a smile.

But he looked weary. And old. Her daddy was looking old.

When had that happened? Kristin went to him, feeling as fragile as glass. Although they rarely spoke of it, this time of year was hardest on him, too. "You look like you need a cup of cocoa and some help. You're in luck."

"I've been known to be handy with a wrench, in a pinch." Ryan's deep voice vibrated through her, and it felt as if for an instant they were connected.

Maybe it just felt that way because they were united in purpose. Kristin made cocoa and gave her opinion on various interpretations of the instructions while the men worked. Dad, with tension etched deep into his face. Zach, frustrated and checking the time as the evening vanished. Ryan looking less troubled with something to keep him busy.

Yet she could still feel his sadness as if it were her own.

There had been something calming about the frustration over the construction of the tricycle. Ryan rubbed at the tension in his neck from leaning and twisting trying to get the handlebars in place. It had taken a mechanic, a farmer and a surgeon nearly forty minutes to reach success. Zach had left with a perfect pink-and-white trike covered with a tarp in the back of his truck.

"Well, good night to you, young man." Mr. Mc-Kaslin set empty mugs on the counter, lost in shadows. "I'm goin' on up to bed. Don't you forget to take my truck."

"Thanks, sir." The winds were dying, the blizzard beginning to wind down. He needed to get back, it was nearly midnight. Since the phone lines were dead and his cell wasn't picking up a signal, his mom was likely to be worried about him.

Celebration marked this room, too. The kitchen and eating area were huge and homey. Multicolor twinkle lights flashed in a cheerful rhythm from the archways and the tops of cabinets, threading over plant shelves and draping from valences. A ceramic nativity scene waited patiently on the polished wood of the window seat. Why the sight of the porcelain mother and child made Ryan's chest hurt, he didn't know. Too many feelings, too much regret? Probably.

There was something about this house, too. This home with its feeling of family in the very air. Of closeness. He could sense what tomorrow would be like. Of the women laughing and working and filling up the kitchen, preparing the Christmas meal. The little kids underfoot, with new toys and limitless energy and munching on those great Christmas cookies. The shouts of the men in the living room and the sound of a game would fill the house.

He remembered on Thanksgiving how it was. A family come together to celebrate.

His chest felt wide open. He'd been wrong to come. Wrong to stay. Foolish to think that he could escape by coming here. Blindly, he grabbed his dad's old coat from the back of the kitchen chair, where it had been drying. He'd come here for a reason.

He unzipped the side pocket, where a small thin box was buried. It had been there all day. He'd grabbed it when Kendra had been by to pick him and Mom up in her sleigh, and he'd totally forgotten. And by the looks of it, it had survived.

It wasn't the only thing in his pocket.

Ryan set aside the box. His heart began to pound in double rhythm. His fingers fumbled as he withdrew the envelope. Ryan was written in a man's hand—Dad's handwriting—on the front.

Why hadn't he noticed this before? Hands shaking, knees weak, he sank into the nearest chair. His fingers working the card loose from the envelope without thought. In the glow of the twinkle lights, he saw it was a card meant for a kid. There was a cartoon dog on the front and big block letters proclaiming, Happy Birthday to the Best Son Ever!

Oh, God. Why hadn't anyone found this? Ryan put it down. Picked it back up. It looked as though there was handwriting inside the card—more of Dad's handwriting.

He squeezed his eyes shut, holding his breath. Freezing every emotion inside him before he broke apart. Before the little boy inside him could remember.

He concentrated on the faint clink and clunk from the next room. The rush and rustle wrapping paper made when it was unrolled. The snap of Scotch tape. The squeak of a bow as it was stretched and twisted. Kristin must be wrapping last-minute gifts. He could hear her gentle frustration, "Mickey! I don't need any help, thank you very much!"

The ripple of her chuckle was warm and wonderful. Soft as silver it seemed to hook his senses. The ice scouring the siding faded to silence until there was only the rustle of her graceful movements, the pad of her step on the carpet. It was too late to hide the card or the emotion leaving him unable to move.

He didn't look up to acknowledge her presence. He could see the black toes of her boots at the far edge of his vision. She'd stopped to lean against the arched doorway. Her nearness breezed over him like a touch against his skin.

"It looks as if we were on the same wavelength."

At the sound of her voice, he dragged his gaze upward. He felt raw, wide open, unable to close down his heart or call up his defenses to protect him from her. The sight of her standing like a dream in the decorated archway, the gentle lights twinkling over her like star shine, took his breath away.

She looked like perfection just standing there, in a simple red sweater and jeans belted at her slim waist, a fuzzy gray cat cradled in her left arm, a small wrapped gift in the other. She arched one eyebrow, awaiting his answer.

His mind was a blur. "What?"

"Exchanging presents. I've got one for you. I'm guessing that one's for me."

Words tore like claws in his throat. Unable to speak, he watched, unable to stop her, as she padded toward him. It felt as if her every step closer was a raw scrape against his exposed heart. Something thudded against the card in his hands. A water droplet. A second. A third. The envelope slid from between his fingers and sailed to the floor, skidding to a halt at Kristin's feet.

"What's this?" She knelt, back straight, keeping the kitty balanced. The paper rasped against the linoleum as she rescued the envelope.

He hung his head, unable to make the wetness in his eyes go away.

Or the explosion inside his heart. What he ought to do was to suck it up, paste a normal look on his face, so she couldn't guess what was going on. Give her the gift, tell her goodbye and march straight into the night. Keep on going until the night numbed him enough so that he could go home, go on with his life per usual.

The card trembled in his hand.

He couldn't let her see. Couldn't let her in. She'd want to soothe him, comfort him with platitudes, and what good would that do? His dad was forever gone. It would never be okay. Never be anything but an unhealed wound inside his heart.

Kristin's hand covered his.

He couldn't look at her. He couldn't talk. He couldn't make himself push her away. The pain swelled in his chest, like a wave breaking against the shore.

"This is from your dad." She sounded gentle. "Where did you get it?"

He scrubbed his eyes, willing the pain away. Failing. "In the pocket. It was his coat."

"Did you read what he wrote?"

He breathed in. His entire being shuddered. Hot grief burned on the back of his eyelids. No, he didn't want to read it. He couldn't bear to bring in any more pain. He was drowning in it. It did no good to dig up the past. To look back at what could never be changed.

"I think you should." Her words came softly. She held open the card.

He yanked it from her grip. His eyes couldn't focus at first. Head down, he jammed it into his pocket. "I'd best be going."

"You want to open your present first?"

She was remarkable. That's what she was. He swiped his eyes with his fingertips, hiding the fact that his face was wet, and did the best he could to turn away. He felt trapped in purgatory with the past a heavy rock around his neck, drawing him down an endless hill and he was helpless to stop the fall.

"Ryan, you're not okay. Why don't I drive you home?"

He was at the back door. He didn't remember standing up. Walking away. Crossing the room. He leaned his forehead against the cold panel of glass and willed the sob building in his windpipe to stay down. But it was rising up. He couldn't let it.

She was behind him, her hand on his back. A calm steady comfort that he didn't want and couldn't stomach. But he needed it like air.

"No, I'll be fine." He was relieved that his words sounded normal. A little strained, but good enough. He looked down to find Pete's truck keys in his hand. There was nothing to do but leave, while he still had a scrap of dignity. "Merry Christmas, Miss McKaslin."

She slid the gift into his pocket. "Merry Christmas, Dr. Sanders. Drive safe. It's cold out there."

The thick layer of clouds broke apart, sending the snow scattering. A white shaft of moonlight lit the steps ahead, as if to guide him. Kristin watched him slip away, a tall hulk of a man in the parka he didn't bother to zip, and that worried her as she held the door after him.

She could feel the weight of his pain like the press of the frigid air. A pain that staggered her, and as she closed the door, she felt the furnace kick on and the rush of hot air at her ankles. Mickey squirmed in her arms, he wanted down, so she released him.

The grief inside her crescendoed—and it wasn't her own. She could feel his pain. It was odd, as if he were a part of her. She couldn't explain it as she brushed tears from her eyes. *Please, Father, help him to read the card. Comfort him.*

There was no answer as the big shadow of a man ambled down the walkway and toward the garage. He vanished from her sight, but she could feel him still in the center of her heart. So much agony. She rubbed her sternum with the heel of her hand.

Maybe she'd been wrong in letting him go. But he was so capable and he'd stood so strong and straight. As if he didn't need her. Why would he? They weren't even friends, not really.

A blur of movement caught her gaze. There he was, inside Dad's truck. He'd pulled the vehicle out of the garage and, judging by the plume of exhaust, was letting the motor warm up a little before taking off.

The needle on the thermometer tacked on the

trunk of the snow-draped maple pointed toward the low minus twenties. Way too cold to take off after him. He sat straight and tall behind the wheel, silhouetted by the slice of moonlight through the clouds. He looked all right.

She didn't know what to do. Only moments ago he'd been seated in the dark, his head bowed, pain radiating off him. She remembered how one drop had marked the card he'd handed her. One tear.

She wasn't sure how to handle that at all. He'd been so restrained then, as he was now, a shadow in the night as he leaned forward, probably to adjust the defroster. He straightened, and the pain inside her swelled until her ribs ached.

Was it her pain? Or his?

Was it possible to feel someone else's emotions?

She didn't know. She stood on tiptoe, trying to see. Ryan's head bowed forward. Was he reading the card? She reached for her coat and let her heart lead her into the cold and night.

Chapter Ten

The past was like a monster reaching out of the dark to choke him. Ryan tossed the child's birthday card on the bench seat. He couldn't look at it. He wasn't a coward or anything, but what was the point? Molten hot emotion built in his chest, threatening to erupt and he couldn't let it. There was no point in giving in to something that couldn't be changed.

What he needed to do was to go home, go to bed, make it through the day and pray for a reason to leave ahead of schedule. Maybe he'd call in for messages. See if there was some emergency he could volunteer for, so he could head home.

He could leave all this behind. Wouldn't that be better? Yeah, he'd give anything right now to be able to be in Phoenix. There were no memories of Dad there. Nor the wild beauty of Montana's icy winters. Just temperate sunshine and rustling palm trees. Yep, that's what he needed.

A knock on the window came out of nowhere—

and sent waves of adrenaline sparking through his veins. The door opened before he could react, and a hooded figure tumbled inside along with the frigid air. Kristin.

"Hey, there." The door shut, and she shivered in her coat and gloves. She didn't appear to notice he wasn't in the mood for company. "I haven't been in this kind of cold since last Christmas. I figure I might as well drive over with you and bring the truck back."

"No way. Then you're out here alone with all this snow. The roads haven't been plowed yet."

"I'm a Montana girl. What's a little snow?"

Silvered by the moonlight, framed by the night, she looked as beautiful as a dream. He swore he could feel more than her physical closeness. Her sympathy, soft as the tiny bit of moonlight reflecting on the miles of snow, chased away the dark. Eased the shadows.

Shame twisted bitterly in his stomach. He couldn't believe how he'd acted in front of her in the kitchen. He'd been way too vulnerable.

Way too...*weak*.

That's what it was. He'd lost his dad as a kid. Sure, it had devastated him, but life went on. Worse tragedies happened every day. He was a man now. A man didn't go around crying like a little boy over what could never be changed. Right?

"Go back in the house, Kristin."

"No. I was feeling lonely tonight, so I thought I'd join you."

"How can I say this nicely? I want to be alone."

"Too bad. Are you going to drive or do you want me to?"

He looked her up and down, as if he wasn't sure what he was going to do.

Kristin's pulse skipped. Was he angry at her? Or was she right in thinking that he was the one who didn't want to be alone? Seconds ticked into minutes as the defroster began to kick out warm air and the clouds overhead sailed in front of the moon, blotting out the light. Leaving only the soft luminescence from the dash controls to see by.

"Stay if you want to." He sounded careless, but he wasn't.

No. Kristin's chest ached with a building pressure. Hurting for him, she opted for silence as he put the truck in gear and hit the headlights. Twin shafts of brightness lit their way as the truck shot forward.

Snow swirled on the ground, drifting, disguising the familiar curve of the driveway. But Ryan forged a path where the road used to be, handling the truck with expert patience whenever the tires lost traction. Without a word, he drove the half mile to his mom's driveway, where the snow had drifted into the cut of the hillside to block the roadway.

He eased the pickup around and pointed her homeward. "I'll hike it the rest of the way."

"It's too cold to walk. You're not dressed for this weather."

"I know what I'm doing. I'll make it in just fine." He set the emergency brake, leaving the truck in neutral. "I don't feel right about letting you drive back."

"I know what I'm doing." She repeated his words. "Apparently we're two people who don't need any help from anyone. Or one another."

That cracked the tension tight around his jaw. A hint of a grin hooked the corner of his mouth. "I'm glad we understand each other."

"Right." She flicked off her hood, since the cab was growing warmer. "Are you going to read your card?"

"That's none of your business."

"True. It's strange, don't you think, that your mom kept your dad's coat—that coat—for so long?"

"I see where you're going with this. And no, Mom's practical. She said to me this morning, before we went out tree cutting, that she knew one day I'd need his coat. The one I brought up from Phoenix wasn't warm enough. That's why she kept it. Just in case. Mom's like that."

"Didn't you notice the card earlier? You could have felt it in the pocket any other time."

"It's a thick goose-down parka. I couldn't tell it was there."

"So why did you find it when you did?"

"Because I was getting your gift out of the pocket.

I know what you're doing, and you're wrong. God isn't trying to tell me something. It's a coincidence. It's just a card."

"It's from your father."

He appeared so strong and steady, as if made from granite. A shadow in the darkness, he lifted the card between two fingers and stared at the colorful front, hardly visible in the dash lights, but substantial nonetheless.

"I'm done with the past. There's nothing there for me." He stuffed it into his pocket, out of sight.

To be forgotten? Her heart breaking, she felt the wash of his grief. She'd known that devastating pain once, too. Did she tell him what had helped her? Or was he right, that it wasn't her business?

It was as if an angel whispered in her ear and she spoke without knowing what she was saying—she reached across the void between them and brushed a kiss to his cheek. A buzz of sensation flitted through her entire being. The part of her heart that could feel his strengthened.

She leaned back, spinning with the feel of his five o'clock shadow and the clean scent of him. "We're a product of our past. You never accepted your father's death, did you?"

"What was there to accept? It happened. There's nothing I can do to change it."

"No. But you carry that loss with you. I know I do. I wrestled with it for a long time. I just wanted my sister back. My family had fallen apart. Mom had sunk into a depression so deep, we didn't think she'd ever come out. Dad just drifted away. Deciding not to cope at all. He just…kept his distance."

"Sometimes that's the best way. Keep away from what's hurting."

"Yes. That's why I moved to Seattle. Part of the reason." She closed her eyes. Thought of the day that had just passed, different because Allison wasn't there. "Nothing is the same. We've all dealt in our own way. I think my sisters are compensating for the past by marrying and having kids."

"Compensating?"

"Trying to recreate what was lost. We were all so close back then. Our family had a real togetherness. Summer vacations and weekend trips up into the woods to camp. Going to watch both Michelle and Kendra compete—they barrel raced. Friday night gatherings and Saturday horse rides and picnics after church on Sunday. Making snowmen and hiding presents around Christmastime and spending Christmas Eve at the piano while Mom played carol after carol. We'd sing until midnight—"

Grief vised her chest, like an iron band twisting tighter with each breath. "Then there was the plane accident. Allison and Kirby were headed with the church group for a retreat."

"I remember." Ryan's baritone rumbled deep with sorrow. With understanding. "You were lucky Kirby survived."

"We were all so grateful. And at the same time,

destroyed. Allison was gone, and our family shattered. As strong as our parents' marriage was, it couldn't stand that loss. And the rest of us just did the best we could. Sometimes the pain feels so fresh. Like on holidays, like tonight. I can't look back because it hurts. I'm sad that nothing is the same. That the future will be forever changed."

Ryan swiped his hand over his face. "Look, I can't do this. I've got to go. Good night."

"Ryan—"

It was beyond rude and he knew it. But he was breaking inside and he had to go. He'd rather face the frigid cold and the hopeless night than to let her in. Let her close. She was coming after him. He could see her in the brief shine of the dome light, which was illuminating the honest compassion on her sweet face. It was too much—too honest, too intimate and too close to breaking open the scars inside him.

He winced as he slammed the door shut, the pain so stark it was as if the grief inside him had broken his ribs. The brief shine from the dome light faded, leaving only the haunting shadow of Kristin, her jaw falling open with surprise at his behavior.

And he hated it. He didn't know what was happening to him. How would someone as perfect as Kristin understand? He sank into snow up to his thigh. Stepped again, cold sliding through his clothes. He cut through the beams of the headlights and faced the dark. Headed to a place that hurt as much as it sheltered. But it was better than going back, although something inside him felt stretched, as if an unseen force was pulling him back. Holding on. Never letting go.

Was it Kristin? Why could he still feel her kiss on his cheek? Not even the icy wind was able to numb the tingle on his skin. The night could not diminish the glow in his spirit when he thought of her.

Look after her, Father. Please. Ryan couldn't turn around, but he could feel her watching him. Praying for him. He had to keep going—it felt as if his survival depended on it. On putting as much distance as he could away from her. Away from her kindness. Her caring. Her softness.

How had she gotten so deep into his soul? He only knew he didn't want her there. He didn't want anyone that close. He tromped through the drifting snow, sinking and struggling. It was tough going, but he didn't care. He just wanted as far away from her as he could get. His heart was bursting, his spirit fracturing and he was thankful when the shadows swallowed him from Kristin's sight. He heard the truck's idle change—she was shifting into gear. The increased hum of the engine reverberated through the silent night as she gave it enough gas to pull out onto the lonely road and then the sound faded into nothing.

Only then did he turn and watch the faint beam of taillights grow smaller in the vast darkness until they disappeared. He was alone, and the bitter cold hadn't eased the agony inside him. Hadn't erased the grip Kristin had on his soul.

With his step crunching on the new snow, Ryan's breathing came loud as the night seemed to draw more silent. As if it lay in quiet anticipation. He'd never heard such silence. Endless and echoing and hushed.

By the time he'd made it to the back steps, he was frozen clear through. His hands and feet were numb. His face chapped and burning. The card and gift in his pocket felt like lead weights, growing heavier with every step he took.

He'd been so wrong to run to her tonight. That's what he'd done, wasn't it? Hauling his tail through a storm to the warmth of her presence. Why had he done it? It had made sense at the time, but now—now everything was worse.

Grateful for the porch light guiding him in, he stumbled up the buried porch steps, kicking snow away as he went. It had drifted up against the back door, even though Mom had probably cleared it away before she went to bed. He grabbed the shovel leaning against the siding and gave a few swipes to clear a path.

Not that the inside of this house was a sanctuary. If anything, his chest hurt worse. His heart broke apart even more. He kicked out of his boots, his numbed feet feeling thick and unresponsive. His fingers were no better. He headed straight to the woodstove in the corner, which crackled and popped as it radiated wonderful heat.

Unzipping, he sank onto the hot floor bricks and

let the warmth wash over him like bliss. He was so cold, he couldn't feel it. His entire body started to shiver.

Okay, he'd been desperate to go out in the cold dressed like he was. Even his bones felt frozen. He thought of Kristin when he climbed to his feet. The clock said ten minutes to midnight. That meant she ought to be just about home now. The roads were pretty much impassable. He never should have agreed to let her come. If he'd been in more control of his emotions, he certainly wouldn't have allowed such a thing.

And at this late hour, he couldn't call and wake up the entire house to make sure she was safe.

Worry churned through him. He grabbed a cup from the cupboard and filled it with water, hating his clumsy movements. He heated water in the microwave and dug through the drawers until he found where Mom kept the tea. She had a whole drawer full of different boxes of the stuff.

He grabbed a fruity-flavored one, dunked the bag in the steaming water. Just cupping it in his hands made him feel warmer. He drank it right there in one long draw and refilled the cup and nuked it again.

He felt marginally better. Still shivering, the minute and a half it took for the machine to ding felt like an eternity. He watched the wall clock's hands move closer to midnight.

The ringing phone surprised him. With adrenaline still knocking through him, he grabbed the receiver before it could ring again. "Kristin?"

"Just checking to make sure you made it indoors safely," she answered.

Relief slid through him that she was also okay. He stopped quaking. Then again, it might have been from the hot tea. The microwave dinged in the background. He couldn't think of what to say other than, *Sorry I was a moron and ran off like that. Sorry I couldn't handle finding a piece of paper in my pocket.*

But she spoke, breaking the silence between them. "Well, I just wanted to ease my mind. I had visions of you frozen in a snowbank in midstride. When I got home, the thermometer read twenty-four below. I shouldn't have let you walk off like that."

"The driveway was full of drifts. The truck would have gotten stuck. Did you have any problems?"

"Nope."

She sounded sad, and he hated that. Ryan took a second to gather up his courage. "I left kind of quick back there."

"It's okay. I overstepped. You're right. I never should have—"

Ryan's conscience winced. He didn't want her to go blaming herself when it was all his fault. His failings. Hadn't Francine done the same thing? Always trying to be there for him, when he couldn't take the pain of letting anyone that close?

He was wrong. "No, you were great. You were a

good friend tonight. I just— I just handle things on my own. It's the way I am."

"Okay." She sounded relieved, less strained. "You take care of yourself. And have a good Christmas with your family."

"You, too." His windpipe collapsed and he could barely get out a goodbye before he hung up. The phone cord dangled long and coiled up, the way it always used to.

The years rolled back against his will and he could remember his dad standing right here, hand on the receiver as he hung up, the last time Ryan had seen him. How big and strong and manly his dad was, the quiet capable type. Dad's deep gravelly voice seemed to rumble through the years and echo all around Ryan.

He saw the past and the present at the same time. The shadowed room where the fire sparkled in the tempered window of the woodstove. The little boy's view looking up at his dad, who was saying they had the prescription ready in town, he'd be back with it and their favorite carton of ice cream. *You be a good boy for your mom, and I'll be right back. We'll get some medicine in you, and you'll be feeling better soon. I promise.*

The darkness swallowed him and Ryan sank to his knees. The hard edges of the brick hearth bit into his kneecaps. Knowing it would break him forever, he pulled the card from his pocket. When he opened the envelope, the orange-and-black cast from the fire writhed upon the page. There was Dad's writing from the past filling the present. *I love you, son.*

The weight of the past broke free. *I love you, too, Dad.* Hot waves of sorrow crashed through him. *I just want you back.* He fought to hold on, but he couldn't. Tears burned in his eyes and brimmed. The first sob escaped, scraping painfully up his throat. A second. A third.

He buried his face in his hands, which were no longer numb. Hurting with a heart that was no longer shielded.

Christmas came with a whisper. The wall clock gently bonged once, as if in welcome. Ryan ignored it. He'd never felt more hopeless or alone.

He didn't see the tiniest bits of snow begin to drift down from the black velvet sky. They were delicate flakes, crested by starlight and glowing like hope.

As if God were listening on this wintry, holy night.

Kristin waited until the final chime of the grandfather clock in the living room silenced. Christmas came on the wings of snow that fell in dazzling reassurance to the frozen ground. Starlight eased between the breaks in the clouds to make the fields surrounding the house shimmer like an opal. Wetness burned in her eyes, and she couldn't say why.

Maybe she was tired. Maybe it was stress. Or the worry over what tomorrow would bring.

So many worries weighed down on her.

It was Ryan and the way he'd practically leaped out of the truck and run away as fast as he could plow through the snow. How could she blame him? She'd leaned across the seat and kissed him. She'd done it without thinking, on impulse. She'd never done such a thing before. She'd called him to apologize, and had lost the nerve to say, "Sorry I threw myself at you."

She wrapped her arms around her middle. It was her family, and worrying about tomorrow, which was already here. Christmas, alive and solemn.

Snapshots from Christmases past clustered the end wall in the breezeway. She stopped to study them. Framed in gold, reflecting the wink of the tree lights, she looked at the past. At the scrawny little girl with her long hair and straight-edged bangs, thanks to Mom's home cut. She sat in the middle, surrounded by all her sisters, crowding close with the Christmas tree in the background. They were all beaming from their exciting morning of ripping open Santa's gifts.

Each year Mom had framed a similar snapshot of the six of them crowded together in front of the tree. Happy and laughing. Allison, the tallest, was always in the back of their group. Slim and sleek and beautiful. She'd been kind and good every day of her life. There were so many pictures without her.

There was last year's picture—just the five of them. Mom always wanted a snapshot of her girls.

But in the corner of the frame, there was another. The grandchildren in their new Christmas clothes for church. They'd gathered here and snapped the Polaroid in front of the tree. Mom must have taken several, reserving one to tuck in this frame.

Life was going on, rolling like the earth in the universe. Tugged along on a path that could not be stopped. It hurt, what was left behind.

She went to wipe the dampness from her eyes and the shocking sound of the mugs clinking together startled her. She'd forgotten she was holding them in her left hand, lost in her thoughts when she should be shutting down the house for the night.

She unplugged Christmas lights in the kitchen. Rinsed the cups and tucked them into the top dishwasher rack. Watched the colorful lights hooked over the bay window valances blink out as she hit the switch. Something moved out of the corner of her eye, a rustle of movement. One of the cats?

She checked the cushions on the window seat. No feline was hiding there or beneath the table. Strange. For some reason the cushions looked inviting and she eased down on them. Ryan's gift, as small as a jewelry box, sat on the center of the table, where he'd left it.

She'd forgotten about it until now. The silver-and-gold wrapping was crumpled in one corner, and the frilly bow was squished from being in his pocket.

Ryan. She wished she could rewind time like a tape and replay it. What had he said? That she'd been a good friend. A friend. That was nice. Maybe he didn't hold her impulsive kiss against her.

So, what had he gotten her? She removed the bow and set it aside, tugging the ribbon until it unraveled. She lifted the lid and gasped. Elegant gold dangle earrings in the shape of snowflakes glinted in the faint starlight. Oh, this was too much, it was too expensive—

A small card was inside, too. She pulled it out. He'd written, *To the storm that brought old acquaintances together and made us friends.*

Yes, that felt right. *Friends.* The warm glow in her spirit remained. As if a door had opened to a place within her heart. To what, she didn't know. Ryan lived in Phoenix. She lived in Seattle. The most they could be would be long-distance friends. It seemed as if the only thing they had in common were their visits home for the holidays.

On the wide wooden sill behind her, the delicate porcelain figures sat in eternal worship. The barn animals, the wise men and mother and father. All knelt before the simple manger where the Christ child lay.

Her breath fogged on the cold window, but she couldn't move. Couldn't look away. Cold radiated through the windows. Warmth from the heat vent curled around her ankles. Tiny snowflakes flitted against the window.

Slowly the grief inside her ebbed away, leaving in its place peace.

Chapter Eleven

Christmas Day

Kristin's cell phone rang. Yanking her favorite Christmas sweater over her head, she dug through her bag on the floor until she found it. She checked the ID on the screen before answering. "Hey, Karen. How did Allie like her trike?"

"She's squealing and pedaling around the living room as we speak. I tried to get her off to eat breakfast and she raised such a fuss, I just handed her a waffle and let her eat and drive."

"Sounds like it was a hit. Did Zach tell you how hard that thing was to put together?"

"Yep. 'Santa' is still assembling some of the other toys. He's been at it since sunup." Karen's voice sparkled with happiness. In the background, a little girl's squeals of delight rang like merry bells, accompanied by a loud crash. "Oops, I gotta go. Disasters abound. I'll see you around noon. Merry Christmas!"

She sounded so happy, Kristin thought as she tucked her phone into her back jean pocket. Good. Karen, who'd been closest to Allison, had a hard time with her death. Now, she was laughing and happy again. That was a good thing. But Kristin couldn't help worrying. She prayed Karen had one of those special marriages that would last. She wished that for all her sisters.

She didn't know how they could do it, but she was thankful they were all thriving and content.

She hopped over Minnie, asleep on the sunny landing, and down the stairs. Presents were heaped under the lit tree, and the fragrance of wood smoke and fresh pine was like every other Christmas in her memory. She followed the scent of sizzling bacon to the kitchen, where Mom was at the stove, spatula in hand.

"Merry Christmas. Is Dad in the barn?"

"Yes, indeed. The snow had drifted over the back door and he had to dig his way out. What a storm we must have had last night." Mom flipped the bacon, the hollows beneath her eyes, bruised with exhaustion, told a different story. "Did you want one egg or two?"

"Are you kidding? Two. It's not every day I get treated to your eggs Benedict." She kissed her mom's cheek as she slipped by.

Mickey was purring, content to lie on the heat

register beneath the table. She stooped to give him a stroke, wondering. Mom looked so worn out, as if she hadn't slept at all. And what about Dad?

A knock at the back door—it was Dad. He poked his head in, his skin was red from the cold. His lined plaid hat with the earflaps was dappled with ice pellets. "Kris—get your boots on and help me. The water's froze up solid at the barn."

"Are the animals all right?"

"For now, but that heater conked out sometime during the night. Don't know how long they've been without water. We've got to start packin'."

"Okay." She reached for her coat, unhooking it from the back closet. The frigid draft from the partially opened door had her shivering. She dug through the closet for insulated gloves. There had to be an extra pair lying around somewhere.

"Pete." Mom's voice felt as chilled as the outside air. "Will you be long? I've just put the eggs on."

"Well, now, I don't rightly know, Alice." Dad sounded tired. Irritable. "It'll take as long as it takes. You know that."

Her parents arguing—it used to be a rare thing. She hated it. Her stomach clenched tight. *Please, stop,* she wished with all her might.

But Mom didn't. She kept right on going. "It'll ruin the eggs to keep them warming."

"What would you have me do? You'll just have to wait, Alice." With a tired sigh, Dad closed the door with a click that echoed through the tense silence in the kitchen.

Kristin released a shaky breath. That was why she never wanted to get married. If her parents, who'd had the perfect marriage and life together, couldn't make love last, then no one could. From the outside, they looked content enough. But behind closed doors, the distance and the hurt separated them. How long would it be until the anger progressed to bitter hatred? Would they divorce?

Her stomach burned. No, that was unthinkable. Her parents wouldn't do that. They wouldn't walk away from their holy vows in that final way. She jerked on the pair of gloves she'd found. They were too big, probably an extra pair of Dad's.

What difference did it make? She just wanted outside. She was choking, and Mom was muttering to herself as she put the eggs on to cook. Words that Kristin didn't want to hear. Turning away, she pounded outside and into the brutal cold before she realized she hadn't zipped up.

She didn't even remember pulling her coat on. Ice dried on her cheeks as she bent to zip up, the thick gloves making it difficult.

No, her parents wouldn't divorce, she realized as she looked around at the sprawling home and well-kept outbuildings, at the horses milling around the open barn doors. Mom and Dad had built something good here together. They wouldn't divide it up into his and hers. They'd just live like this forever, silently angry and quietly hurting.

Marriage was such a blessing? Not from where she stood. Disillusionment twisted in her heart on this most sacred of mornings. She tried to push it aside but she couldn't. Since Dad had left two ten-gallon buckets by the back steps, she swept them off and sidled back inside to the laundry room, off the mudroom, where she hefted the buckets into the oversize sink and hit the faucet.

There was no way she was ever going to get married. No way she was ever going to trust that one day her world wouldn't be pulled out from under her like a rug beneath her feet. Leaving her in pieces and hurting as Mom was. She tried not to listen to the sounds of Mom's anger. The harsh ring of a pot or the harder than necessary thud of a cupboard door closing

The buckets were nearly full. Kristin, used to the drill, turned off the water, hiked the buckets with care and lugged them to the back door. It felt like a two-mile trek to the barn hauling twenty gallons of water. Her nose, throat and lungs burned from the icy wind as she struggled across the backyard. Dad had broken a path, but she still sank into snow up to the top of her boots.

"Say, thanks for your help, Kris." There was Dad, hurrying to take the heavy load from her.

He was such a kind man. Why couldn't he and Mom just get along?

"I've got a space heater working in the utility room. Temporary fix." Dad gestured with a curt nod toward the corner room, where the water heater and industrial furnace were housed. "Could you do me a favor? Run in the house, would ya, and fetch my phone. I left it in the living room."

She heard what he didn't say. He didn't want to face Mom. "Fine. I'll do that."

"Good. I figure all our little ones are up by now. All that excitement with Santa Claus comin', you know." His blue eyes twinkled and for a moment he looked young and alive. But the brightness slipped away and left a tired, aging man. An unhappy man.

"I might as well warn the boys I'll be needin' their help today. Sure is good havin' them in the family. You wouldn't be lookin' to give me another son-in-law, would you?"

"Dad! Not you, too." She snatched up empty buckets from the ground, ones Dad had just emptied. "I expected better from you."

"I'm just sayin'. It doesn't hurt to mention it." Dad upended a full bucket over the top of the gate and into his mare's water trough. "Noticed you and Ryan are getting close."

"We're *friends*. You know. We're *friendly*."

"Well, sure, but he'd make a fine son-in-law. He's smart, works hard, respectful to women and his elders. It'd be awful handy to have a doctor in the family."

"Dad! I'd much rather haul twenty gallons of

water in the freezing cold than stand here and listen to this." With the buckets she held clanking, she marched straight to the door without looking back.

Although she couldn't stop from wondering— why was her dad doing this, too? Putting so much attention on her and Ryan's friendship that could never be anything more.

Maybe because it helped them to forget for a while their own unhappiness.

Snow tickled her nose as she negotiated the treacherous path to the house. She could see Mom through the big bay window busy at the stove, the bow of her apron at the small of her back. Her left shoulder hitched high to keep the phone at her ear while she worked. Probably hearing about her grandchildren.

Kristin popped open the door to the sound of Mom's voice, falsely cheerful.

"Oh, I'm sure Allie will get the hang of it in no time... I suppose the couch will have to face a few more head-on accidents before the day is through. How's little Anna? Loves to rip the paper..."

Talking with Karen, Kristin concluded, as she elbowed into the laundry room and set the buckets in the sink. Bits of conversation rose over the rush of the water. "Oh, dear, Kirby's calling on the other line. Yes, I'll tell her. See you in a bit... Kirby, Merry Christmas. Michael did *what?*" Mom laughed, shallow and forced, the note ringing hollow on this holy day.

The tension between her and Dad lingered.

Once they'd all come together in celebration and joy. Christmas would never be that way again. Her family was forever changed.

Ryan followed his nose down the hall, yawning. He wasn't even really awake yet, but his stomach was growling. He shuffled in his socks and his flannel pj's, lured by the scents of coffee and sausage and maple syrup.

"Hey, sleepyhead." Mom sat in her favorite chair by the window, smiling up at him as her knitting needles flashed. "Mia's still asleep, too. Boy, does this take me back to when you two were teenagers on a weekend morning."

"Weekends and holidays are made for sleeping in. You know that." He raked a hand through his hair. Yawned again. He was still tired. He couldn't say he got much sleep last night.

Christmas was everywhere. The solemn carols humming from the little stereo system he'd gotten Mom for her last birthday. The blink and glisten of the tree lights. The presents piled beneath the branches. A mix of the presents for each other and ones "Santa" had left overnight. The serene glow of love that lingered in this house. Why hadn't he noticed that before?

"I have your breakfast keeping warm in the oven. Don't forget to rinse your plate!"

"Yeah, yeah." He stooped to brush a kiss to her forehead. "Merry Christmas."

Mom's eyes filled. "Oh, you're my favorite son."

"I'm your only son, but I am your favorite." He winked, enjoying the sound of her chuckle as he left the room. One thing about his mom, she loved both Mia and him equally. But he was uncomfortable with what he'd wanted to say. Like, I love you, Mom.

With the fire snapping in the woodstove, the kitchen was blissfully warm. He found two plates keeping warm in the oven, the smaller one was Mia's. He took the big serving plate, heaped with scrambled eggs, pancakes and sausage links to the table.

It was a very white Christmas. Snow clouds rolled along the sky like waves in an ocean, undulating and white-capped and stunning, crashing upon the frosted mountains. The roll of land, the draw of valley and silent firs snowcapped and still, tugged at his heart, summoning the past. Memories surged through him. Of Dad at the table, nose in the paper as he dragged out that last cup of coffee and used the last sausage link to wipe up the puddle of maple syrup from the pancakes.

Mom, younger and more lively, taking the empty plate from him. "No, you just relax. You work enough for two men the week through."

Mia hopping up from the table—spritelike and freckle-faced as she'd been as a little girl. "I wanna open the presents now. Can we? Can we?"

"After your father finishes his coffee," Mom had answered from the sink. "Ryan, are you still eating? Haven't you filled that hollow leg of yours yet? There's one more pancake. Go ahead and eat it."

That had been their last Christmas together, Ryan remembered as he sat down to the table with the syrup bottle in hand. He'd gotten skis as part of his cache and after Christmas dinner, Dad had taken him outside. Showed him how to cross-country.

The years fell away and he was an eight-year-old bundled well in bulky winter gear. The thick scarf and the parka's hood made it hard to tip his head back far enough to look up at his dad. Dad had seemed so tall and invincible. A superhero of a man who could do anything.

With endless patience, Dad showed him how to use the poles to kick off and glide. "With a little practice, you'll be good enough to go up in the backcountry with me."

"Can I, can I?"

"Sure thing, Son. I promise. We'll make a day of it. We'll use the new binoculars you and your sister got me. I bet we'll even see a few wildcat tracks, if we're lucky."

A promise that Dad never got to keep.

Ryan could almost feel the pure thrill of anticipation he'd felt that Christmas. How like a man he felt skiing alongside his dad. Being big enough to get to go up into the mountains. Of swelling up with love until he'd felt like bursting, as his dad's hand came to rest on his shoulder.

"That's my boy," Dad had said.

In the warmth of the kitchen, Ryan took a steadying breath. His vision was blurry, and he swore he could feel the weight of his dad's hand on his shoulder still. Could still sense his father's love and pride.

Something he hadn't felt since that long-ago day.

Why? He'd never faced his grief before. He'd been a kid. He hadn't known how to handle his father's death. And through the years, it had been easier to push those feelings down. Until last night. Until he'd found the card.

Because of Kristin. She was the reason. If his mom hadn't been trying to fix him up with her and arranged for them to cut Christmas trees, then he wouldn't have used Dad's coat. And he wouldn't have put Kristin's gift in the pocket where the forgotten card had resided.

Kristin. He thought about her. About how she'd looked last night in the truck's dome light, full of compassion and caring and beauty. How she was like the gentle peace of a winter morning, and he wanted to see her. He missed her company. There was a place deep in his heart that warmed. It was like the connection he'd felt last night between them, and he wondered if she was thinking of him, too.

Oblivious to the tension in the living room, little golden-haired Allie galloped in circles around the couch, holding on to her new toy horses with real manes, who were "galloping" with her. Her little sister, Anna, ran after her with one hand outstretched and the other clutching the couch for balance, making a shrill sound of glee.

Kristin moved her left foot in time to save it from being run over by little Michael's dump truck that raced on the edge of the cold hearth bricks. With the help of Michael's sound effects and guiding hand, the truck took a tragic head-on into the wood box, flew through the air to roll to a stop where Kristin's foot used to be.

"Uh-oh!" Baby Emily commented as she hugged her Sesame Street doll that was laughing hysterically.

Wearing a very fashionable red-and-green Christmas sleeper that said Santa's Favorite in candy-cane striping, Baby Caitlin yawned, stretched her little fists and nestled deeper into her mommy's arms. Seated side by side, Kendra and her husband Cameron watched their infant daughter sleep with sheer love on their faces.

Kristin prayed that their love would last. She wished that for all of her sisters. And for her parents, who sat on opposite sides of the room, Mom staring at the brochure that held the tickets and paid hotel-and-tour vouchers. That wish was looking more and more like an impossibility.

"Look what the girls got us, Pete." Mom held up the picture of a lush Maui resort.

Mom didn't look too happy. Kristin glanced at her sister Michelle, who was seated on the chair next to her.

"Disaster," Michelle leaned over to whisper.

"Uh-oh!" Emily commented from Michelle's lap.

Exactly. Kristin watched as Mom struggled to smile. Not a real smile. And the last of Kristin's hopes—and, she was sure, all of her sisters'—broke into a thousand pieces.

"Well, now," Dad commented as even the children silenced. "That was real thoughtful of you girls."

"You always used to talk about a second honeymoon in Hawaii, but with the running of the farm, there was never any time," Kirby gently explained. "So we thought—well…"

"Since you never got the chance to go," Michelle broke in. "We'd help you along. Merry Christmas."

"That's real fine." Dad's smile was too tight, but he was trying to be gracious.

As Karen and Kirby huddled around Mom, showing her all that the two-week vacation included, Dad stood from his recliner and began clearing away the wrapping paper. Brody and Cameron got up to help him. The TV flashed to life. Little Michael had abandoned his dump truck to take command of the remote control.

Sam blew a raspberry on his boy's cheek and they chuckled together, father and son. "If you're going to take charge of the remote, you've got to make sure to turn it to football. That's it, hit that button right there. Good boy."

The black-and-white Jimmy Stewart movie switched to a game in progress. The men froze, staring at the screen as a football sailed through the air—

"Incomplete!" the commentator announced and the men moaned in agony.

"How badly do you think we goofed?" Michelle whispered, keeping one eye on Mom. "I should never have pushed for this. I just want them to be happy."

"That's what we all want. We want our mom and dad back the way they were. In love again." Love, once lost, could never be found. That's what Kristin was beginning to see for certain. "You meant well, and it was a great idea. Everybody thought so."

"I'm still holding out hope. I say they'll go on this second honeymoon and fall madly in love the way they used to be. It, like, happens in movies and stuff."

"Uh-oh!" Emily shrieked, just for the fun of it.

My thoughts exactly. Kristin knew all too well the look of suppressed pain on her mother's face. A second honeymoon was the last thing her parents wanted. Maybe their love had finished for good, and they would settle for distant indifference for the rest of their married lives.

Sad. Kristin's stomach clenched so tight, she winced.

"I thought it was a fine idea!" Gramma sidled in behind them. "Just what they need. Once they spend their first evening dining on their lanai gazing out at that tropical sunset, they'll thank you. You wait and see. Kris, who gave you those earrings? They're just lovely."

"A friend." A friend she'd been trying not to think about all day.

"Oh? Which friend?"

"Ooh, Gramma, she won't tell us!" Michelle protested. "I asked. Kirby asked. Karen asked. Kendra asked. Mom asked. She just gets that panicked look on her face, which can only mean one thing. It's from a man friend. A *boyfriend!*"

"No! I never said that." Kristin knew she was walking the edge of a lie, but—

"I heard you and Ryan Sanders were spending time together." Gramma seemed so pleased. "First you spend time with him when you were home at Thanksgiving—"

"We drove together. We didn't go out on a date—"

"And now he's giving you expensive jewelry. Of course he's only a friend." Gramma was beaming as she scooped Emily from Michelle's arms. "Come to great-gramma, precious girl."

"Those are expensive-looking earrings." Michelle chimed in appreciation. "Ryan sure must like you."

Kristin leaped out of the chair. It wasn't because she was panicked. "I think I hear the phone ringing."

"You know what Gramma says. One day the love-bug's gonna bite you. Watch out, sister dear!"

"Yeah, maybe I have immunity to the love-bug bite." Kristin escaped while she could into the kitchen where the whir of the dishwasher was a welcome relief. Alone, she grabbed a can of diet cola from the fridge.

Ryan. She'd been trying to keep him out of her mind all day. That couldn't be a good sign. Had she ever thought about a man so often? Not in all her life. Not once. What could that mean?

"Oh, Kristin. Would you mind taking out the pies? Your dad is asking for dessert." Mom padded in and pulled a knife and a pie server from the utensil drawer. She looked so sad, even when she smiled.

If only there was something she could do. She set aside the can of soda to give her mom a hug. In the twinkle lights of the kitchen, with the sounds of Christmas all around, Kristin was grateful for her mom and her dad. Grateful for their health and prosperity. Thankful for the family that filled this house.

"I told Kendra I'd bring out the high chair." Mom hurried away, busy as always, leaving Kristin alone.

As she was setting out the homemade chocolate-cream pies, the phone rang. The TV blared as the Cowboys gained four more yards on their second down. The men in the living room cheered, drowning out the sound of a bell ringing.

The phone. Kristin reached for the receiver, then waited. The caller ID said Sanders. Was it Ryan? Or his mom? Over the noise in the living room, no one else heard the phone ring three more times. Kristin waited in the glow of the twinkle lights as the recorder beeped to life.

"Hey," came Ryan's smooth baritone, deep and wonderful. "Merry Christmas, McKaslin family. I'm trying to get a hold of Kristin. I'll be in town until Saturday night. Give me a call. There's the matter of a chocolate milk shake we need to discuss. Okay? Bye."

She could really like him. Maybe she already liked him too much. The tug of pain in her chest, deep in her heart, was regret. Not love. The connection she felt to him wasn't what she wanted at all. She refused to get carried away and let caring turn to something more dangerous. She had to stop this and stop it now.

She hit the Erase button, wiped away the evidence of Ryan's call, yet the link remained. It was a glow in the center of her chest that didn't fade but remained long into the night as she lay awake, listening to the wind at the eaves.

A fitful sleep claimed her and, when she awoke with the dawn, still the connection stirred within her.

Chapter Twelve

December 31

Ryan hit the lights the minute he walked in the kitchen door. His keys landed on the tile counter and his shoes echoed in the quiet room as he glanced through the mail. A few bills, his school loan payment, an invite to some charity event and the flier from his local church. The last envelope in his hand froze him in place.

It was from his friend Mark, at the clinic in the Seattle area. The one he'd interviewed with in November. He ran his thumb over the tasteful embossed blue-and-green lettering of the return address. Mark had e-mailed him yesterday. Said they were still shorthanded and had a growing practice. They sure would be interested in bringing him on board.

Yeah. He was more interested than ever. His trip home for Christmas had wound up changing everything. Not that he would ever stop missing his dad, and nothing would ever stop the pain of losing his father. But at least he could remember the good times. Like the sun through storm clouds, there was light, and it was easier to see a lot of things he hadn't before.

He liked Phoenix, but he missed the seasons. He missed being able to ski without hopping into a plane first. He wanted to be closer to his mom. She wasn't getting any younger.

Seattle was green ánd tidy and metropolitan enough to give him a choice in his work. It was located on the water. He could boat, windsurf and ride a Jet Ski during the summers. In less than an hour's drive, he could be on the slopes in winter.

It was a fairly short flight to Montana. He could pay for his mom to visit as much as she wanted.

And, best of all, he already had friends in the area. Jeremiah and Mark and Kristin. Kristin lived in Seattle.

What was he going to do about Kristin? He pulled the folded tie out of his jacket pocket. The colorful sails of the sailboats and Windsurfers soared on a soft blue background. It had been Kristin's Christmas gift to him. He wore it today and thought of her. Nearly every minute of the day.

She'd never returned his call on Christmas. He'd left two messages the next day and nothing.

No. He'd messed that up. He'd pushed her away deliberately that night he'd fled from the truck, when she'd been offering him her help. Her friendship. Maybe more.

He'd blown it, like he always did. He'd been alone for so long, deliberately keeping people away, maybe he didn't know how to do anything else.

Maybe that was for the best.

He wandered into the bedroom, wondering. Maybe he'd make a few calls on Monday. Find out if this offer was in his best interests. What would it cost him to move? He'd have to arrange for movers and look for a new residence to rent or buy. And his work—he had surgery scheduled out two months. He couldn't move before then.

It was a lot to consider.

He grabbed the remote off the corner of the dresser, where the housekeeper always placed it when she'd been in. The silent TV burst to life and a fireworks celebration exploded across the scene. He glanced at the clock. It was four minutes into the new year.

It felt like a new beginning. What was ahead of him for the coming year? he wondered. Would he find real happiness?

With her stomach in knots, Kristin snapped off the small TV in her living room and the New Year's festivities on the East Coast faded into black. Minnie, drowsing on the back of the couch, slit one eye as she passed by.

The kitchen was dark. She made her way to the

microwave by memory after grabbing her favorite mug and filling it with water. Her nightly ritual—she heated the mug and water and grabbed a bag of her favorite chamomile tea. The luminous green numbers on the stove told her how late it was. Where was Michelle? She should have called by now.

As if in answer, the phone rang and she snatched it up. "Please, don't tell me they refused to go."

"Okay, I won't." Michelle sounded cheerful. That had to be a good sign. "Brody and I drove them to the airport. They got on the plane this morning as planned. But I got some really awesome news and I spent the rest of the day at Kirby's place."

"What kind of awesome news?"

"She and Sam decided to wait to tell everyone, until they knew for sure and there were no complications. But she's—"

"Pregnant?"

"With twins, thanks to in vitro! Isn't that totally cool? I mean, imagine Christmas next year. My little one will be here. Kirby's twins will be here. Isn't it totally amazing? Remember how sad it used to be, after Allison left us?"

"I remember. Nothing was ever right again."

"But now it's like that's healing. We're all married and starting our own families. It's like coming full circle. Well, except for you. You're the last holdout."

"And that's a plan I intend to stick to."

"Sure, okay. Be stubborn. I'm sure when God's

ready He'll send the perfect Mr. Right into your life. If He hasn't already."

"Stop that! You're sounding way too happy. I like being on my own."

"Good. But being married to your soul mate is *so* much better. You'll see. Anyway, maybe this trip alone together is exactly what Mom and Dad need. True love can heal anything. Don't you think?"

No. Kristin didn't believe in true love. Not anymore. But it was a nice thought, and Michelle had always been optimistic. Maybe that's why she had the courage to marry—she imagined the best that could be.

Where Kristin was too much of a realist. "I'm certainly praying that it does."

"Ooh, me, too! Oh, there's Emily. I gotta go. Happy New Year! Later..."

The microwave dinged, an echoing beep that emphasized the silence and the shadows. Kristin popped the door and set the tea bag to steep in the steaming water. See how quiet it was here? How calm? How safe? Love wasn't safe, that was for sure. It wasn't sure and solid at all. She hoped Mom and Dad could find their love for one another again, but she didn't believe they would.

All it had taken was one tragedy to rip their world apart. Kristin had never recovered from Allison's death, either. She'd found a way to go on. Learned from that hard life experience that people of faith weren't immune to tragedy. It was a part of life. But you could make good common-sense choices. You could be smart and protect yourself.

That's why she was happy here. Maybe not blissful, the way her sisters were, but the upside was that she wouldn't experience the deep lows that her siblings might encounter one day. The fall into despair. The life she'd built for herself was a sensible one. She owned this lovely home, modest, but a sound investment. She'd built equity and refinanced with an incredible interest rate. She worked hard, spent her money wisely and had built a very sound savings making a solid rate in bonds and CDs.

Yes, she had a good practical life. One that made her content. And content was enough. It had to be.

And Ryan? Well, she'd tucked his earrings away in her jewelry box. She'd added him to her prayers, wishing for him the best possible future. But she wasn't going to let her regard for him turn into anything as untrustworthy as love.

No, she was better off alone. That's the way she liked it.

January 19

Ryan's day could have gone better. Two hours behind schedule, he was stuck in traffic in the middle of one of Seattle's floating bridges. The barely measurable forward progress he was making in the left lane had stalled to a dead stop for the last twenty-three minutes.

The downpour turned torrential, and he flicked

the windshield wipers on high. Hit the brake. Great. Now the traffic wasn't moving at all. His interview had gone way late, but it had gone well. He liked the clinic and their philosophy, and their waterfront offices were a definite bonus. He'd even checked out the affiliated hospital. It was all great, but it had taken time.

He had a seven-fifteen flight. If the traffic was going to be uncooperative, then he wouldn't have time to look up Kristin.

The truth was, he was almost glad. Maybe the problem had solved itself. He'd been struggling with whether to call her, or whether to let their so-called friendship go.

He tugged Mom's letter from his coat pocket and unfolded it, keeping one eye on the road, but the traffic was gridlocked. A gust of wind roared around the car and the concrete and steel beneath the car shook from the force. White-capped waves sloshed over the concrete barrier.

He studied the numbers she'd sent. Kristin's home, work and cell-phone numbers. He certainly had the information he needed to contact her. Should he? Or would she refuse to take his call again?

He didn't know what he felt. He didn't know what he wanted. He only knew that the thought of calling her and seeing her again made his palms sweat. Nerves. Anxiety. Stress.

He'd leave it up to heaven to decide. If the traffic started moving, and he had enough time to see her, he'd call. Easy as that. But if the traffic stayed like this, he'd creep and crawl right on past the downtown high-rises.

An hour later, he had his answer. Twilight came and he'd moved to the far side of the bridge. Rush hour had officially started. He crumpled Mom's letter and tossed it into the car's little plastic garbage bag.

Problem solved.

April 11

"Do I have the best sisters, or what?" Michelle swiped her eyes as she gazed around the coffee shop decorated for a baby shower. "Oh, look at me. I'm bawling again. Oh, I didn't expect this. I thought it was Bible Study as usual. You fooled me!"

"No, we surprised you." Kristin wrapped her arm around Michelle's slim shoulders and guided her to the chair reserved just for her. "You told me you would be needing all new things for this baby."

"I did!" Michelle glowed as she eased into the chair, her hand rubbing her swollen tummy that looked ready to burst beneath her pink maternity T-shirt. "Oh, this blue comforter set is so wonderful, Kristin."

"It's from all of us." Karen circled behind the counter with a tray of iced drinks. "Your favorite Italian soda. Oh, and there's Mary's car driving up. Kristin, would you help her carry in the food?"

"Sure." More than happy to let her sister show off

the new crib set, Kristin escaped out the front door and into the warm spring day. She loved her sisters, but she'd already been asked about Ryan nearly two-dozen times since she'd arrived yesterday. That was two-dozen times too many.

"Kristin." It was his voice. Had she imagined it?

No, there he was, rising up from behind his mom's sensible sedan. He looked *good*. Bronzed with a tan as if he'd been getting more time out of the office. Unlike he'd been at Christmas, he looked relaxed. At ease.

Her heart hitched hard, and it hurt to breathe. He was the last man she wanted to see. How could Karen have sent her out here? Had her sisters done it on purpose?

He held a covered pot in his broad hands. "I'm the official Crock-Pot carrier. My mom appointed me. I'm not just a doctor. I serve other useful functions."

"You? Useful? Doing what?"

"Cookie carrier. Errand runner." He couldn't believe she was here. That Kristin, whom he'd been thinking of and trying not to think of for months, was standing in front of him. Kristin, who seemed to glow with beauty. She wore a feminine soft yellow outfit, and the quiet color made her as lustrous as the first light of dawn.

What he felt when he saw her wasn't normal. It wasn't friendship. It wasn't even that zing of interest. It was…he didn't know what it was. His soul sort of gave a hitch of recognition whenever he looked at her.

What did that mean? Why, when he'd filled his life with work and responsibility and more work, couldn't he forget her? He'd never stopped feeling sad that he'd never made that call when he was in Seattle.

No, it was for the best. He'd learned the hard way. He was terrible when it came to relationships. He wasn't good at letting people close. It wouldn't work out anyway, and look how incredible she was. So amazing. She deserved a man who could love her with all his soul.

Why was he thinking about love anyway?

He watched the wind tousle her short blond hair, ruffle those golden strands. Furrows dug into her forehead, as if she wasn't sure what to do with him. As if he was the last man she wanted to see. "Why are you doing this?"

"Mom said I had to help."

"Do you always do what your mom says?"

"If I know what's good for me." He grinned, hiking the Crock-Pot safely into the crook of his arm. "If I don't, she beats me."

"Why, hello there, Kristin." Mom came around from the driver's side, looking way too proud of herself for an innocent woman. She was pleased with her efforts to bring them together. "What a pleasure to see you again. Ryan, isn't she looking very beautiful today?"

"Yes, she is." It was only the truth.

Kristin blushed. "Thank you, Mrs. Sanders. Your new hairdo looks wonderful."

"I got it frosted. And you, young man, stop telling lies about me." As pleasant as could be, Mary thwacked him on the shoulder. "Stop it."

"See?" There was no mistaking the affection in his gaze. "Mom is only starting to forgive me for still being a bachelor."

"I want grandchildren before I die!" Mary called out as she marched along the sidewalk toward the coffee shop. "It doesn't seem too much to ask."

"I'm waiting to procreate until after I'm married." Ryan called out. "But you have a long wait. Marriage is too much to ask of a man."

Mary stormed up to the front door, too dignified to answer.

Kristin took the opportunity to take a covered casserole from the floor of the trunk. All this talk of marriage between mother and son. Had Ryan been waging the same battle with his mom as she'd been having with hers? How could her mom keep doing this to her?

"I'm so glad my mom loves me." Ryan winked as he closed the trunk. "She's in this difficult phase. I do my best with her, Lord knows."

"What phase would that be?"

"Grandchild envy. A very dangerous phase. As a doctor, I recommended counseling but she's been very rebellious. Then I told her to try pressuring Mia for a change. That's what a sister is for. To take the pressure off of me."

"It's never worked for me."

"I guess I'm doomed." He didn't feel doomed. Why was his gaze sliding upward to notice the slender curve of her calves and the sway of her lace-edged dress? The swing of her short hair and the elegant line of her back? Because she was the reason he'd decided to come home again.

He held the door for her and watched as she breezed by. She was delicate, fine boned and petite. He bet he could span her waist with his hands. Tenderness—where was it coming from?—ached hard beneath his sternum. What would it be like to hold her against his chest? To tuck her against him and shelter her—just a little—from the world?

Why was he wondering?

The coffee shop was busy as more women arrived. Some of them he recognized from his school days, some he didn't. They crowded into the room in that way women have, of talking and excitement and hugging in greeting. Gifts piled on a table against the wall, and there was Mom, waving to him from the corner, where a table just for the food was waiting.

Unfortunately Kristin was heading there, too. He followed her and still managed to keep from dropping the Crock-Pot until he delivered it safely onto the table where Mom indicated. He looked up. No

Kristin. Where had she gone in the ten seconds he'd taken his eyes off her?

"Ryan." She reappeared, winding her way to him. The dress she wore was the color of pale daffodils. It made her look elegant and beautiful in a classy timeless way. She carried a stack of plates from the kitchen. She unloaded them on the table and thrust one at him. "You might as well dig in. You'll be our test guinea pig."

"If I keel over, then you know to stay away from the macaroni salad."

"Something like that."

How had he gotten more handsome? The months had rolled by, so busy with work and hoping for a new promotion, that she'd hardly been aware of the days slipping away like water. But seeing him made her aware of the time. He looked well-rested. He looked as if he'd been getting in some windsurfing time.

Not that it was any of her business. If her mom were to walk in at this exact moment and notice how she was studying the handsome doctor, think of what new levels of determination that would push her to.

She pivoted away and headed in the opposite direction. A hand on her arm stopped her.

Ryan's mom seemed to have noticed. "He could be moving to Seattle, did he tell you? He's been hemming and hawing and this week that fancy clinic made him an offer he shouldn't pass up. I think he should take it. Don't you?"

Her brain stopped working. Odd, because the cheerful excitement in the room seemed to diminish, as if someone had turned down the volume on a radio. Whatever this was, she had to stop it right now. She had to protect her heart. She had to make sure—

A loud, excited squeal kick started Kristin's mind. She blinked, the sound crescendoed.

It was Michelle making that excited laughter. Her hand settled on her huge abdomen. "Oh! I can't believe it! I'm in labor!"

Shrieks of excitement filled the shop. Kristin stood as if transfixed as everyone jumped to life around her. Jenna, Michelle's best friend, made a call on her cell. Karen raced over and made Michelle sit down. Ryan's mom ran for her purse on the counter.

"Hey, Kristin. Don't look so shaken. She'll be all right. Promise." Ryan's hand settled against the small of her back, offering her assurance.

She believed him. How could she resist? He was everything manly and rugged and dependable. He towered over her. She should have felt dwarfed, but she felt protected. Safe. As she knew Michelle would be, too.

A strange thing happened to her heart. As he moved away, to cut through the crowd of women to kneel down at Michelle's side, it felt as if he was still at her side. Touching her. Linked to her. She felt his compassion and his care as he took Michelle's hand and leaned to whisper something in her ear.

Oh, he's wonderful. If Michelle didn't look happy enough, she lit up with more joy. Breathing deliberately, the pain seemed to pass and she relaxed. Kristin's heart filled with a floaty, airy sensation.

"Oh!" Michelle let Karen and Ryan help her to her feet. She surveyed the family and friends who had gathered just for her. "I hate to run out on, like, an awesome party. I love you all so much. But I get to go have my baby now!"

Amid cheers of excitement, Kristin stood still, riveted by the way Ryan held Michelle's arm in his. She was perfectly capable of walking to the door, but he took such care with her. Michelle, her baby sister, was all grown up, waving goodbye at the door and throwing kisses.

"Come see us in the hospital! Oh!" Her hand flew to her tummy. "You may not have to wait very long!"

"Kristin?" It was Mary, pressing something cool into her palm.

She looked down at a set of keys.

"Take my car, sweetie. It's parked the closest to the door, I think, and if you drive, then Ryan can keep watch over Michelle."

Yes, it sounded sensible. Why she felt utterly overwhelmed, Kristin couldn't say. She only knew the room silenced to her ears when it should have been loud with the din of friends' and family's excited shouts of good wishes and joy.

She moved without thought, striding into a world where the sun wasn't as bright as the sight of one man. It was as if her entire being waited until his gaze met hers. Then air rushed into her lungs and blood pumped into her heart.

When he smiled, her soul opened wide.

Chapter Thirteen

With every breath she took, it was worse. This agony of awareness beating within her spirit. It was like gazing into a too-bright light and being unable to look away. And that light was Ryan. When he spoke, his voice vibrated deep within her. When he was silent, his silence was peace in her soul.

She didn't want him there, a part of her. Affecting her. She fought as hard as she could to concentrate on driving and *only* on driving. It was impossible not to notice the man's reflection in her rearview mirror when she checked traffic. She tried to ignore him. She truly did.

But every time she breathed, she noticed the faint scent of his aftershave. It reminded her of spice and smoked wood and winter nights spent at home.

The ribbon of highway unrolled before her. The miles spun away and they were pulling off the exit in Bozeman in no time. Certainly not long enough for Michelle to finish up on her phone. She was calling everyone important, including several calls to her husband to make sure he'd be waiting for her.

And he was. As dependable as a knight of old, Brody was waiting by the entrance door. He had the car door open the moment it stopped and he took his wife's hands in his big strong ones. Their love and joy was as unmistakable as the scent of spring on the breeze. Brody slipped a protective arm around Michelle and let her lean on him, a strong rock of a man.

That was what true love looked like. The quiet gazes, the comforting touches, the deep bond that had them walking with the same stride, exchanging words without saying anything at all.

An orderly came with a wheelchair, just in time as Michelle winced in pain. Brody helped her off her feet, held her hand and they breathed together until the pain passed. Michelle relaxed, leaned her forehead to his.

"Wow." Ryan felt so close. He settled into the front passenger seat, all six feet of him. "Is that something, or what?"

"If you believe in that kind of thing."

"You don't believe in love?"

"Sure. I just don't think it lasts."

"You don't? Really? Boy, what Michelle and Brody have. That looks like forever to me." Ryan had never let anyone that close to him. He couldn't seem to remember why as he watched Brody and

Michelle make their way into the hospital, hand in hand, heart to heart.

Man, it was obvious. They were deeply in love. Wrapped up in each other, they clearly shared a deep bond. They sure made it look good. Watching them made him feel not exactly envious. He'd tried the relationship thing. He'd failed at it.

But it made him consider his possibilities. He had to consider there was the potential for that kind of link between him and Kristin.

Icy fear hardened in his veins. He shivered and pulled the door closed. No, he had to stop thinking like that. He couldn't make it work. He'd tried before and found disaster. His former fiancée had been right. He wasn't good at intimacy. He'd never let her, or any other woman he'd dated, get close enough.

So why, whenever he gazed at Kristin, did his soul stir?

He remained silent as Kristin pulled away from the curb and circled around in search of a parking spot. A couple climbing out of a new SUV waved. He recognized Kristin's older sister Kendra and her husband, who was carrying their baby daughter.

Kristin stopped and rolled down the window. "How did you two get here so quick?"

"I was loading up to come to the shower when Michelle called from Mary's car." Kendra hit her remote locks and tucked the keys in the diaper bag slung over her shoulder. "So I headed here instead of town. I hear Michelle had the best medical care on the ride over here. Thanks, Ryan."

"Hey, my pleasure. I didn't do anything. I'm an orthopedist. Good to see you again, Kendra."

"Make Kristin bring you on up. Come wait with us if you want."

Kristin glanced in the rearview. "I've got someone coming up behind me. See you inside, Sis."

She pulled into the first available space and turned off the engine. A hard pressure jammed behind her sternum. With every breath she took, it seemed to expand. She felt ready to explode. She was worried about Michelle. She was happy for Michelle. She was glad to see Kendra looking so good and content walking alongside her husband. A year ago, they were newly married. Now they were a family.

Back in Seattle tucked in her little town house with her busy life and her demanding job and errands and housework and dinner out with friends, she didn't have to think about it.

It wasn't until she was here that it hit her between the eyes like a blow. Her sisters were married and mothers. Making lives of their own. With their own families. She didn't know how they could do it, how they could risk so much.

"Kristin?"

She blinked, realizing that Ryan had circled around and opened her door. He was offering his hand like a gentleman of old. Like a man courting.

No, that couldn't be right. Ryan wasn't interested

in her like that. Just as she wasn't interested in him like that. But his hand, palm up, looked so dependable and *right*. She was already moving to lay her hand on his, before she realized she hadn't meant to. It just happened. When her palm met his, his bigger fingers wrapped around, holding on. Something clicked in her heart.

A perfect fit.

Dazed, she was somehow on her feet, squinting in the vibrant spring sun. Watching him, senses spinning, as he closed the door, took the keys, pocketed them, and then moved away. She let go of him, and her hand had never felt so empty.

The wind ruffled his dark shanks of hair as he slowed his pace to match hers. "It looks like your mom just drove up. It looks like she's alone."

"Yeah. That means Dad will probably come along later." Kristin could see clearly that Mom was alone in her car. The big white sedan slowed two parking aisles over. Mom waved behind the sun-streaked glass, then drove on in her hurry to find a parking spot.

The emotion pushing against her rib cage hardened. Like a cooling ball of lead, it began to sink downward, settling into her stomach. She took a step farther away from Ryan. Their shadows traveled in front of them, and she saw them in silhouette. Two separate entities.

"Dad's busy this time of year in the fields." But that wasn't the whole truth. He and Mom hardly ever drove anywhere together, and since their two weeks in Hawaii in January, it had gotten worse. The silence between her parents was louder. The breach in their marriage painfully obvious and how sad was that?

As if he could sense her thoughts, Ryan inched closer until their shadows hovered on the blacktop side by side. "Mom mentioned that your mom is thinking about divorce."

Divorce. That word hit like an unexpected blow to her abdomen. Her mom didn't believe in divorce. Both her and Dad had to be desperately miserable to even consider such an option. She took a steadying breath.

"Oh, great. I shouldn't have said anything. You didn't know."

"No, but it's not that big of a surprise, either. It's just to hear it said out loud like that. It sounds *real.* As if there's no more hoping things might work out."

"Wow, and your parents once had a solid marriage. The best. Like my folks had, until Dad died."

"Yeah, that's the problem with love. It doesn't last. When you think about it, how can it? Life is full of hardship and disappointments and devastating loss. How can something as fragile as love survive that?"

Ryan felt something nudge his cheek, soft and silken and warm. A brief brush, and then it was gone. He looked up. The wind shivered through the old flowering cherry trees lining the parking lot, and pink blossoms fell like rain.

Kristin held out her hand, palm up, to catch the silken petals. They rained down on her, clinging to her hair, her face, her dress. Carpeting the cement at her feet.

As if heaven had overheard her and sent a sign to disagree.

The wind calmed, and the downfall stopped.

"I have these all over me. They're like little bits of silk." She stopped, her slim skirt swishing around her thighs, to brush blossoms stuck to her clothes. Her golden hair fell forward to frame her face, revealing more blossoms there.

"Here. You have some—" He reached without thinking, moving close as if he had the right. Her hair was as soft as the pink petals he carefully separated away.

"Oh," she breathed, turning to him.

Drawing his attention to her mouth. Ryan cupped her lovely face. Cradled her delicate jaw in his hands. There was no thought. No plan. No intention. Just a feeling so strong and true, it overwhelmed him. Drove him forward. He watched her bow-shaped mouth part slightly in surprise, but it was too late. He wanted to know her warm kiss. She was like spun sugar and spring light. Hope like no other.

He brushed her lips with his.

What did he think he was doing? Kristin wanted to argue, but she didn't seem able to push him away. Instead her hands closed on his shoulders, holding on. His kiss was a storm tearing across the western sky. Like lightning crackling along the horizon.

When he broke the kiss, his hands remained a tender claim against her cheek. The sun behind him haloed him, gracing him with a rare, brilliant light.

Everything within her stilled.

Afraid to breathe, afraid to break the magic, she closed her eyes. His touch sparked like fireworks popping in a midnight sky. Bold and bright and unmistakble.

A longing, sweet and intense, knifed through her. Longing for what could never be.

She stepped away, tuning into the real world around her. The place where love was not perfect, where impatient horns blared, where her mom was hurrying, her shoes clacking on the concrete. Where a siren announced the arrival of an ambulance at the emergency entrance down the way. This was a world where love couldn't last.

"Ryan." It was her mom, hurrying up, her big black purse swinging from her forearm, her free hand holding the scarf on her head with the other. "I can never thank you enough for staying with Michelle during the drive to the hospital. I didn't worry a bit knowing you were with her."

"I was glad I could help, although I didn't do a thing. Michelle seemed to be handling everything just fine."

"That's my Michelle," Mom said fondly, spar-

kling. And not only at the thought of the new grandchild ready to come into the world.

No, Mom was near to bursting. She had to have
witnessed the kiss. There was no way she could have
missed it.

Panic set in. Kristin started walking. She needed
space. She needed perspective. She needed to oblit-
erate the memory of that fantastic, emotion-filled
kiss from every neuron in her brain. Because there
was no way she was going to get carried away or let
her feelings spiral out of control.

She didn't need anyone. Especially not Ryan. He
made her feel way too much. And he just thought he
could kiss her any time he wanted? She ought to be
insulted.

She wanted to be angry. She wanted to be so consumed with fury she didn't have to think about what
she'd done. About how she'd practically run into the
building, dashed through the lobby and bolted into
the first elevator to open, even though it was going
down, because she wanted to put as much distance
as she could between her and Ryan.

But she hadn't left him at all. Not really. He was
right there, in her heart and in her soul. Linked.

What was she going to do about that?

Since she took the long way to the maternity
floor, down to the basement and back up again,
Mom was already in the family waiting area.

One quick glance told her that Ryan wasn't there.
He must have gone back to his mom's car and gone

home. Good. She had enough to worry about without him around.

"Kristin, come sit with me." Kendra patted the hard plastic chair next to her. On her other side, her husband, Cameron, was talking on his phone, his low mumble hardly audible above the excited conversation.

Kirby and Sam arrived, with Michael leading the way. He still carried his plastic dump truck everywhere he went, but he was bigger. Taller. A little boy with thick dark hair and big blue intelligent eyes.

"Kristin!" It seemed impossible for Kirby to look any happier, but she did. "Oh, it's so good to see you! This is what I get for being late to the shower. I missed all the excitement, and seeing you. You look good. Tired. You're working too hard."

"Guilty, but I'm up for this cool promotion. I really want it." Love for her sisters was the kind of love a girl could count on. She hugged Kirby, careful of her growing girth. "How are mommy and babies?"

"Healthy and happy."

Kirby looked it, too. She seemed to glow from the inside out, and the joy on her face doubled when her husband took her hand to help her into a chair. "Oh, that feels better. Thanks, handsome."

"Anything for you, beautiful." Sam kissed her, the way a husband kisses his wife, and means it. That's true love.

Ryan had kissed her like that. Kristin's throat

ached with too much emotion, a wild jumble of feelings that she didn't want to name and didn't want to
feel. She remembered Ryan's kiss. How could she
forget it? Her lips sparkled. Her soul sparkled. That's
how Ryan had kissed her.

Panic shot through her and she bounced out of the
chair. "I'm going to the cafeteria," she announced
too fast, already striding toward the elevator. "Any-
body want anything?"

"Tea," Kendra answered. "Want me to come with
you?"

"No!" She wanted to be alone, but she wasn't fool-
ing Kendra, who was watching her with concern. Or
Kirby, who was gazing up over the top of her little
boy's cowlick, an unasked question clear on her face.

She loved her sisters, and she knew they loved her
back, but they wouldn't understand. They couldn't.
They had chosen to hide from the fact that you were
born into this world alone, and you left it alone. That
no matter how much you loved someone, that didn't
stop them from dying. Loss was a part of life she
didn't want, no way. And she wasn't going to close
her eyes, open her heart and love as if loss wasn't
inevitable.

No. She'd been there once. Allison's death had
brought Mom to her knees in despair. Broken Dad's
spirit for good. And it was all Kristin could do at
the time to keep going through life with the grief.
Taking her exams and the SAT she'd already paid
and signed up for. Cooking meals that no one would

eat, because her mom couldn't. Of trying to hold on to the broken pieces of her life, her heart, her family.

It had taken years before she'd been on an even keel again, before Mom came out of her dark depression and Dad began to talk a little, even if he spent most of his time in the fields or in his workshop.

Grief took a hard toll. Kristin only had to look at her mom to see the cost. The woman who'd been so vibrant and bustling and humming everywhere she went. It was as if a light had forever died inside her.

The cafeteria wasn't crowded and she took her time making up a tray of tea and coffee for everyone. Chai tea for Kendra, chamomile for Kirby, mint for Karen. Coffee with sweeteners and black tea with honey for the brothers-in-law. She didn't know them well enough to know what they would want. For Mom she waited for the apron-clad girl behind the counter to whip up a mochaccino. It helped to do this, something normal, something useful. But she couldn't forget her thoughts completely.

The kiss. That's the way she was going to think about it forever. Her first real kiss. Wow, and she hadn't even wanted it. If only she could erase it from her memory entirely. She wished she could hit the rewind button on her life and do that one moment over when he cupped her face with his amazing hands and claimed not just her mouth, but her heart and soul. How could a simple brush of lips be everything? The past, present and future all in one moment?

Stop thinking about it. That's what she had to do. Figure out a way to blot it from her mind. *The kiss* was never going to happen again. *The kiss* was a single aberration in her life centered around quiet, sensible choices and a serious work ethic. Before *the kiss,* she was a person who balanced her checkbook, set aside savings every month, paid her mortgage before the due date and was in bed by ten every night. She wore sensible shoes and a wild night out on the town was dinner with her cousin at their favorite burger place.

And she intended to be exactly the same person after *the kiss.* It wasn't a life-changing moment. It wasn't a soul-shattering experience. It was *never* going to happen again.

Because if it did, then the power of it would shatter everything she'd spent her life building. It would unbalance her carefully ordered world. It would make her want something she could never put her faith in—love.

By the time she made it back to the waiting area, the rest of the family had arrived. Karen with her husband Zach and their daughters. Gramma was reading Allie her favorite picture book.

Allie had changed, too. She'd grown taller and willowy, the toddler softness gone. Her shoulder-length straight hair shimmered like sunlight on the finest gold. She chattered away to Gramma; having the story memorized, she took over the telling. A preschooler.

Dad appeared around the corner, leaning a bit to the left where Emily held his hand tightly as she skipped on her pink strappy sandals. A toddler now. He looked younger, happier, in the company of his granddaughter.

He spotted the drink carriers. "There's my girl. You wouldn't happen to have a black coffee in there for me?"

"The biggest one is for you, right there in the corner." Kristin balanced the eggboard carrier while her dad helped himself to the large-size cup.

Dad seemed better. He kept his distance from Mom, but at least he looked content, almost like his old self as he led Emily to the play area in the corner. Together, Granddad and granddaughter constructed a house of blocks, which Michael and his truck crashed into with appropriate sound effects.

"Kristin, see what you're missing." Gramma winked over the top of Allie's blond head. "Life without love is just existing. Life without family is like being lost on an island. Life passes a person right on by and keeps going."

She'd take the island any day.

Except right now, at this moment, as she handed out the drinks, she couldn't deny the horrible pain stabbing her directly in the heart. A pain that felt like grief. Not over her sister's death, she realized.

Grief for herself. For the life she'd lost.

She examined the life her sisters had chosen. Fragile or not, they had husbands who gazed at them as if they were the only women in the world. They had children who played and laughed and gave sweet kisses. True love, the kind that was the most fragile of all, was in this disinfectant-scented room with the hard plastic chairs and the stark cold tile floor. The love they'd brought with them. The love they held in their hearts. The love they shared for Michelle as they gathered to wait. To pray for her. To be there to celebrate the new life she was being given to love and guide and protect.

How many gatherings like this had she missed? Every single one of them. She'd missed every one of her nieces' and nephews' births. Except this one.

Ryan, he was the reason she was feeling like this. His kiss…what had it done to her?

Confused, she took the empty carriers to the garbage can in the hall, poured two packets of sugar into her chai tea and sat down to wait. She couldn't help wondering. Where was Ryan now? Was he regretting kissing her? Or had she hurt him by running away?

Two hours and eighteen minutes later, Brody appeared to announce the birth of their son. Ten-pound, eight-ounce Gabriel Peter, named after his daddy and grandfather.

Ryan watched the sunset bleed like a wound. The proud rugged peaks of the Rocky Mountain Front glowed crimson beneath a troubled sky. The hospital parking lot felt abandoned. Although it was crammed with cars, he was the only one making his way across the petal-strewn pavement.

The gusty winds had stripped all but a few petals from the trees. Dark limbs reached upward, through the haze of light from the tall structure. The first cold raindrops fell as he dashed inside.

There was no wait for an elevator in the lobby, which was nearly as quiet as the parking lot had been. As he jostled the packages and gifts for Michelle's baby, he punched the button for the maternity floor.

Kristin had been on his mind for hours. The memory of their kiss remained like a whisper in his soul. The sort of whisper that was too quiet to hear the words, no matter how hard he listened. All he knew was that it had brought him here.

All was calm as he strode down the hallway. His boots beat like his pulse down the long corridor. He followed the shine of fluorescent lights on the tile to the last door on his right. It was half open and, hidden in the shadows, he raised his knuckle to knock but froze at the sight of Kristin. She was seated in a chair, graced by the glow of a lamp, so still and calm he could see the rare and beautiful love within her as she gazed down at the tiny bundle she cradled in her arms. A newborn child.

In the space between one heartbeat and the next, he saw the world shift around him and time roll forward. For one brief moment he saw her holding a different child wrapped in a similar blue receiving blanket, dark downy hair curling beneath the blue infant cap.

His son.

In her arms.

She was his fairy tale—enchanting and kind and a vision of everything good and dear. She stole his heart and he couldn't have stopped his feet from moving forward anymore than he could have stopped his heart from beating.

He lost his heart. It was gone. No longer his.

More sure than he'd ever been in his life, he walked into the light.

Chapter Fourteen

What was this ache inside her, so sharp and fierce it was like a great pain?

She felt as if places within her spirit were being opened for the first time. Places open only to the man who emerged from the shadowed doorway, with flowers in one hand and helium balloons trailing behind. He seemed like a dream, her dream. Had she been thinking so hard about Ryan that she'd conjured him up from her imagination?

No, he was real. His step a hush on the floor, his presence as tangible as the pain in her heart. Wearing ordinary wash-faded jeans and a black T-shirt, he was manly, all right. Just watching him made the woman in her give thanks.

Strong and steadfast, he towered over her. He was all she could see. All she wanted to see. Her spirit silenced. The places within her swelled with a strange force that was like pain. But no, it wasn't pain exactly. She didn't know what it was, but when Ryan knelt before her, it brought tears to her eyes.

"Look what a precious gift you're holding." When he spoke, it was as if he tugged at strings stuck to those tender places deep within her.

An odd pulling at her heart and her soul that made her ready to shatter. She couldn't bear to look at him, it hurt so much. She gazed down at the new life cradled in the crook of her arm. Looking at her new nephew made a different place within her spirit hurt, too.

She cleared her throat before she answered, and her voice came out as a rough whisper. "This is our newest blessing from God."

Ryan leaned closer to study the sleeping infant. His eyes tightly shut. One fist visible. "It blows me away every time I see a new baby. Look at those tiny fingers. They're just so…new."

"And precious." Kristin's eyes burned, and she didn't dare disturb Gabe, who'd had a hard time drifting off to sleep. "I've got another incredible nephew. I'm a pretty lucky aunt."

"You surely are." His rumbling baritone was like a kiss to her soul.

She shivered. The pain within her, that wasn't a pain at all, became something more. An emotion she would not acknowledge. She *couldn't*.

"Michelle and Brody are just down the hall, if you want to give her those flowers."

"Down the hall? I can't imagine they'd want to leave this little guy."

"Only because I swore I wouldn't take my eyes off him. They're having dinner. It's a special thing the hospital does, serves steak-and-lobster dinner to the new parents. They have it catered. It's really nice."

"They should get some time together, because they may not have a quiet romantic dinner for some time to come."

"Exactly. That's why I volunteered to stay with him. Besides, tomorrow I head home, right after Easter dinner. I have a big day on Monday. It's work stuff. So I thought I'd get in as much baby holding as I could. Next time I see him will be, gosh, next Thanksgiving, when I come home again. He'll be seven months old. He'll be so different than this."

"Yep. Babies have a tendency to do this. Grow up."

"Yeah." The intense emotions she refused to feel became sharp enough to spike through flesh and bone, that's what it seemed like as baby Gabriel's sweet round face blurred. Everything became a fuzzy cloud as she blinked hard and fast.

What was wrong with her?

"He sure is something. I bet holding him makes you think about having one of your own one day."

"He sure is precious. Michelle and Brody are blessed to have him."

"Yeah. Aren't they?" Ryan's chest thrummed

with a yearning so strong, it felt ready to blow him apart. He thought of how he'd been sitting on the back steps, feeling the night come. Missing his dad.

Seeing the past, present and future in the same moment, what was and what could be, made him sure. As if his dad was watching out for him from heaven after all. Once, Dad had been like this, gazing at the woman he loved with a newborn in her arms.

The seasons of life come full circle. He understood it now. What was the quote? There is a time for every season. As one season was linked to the next, so was one life linked to another. His father to his. And, one day, God willing, his life to his son's. Love was the glue that bonded them together for good.

This world was full of hardship and tragedy, accidents and illness, of loss, but of renewal, too. And God's great gift of love.

That's what this was in his heart, in his soul. Love, honest and true. As infinite as heaven. As precious as grace. And it filled him with tenderness so rare, it overpowered everything. Made everything clear.

All that mattered in his life was right in front of him. Kristin. Deep furrows dug into her forehead. Her eyes shimmered with unshed tears. He could feel her sadness, for his heart was hers. A life not lived was its own sorrow. He knew, because that's how he went through his days, too. Existing, and it was no way to live.

He was already reaching. His fingers already aching for the different texture of hers. He covered her hand, and the link between them strengthened. His soul sighed.

Now, all he had to do was to come up with the right words. How did he start? "I'm absolutely sure of one thing. I'm going to be moving to Seattle."

"Your mom mentioned that you were thinking about it."

"Yep. Phoenix is just too far away."

"From your mom?"

"From you."

The spikes in her rib cage lengthened. Sharpened. She felt this way because of the baby she was holding. The beloved new life asleep in her arms, trusting and innocent. Maybe it was her biological clock starting to tick.

Or maybe it was that she was afraid if she met Ryan's gaze, she would want everything she couldn't believe in. Even if she wanted it, she couldn't. Not knowing what she knew about life. About loss.

No, she wasn't going to let him go any farther. She had to hold on to her heart. She took a steadying breath although she felt as if her ribs had shattered. As if a part of her were dying, but it had to be said. "We're only friends, Ryan. You shouldn't move just to be closer to me."

"Don't you feel this between us?"

No, she should say. But the truth rang within her.

Yes. If only he could be the one. The one man she could love for every day of her life to come.

Could he be?

All she had to do was to look into his eyes to see it. Yes. This all-consuming agony within her was love. Love for this man kneeling before her, and she couldn't let herself feel it or it would move through her like a mountain creek, refreshing and sweet, and it would tear her stable world apart.

"Excuse me." She waited for him to remove his hand and stand so she could lay baby Gabriel in his bassinet. With her arms empty, it was easier to close her heart. To face him, even though he'd let the balloons go. They hopped along the ceiling toward the other bouquets of balloons in the corner.

He held the flowers, white lilies and pink roses, to her. "I've got to say this. I don't know if the moment is right, but I know your sister and her husband are going to be walking through that door soon. And you'll be surrounded with your family again and tomorrow, with Easter. And then you'll be gone."

"Don't, Ryan." She had to be smart about this. She had to stop him before he went too far. Her entire life depended on it. "I don't want you to say—"

"I love you."

For one split second she felt as light as the balloons he'd brought. She seemed to be floating. When Ryan took her hand, she felt dizzy and joyous and terrified all at once. As if she were falling through the stratosphere without a parachute. With only the earth far below to break her fall.

His kiss sparkled across her lips. Soft and warm and wonderful. Like a dream she wanted to hold on to as tight as she could and never let go. But how could she? She broke away from his amazing tenderness, feeling her heart buckle and her soul crack.

She'd chosen her life for a reason. Look at the baby, so infinitely precious. If she kept following this new path, it was too much to lose. Life was like that. Look at Mom and Dad. Love didn't last. Not even the best of loves. People let you down, death happened. The steel she'd found in herself, that had gotten her through her family falling apart, Allison's death and losing the parents she used to have, was strong.

Very strong. She could feel what was next as Ryan's heart opened more. He was going to propose. She could feel it. She could see his dreams as if they were her own. Married, life along the lakeshore in Seattle, children and car pools and quiet evenings after the little ones were sleep.

No! It took all her effort to take one jerky step away. To put distance firmly between them. She swore she could hear what remained of her heart crumbling into dust. "I think I hear my sister."

She felt Ryan watching her as she circled away from him. Swore she could feel his heart turning to dust, too.

Desperate, she popped into the hall and there was Michelle, hand in hand with her husband. The two of them walking slow and leisurely, moving as if one, caught up in each other. True love.

Kristin tore her gaze away. Ryan was right behind her, his hands falling to her shoulders. It was the sweetest thing, his love. His unwavering devotion.

Emotion wedged tight in her throat made it impossible to speak. Everything within her begged her to turn into Ryan's arms and reach out to him. To kiss him the way she longed to. With all the tenderness she had. With all the love stored up just for him.

"This isn't over," he whispered.

"Yes, it is." She meant it. She had to. This man would be so much to lose. Whether over time as love faded to nothing. Or from the inevitable truth that this earthly life wasn't forever. Ryan already had a piece of her soul. Losing him would be losing *everything*.

How could she put her faith in that? She couldn't do it. No. She stepped out of his touch, turned away and gave thanks when Michelle and Brody arrived in the room, chasing away the tension, bringing their joy.

Kristin left the moment she could and was grateful when she stepped out into the night. Alone, she raced the first raindrops to her mom's car and collapsed into the driver's seat. While the defroster chugged away at the foggy window, she watched Ryan emerge from the building and disappear into the black curtain of cold rain, taking her heart with him.

* * *

She was one raw nerve by the time she reached her parent's house. Wrung out and soul weary, she didn't care that she was drenched to the skin on the walk between the detached garage and the house. The world around her was as pitch-black as hopelessness, but the light from the kitchen window glowed, drawing her gaze.

Easter decorations were everywhere. From the basket of candy eggs on the counter to the colorful clings in the window, to the cross as the centerpiece on the table where Mom was standing. She had Emily at her side, kneeling on a chair, their heads bent together decorating sugar cookies.

"Pink! Pink!" Emily was chanting as Kristin opened the door.

"Yes, you did a good job with the pink buttons. Now, let me give our bunnies happy smiles. See?" Mom patiently squeezed frosting onto cutout cookies laid out in neat rows on a cookie sheet. "Oh, Kristin. There you are. Ryan called looking for you. I tacked his cell number up on the bulletin board."

This isn't over, he'd told her. He was certainly a man of his word. Too tired, feeling half-dead inside, she dropped her keys on the counter. She'd deal with Ryan later. What she wanted more than anything was to lie down. Maybe she'd take a book and a cup of tea and—

The oven timer beeped. She reached over to turn it off.

"Kristin, honey, could you take the loaves out for me. I've got my hands full. If you don't mind?"

"Loaves? Of bread? What are you doing baking bread at this hour?"

"Tomorrow's going to be a busy day. With everyone coming for Easter dinner, and Michelle coming home in the evening, and her house to get ready, and all the cooking." Mom set aside the tube of frosting. "Emily and I sure have been busy."

"Yum," Emily agreed, licking the finger she'd swept through the bowl of colored sugar. She was adorable and she knew it. She wiped her hands on her ruffle-edge pink shirt and grinned like the princess she was.

"And you!" Mom's chuckle was thin edged, but there was no mistaking the joy she took in being with one of her granddaughters. "What color should we make the bunnies' shirts?"

"Yum!" Emily answered with glee, reaching for a second helping to the sugar topping.

Too cute. Kristin grabbed the oven mitts and took the first loaf from the oven. She popped the golden loaf from the pan and flipped it onto the cooling rack. The second loaf stuck and she shook gently, waiting for it to release.

That's when she noticed the bottle of antacid on the counter. It was safely out of Emily's reach, but hadn't been put back in the cupboard. One thing Mom never did was leave clutter anywhere, even one bottle. She really *must* be tired.

And it was Kristin's fault. Instead of coming right home from the hospital, she'd driven around in the rain and lightning for hours until her emotions had settled into a quiet wooden numbness. That wasn't good, either, but it was better than feeling as if she'd been broken wide open from the inside out.

If she'd come straight home, then she would have been able to help Mom.

The loaf tumbled into her protected hand, and she turned the bread over to cool. She'd left a dent in the top and she patted at it, hoping it would go back into its original shape.

"That's all right, honey." Mom sounded tired as she circled around the island. "Can you keep an eye on Emily for me?"

"Sure. I haven't lost my touch at decorating cookies."

"That sure would be a help. The potatoes should be chilled long enough, and if I whip up the salad now, it would be one less thing to do tomorrow morning." Mom hefted the big bowl of diced potatoes from the refrigerator shelf and winced. Her hand flew to her chest. "Goodness, my stomach's acting up again."

"You do too much, and you keep everything inside. Just like me." Kristin took the bowl from her mom and glanced over to check on Emily, who'd helped herself to a handful of M&M's and was eating them one at a time by color. She handed the bottle of antacid to her mother. "Take a few, and then let me make you a cup of tea. You rest, I'll finish up here."

"What about Emily?"

"She can help me, right, Emily?"

Emily's mouth was too full of chocolate to answer, but she looked agreeable enough.

"See? We're more than capable." Kristin's stomach took a tumble. Mom was really pale. And the bruised circles beneath her eyes told of her stress. While she'd refused to talk about what happened in Hawaii and what happened between her and Dad since, she clearly wasn't sleeping well.

"Go upstairs, that's an order. I'll bring you up a cup of tea as soon as it's ready."

"But the potato salad—"

"I'll follow the recipe. I have a college degree. I know how to read." Gently, she kissed her mom's ashen cheek. "Please."

A knock thundered at the back door.

"Who'z it?" Emily hopped off the chair.

"I'll get Emily *and* answer the door. Sit down." Kristin knew who was standing on the other side of the door. Even if she couldn't see him through the glass panes, she could feel his presence and his determination.

The little girl stood on tiptoe, using both hands, but she wasn't quite tall enough to turn the knob. With one swoop, Kristin hefted the toddler onto her hip and opened the door.

He stood there, as dark as the night, soaking wet. "We have to talk. I want to finish this. I need to."

"Now's not a good time." She glanced at her mom, who had sunk into one of the breakfast bar chairs. Her head was in her hands. "Mom?"

"Oh, I'm just not feeling well. I'm tired, that's all." Mom's voice came thin and breathy. A few beads of sweat clung above her upper lip. "I just, oh, need to go lie down, I guess."

"What is it, Mrs. McKaslin?" Ryan was at her side in a second, his jaw tense, his gaze concerned. "Been working too hard, huh? What seems to be the trouble?"

"Upset stomach. I took some of these tablets my doctor recommended."

"How long ago?" Ryan sounded casual, calm.

He wasn't. Kristin could feel his tension. She closed the door, afraid to move as Ryan gently took Mom's hand in his and felt her wrist. Waited as he timed her pulse.

"Any dizziness? Does your jaw hurt? Or your neck?"

"My neck. It's nothing, just my stomach, you know how pain travels."

"Yes, I do. Kristin, get me a bottle of aspirin, would you? And call for an ambulance." He could have been asking for a cup of tea, he didn't seem alarmed at all. But when his gaze met hers, she knew that he was.

Something was wrong with her mother. Keeping

a tight hold on Emily, she rummaged through the cupboard, knocking aside vitamin containers until she found the aspirin. She tossed it across the counter to him, reached for the phone and hit the numbers without thinking. As she anxiously waited for the county dispatch to pick up, it seemed to be an eternity between the first ring and the second.

"Just lie right here on the floor, that's right."

"Goodness, there's just nothing wrong that a good night's sleep won't cure." Mom argued, even as Ryan helped her to the floor. "Oh, I *do* feel weak."

"That's because you're probably having a mild heart attack. At the very least an angina attack. Just relax. I'm here. I'll take care of you."

"What a good man you grew up to be," Mom said shakily as she placed her hand on Ryan's big capable one. "It's my stomach. There's no need to fuss."

"Just humor me." Ryan's kindness shone like a rare light.

"Hello—9-1-1. What is your emergency, please?" came a woman's capable voice across the line.

It was a blur, time taking on a strange slowness as she verified the address, and held the line as Ryan held Mom's wrist, keeping track of her pulse, keeping her calm. Ready and vigilant.

Where was Dad? Why wasn't he in the house at this time of the evening? Kristin couldn't hang up to try the outside shop or barn lines. She could only wait until the ambulance arrived and the medics poured into the house, with their equipment and their gurney and their squawking radios. Emily started to cry at the noise, and trying to comfort her, Kristin made a few quick calls. No answer. Where was he? What if Mom...*died?*

No, she couldn't think about that. Or how pale and weak Mom looked, surrounded by men and monitors as they rushed her out of the house and into the night. Lights flashed, cutting through the rain as the firemen and paramedics took her mom away.

Praying as she went, Kristin turned off the ovens, grabbed the car keys and Emily's diaper bag. She was shaking so hard, she couldn't get Emily's coat zipped, so she left it, huddling the little girl against her for warmth.

Her sisters. She had to call her sisters. Trembling, she took a steady breath, wiped the rain out of her face, and saw Ryan. He was in the back of the ambulance, his gaze like a force that drew her.

Without a word, she *knew.* She could count on him to do his best for her mom. She knew, too, as lightning raced across the sky, that she wasn't alone. God was watching over all of them on this dark, hopeless night.

Easter Sunday

The McKaslin family gathered in the ICU waiting area. Ryan wasn't surprised to see everyone there but Kirby, who'd stayed behind to keep watch over the children. Only the adults were there—the sisters and their husbands, the grandmother and grandfather, in various states of dress. Those who had been pulled out of their beds wore pajamas underneath their coats.

The oldest sister, Karen, still wearing the fuzzy slippers she'd received Kristin's call in, spotted him first. She clung to her husband's steadying hand, fear stark on her face.

Kristin, holding a sleeping Emily, rose quietly, careful not to waken the child in her arms. It was a sweet sight. Ryan's hopes warmed. Yeah, he had hope. Because there was only one outcome to this. And he was going to do whatever it took to make it right between him and Kristin.

"We haven't heard anything." She kept her voice a low whisper. "No one's said anything. Dad is trying to get some answers, but he's not back yet."

"I saw him. He's talking to the doctor, who should be out to talk to you all shortly. She's all right."

Relief shuddered through her. He felt it, just as he could feel her pain. And her love. "It's because of you. You were there. You knew what to do."

"I'm handy to have around. I was hoping you might have noticed that by now." Gently, because now wasn't the time, he ran his hand over her hair. He'd never seen her look so disheveled. Her hair was tangled and had dried however the wind had last left it. Her mascara was smeared away and her eyes were red from tears.

He'd never loved her more.

"Just relax, okay?" He inched close enough to rest her cheek on his chest, loving the way she leaned against him.

It was sweet, holding her. And Emily, too, sleeping so soundly. He just opened his heart to the moment. To Kristin. And he felt the love inside, intense and brilliant and overwhelming.

Love of a brighter hue than he'd ever imagined. So radiant, his soul ached with the power of it.

As if she felt it, too, her fingers curled into his shirt. She held on to him as if she never wanted to let go.

Chapter Fifteen

Every minute that had passed since she'd pushed away from Ryan's arms was torture. And it had only worsened after Zach offered to take Emily with him to drop her off with Kirby who was watching all the children. At least when she'd had Emily to hold, she had someone to think about besides Ryan. But the little girl was probably tucked in for the rest of the night, and Kristin wished she could feel as safe and insulated.

Mom's condition could worsen. She could die. And then what? Just thinking of that possibility for half of a nanosecond brought suffocating black pain that made it hard to breathe. Would she lose Mom, too?

Sitting on the edge of the hard plastic chair, Kristin swiped the wetness from her eyes. *No, don't even think like that. Mom is going to make it.* She'd had a mild heart attack, and the doctor who'd been treating her came out to assure them she was stable. They were very pleased how well she'd responded to their treatment.

What if their prayers and the doctors' care weren't enough? What if she had another attack? A thousand horrible possibilities flashed through her mind. Frightening scenarios. She *so* wanted to slide into the vacant chair next to Ryan, lean her head on his shoulder and soak in the comfort of his strong arms tightening around her. Shivering with panic, she couldn't sit still for another minute. She was terrified a doctor was going to come around the corner and tell them that Mom was gone.

She darted past Ryan and kept on going. She could feel his questions—why was she going, where was she going, why hadn't she turned to him? Although his gaze was like a magnet pulling her back, she didn't stop until she was safely around the corner and out of his sight. Then she slumped against the wall, the faint beep of monitors echoing down the sterile corridor.

Had Ryan felt the same shifting in his soul when they kissed? The same harmony when he held her? The link between their souls? She wanted to stay in his arms forever. With everything inside her, she fought to stay where she was instead of running around the corner to him. To know the sweet perfection of holding him.

She'd done it once. Twice would be too scary to think about.

A prickle of awareness flitted through her, and

she heard the pad of his boots coming closer. He was coming after her. She was way too vulnerable, her every nerve exposed. Panic had her zooming down the hall before he could find her. Afraid because she yearned for this man with all the deepest parts of her soul.

She whipped around a second corner, knowing all she'd done was buy herself time. She had to deal with wonderful, tender, incredible Ryan. There could never be a future for them. No way—

She skidded to a halt on the tile floor. The sight of a lone man sitting on a chair jerked her out of her thoughts. He sat with his elbows on his knees, his face in his hands, his fingers anxiously combing through military-short graying hair. The man looked so grief-stricken as he lifted his head to swipe at his eyes. Tears stained his cheeks. Blind in his sorrow, he lowered his face again. He was wearing a flannel blue-plaid shirt and old jeans with a rip at the hem.

"Dad?" Fear racked through her. Shaking, she made her wooden, quaking legs carry her to the man's side.

The man who looked so alone. When he looked up at her, there was no light in his blue eyes. There were only the shadows and dull darkness of a man who had lost everything.

Mom's dead. That was the only thing that would make Daddy look like that. Kristin knew, sinking to the floor, remembering the last time she'd seen him like this when Allison died.

Had they lost Mom, too? The tile was cold, the overhead fluorescent lighting a bright surreal shine that blurred as tears roared upward with the pain of complete loss.

"Oh, Kris." Dad's deep voice broke. "They said I should g-go on in and sit with her. She needs me to c-comfort her."

Comfort her? Hot tears scorched her throat and burned her eyes as relief took the last of her strength. Mom was alive. She was okay. *Thank you, Lord.* She still had her mother.

But not her father. Her dad was breaking apart. Pinching the bridge of his nose to hold back the wetness pooling in his eyes.

"I can't go in there." Dad's mouth trembled. Fighting to hold everything in. "I thought when I buried Allison, that's it. I just can't take any more. It killed me, I tell you. It killed your mother, too. She kept trying to hold on to me, and I just kept moving back. I know she needed me, you girls needed me. But I loved you all so much. I couldn't take any more."

"Oh, Daddy." Kristin's heart broke although it was in pieces already. She gazed at her quiet father who'd felt so deeply but had kept it bottled up inside for so long.

"I don't think I thought it all out, but I know this for sure. I couldn't take another loss like that. The Good Lord had his reasons for taking Allison home. She was so good and pure, like every one of our girls. Why wouldn't He love her so much, He wanted her with Him? But I was just a dead man walkin'. Walkin' and workin', and barely gettin' by. And I thought, this is what comes from loving. So I guess I just stepped away. Figured it was the best way."

"I understand, Dad."

"I thought you would. You're like me in a lot of ways, Krissie. But listen to me. I'm sitting here choking on my own sorrow. I kept safe, that's what I did, and the grief is just the same. Only this time around, I see the truth. I've got nothing but regret. All that time I wasted. For the years I could have loved that woman and was too darn afraid. Now, all I've got is the same killing grief and no love in between."

"Oh, Dad." Kristin laid her hand on his. He was cold and trembling, his pain etched deeply on his face. "Just go in and sit with her."

Dad struggled to blink back his tears. "It didn't stop me from this hurtin'. I didn't wind up loving that woman any less. But it did stop me from living life with her.

"Don't make my mistake, baby girl. That man there—" Dad nodded toward the end of the hallway. "He's come with his love to offer you. You can't stop life from happening, it happens just the same. But take what care you can with these fragile blessings God has given you. Love with all your heart. It's all there is. It's everything that matters."

"Okay, Daddy." Kristin wrapped her arms around her middle. The knot of tears wedged in her throat broke apart. She hung her head as her father stood and walked away. But he was really walking toward something. To Mom. To life. To true love.

Kristin closed her eyes. Laid her face in her hands. Every part of her hurt. Daddy was right. She knew he was. But how could she risk it? There was so much to lose

So much to have, if she could reach out.

Ryan. She felt him draw nearer, for her soul turned like a season, like the ice of winter cracking away to expose the tender new earth beneath.

Her tender, fragile heart ached from the brightness, but she turned toward the light, toward Ryan's love. He came to her and gathered her to his chest. It was like coming home to stay forever after a painful eternity spent in the cold. What would it be like to be held by him forever?

"He's a wise man, your father." Ryan's lips brushed her forehead. "I think you should take his advice."

"And love you with my whole heart?"

"As I will love you for the rest of my life. And beyond." His kiss was perfection. A promise of commitment and honor and quiet evenings spent beside him. Of love through good times and hardship. "You are my everything. That's what this is between us, this bond, this down-to-the-soul love. Will you marry me?"

It was there, his endless love for her, in his eyes, in his touch, in his dreams. She lost her heart. It was gone. No longer hers. "Yes, I want to marry you. I love you so much."

When he claimed her lips with his, she saw the fragile blessings yet to come. She saw their future. Their God-given love was like the joy of a warm spring day. Ever blooming and ever precious. Strong enough for this life and ever after.

"C'mon. Let's go check on your mom." Ryan helped her stand, wiping her tears with this thumb.

They walked away hand in hand.

Epilogue

Christmas Day, two years later

"Kristin!" Gramma called from the kitchen door. "We're waiting for you, honey. The girls have the game board all set up and ready to play in the dining room. Come and bring the cookies with you."

"Sure." The last snap fastened, she smiled down at her freshly diapered son. Matthew, two weeks old, scrunched up his face, the same way his daddy did before he yawned hugely. "Nap time for you, little one."

"I'll take him in with me." Ryan's hand settled on her shoulder.

Together they gazed down at their baby. His dark hair was Ryan's. He had eyes so blue, Kristin knew they would deepen into her family's trademark violet-blue.

"I don't think it's ever too early to expose him to football."

"Football? That's not nearly as important as starting him out young playing Monopoly. Maybe I'd better take him in with me."

She loved that she made her husband chuckle, low in his throat. He rewarded her with a tender kiss. Her soul moved, as it always did. As it always would.

"No way, babe. The third quarter is about to start, and I don't want him to miss the kickoff." With care, he scooped his son into his big protective arms. Love for Matthew shone deep in his eyes, as did his love for her.

The love she valued more than anything, for it had changed her life. Changed her.

"Kristin!" Michelle stood in the doorway this time, her new baby, Brittany, in her arms. "We're waiting!"

"Okay." She brushed a kiss on her son's forehead, so sweet and soft and perfect. Pure love lifted her up as she watched her husband and son head off for the exciting second half of the game.

"Excuse me, Aunt Kristin." Allie, in grade school now, held up one end of a blanket. "Are you done? Cuz I gotta finish makin' our tent."

"Sure." She hefted the diaper bag out of the way as the slim little girl who looked so very much like their dear sister Allison, studiously secured the end of the blanket, successfully finishing the huge tent beneath the wide round oak table.

"Okay, everyone, it's all done!" Allie flipped the edge up that was to serve as the door, and children came running. Michael, a tall sturdy preschooler, abandoned his racecar track. Hauling their baby dolls, Emily and Anna were the first to crawl into the tent.

Kristin stepped around Kirby's twins, both little girls struggling to push the same toy vacuum cleaner around the kitchen. Too cute. She snatched the cookie tray from the counter, sidestepped Gabriel, who was happy throwing his Play-Doh on the floor and at the twins, who stopped vacuuming to throw it right back.

The football game blared in the living room as the men gathered around the big screen, shouting encouragement and advice and reprimanding the refs. Mom sat next to Dad, contentedly crocheting on her latest afghan. Their love renewed.

Ryan must have felt her presence because he turned from the game, their new baby drowsing against his wide chest. Their gazes met and the link between them, soul to soul, brightened. "I love you," he whispered.

"I love you back."

"Kristin." It was Karen this time come to steal the cookies away. The pictures on the wall caught her attention. She nodded toward them. "Look. Mom has your little Matthew's picture framed and up already. There are a lot of us now."

"Yeah." Kristin noticed the pictures that were missing, but the past couldn't be changed. Only laid to rest. And her love for Allison didn't have to stop.

"She's watching over us, don't you think? At least checking in to see how we're doing."

"I'm sure. We'll see her again one day, you know. That's why it's called heaven."

Kristin swallowed hard to hold back the tears. The sounds of family, of laughter and playing children and the groan of the men at an unfortunate interception rose and fell. The tides of life, of homecoming, of all that was important in this world rushed through her.

The room shifted, and it was memory she saw. Grade-school girls crowding around the dining-room table, baby Michelle toddling after them, cookie crumbs everywhere as they hurried to start the Monopoly game Santa had brought them for Christmas. In the next moment teenage girls, laughing and disagreeing just to disagree as properties were traded and money lost.

The past dissolved, leaving the present. Kirby and Michelle setting up the game. Kendra, expecting her second daughter next month, sorted through the tokens and lined up all of their usual ones on the Go square. Karen joined them, trying to distract Kirby by offering her a cookie, so she could try to grab the bank's money.

"Hey!" Kirby protested good-naturedly. "No fair. I get to be banker this time. Mom!"

"Girls, girls!" Mom scolded from the couch. "Don't make me come over there."

"*I'll* be good." With a wink, Karen successfully

stole the box with the money in it. "Just tell Kirby it's *my* turn."

The old disagreement had them all laughing. Some traditions were more treasured for all the ways they stayed the same.

There was nothing like coming home. Kristin swiped the tears from her eyes, took her place at the table and rolled the dice.

* * * * *

Dear Reader,

All of her four sisters have discovered true love, and now it's Kristin's turn. I hope that you will be reminded, through this story, of how truly precious God's blessings are. That this earthly life may not be an easy one, but it is a beautiful gift. But Kristin's is not the final McKaslin story! The McKaslin cousins are about to find their happily-ever-afters. Please watch for Amy's story, *Sweet Blessings,* which shows how real love happens, even when a person has given up all hope.

I wish you the sweetest of all blessings,

Jillian Hart

A SOLDIER FOR CHRISTMAS

I wait for the Lord, my soul waits,
and in His word I put my hope.
—*Psalms* 130:5

To Frank Heidt. Thanks for taking the time to
answer my questions about Force Recon,
I'll keep your family in prayer, always.

Chapter One

Kelly Logan closed the textbook with a huff and blinked hard to bring the Christian bookstore where she worked into focus.

Math. It was *so* not fair that she, a twenty-four-year-old college student, had to take the required course so she could graduate. She intentionally hadn't thought about quadratic equations since high school, which was six years ago. Hello? Who would want to have to think about this stuff? Unfortunately, she was paying good tuition money to have to think about this stuff. She rubbed her forehead in the hopes that her equation-induced headache would go away.

No such luck. Pain pounded against her temples as though someone was inside her skull, beating her with a mallet. Lovely. She'd been studying algebra for thirty minutes in the quiet lull of a Friday afternoon. Thirty minutes was all it took for her neurotransmitters to quit working in protest. Not that she blamed them. Definitely time for a study break before her head imploded. She leaned a little to the left over the counter to check on the store's only customer, busily browsing in the devotionals display. "Do you need any help, Opal?"

"Any more of your help and I'll break my budget, honey." Elderly Mrs. Opal Finch wandered away from the decorated table with a small book in hand. "I got this one. The one you recommended. I see one of your bosses put up a written recommendation on it, too."

"Katherine has exquisite taste."

Opal slipped the book onto the counter. "Since when have you two steered me wrong? It's such a pretty cover, I couldn't resist."

"Neither could I. I bought it today—payday." Kelly gestured toward the identical small pink book next to her textbooks before she rang up the sale. "I already took a peek at it. The first day's devotion is awesome."

"Wonderful. Are you going to want to see my identification? That new girl did last time I was here."

"Nope, I know your account number by heart."

"That's not what I meant." Opal's merry green eyes sparkled with amusement. "So you can verify my senior citizen discount! It's a hoot, that's what it is, questioning my age. Oh my, it's good for the soul."

"You look eighty-three years young to me," Kelly

assured the lovely octogenarian as she scribbled down the purchase on an in-house charge slip.

"Bless you, dear, I surely appreciate that. And I don't need a bag, sweetie. Conservation, you know." She opened her wide paisley-patterned purse, hanging by sturdy straps from her forearm.

Kelly leaned over the counter to slip the book and receipt into the cavernous purse. "Thanks for coming by. You stop in and tell me how you like the devotional, okay?"

"I most certainly will." Opal snapped her purse shut, her smile beaming and her spirit shining through. "Don't study too hard. An education is important, but don't you forget. There are greater blessings in this life."

In yours, yes. Kelly filed the in-house copy of the charge slip in the till and held back the shadows in her heart. She feared that a happy family may not have been in God's plan for her. Sometimes it was hard to accept, to see the reason why she'd been given the parents she had.

Some days it was all she could do to have faith.

"Kelly, dear," Opal called over her shoulder on the way to the door. "Be sure and tell Katherine goodbye for me. That girl works too much!"

"I'd tell her that, but she won't listen."

The bell over the front door chimed cheerfully as it swung open with a force hard enough to keep the bell tinkling a few extra times.

"Let me hold the door for you, ma'am." A man's rugged baritone sounded as warm as the intense

August sunshine, and the bell jingled again as he stepped aside, holding the door wide as Opal passed through.

Something puzzled her. His voice. There was something about it. Kelly couldn't see him well because of the glare of bright sunlight slanting through the open window blinds lining the front of the store.

All she saw of the newcomer was his silhouette cutting through the strong lemony rays of the western sun. It was a silhouette cut so fine, everything within her stilled, awestruck by the iron-strong impression of his wide-shouldered outline.

"Why, thank you, sir," Opal's genteel alto rang with admiration. "You're a fine gentleman."

"You have a nice afternoon, ma'am." He stepped out of the touch of the light. His shadowed form became substance—a fit, capable soldier dressed in military camouflage, who looked as if he'd just walked off the front page of the newspaper and into the bookstore.

Wow. Definitely, one of the good guys.

"Good afternoon." The soldier removed his hat, the floppy brimmed kind that was camouflage, too, revealing his thick, short jet-black hair. He nodded crisply in her direction.

"Uh. G-good afternoon." Was that really her voice? It sounded as if she had peanut butter stuck in her throat. Totally embarrassing. "Do you need any help?"

"I might. I'll let you know." He stood too far away

for her to see the color of his eyes accurately, but his gaze was direct and commanding.

And familiar. There *was* something about him. It wasn't uncommon for soldiers to find their way in here, down from the army base up north.

Could he be a repeat customer? She considered him more carefully. No, she sure didn't think he'd been in before. His face was more rugged than handsome, masculine and distinctive with piercing hazel eyes, a sharp blade of a nose and square granite jaw.

Kelly, you're gawking at the guy. Again, a little embarrassing, so she went in search through her backpack instead. Her aspirin bottle was in there somewhere—

"Hey, I know you. You're Kelly, right? Kelly Logan?" The handsome warrior grinned at her, slow and wide, showing straight, even white teeth. Twin dimples cut into lean, sun-browned cheeks. "South Valley High. You don't remember me, do you?"

Then she recognized the little upward crick in the corner of his mouth, making the left side of his smile higher than the right. Like a video on rewind, time reeled backward and she saw the remembered image of a younger, rangy teenage boy.

"Mitch? From sophomore math class. No, it can't be—" Like a cold spray from the leading edge of an avalanche, she felt the slap and the cold. The past rolled over her, and she deliberately shut out the painful blast and held on to the memories of the man standing before her. The shy honors student who'd let her, the new girl, check her homework answers against his for the entire spring quarter.

"Yep, it's me." A very mature Mitch Dalton strode toward her with a leader's confidence. "How are you?"

"Good." A sweet pang kicked to life in her chest. She remembered the girl she used to be. A girl who had stubbornly clung to the misguided hope that her life would be filled with love—one day. Who had still believed in dreaming. "You have changed in a major way."

"Only on the outside. I'm still a shy nerd down deep."

"You don't look it." She glanced at the pile of textbooks on the counter. She, on the other hand, was still a shy bookish girl—and looked it.

"You haven't changed much." Mitch halted at the edge of the counter, all six feet plus of solid muscle, towering over her. "I would have known you anywhere."

"Why? Because—wait, don't answer that." She saw the girl she'd been, so lost, so alone, in and out of foster care and relatives' homes. She belonged nowhere, and that had been a brand she'd felt as clearly as if it had been in neon, flashing on her forehead. She still did.

Forget the past. Life was easier to manage when she looked forward and not back.

Mitch jammed his big hands on his hips, and the pose merely emphasized his size and strength. "It's been a long time since we sat in Mr. Metzer's advanced algebra class."

"Math. You had to go and remind me of that particular torture. I was lost until you took pity on me and gave me a little help. I wouldn't have passed Algebra Two without you."

"Math's not so bad. I'm planning on getting a math degree after I get out next summer."

"Out of the army?"

"Please. I'm a marine."

"I should have known. The distinctive camouflage outfit gives it away. Not."

His left eyebrow quirked as he glanced down at his uniform and then at his name on his pocket— M. Dalton. "Did you really remember me, or did you just read the tag?"

"You were too far away when you walked in. So, this is what you've been doing since high school?"

"Yep. Being a soldier keeps me busy and out of trouble."

Kelly wasn't fooled. His hazel eyes sparkled with hints of green and gold, and humor drew fine character lines around his mouth. He didn't look as if he caused trouble. No, he looked as if he stopped trouble when it happened. "Are you stationed up north?"

"It's only temporary. I'm here for more training. Then it's back to California, and the desert after that. They keep me pretty busy."

"The desert, as in the Middle East? Like, in combat?"

"That's what soldiers do." His smile faded. He

watched her with a serious, unblinking gaze, as if he wanted to change subjects. "How's Joe doing?"

"J-Joe." She froze in shock. Didn't Mitch know what had happened? Her chest clogged tight, as if she were buried under a mountain of snow. She wanted to be anywhere, anywhere but here. Talking about anything, anyone.

It felt as if an eternity had passed, but it had to be only the space between one breath and the next.

Silent, Mitch loomed over her, the surface of the wooden counter standing between them wide as the Grand Canyon. The late-afternoon sun sheened on the polished counter, or maybe it was the pain in her eyes that made it seem so bright. Looking through that glare and up into Mitch's face was tough. It was tougher still to try to talk about her broken dreams. They were too personal.

She'd stopped trusting anyone with those vulnerable places within her when she'd buried Joe.

And that's the way she still wanted it.

She slipped her left hand into her jeans pocket so he wouldn't see that there was no ring. She could not bring herself to answer him as the seconds stretched out longer and longer and she looked down at the counter, too numb to think of anything to say, even to change the subject.

The truth of the past remained, unyielding and something she could not go back and change. There were a lot of things in her life she would have wanted to be different. A man as forthright and strong as Mitch Dalton wouldn't understand that. Not at all.

The phone jingled, like a sign from above to move on and let go. She had a reason to step away from the tough marine watching her, as if he could see right into her.

"Excuse me," she said to him and turned away to snatch the phone from the cradle. "Corner Christian Books. How can I help you? Oh, hello, Mrs. Brisbane."

Mitch retreated from the counter, captivated by Kelly's warm, sweet voice. It was still the same.

She was not—quiet, yes, sweet, yes, but wounded. So, what had happened?

Years ago, the first time he'd come home on a much-deserved quick break from his Force Recon training, he'd gotten up the courage to ask his mom first about any hometown news. And then about Kelly in particular.

She's marrying that McKaslin boy she's been dating, Mom had said.

Married. That word had struck him like a bullet against a flak jacket and he'd hidden his disappointment. That had been the last time he'd asked about Kelly Logan.

She wasn't married now, whatever had happened. As he sank into the rows of books, he cast another glance in Kelly's direction. Her gentle tone continued. Clearly she knew and liked the customer who'd called. But this didn't interest him so much as what he could read by simply looking at her. The way she held herself so tightly and defensively, as if she were protecting the deepest places in her heart. The way her smile didn't reach her pretty blue eyes. Sadness clung to the corners of her soft mouth and made her wide almond-shaped eyes look too big in her fragile heart-shaped face.

How much of that sadness had he made worse by putting his foot in his mouth? Troubled, he turned his back, determined to leave thoughts of the woman behind, but they followed him through the long shelves of Bibles and into the Christian fiction rows. He still reeled from the raw pain he'd recognized in Kelly's eyes.

He'd been so wrapped up in his life, in his demanding job and nearly constant deployments, that he'd almost forgotten that heartbreak and tragedy happened off the battlefield, too.

Pain. He hated that she'd been hurt. He hated that he'd been the one to bring up the past. He should have looked at her hand first, the ringless left hand she'd been trying to hide from him, before he'd said anything. Something had happened to her, something painful, and he was sorry about that.

Wasn't pain the result of relationships? He saw it all the time. Marriages failed all around him, it happened to his friends, his team members, marines he barely knew and to his commanding officers.

Between the betrayal when a spouse broke wedding vows or changed into a different person, and the grief when love ended, he didn't know how anyone could give their hearts at all, ever, knowing the risks. Knowing the pain.

That was why he kept clear of relationships. Not

only did he not have much free time to get to know a woman, but he wondered how anyone knew when it was the real thing—the kind of love that lasted, the kind his parents had—or the kind of relationship that ended with devastation.

Either way, it was a lot more risk than he'd felt comfortable with.

So, why was he searching for a view of Kelly? From where he stood, the solid wooden bookshelves blocked the front counter, so he stepped a little to his left until he could see her reflected in the glass like a mirror. Perfect.

He wanted to say it was guilt, of bringing up something painful that had happened with Joe, that made him notice the way the soft fluff of her golden bangs covered her forehead and framed her big, wide eyes. And how the curve of her cheek and jaw looked as smooth as rose petals. Her hair curled past her jawline and fell against the graceful line of her neck to curl against the lace of her blouse's collar.

But that wasn't the truth. Guilt wasn't why he was noticing her. Concern wasn't the only reason he couldn't seem to tear his gaze away. He was interested. He was stationed here for a short stint, that was all, and he wasn't looking for anything serious—that was a scary thought.

No, he wasn't ready for that. He didn't have time for that. He wasn't a teenaged kid anymore with an innocent crush, and by the look of things, Kelly'd had her heart broken. She probably wasn't looking, either.

He'd come here to find a gift—nothing more—and he'd be smart to get to it. That was the sensible thing to do. He wandered back to the aisle of Bibles, determined to keep his attention focused squarely on his difficult mission: finding a suitable birthday gift.

The rustle of her movements jerked his attention back to her. He was at the end of the row, giving him a perfect view of Kelly. She'd hung up the phone and was circling around the edge of the long front counter. She was keeping her eyes low and intentionally not looking his way, but he kept observing her as he went on with his browsing.

He couldn't say why he watched her as she padded to the far edge of the store. Or why he noticed how elegant she looked in a simple pink cotton blouse and slim khaki pants. It was a mystery. He wanted to attribute it to his training—the marines had trained him well and paid him to observe, but that wasn't it at all. Not truthfully.

He couldn't say why, but he listened to the whisper of her movements and kept listening…even after she'd disappeared from his sight.

Chapter Two

Was it her imagination, or was he watching her?

Kelly slipped the inspirational romance from its spot on the shelf. Her gaze shot between the open book bay to watch the hunky soldier's broad back, which was all she could see of him. Mitch stood with his feet braced apart, browsing through the devotionals display midway across the store.

No, he's not even looking my way, she thought, shaking her head and hurrying back to the cash desk. Besides, he seemed totally absorbed in his browsing as he set down one book and reached for another. He was the only customer in the store, and if he wasn't noticing her, then no one was.

Okay, so she was nuts, but she still felt...*watched*. She remembered the impact of his gaze, and how tangible it had felt. She kept a careful eye on him as she returned to the front.

Although he didn't lift his head or turn in her direction, she felt monitored the entire time it took for her to write Edith Brisbane's name on a slip of paper, rubber-band it to the spine of the book and slip it onto the hold shelf.

I know what the problem is, she realized in the middle of shaking an aspirin tablet onto her palm. *She* was the one noticing *him.*

Who could blame her? He cut a fine figure in his rugged military uniform, and back in high school she'd always had a secret crush on him. He'd always been a truly nice boy. It looked as if time had only improved him.

As she chased the aspirin down with a few swallows from a small bottle of orange soda, her gaze automatically zoomed across the floor to him. Head bent, he had moved on to amble through the gift section of the store, his attention planted firmly on the rows of porcelain jewelry boxes in front of him. There were two inspirational suspense books tucked in one big hand.

When she looked at him, she could hear his gravelly voice asking again, *How's Joe doing?*

It wasn't his fault, Mitch obviously didn't know what had happened. But that didn't make the raw places within her heart hurt any less.

She was no longer a girl who could dream.

She climbed back onto her stool and debated tackling more of her homework, but she wasn't in the mood to face her math book. She knew that if she sat here trying to solve for x, her attention would just keep drifting over to the impressive warrior. To the past.

What good could come from that?

"Hey, Kelly." Her boss's solemn baritone cut through her thoughts, spinning her around to face him. Spence McKaslin pushed open the door on the other side of the hold shelf. He emerged from the fluorescent glare of his office, looking gruff, the way he always did when he worked on the accounts. "I'll be in the back going through the new order. Katherine's still out, so if it gets busy, buzz me."

"Sure, but it's been really quiet. Do you want me to start restocking or something?"

"No, we're all caught up. Just watch the front until your dinner break. Study while you can. It could get busy later."

"It never gets busy on a Friday night."

"Don't argue with me, I'm the boss." He gave her an extra-hard glare on his way to the drawers beneath the till, but he didn't fool her.

Spence was strong and stoic and tough, but also one of the kindest men she'd ever met. Her opinion of him had been pretty high ever since he'd hired her, which had saved her from losing her apartment when she'd been laid off from her previous job. Spence would have been her cousin, had things worked out differently with Joe.

A lot of things would have been different if she'd been able to marry Joe.

Feeling as if she'd been sucker-punched, she tried hard not to let the pain show. She didn't know how something so powerful would ever go away, but she did her best to tuck her grief down deep inside. Her gaze strayed to where Mitch still browsed, looking like everything good and noble and strong in the world.

But she also saw memories. And she wanted nothing to do with the past.

Spence grabbed the key ring from its place under the counter and studied her in the assessing way of a good big brother. "Did you manage to fit in lunch today?"

"Well, I ate a granola bar while I was stuck in traffic in the big parking lot on campus."

"I knew it. Take your dinner break at five, and I'll go when you get back," he ordered over his shoulder, already marching away.

Mitch watched the older man pass by the gift section and disappear through a door in the back. It was less than an hour before her dinner break. Interesting. He couldn't say why, but he felt out of his element. And it wasn't because he was in a store full of flowery knickknacks and breakables.

A plan hatched in the back of his mind, and it had nothing to do with his shopping mission.

Kelly remained in his peripheral vision. She made a lovely picture, sitting straight-backed with her head bowed over a book. The math text was still in the stack, so she must be working on another subject. Absorbed in her reading, she tucked a strand of rich honey-blond hair behind her ear, revealing a small pearl earring and her bare left hand.

While he was at home creeping through enemy territory in the rugged mountains of Afghanistan or the deserts of the Middle East, his extensive training did not include what he was about to do.

He kept her in his line of sight as he approached the register. The light from the window seemed to find her and grace her with a golden glow. She kept her head bowed over her book as he approached, but her shoulders stiffened with tension. Telling. But he continued his approach, taking in other details. The soda bottle, her nearly worn-out leather watchband, the pink barrette in her hair that matched the tiny flowers on her blouse. The two sociology textbooks stacked neatly at her left elbow.

He wondered about her life. Did she like being a college student? Did she live on campus in a dorm room or in a nearby apartment? Alone, or with a roommate?

When she looked up from her reading, her smile was cordial but he didn't mistake the sadness, like a shadow, in her dark-blue eyes. He felt a tug of sympathy from his heart. "You look pretty busy," he noted, easing the books onto the counter by her register.

"It's the life of a college student. I have a test on Monday." As she leaned to scan the books, her hair bounced across the side of her face, leaving only a small sliver of her profile visible. "Did you find what you were looking for?"

"I found more." He wasn't talking about the books.

"I do that all the time." Her gaze didn't meet his

and her polite smile was too brief. She turned her attention to the cash register. All business.

Okay, he got the signal, but he didn't let it deter him. "How long 'til you get your degree?"

"After this summer, I have two semesters left." She paused to study the cash register and searched for a key.

"It's gotta be slow going, working your way through."

"It's taking twice as long, but at least I don't have a major loan to pay back when I'm done."

"That's one perk of enlisting. My college will be paid for."

At least he wasn't mentioning the past or Joe again, Kelly thought thankfully as she totaled the sale. Her chest was still clogged tight, like the fallout of an avalanche still pressing her down. "Twenty-one ninety-three, please."

Mitch held out his credit card.

When her fingertips caught the other end, she felt a flash, like a shock of static electricity in the air. The sunlight changed to a bright piercing white. The floor rocked beneath her feet. It lasted only for a second. Then the earth steadied, the sunlight turned golden and there was Mitch, unmoved, looking calm and as cool as steel.

That was *so* not a sign from heaven. Just the pieces of what remained of her dreams, longing, in the way faint embers from a fire's flame could glow briefly to life when exposed to air. Her fingers trembled as she swiped his card and plunked it back onto the polished counter between them.

If there was a way to breathe life back into her dreams, she would ask the Lord to show her how. But she didn't bother. Some things really were impossible. "I still can't believe you're a soldier. What happened to your pocket protector?"

"No place for it on this uniform. I love what I do."

"What exactly do you do?"

"Well, I started out at oh-six-hundred with a ten click—kilometer—run in full gear and spent the day mountain climbing to five thousand feet."

"You get paid to climb mountains?"

"That's not all. I get to do things like scuba dive, parachute, drive around in Humvees and play with explosives." He said it all as if it was no big deal, just in a humble day's work. "Keeps me out of trouble."

"Seems like that would get you *into* trouble."

"Nothing I can't handle."

Wow, Kelly thought, as she bagged the books. He's grown up into quite a man. "See, my day is a piece of cake by comparison."

"Except for the math."

"Oh, you *had* to mention that again. I was trying to forget for a while." She hadn't laughed out loud in a long time. "Where you get paid to do things that you think are fun, I pay out good tuition money to be tortured by algebra."

"I'll be in your boat in eighteen months."

"That's right. That math degree you're going to get." The machine spat out the charge receipt and she held the two-part paper steady while it printed. How her heart ached as those embers of old dreams struggled for life. She tore off the printed receipt and slid it across the counter. "I need your autograph, and then you're free to go, soldier."

"*Free's* a relative term." He grabbed a pen from the cup by the register. "My time's pretty regimented."

"I bet it is. Are you headed back to your base?"

"In a few hours. I'm free until then." He scrawled his signature at the bottom of the slip.

Too bad she'd given up on dreams. She didn't know if she felt relief or regret.

"I hope you enjoy your books." She slipped his receipt into the bag and presented it to him. "I'm glad to see you're doing so well. I wish you luck, Mitch."

"You're letting me go, just like that?"

"Well, what else am I supposed to do? Generally we let customers leave our store. We seldom hold them hostage."

"I'm not talking about other customers. I'm talking about me. We could renew our friendship."

"We were never really friends, you know."

What did that leave him with? Renewing his secret crush on her? He took his bag, but the last thing he wanted to do was leave. She was still the nicest girl he'd ever laid eyes on. He could use a little nice in his world. It wasn't something he saw much of.

"We could be friends now," he suggested with his best grin.

"But you said you were headed back to California." Sweetly, she studied him through her long lashes.

A mass of emotions struck him like shrapnel to his chest. Emotions weren't his realm of expertise, but he felt strong with a fierce steely need he'd never felt before—to protect her, to make her smile, to make her every sadness go away.

Not really in his comfort zone, but a crush was a crush. What was a guy to do?

He tried again. "I'm not leaving for a while. We could still be friends."

"I have enough friends." Her eyebrow crooked up in a challenge.

So, she was giving him a hard time on purpose. "You get a dinner break, right?"

"Now and then they loosen the chains and let me out for a bit." Kelly folded her arms in front of her, considering him.

"You get a dinner break, and I'm hungry for dinner. It's a coincidence."

Kelly couldn't believe how he was just watching her with those intense, commanding hazel eyes of his, so wise and perceptive. She felt the impact as if he could see directly into her. "You're asking me out, aren't you?"

"No, not out. No. Of course not." He held up his free hand, as if he were innocent. Completely guilt-free.

"That's good, because I don't date anymore. I'm sorry."

"That's okay, because I'm not looking for a date. I was asking you to help me out."

"As if a big strong soldier like you needs any help at all?"

"Sure. I need a favor. I'm a lonely marine."

"A lonely marine?" Oh, she was *so* not fooled.

"Sure. It's only dinner." Amusement quirked the left side of his mouth. "C'mon, you gotta eat."

"True, but you probably have better things to do on a Friday evening."

"I can't think of one."

It's gotta be the uniform, she told herself as she assessed him carefully. "They must not let you out much if you think sharing my dinner break is your best option."

"What can I say? I could use a friend. How about it?"

Kelly's heart twisted hard. There was no mistaking the sincerity in his steady gaze. He meant those words. How could she say no? She knew a thing or two about wanting a friend. "You've got a deal."

"Excellent. How do you like your hamburger?"

"With cheese and mayo, no onions and tomatoes."

"I'll be back in an hour. Thanks, Kelly. I'm glad I ran into you."

"I'm glad, too."

He was military-strong *and* nice. What a combo. She couldn't help liking him. Who wouldn't?

She watched him stride away, cutting through the long rays of sunlight and disappearing into the glare.

She couldn't help the little sigh that escaped her. The bell jingled and the door swished shut and he was gone.

The dying embers in her heart ached. Be careful, she warned herself, holding on tight to her common sense. A man like Mitch could make her want to believe. And it was the wanting that got her into trouble every time—the longing to belong, to be loved, to know that soft comfort of a loving marriage and family.

"Hey, who was that?" Back from her run to the bank, Katherine, Spence's sister, swished behind the counter. "He looked like a very nice, very solid, very fine young man."

"Oh, that was just a customer."

"No, he was trying to ask you out. I happened to overhear. Accidentally, of course." Katherine leaned against her closed office door, looking as if she'd just received the best news.

That was Katherine. Always wishing for happy endings for other people. "It's not how it looks. We're just friends."

"Right, well, that's the best way to start out. You never know what will develop from there. I'm saying prayers for you. No one deserves a happy ending more than you."

"There are no such things as happy endings." Kelly knew that for an absolute fact. "This isn't a fairy tale. He's only in town for a little while."

"You just never know what the Lord has in store for you. It wasn't fair what happened with Joe."

She had to go and mention it. Kelly swallowed hard, wrestling down painful memories—the weight of them heavy on her heart, along with too many regrets. Too many failures. "Life is like that. It's not fair."

"No, but in the end, good things happen to good people. I believe that." Katherine breezed into her office, sure of her view of the world.

Kelly didn't have the heart to believe. She could not let herself dream. Not even the tiniest of wishes. She was no longer a girl who believed in fairy tales, but a grown woman who kept her feet on the ground.

She had no faith left for dreaming.

Chapter Three

"I think it's gonna be a quiet Friday night." Spence emerged from one of the fiction aisles with a book in hand. "How's the studying coming?"

"I'm less confused, I think. I haven't taken math since high school and I've forgotten just about everything but the basics."

"That's why I use a calculator." Spence nodded toward the front windows. "The soldier who was in here earlier? He's back."

"He is?" It took all her effort to sound unaffected. She turned slowly toward the front, as if she hadn't been of two minds about their upcoming dinner. She squinted through the harsh sunshine that haloed the wide-shouldered man.

She recognized the silhouette striding away from a dusty Jeep, carrying a big take-out bag and a cardboard drink carrier in one hand. The light gave him a golden glow, and he was all might and strength and integrity. She remembered what he'd said about needing a friend. It had to be a lonely life he'd chosen.

Spence cleared his throat. "I'm glad you're dating again."

Heat crept up her face. She busily set the alarm on her watch, so she wouldn't go over her allotted break time. "It isn't like that, Spence. Really."

"Okay." Like Katherine, he didn't sound as if he believed her. "Go ahead. Have a nice time."

It was Mitch. How could she not have a nice visit? As he strode her way, she beat him to the door. His welcoming smile was lopsided and friendly—definitely a smile that could make a girl dream. "I'm free for half an hour."

"I'm glad they loosened the chains." His shadow fell across her, covering her completely. "Wanna eat across the street? I saw a couple of tables and benches. Okay?"

"Sure. I eat over there all the time."

Walking at his side, she realized that he was bigger and taller than she had thought. He was a big powerful bear of a guy, his field boots thudding against the pavement. She felt safe with him. Comfortable. "Isn't Montana a little landlocked for a marine?"

"It would be, if I worked on a ship. That would be navy."

"But you're training at the army base?"

"I'm doing some advanced mountaineering. They train their Rangers there, and they're letting my platoon climb around on their rocks."

"Advanced mountaineering. That sounds serious."

"We're doing tactical stuff while we're climbing," he explained with a shrug.

"You must be pretty good."

"I haven't fallen yet."

She stopped at his side, at the curb, waiting for the few cars and trucks to pass. "What exactly do you do in the marines?"

"I'm like a scout. It's clear," he said, referring to the traffic and, as he stepped off the curb, laid his free hand on her shoulder. Not exactly guiding her, as much as guarding.

Kelly shivered down to her soul. Nice. Very nice. What girl wouldn't appreciate a soldier's protective presence? They stepped up on the curb together on the other side of the road, and his hand fell away. The world felt a little lonelier.

"How about that table?" She nodded toward the closest picnic table in the park, which was well shaded beneath a pair of broad-leafed maples.

"That'll work," he agreed amicably.

It was hard to keep pace with him as they made their way across the lush, clipped grass. He didn't walk so much as he power walked, even though he was obviously shortening his long-legged pace for her. She had to hurry to keep up with him as he crossed the grass. "How long are you going to be in Montana?"

"I've been here three weeks. I've got five more to go." He set the drinks and food on the table, then pulled out the bench for her. "That means I'll be outta here mid-September."

"And then back to California?"

"Like I said, they keep me busy." Mitch could only nod. He waited while she settled onto the bench, and the breeze brought a faint scent of her vanilla shampoo. The warmth in his chest changed to something sweeter.

She watched him with gentle blue eyes. "I didn't know marines climbed mountains."

"We climb whatever we're ordered to climb." He freed a large cup from the carrier. "I brought orange soda or root beer. The lady picks first."

"I love orange soda. Good guess."

He didn't mention that he'd noticed the pop bottle she'd had on the store counter beside her schoolbooks. He set the cup beside her. Had she figured out that this was a date yet?

"Cheeseburger, as ordered." He handed out the chow. "Do you want to say grace or will you let me?"

"Go for it." She folded her hands, so sincere.

He brimmed with a strange tenderness as he bowed his head together with hers. "Dear Father, thank you for watching over us today. Please bless this food and our renewed friendship. Amen."

"Amen." A renewed friendship, huh? Kelly unclasped her hands and unwrapped her burger. At least he wasn't trying to make this a date. "Why the marines?"

"That's easy." He dug a few ketchup containers out of the bottom of the bag and as the wind caught the empty sack, he anchored it. "My life has a purpose. I make a difference."

"That matters to you." She took a long look at him. "Making a difference matters to me, too."

"When I was a kid, watching the news coverage of Desert Storm, I was blown away by this segment they did on the marines. They were these powerful men with weapons, and they were taking care of refugees from the fighting. One of the refugees said how amazed he was by these big men. They looked fearsome, but they were also kind."

That pretty much summed it up for her. Kelly blinked and tried to act as if his words hadn't sunk into her heart. He'd grown up and grown well. She only had to look into his clear, expressive eyes to know that he was a very fine man.

Mitch took a big bite of his burger and leaned closer to dig a handful of fries out of the container. "Then it hit me, just how great that was in this world. To be a warrior fierce enough to protect and defend, to stand for what is right. That's honor, in my opinion. And that's how I serve. I do my very best every day."

What on earth did she say to that? She seemed frozen in place. She wasn't breathing. It seemed as if her heart had stopped beating. His gaze met hers, and the honest force of it left her even more paralyzed. The magnitude of his gaze bored into hers like a touch, and she felt the stir of it in her soul, a place where she let no one in. How had he gotten past her defenses?

He grabbed more fries. "How about you?"

"M-me?"

"Sure. Why social work?"

"I didn't tell you that."

"I noticed your textbooks. Are you getting your degree in sociology and a masters in social work?"

"That's the plan. I want to help children. There's a lot of need out there."

"There is." His voice deepened with understanding. There was something about a powerful man who radiated more than just might, but heart, too. "I remember back in high school that you were on your own a lot."

Keep the pain out of your words, she reminded herself. She wasn't willing to confess about the loneliness and the fears of a child growing up the way she did. "I know I can help kids who are in a similar situation. I want to make a difference."

"I'm sure you can." He studied her, his hazel eyes intensified. It was as if he could see the places within her that no one could. "You were in foster care. Is that right?"

"On and off, depending on whether or not my mom was in jail for drugs or if my aunt's bipolar disorder was under control." She forced her gaze from his, breaking contact, but it was too late. She already felt so revealed. "I was lucky. I made it through all right. A lot of kids aren't so fortunate."

"You've done very well for yourself."

"Not by myself."

"By the grace of God?" Mitch waited as Kelly

stared toward the far end of the park. There was nothing there, no people to watch, no traffic, nothing but a row of shrubs shivering slightly in the balmy evening breezes. He knew it wasn't the foliage she saw, but the past.

He didn't take for granted one second of his life, especially his childhood with two loving parents in a middle-class suburb. It was a start in life for which he was thankful. "About six years ago, I was training at Coronado when I got the word my dad had had a heart attack. I made it home in time to see him before he went into surgery. I think the good Lord was reminding my family just how lucky we are. We take nothing for granted, not anymore."

"Wise move."

He washed his emotions down with the ice-cold soda. "I've seen enough of the world to know that I wouldn't be who I am without them. It's a blessing to have parents like mine. Remember that favor I mentioned back in the store?"

She dragged a pair of fries through the ketchup container. "I thought this *dinner* was the favor."

"Nope, this is my apology. For sticking my foot in my mouth and bringing up a subject that hurt you."

"You couldn't have known. It's all right." She froze for a moment, and sadness flashed in her eyes again. "What's this favor?"

"I've been trying to find a gift for my mom. No luck. I'm clueless."

"You don't look clueless. And you can't be serious. You look around, you find things and you buy them. It's called shopping. That's how you find a gift. Our store is full of wonderful gifts. Why didn't you say something when you were in before?"

"I wanted to get a look at the jewelry store down the street first."

"Jewelry is always good. We have some lovely gold crosses."

"That's what I got her last Christmas. She has everything else, a mother's ring, more lockets than she can count. A charm bracelet so full of charms there's no room for more. I need help."

"You certainly need something." He was way too charming for her own good, Kelly decided. And she had a hard time saying no to a worthy cause. "When do you need this gift?"

"Her birthday dinner is Sunday night."

"I should have known. A last-minute gift."

"Last minute? What do you mean?" He feigned mock insult. "This is Friday. I have two more days."

Why wasn't she surprised? Kelly took the last bite of her burger. "Okay, what are your parameters?"

"Something unique. Personal. It has to be fairly inexpensive. I'm thinking around a hundred dollars."

"That's not so inexpensive. Have you tried the mall?"

"You're kidding, right? I avoid those at all costs."

"Why is that?"

"No amount of military training can prepare a guy for the conditions that await him in a mall. I'm mall-phobic."

She seriously doubted that. She couldn't imagine

Mitch being afraid of anything. "Mall-phobia. I *think* I read about that in my abnormal psychology class."

"Funny. So, you'll help me?"

"It's the least I can do for a friend." *Friend* being the operative word. The beep of her alarm made her jump. Had that much time gone by already? "I've got to go."

"Duty calls."

"Exactly. Did you want to come with me? We can go through the sales books together."

"No time." Disappointment settled like lead inside him. "I've got to be back by twenty hundred hours, and I've got over a two-hour drive ahead of me."

Was it his imagination, or did she look disappointed? Good. Now was the time to set up date number two. "I'm coming back to town on Sunday. How about the two of us get together and put in some serious shopping time?"

"Sunday, then." She folded her empty burger wrapper neatly.

He held the food sack open for her, waiting to toss in his wrapper, crumpled into a ball, after hers. "Where do you want me to pick you up?"

She grabbed one last fry from the tub before she twisted off the bench, graceful and lovely. She backed away, studying him through her long lashes with those big stormy-blue eyes. "The Gray Stone Church on the corner of Glenrose and Cherry Lane. Meet me there. Ten o'clock sharp."

"Meet you there? No, I should pick you up."

"It's not a date, remember?"

Have it your way, pretty lady. He watched her jog away, her hair brushing the back of her shoulders and swinging in time with her gait.

Mitch could only stare, unable to move, waiting as she crossed the street. She was like a vision, awash with light. He remained vigilant until she reached the storefront and disappeared inside.

You're heading to Afghanistan in six weeks, he thought, hardly noticing the crinkling sound the food sacks made when he bunched them and tossed them into the garbage can. What he did was dangerous. He'd learned the value of starting each day without regrets.

If he didn't make the most of this second chance to get to know Kelly, wherever that path might lead, he'd regret it. Six months from now, he'd be shivering on some rock in the border mountains of Afghanistan or belly down on a dune in the Middle East, and he didn't want to be wondering *what if.*

It wasn't only exhaustion weighing her down as she climbed the flight of steps to her apartment. Not the late hour or the dark shadows that fell from the whispering poplars. She felt as if the past clung to her with a tenacious grip tonight, like the stars to the black velvet sky.

Kelly sorted through her key ring as she climbed the outside stairs that brought her to her third-story landing.

In the end, good things happen to good people. I believe that. Katherine's words. They were part of what troubled her tonight and made the shadows so dark, the quiet so deep. Those words haunted her last steps and followed her into the soft pool of illumination from the light over her door. She fitted her key into the deadbolt and turned it with a click. The metallic sound seemed to echo in the chambers of her heart.

Everyone she'd ever depended on had let her down, so it was hard to believe in good things. God never promised that life would be easy or fair. A heart can be broken too much. And she'd learned that every time a heart is broken, it is never the same again.

She withdrew the key and inserted it into the doorknob, turning the knob and shouldering open the door. Her heavy backpack clunked against the door as she stepped through the fall of porch light and into the dark quiet of the foyer.

Mitch had stirred up some of this uneasiness, too. What a great guy. At least he was only interested in a friendship. How could it be anything else, with him leaving for California and beyond?

She could relax and not worry about him leaving—it was a given. She knew what to expect.

The luminous numbers of her stove's clock cast a green glow bright enough to see by as she pushed the door shut behind her, turned the deadbolt and slipped her keys onto the small table between the door and the hall closet. Her pack made a thump when she set it on the floor.

Hot, stifling air greeted her thanks to keeping

off the air conditioning. She headed straight for the living room and unlocked the wide window. Cooler air felt heavenly against her overheated skin. She stood for a moment letting the breeze fan over her. Outside the poplars cast dancing shadows from the streetlights and rustled cheerfully. She pressed her hot forehead to the cooler glass, breathed in the fresh night air and let her feelings and thoughts settle.

Mitch. Just thinking of him brought a smile to her face. He was back at his base by now. This was going to be different—interesting, but different—to have him for a friend.

She was actually looking forward to Sunday.

Chapter Four

Mitch scanned the light-veiled sanctuary, crowded with worshippers and loud with their conversations, searching for Kelly. To find her, he only had to follow the sunshine as it slanted through the glittering panels of stained glass.

Kelly. When he saw her, brushed with golden light and goodness, his heartbeat skipped. The sanctuary, full of light and sound and families getting settled, faded away and only the silence remained. She was sitting in a pew near the middle, her head bowed as if reading.

She hadn't noticed him yet, so he took a moment just to drink in the sight of her. Her honey-gold hair was unbound and framed her heart-shaped face. The lavender summer dress she wore shaped her delicate shoulders and fell in a complimentary sweep to her knees. A book bag slumped on the bench beside her. Matching purple flats hugged her slim feet.

He liked the way she looked, so pure and bright.

She made a lovely picture, sitting so straight, with her Bible open on her lap. It wasn't too much of a hardship to look at her. He eased into the row and onto the pew beside her.

She jumped, and her Bible tumbled onto the polished wood bench between them. "Mitch! You snuck up on me!"

"Hey, I'm no sneak."

"Then what do you call that? You didn't make a sound. That's sneaking in my book." Her eyes twinkled like aquamarines.

Enchanted—he was simply enchanted. *And* she looked glad to see him. What was a helpless guy to do? He shrugged. "Sorry. It's habit, I guess. Didn't mean to scare you."

"You are a scary man, Mitch Dalton." Her smile said the opposite as he rescued her fallen Bible from the bench between them. "Do you have a chance to attend a service when you're overseas?"

"Usually a chaplain holds service every Sunday. I attend whenever I'm in camp." He studied the Bible in his hands. It looked like his, treasured and well-read. He handed it over. "This is some church. It beats a tent hands down."

"A tent, huh?" Her fingertips brushed against his, featherlight and brief.

Wow. Her touch stilled his senses. As if from somewhere far away organ music began, and late worshippers hurried to find seats as the minister stepped up to his podium. The congregation rose.

Kelly stood, and somehow he was on his feet

beside her. She was so small and feminine at his side. All he knew was that he liked being with her. Not a comfortable thing for the lone wolf he was. But not bad, either.

She went up on tiptoe to tell him something, and he had to lean so she could manage to whisper in his ear. "I'm wearing my shopping shoes. I hope you can keep up with me."

That was funny. Little did she know what he was capable of doing in a single day. "Bring it on, little lady. I can do anything you can do."

"Be careful. I just might drag you to a mall."

"Hey, we had a no-mall agreement."

"I made no promises, soldier."

Kelly felt as light as air. Happy. She'd been working and studying so hard lately, she was glad she'd agreed to spend this time with Mitch. Besides, it was never a bad thing to have a handsome man—er, *friend*—sit beside you at church.

Mitch. She couldn't help noticing he had a very nice singing voice and yet he didn't attract attention to himself. His voice was quiet and his manner solemn. And he stood powerful and tall. Very masculine.

Not that she was wishing.

As she bowed her head for prayer, she caught sight of the Bible passage on the program. The typed words were the last thing she saw as she closed her eyes and the words from Isaiah emblazoned themselves on her eyelids. "Whether you turn to the right or to the left, your ears will hear a voice behind you saying, 'This is the way, walk in it.'"

It had also been the exact passage from her morning devotional. Coincidence? Probably not.

I'm trying, Lord, to follow where You lead.

But she was so adrift. Even with Mitch at her side. Even in the peace of God's sanctuary with heaven's light falling all around her.

"Whether you turn to the right or to the left, your ears will hear a voice behind you saying, 'This is the way, walk in it.'"

With the minister's message in his heart, Mitch stayed at Kelly's side as they inched patiently down the main aisle. Maybe this was a sign he was on the right path. A new one for him, considering his wariness of long-term relationships. And a strange one, because God's plan for him was thousands of miles away, across an ocean.

Kelly introduced him to the minister, who warmly thanked him for coming. As they followed the departing worshippers down the front steps and out into the bright sunshine, he stayed at Kelly's side, protecting her from any jostling from the crowd.

"Well, soldier, are you ready for your mission? Or do I leave you to survive shopping as best you can?" Her smile was as sweet as spun sugar.

He liked it. "I've already confessed that I'm retail-challenged."

"A big tough guy like you? C'mon, soldier up."

She winked, and couldn't help laughing. "I expect a marine to be tougher than that."

"I'll survive with a pretty girl like you watching my six."

"Your six? Oh, I get it. Watching your back. You're going to need it where I'm taking you. Peril and danger abound."

"I live for danger."

"That makes two of us." Kelly liked the look of worry crinkling his forehead. She guessed he was only halfway kidding her about having mall-phobia. "At ease, sir. I spent some time thinking of a few good ideas for your mom. And we don't have to set foot inside any mall."

"I'm gonna owe you big-time for this."

"No way. What's a little favor between friends?"

Mitch frowned. He had to set the groundwork for date number three. Something gave him a clue that she wouldn't make it easy for him.

He'd just have to wow her so much, she'd want to go out with him again. Maybe even call it a date next time. A man could hope. "You wanna grab a bite first?"

"I didn't think you soldiers took detours when you were on a mission."

"Right, but I'm gonna need fuel. No way can I shop on an empty stomach. Oh, wait. I get it. You don't date. And you're afraid that eating together twice would make it look like we're dating."

"It *could* look that way, but it's not. Right?"

Was that a shadow of fear he saw in her gentle

blue eyes? Why would she be afraid? Then in a blink, it was gone.

He stepped off the curb, looking for traffic, but there were no cars headed their way. He fished his keys from his pocket. "Don't even worry. Friends go out to eat together sometimes."

"I just don't want you to get the wrong idea. I know you'll be leaving in a month or so—"

"Exactly, so don't sweat it. We'll do whatever you want."

"I've got the best shop to show you. I really think you'll find what you want there."

"You mean this could be a one-stop deal?"

"It might even be painless."

She was doing her best to thwart his plans for their date. He was going down in flames. Not good. This had to be about Joe. What had happened? What had he done to her? He hadn't known the guy except as a name back in high school.

Whatever had happened, it had sure made Kelly afraid to try dating again. As he unlocked the passenger door, a mild breeze whispered through the maples overhead and shifted the lemony sunshine over them. In the dappled mix of shadows and light he opened the door and took Kelly's hand to help her up.

She dodged him, as if too independent for such a gesture, but he sensed it was something more as she slipped past him. Her cotton dress gave a whispering rustle, and the vanilla fragrance from her shampoo scented the air between them.

Unaware of how she moved him, she climbed into the passenger seat and settled her book bag on the floor at her feet. She sat there in a swirl of lavender summer cotton and dappled sunlight and sweetness. Feelings came to life within his heart and weren't like anything he'd felt before. They were soft and warm, and as soothing as prayer. Tenderness lit him up from the inside out. He felt every inch of his six-foot-two-inch frame as he closed her door and circled around to his side.

Her smile was calm, her blue eyes bright and friendly. "It's not far from here. If you can pull a U-turn and avoid the traffic jam up the street?"

"Inciting me to break the law, huh?" He winked as he started the engine and belted in. "I'm shocked. A sweet girl like you."

"Ah, the things you don't know about me."

"I'm beginning to get the picture. A hard-working college student who goes to church every Sunday. Yep, you're trouble." He checked the mirrors and the pedestrian traffic before turning sharply out from the curb and down the narrow tree-lined residential street.

Then he saw the sign, allowing U-turns in the wide, turnabout intersection.

"No more trouble than you are, I bet. Sunday service and then dinner at home with your parents."

"Not until six tonight. Until then, I'm a reckless man on the town." A gray tabby cat paraded off the sidewalk about ten yards up the residential street, and he slowed to a stop.

"Yeah, reckless. I see that."

He could feel her gaze like the softest brush against the line of his profile. He'd like to know what she thought about him. Come September he'd be on a bird out of here and he wouldn't be back this way again except for a rare, quick family holiday.

He wanted…he didn't know what he wanted. But he liked being with her.

Once the cat was safely across the street, he hit the gas. A four-way stop was ahead. "Which way?"

"Right. And take the first parking spot you come to."

"It's that easy? I can't believe it." He whipped the Jeep over to the curb and parked. "I just might make it out of this mission without a casualty."

"No casualties, remember? I'm watching your six."

"Then let's do it." He killed the engine and released his seat belt.

Kelly took a deep breath and tried to steady herself, to just breathe. What she couldn't explain was why he'd affected her like this. Why he'd slipped through her defenses as if they were nothing.

She didn't have a clue. He was already out of the Jeep and slamming the door, moving with an easy, latently powerful bearing around the front of the vehicle.

Why was she watching him? Because it was impossible not to. He looked like everything good in the world, honorable and strong. He made the broken places within her heart feel less cracked. He made her laugh and smile.

It was hard not to like him a little more for being a gentleman as he caught the edge of the door when she opened it with his big powerful hand. Golden flecks twinkled in his eyes as he grinned at her. "This might not be a date, but I'm getting the doors for you anyway."

"You're going to spoil me, and then where will I be?"

"You'll be treated the way you deserve." He held out his big hand, palm up and waiting.

She hesitated. He was simply being a gentleman, nothing more, but that's what scared her. There was danger in taking even the first tiny step in leaning on anyone. When you started leaning, you started hoping.

And in the hoping, dreaming.

The pieces of her broken heart ached like shattered bone. Friendship was one thing, but she could get out of the Jeep on her own, thank you very much.

As she tipped off the edge of the seat, his hand shot out, caught her forearm, the tricky guy. His grip was iron-strong and commanding. The warmth of his touch, and the strength of it, rocked through her.

Instead of feeling afraid, peace ebbed into her heart. Even into the broken places.

Her feet hit the concrete sidewalk, jarring her back into reality. Mitch let go, and shut the door with a thump. This gave her the opportunity to step away from him.

That rare, warm peace ebbed away like a tide rolling back out to sea. Although the sun blazed already hot on her shoulders, she shivered, as if with cold.

"I can see the campus from here, just down the street." Mitch pocketed his keys, his movements confident and relaxed as if he hadn't felt a thing. As if this hadn't affected him this way. "Do you live in the dorms?"

Somehow she managed to make her feet carry her forward as though nothing had happened, as though she were perfectly fine. Her voice came as if from far away. "No, the dorms are too expensive. I have a little apartment three blocks from here."

"Any roommates?"

"Just one."

"An apartment sounds good to me. Right now I have the luxury of living in the barracks."

"The luxury?"

"And so much privacy. Not. I'm happier in a hootch—"

"A hootch?"

"A tent—" he supplied, "in a camp somewhere overseas with my team. Give me a cot and I'm home. Better yet, I'd rather be sleeping out in the bush."

"Really, on the ground? You like that?"

"Sure. It's like camping, except for the grenades and C4 explosives. I grew up in these mountains."

"Really? The math whiz I remember from high school didn't look like the outdoors type."

"Looks are deceiving, and I was at an awkward age. Okay, a very awkward age. My dad is a forest ranger. We're gonna take one of these weekends I have free—if I get a whole one free—and hike up into the Bridger Mountains. Spend the night. Camp. Cook river trout over a fire."

"Sounds very rugged. I'm more of a stay-away-from-the-mountains kind of girl."

"You just haven't been properly exposed to the wilderness."

"Where there's no hot water, no plumbing and no electric blankets?"

"Those luxuries are highly overrated. Trust me."

"I'm a little afraid to, with an attitude like that."

When she smiled, sweet as candy, his emotions jumbled into a wedge in his throat. The palm of his left hand still glowed from where he'd taken hold of her arm to help her from the Jeep, and the brightness of her touch remained, calming and terrifying all at once.

Heaven was on his side, because Kelly chose that moment to pause in front of a store window. A striped yellow-and-white awning stretched overhead and he studied the way the hem ruffled in the breeze instead of figuring out what was happening to him.

At the back of his mind, he knew. He had a life, he had a calling, and he had eighteen months left on his contract. So how was this going to work?

"The lady who owns this shop is a good friend of the family—well, of Joe's family." Her voice broke on the sound of Joe's name. "She takes antique gems and resets them in the most beautiful jewelry you've ever seen. I don't know if you'd be interested in something like that for your mom, but Holly's work is so beautiful, it's like giving a little piece of love."

Okay, that was the word he was trying to avoid.

"Do you want to go in and look? Or I have other suggestions. We can just go down the block and there's—"

"No, let's start here." It felt like a definite step on an unknown path in the dark, when there was no light to see by. But he wasn't bothered by the dark.

When he opened the door, he wanted to take her by the hand. But he figured she wasn't ready for that. She breezed past him with a rustle of her cotton dress and the tap of her shoes, and he caught again the scent of vanilla and sweetness.

Impossibly, his heart tightened even more.

Chapter Five

Kelly couldn't help leaning closer against the display case to study the brooch Mitch had taken out of its velvet bed. It was an elegant piece of lacy gold with a baguette-cut ruby looking outrageously fragile against Mitch's broad, callused palm.

Stop looking at the man's hand, Kelly told herself. She was supposed to be concentrating on the beautiful pieces of jewelry, right? Not noticing the deep creases in Mitch's palm. Or how capable his fingers looked. The nicks and cuts and scars marred his sun-browned skin. Such powerful hands he had, just like the rest of him.

She *so* remembered the peace his touch had brought her, when he'd helped her from the Jeep.

"What do you think?" His hazel eyes met hers, and in those green and gold depths she saw glimpses of his big heart. He cared about the people in his life—and he cared about her opinion for some reason.

He's just too perfect. If he wasn't, then she wouldn't feel this turmoil seizing her up. Hard lessons learned ought to be enough to make her step away and stay firmly on the path she believed in. The path where God had placed her over and over again.

Mitch waited for her answer, the delicate and expensive brooch resting rock steady on his palm.

Don't just stand there, Kelly. Say something. Her gaze shot to the other box he'd chosen from among the many in the display cases. Which one did she like better? The dainty necklace shimmered in the sunlight, the delicate swoop of wings and halo around a thumb-nail-sized freshwater pearl made her heart stop. "It's a pearl. What can I say?"

"You like pearls?"

She supposed he was looking for a woman's opinion on jewelry. "I think your mom might like the ruby better, though."

"You didn't answer my question."

Which question? Her mind wandered. No matter how hard she tried to stop the caring from creeping into her heart, she couldn't. She liked Mitch Dalton. She liked him very much.

As a friend. She couldn't dare think of him as anything else.

"Why pearls?" He studied her, waiting.

Oh, right. Pay attention, Kelly. "Pearls are so simple and unassuming. Everyone knows that a pearl starts with a tiny grain of sand, but to me, it's like faith. We are like that grain of sand and it's God's grace that can cloak us and make us shine, if we are humble and faithful enough. In the end, it's a thing of true beauty."

"Yes, it certainly is."

He wasn't looking at the pearl. But at her. Somehow his gaze deepened and there he went, somehow feeling too intimate, as if he could see too much. But how could he look past the layers of defense in which she cloaked herself so carefully?

The pieces of her heart stung like salt in a fresh wound, and she felt so vulnerable and wide open. It was Mitch. He made her feel like this. So wouldn't the smartest thing be to head for the door and never look back?

It would be the safest.

"I'll take the ruby," Mitch told Holly, behind the counter. "But could you put the other on hold? I'd like to think about it. Christmas will be here before you know it."

"Sure." Holly gladly set the pearl angel aside and took Mitch's credit card with her over to the cash register.

They were done. Kelly let out a deep breath she wasn't aware she'd been holding. This was how worked up she was. But now Mitch had found his gift, and he'd be heading back to his base.

I'll be back on safe ground.

She probably wouldn't see him again. She didn't want to see him again, right? It wasn't as if she was looking for a man to love—not anymore. Not ever again. It didn't make any sense.

"Mission accomplished." The way he leaned both forearms on the counter, coming in close to her, made her want to hope—past the ache where no hope lived.

How impossible was it to start hoping? And for what? That kind of hope, that kind of dream, was not meant for her. She thought of what had happened with Joe, and it felt as if the shadows within her lengthened. No, this was her path and she would not step one foot off it.

She cleared the thick emotion from her throat. Somehow she managed some resemblance of a normal smile. "Your mom should love the brooch. I bet she'd love anything as long as it was from you."

"Well, she's biased, being my mom. But you, pretty lady, you saved my bacon."

"Me? I just pointed you in the right direction." Why did her heart flutter in her chest? Maybe it was simply the remnants of that old crush. Maybe. She couldn't let it be anything else.

"I did nothing. You would have done fine by yourself, but I'm glad I could help. I wish your mother a very happy birthday. And you a safe journey back to the base tonight."

She took a step in retreat.

"What? You're leaving me? Just like that?"

"You were the one who said mission accomplished."

"Well, maybe there's another mission scheduled after this one."

"Holly gift wraps, so you're good to go." She took another backward step to the door. "Bye, Mitch."

"Wait." As if he was going to let her escape. She was wrong, his mission wasn't close to being completed. Mitch scribbled his signature on the slip the shop owner slid toward him. "Kelly, don't run off on me."

"I've got to study."

"Flimsy excuse." Done, he dropped the pen but Kelly was already heaving open the old-fashioned wood-frame door. The cowbell over the door clanked as she tried to evade him.

Emotion struck him hard in the chest, and he remembered the fear he'd seen in her eyes. "Ma'am, could you wrap this for me? I'll be back."

He hardly registered the owner's agreement; he was already out the door and into the blinding burn of daylight. He turned toward Kelly instinctively, as if he could feel the tug of her spirit against his.

She'd gained some distance on him, he had to give her that. She speed walked in those purple sandals as efficiently as if they were cross trainers. The hem of her pretty dress swirled around her slender knees, and her long honey-blond hair swung with her gait, like lustrous liquid gold.

Yeah, she was in definite retreat. What had scared her? He puzzled over that as he bounded after her, cutting around a couple holding hands. She had that strict no-dating outlook on things. Was she bolting because he'd gotten too close? What he needed to know was what had happened with Joe. Otherwise, she was going to run off and he'd never see her again.

Maybe that was as it should be. Maybe it would be best just to let her go. His chest tightened. The tenderness and confused emotions inside him tangled up into an unbreakable knot.

What he did was dangerous. There was no denying it. He'd learned the value of making sure to start each day without regrets. To leave nothing unfinished.

If he let her go, he'd regret it. No doubt about that.

So he continued after her. He could have closed his eyes and found her by heart and by the cadence of her gait. In the reflection of a coffee-shop window he could see her profile, her soft mouth downturned, her chin set with determination. Then her slim shoulders tensed more as if she, too, sensed him behind her. She kept going.

There was a clue, but did he get the hint? No. He kept going. "Kelly? Did I do something wrong?"

"No, you didn't do anything." She spun with a swirl of cotton, stark pain clouding her eyes. "I really do have to study."

"Yeah, but you're running scared, I think. And I want to know why." He towered over her like a bear. "Do I scare you?"

She swiped at a shock of blond hair that fell across her eyes, tucking it delicately behind her ear. He knew she was biding time, trying to think of the right answer—one that was still the truth but not the whole truth, either. She wanted to hold that back, the real reason she was afraid. Maybe because it was too personal or too painful.

But if he wanted to have a chance of seeing her again, then he had to know. He folded his arms over his chest and waited.

She stared long and hard down at the crack in the sidewalk between them. "I know you said you wouldn't mind having a friend, but this doesn't feel like friendship. I don't know, maybe it's just me. But there's something—"

He knew exactly what she meant. It should be a relief that she felt this, too. It wasn't one-sided. But the tangled mess of emotions in his chest clamped tight enough to make him wince. "You know what we can do? Let's find a place to sit down, have lunch and figure this out."

"Figure what out? I don't want to figure anything out."

"Running away from this isn't going to make it go away. Or keep it from happening the next time we get together."

"The next time?"

"See? That's something else we can talk about. There's a taco place right behind you. How about it?"

"No way am I going to let you turn this into a date, Mr. Dalton." Her words were kind, but strangled. He could see the sadness in her honest blue eyes.

He definitely had to know what had hurt her so much. What had that Joe McKaslin done to her? He thought of all the things that went wrong in the world, in relationships, between two people, that caused that much hurt. Hated to think of her exposed to anything like that. "Why? Why can't you date me?"

"I told you right up front. I have a no-dating policy—"

"And I'm asking why. What happened to you?"

"Life. Just like it happens to everyone else." She lifted her chin, as if determined to hold back her secrets and onto what she felt was private. "Surely you've seen enough of life to know what I'm talking about."

"I have." He pushed aside too many images of the world he'd seen up close. Images so far removed from the safe streets of this little college town and luxury unimagined in some of the places he'd been. But young or old, rich or poor, Christian or not, here or in some desperate country, life happened, and there was no stopping the pain that came right along with the living. "This has to do with Joe."

She took a step back, then another, as if wanting distance. "He's at the Mountain View Cemetery. He's buried there."

"I—I'm sorry. I didn't know."

"Now you do." Kelly's chest clogged tight, as if she were buried under a mountain of snow instead of the pieces of her broken dreams.

She left him standing there, in the middle of the sunswept sidewalk, with life teeming all around him. Students from campus were pacing the sidewalks now that the shops were open. People fresh from church were looking for a place to have lunch and discuss the service. Young mothers pushing strollers and young married couples holding hands, their backpacks heavy on their shoulders as they sought out places to sip coffee and study.

Life swirled all around him, and yet he seemed darker than the shadows.

Kelly felt the same shadows in her soul, and she kept on going, woodenly forcing one foot in front of the other until she'd reached the end of the block. When she turned the corner, he was out of her sight.

But, strangely, not out of her heart. She could feel him there, like the shadows.

And the light.

Okay, that wasn't the answer I expected, Mitch thought, still troubled hours later as he helped clear the dishes from the table. He hadn't forgotten the look in Kelly's eyes—not one of grieving as would be expected—but of hopelessness.

He heard the waltzing rhythm of his mom's gait in the kitchen behind him. As he gathered up a stack of dinner plates, he tried to put his thoughts aside. His mother could probably sense that he was thinking about a woman, possibly daughter-in-law material. "Don't even think about asking."

"Why? What was I going to ask?" Barbara Dalton paused in the archway and planted a hand on her hip, but the gleam in her eye clearly said, "Fine, I'll just ask later." "Come out onto the deck. Your father is setting up the ice cream maker."

"This'll only take a minute." Like he was going to leave the dishes for his mom to do. "Go help Dad. Go on."

"Who do you think you are, giving orders?" She hefted the stack out of his hands—she was stronger than she looked. "You might be part of an elite force, Sergeant, but in this house you're still my boy and you'll do as I say."

"Yes, ma'am." He liked it when she pulled rank. He loaded up another pile of serving bowls and joined her in the kitchen, where she was stacking the plates in the dishwasher.

"I love my brooch, Mitch." She beamed as she worked. "Wherever did you find it?"

"A little shop near the university."

"You did good." She studied at him as he went in search of the plastic containers she stored leftovers in. "So, is she a nice girl?"

"What makes you think there is one?"

"Mother's intuition."

"Either way, that's filed under the topic of not-your-business."

"Well, I had to try." Mom went back to loading the dishwasher. "I am praying for you to find someone. I would so love a daughter-in-law to spoil."

"I'm still not going to discuss it." He dug a spatula out of a nearby drawer. "Do you remember Joe McKaslin?"

"He went to high school with you, didn't he?" She rinsed flatware beneath the faucet before plunking them into the basket on the bottom rack. "There was something about him in the local paper years ago. He passed away fighting forest fires."

Wow. No wonder he'd felt Kelly's sadness so powerfully.

"So sad, to lose someone that young," his mom went on. "I worry about you every day. You're the reason behind all this gray hair."

"It looks stunning on you, and you shouldn't worry. I can take care of myself." He dropped the container of leftovers in the fridge. "There. Done. What next?"

"Go take those bowls out to your father." She nodded toward the counter. "He should be about ready to dish up."

"Then leave the dishes, Mom. I'll do them later."

"You'll do no such thing. Now go, before I get out my switch."

He laughed at the joke between them, a threat she'd been using for as long as he could remember and a promise she'd never made good on. He grabbed the bowls and headed to the deck where his dad was fiddling with the lid of the ice cream maker.

Beside him his sister, Suz, a corporate lawyer in Seattle, was out of her area of expertise. "I don't know, Dad. You'll have to ask Mom."

His dad scratched his chin, as if considering the matter. "Maybe Mitch knows."

"He knows nothing," Suz winked at him as he joined them on the deck. "As usual. I'll get Mom."

"Hey now, move aside, Dad." Mitch set the bowls

on the patio table and knelt down in front of the ice cream maker. "What's the problem?"

"We'd best wait for your mom. We bust this new-fangled thingy of hers, I'll get in trouble." Dad didn't look too worried as he straightened. "It's good to have you home, son."

"It's good to be here for a change."

Memories surrounded him of all the summers Dad had barbecued on the grill and they'd eaten at the patio table, gazing out at the Bridger Mountains. The pool glittered in the sunshine and beyond the freshly mown lawn evergreens seemed to go on forever. Growing up here had been good; maybe the years to come would be even better.

Why was it, miles away and hours later, he could still feel Kelly in his heart? Because, he suspected, there was a chance that she could be his future.

Give it up, Kelly. It's no use. She was *not* into studying, no matter how hard she tried to focus. Kelly slammed the book shut and the sound echoed around the dark house. She was babysitting for one of her regulars, Amy—one of Joe's many cousins—and the little ones were snug in bed. When she checked the clock, she realized Amy and her husband would be home in less than an hour.

Why couldn't she concentrate? That was easy, because of Mitch. He was on her mind. Too much and inexplicably. She rubbed the heel of her hand over her hurting heart. Why did Mitch make her feel again in these broken places?

She had no idea. Aimless, she headed into the kitchen. She put a cup of water in the microwave and while it heated, she fished through her backpack until she found the zipper sandwich bag where she kept her teabags. The cinnamon aroma of the tea comforted her, but who was she trying to fool?

Only herself. There could be no comfort for what troubled her tonight. Everything she wanted with all of her soul—it surrounded her in this homey kitchen with bits of love and family everywhere. Crayon drawings and magnetic alphabet letters were tacked on the refrigerator door. Framed snapshots of the babies hung on the walls and were propped on the windowsill over the sink.

The broken pieces of her dreams and of her heart felt enormous in the comfortable silence of the cozy kitchen. And still, like a survivor beneath an earthquake's rubble, she could feel hope struggling to stay alive in her soul.

Chapter Six

In the middle of reading her assigned sociology chapter, Kelly felt a soft breeze move through her. Awareness flickered to life within her heart, an awareness that was warm and sweet. Highlighter in hand, she looked up over the rail of her top-floor deck, through the rustling, sun-drenched poplar leaves to the street below. A familiar tan Jeep was parked by the curb.

Mitch. Aviator sunglasses hid his eyes and he seemed to gaze along the block. What was he doing here? She hadn't heard from him in a week. She recapped her highlighter and slid out of the plastic deck chair. Remembering how she'd left things between them, part of her was glad to see him, the other part wanted to scrunch down in the chair, hide behind her book and hope he didn't see her.

No such luck. "Hey, Kelly. Are you studying up there?"

"Guilty as charged." She stood, leaving her book open, pages ruffling in the warm breeze.

"It's Saturday evening."

"So? You say that as if it's a bad thing. I like studying." She leaned against the wooden rails. "What are you doing here? And how did you find me?"

"You're listed in the phone book. I know how to read and I am fairly good at finding my way around." He lifted his glasses off his nose enough to meet her gaze. "You went AWOL on me, so I had to hunt you down."

"So, is that a punishable offense?"

"Yep. I've come to impose dinner on you. I hope you like the works, because that's what I got." He withdrew a large pizza box from the back seat. "I'm comin' up."

As if she would want to stop him. "I never say no to a man who comes bearing pizza."

"Lucky me." He piled a cardboard carrier with soda cups and two smaller pizza boxes on top of the one he already carried.

"I like a man who comes prepared."

"Good. I take pizza seriously."

Mitch took one look at her smile, as sunny as the bright summer evening, and the tangle of emotions in his chest yanked so tight he couldn't breathe. She was smiling at him, okay, maybe she was glad to see him…or she really liked pizza, but it was nice to see. As he headed around the small, seventies' apartment building, following the walkways through the mature poplars lining the complex, he spotted Kelly in the open doorway of the top-floor corner unit.

He took in the sweet glint of her dark-blue eyes and her girl-next-door wholesomeness. She looked great with her hair pulled back in a careless ponytail, wearing a light summer T-shirt in the palest shade of blue and comfortable-looking, dark-blue drawstring shorts.

He knew when she'd spotted the flowers because her smile widened. In his enthusiasm, he took the steps two at a time all the way to the top. "I tried calling a couple times, but your line was busy."

"Oh, I was online doing some research at the library. I've got a paper due." She backed into the unit and held the door for him. "I *always* have a paper due, or it seems that way."

She looked nervous. He didn't want that, so he handed her the flowers. "I promise I won't say anything to chase you away this time."

"Deal." She took the bouquet and breathed in the scent of the purple flowers. "I love freesias. How did you know?"

"They just made me think of you. That's a thank you. My mom loved her gift."

"I was glad to help."

He spotted the kitchen straight down the little hallway to the right. Definitely a girl's apartment, he thought as he slid his fragrant load onto the beige-colored counter and nudged a bowl with dried flower stuff aside so the extra-large box would fit. The pepperoni and garlic scent competed with the potpourri. "You haven't eaten yet, have you?"

"No. My shift at the bookstore was over at four-thirty, but I'm waiting for my roommate. We sorta had dinner plans." She joined him in the kitchen and pulled a glass vase from the cabinet beneath the sink. "Do you mind if Lexie joins us?"

"Sure, I'm the one who showed up unannounced."

"Yes, but with pizza and, oh, is that a box of cheesy sticks?" she asked over the rush of the tap water.

"Cheesy sticks and a dessert pizza."

"The blueberry cheesecake swirl one, by chance?"

He nodded confirmation as he removed the drinks from the carrier. "Did I do good?"

"Are you kidding? You did perfect. That's the best pizza in town. Do you mind if we wait? Lexie should be here any minute."

"Sure." He slipped his sunglasses onto the counter. "Pretty nice place you got here."

"Decorated on a budget, but it's home." She unwrapped the flowers and began arranging them in the vase.

He checked out the living area. The furniture was mismatched pieces in different shades of brown and blue, well-worn and comfortable, and aimed at a small wide-screen TV. A sturdy green plastic table sat squarely in the middle of the little deck that looked out over the poplars at the busy street below. A textbook's pages ruffled back and forth in the wind.

"Sit wherever you want," Kelly invited as she arranged the flowers. "How is the mountain-climbing going?"

"I still haven't fallen."

"You must have developed a certain competence at it by now. You said it was an advanced training thing you're doing, right? What's advanced about it?"

"Next week we get to train on glaciers. There's nothing like ice-climbing."

"I haven't ice-climbed in ages." She carried the vase past him to the scarred pine coffee table between a mismatched brown couch and blue striped chair. "Okay, never. It has never occurred to me that people actually climb across mountain glaciers."

"Well, they do if they want to get to the other side."

"Tell me that's not your idea of a joke."

"My sense of humor. It's why no woman will have me."

Oh, I doubt that, Kelly thought as she studied him. She imagined plenty of nice women would definitely consider him a fine catch.

The door opened, and Lexie's voice filled the little foyer. "Kelly? I couldn't believe it! I got the last copy on the shelf—"

Kelly watched her roommate skid to a stop midsentence, stunned by the sight of the guy standing in their living room. Before Lexie could jump to the wrong conclusion, Kelly made it clear. "Mitch and I went to the same high school. He's an old acquaintance, because we were never really friends. I was too shy."

"So was I," Mitch added, slipping his hands into his back pockets, which only emphasized the corded muscles in his arms. "It's good to meet you."

"You, too." Lexie swiped a chunk of wayward black hair behind her ear and looked utterly shocked. "I, uh, am just on my way back out. You two have a nice date—"

"Not a date," Kelly emphasized. "Mitch and I were waiting for you. He brought cheesy sticks. C'mon, let's grab some plates."

His ego was *not* getting a boost. Good thing he was tough, Mitch thought. There was nothing a guy liked better than being a friend, when that wasn't what he had in mind at all.

But it really was, he realized. The least he wanted with Kelly was friendship, and that was a good place to start. He noticed the rental DVD case the roommate was holding. "Is it movie night?"

"You can stay and watch it with us." Kelly offered, handing him a plate over the counter. "Lexie, did you say that you got the last copy?"

"Yeah, of the new romantic comedy that just came out for rent." Lexie still looked uncertain, even as she dumped her backpack and the video case on the edge of the couch. "I bet you're not into romantic comedies, Mitch."

"Not my thing, but I'm up for it."

He really was a nice guy. Kelly knew he probably wasn't jumping for joy to spend his Saturday evening watching a girl movie, but he was here as a friend. He'd come all this way—maybe he really was lonely, just as he'd said last week, when he'd brought burgers for her dinner break.

She was glad he'd come. "This is so much better than what we had planned. Barbecued hot dogs on our hibachi. Thanks, Mitch, for bringing the pizza."

"And the cheesy sticks." Lexie chimed in as she started loading up her plate.

"Any time, ladies."

Yeah, Kelly couldn't help thinking, he was *definitely* one of the good guys.

Nightfall darkened the dome of the sky as Kelly opened the door. "You were a good sport about the movie."

"It had some funny parts. It was a nice, wholesome movie. It was good for me."

"I doubt that, but thanks for coming. Maybe you'll want to stop by again."

"If that's an invitation, I'll take you up on it. Say, next Saturday night. I'll bring pizza again, if you want."

"My treat since you brought this time. We're friends, remember?"

"All right, then." Somehow, he would survive this friendship thing. He hesitated on the top step. "Same time same place next week?"

"I'd really like that." She trailed him out onto the covered landing. "It's pretty late. You have a long drive back."

"Don't worry about me. I've only been up and going full-bore since oh-five-hundred."

"Your hours seem as long as mine. Except ice-climbing is sadly lacking from my daily workout regime."

"You don't know what you're missing."

"Seeing as I'm more of an indoor girl, I'm more than happy to pass on the glacier-climbing. You really like it?"

"I do." That was an understatement. He started down the steps, slowly, going backward so he could watch Kelly standing in the shower of light from inside the door. "Monday, when you notice the whitecaps on the highest mountains, think of me."

"I'll send a whole bunch of no-slipping prayers your way."

"I'd appreciate it." Mitch stopped at the landing, gazing up the length of steps between them. It was late, he needed to head back but the last thing he wanted to do was to go. "How's the math class?"

"Good, but then I haven't looked at that homework all day. When I crack that book tomorrow, I'll be singing a different tune."

"You having trouble with the class?"

"It's math. Math equals trouble. Wait, you love the subject, so you don't understand delaying torture whenever possible."

"You just don't have the right attitude when it comes to math. You wouldn't happen to have a pen handy?"

"You're not going to look at my homework, are

you?" Her brows knitted and made an adorable crinkle between her eyes. "It's late. It's Saturday night. I have a strict no-math policy on Saturday nights."

"You have a lot of strict policies. First no dating, and now no math on certain nights. I'll be back in town tomorrow. Mom's dragging me to church with her and Dad so she can show her friends I really do exist and I'm not a figment of her imagination."

"You don't make it home much, I take it?"

"I've made it home for one Christmas, and about ten days total, and that's after boot camp. I spend ninety-nine percent of my life on a mission or waiting for one. Hey, how about I give you my cell number and my e-mail address? You can call if you want me to stop by. Or just e-mail a question."

"You've got to be kidding. You're busy enough."

"Sure, but I always have time for my friends. And for the thrill of math."

"All right, hotshot, but don't say I didn't warn ya."

"Bring it on. I'm used to a certain amount of hardship."

Kelly darted inside to grab the little spiral notepad by the phone. As she scavenged around the kitchen for a pen, delicate freesias scented the air with incredible sweetness.

"Use mine," Lexie offered, hopping up from the couch to hand over a purple glitter-gel pen. "He's awesome. You should date him."

Kelly shook her head. "Too complicated. He's leaving soon. He's stationed in California. Plus, I'm done with romance."

"Bummer." Lexie returned to the couch where the TV droned the latest local news.

Bummer was an understatement, but that was life. Kelly stepped out onto the front porch and her gaze found Mitch by feel rather than by sight. He'd retreated to the darker corner of the landing, but he radiated such a strong essence of might and honor that she saw him clearly, even when the twilight shadows hid his features.

She came closer and could just make him out leaning against the railing, his arms crossed over his chest. The embers within her heart breathed to life. Just a flicker, but it was bright and joyful.

This is happiness, she told herself. Mitch was a good friend, the pizza-bringing, kindly, offering-to-help-her-with-her-homework type of friend. Why shouldn't she feel gladdened by that?

Mitch met her halfway, reaching out for the pad and pen. "If I hear you had trouble and you didn't ask me for help, I'm gonna be pretty mad at you."

She wasn't fooled; she spotted the good-natured crook of his grin, even in the shadows. "It's my strict policy never to get someone as big and strong as you mad at me."

"Good policy." His grin widened as he wrote and handed her back the book and pen. "I'll provide the movie next time. Deal?"

"Something PG."

"There's a challenging mission, but lucky for you, I always prevail. Good night, Kelly."

"Night. Drive safe."

He raised one hand in answer, moving down the stairs silently. Not even the bottom step squeaked as he disappeared from her sight, taking the brightness of his presence with him.

In his Jeep, heading north over the moon-drenched Montana landscape, Mitch thought over the evening. Not bad. It had gone much better than he had the right to hope for. Kelly had relaxed around him, especially with her roommate there.

Over pizza consumed at the balcony table, with the rustling trees, the wind and sun, he'd asked questions about college life. About Kelly's life. He learned that she worked full time at the bookstore and supplemented that with babysitting jobs. That she was a straight-A student. She was starting to do extra study for the exams to get into graduate school. And that she daintily picked green peppers off her pizza.

She amazed him. Life had brought her a lot of twists and turns. The image of her standing on the top step, the light from the apartment behind her, the moon's glow falling over her in the dark night, remained. She was pretty determined that all the two of them had in store was friendship.

He considered her side of things. It sounded as if she'd been alone for most of her formative years. And just when she thought she'd found a place to belong and someone to love, it had been ripped from her.

Pretty devastating. No wonder Kelly had given up

on dating. On trying to find love again. No wonder the friendship-only thing was so important. He could understand that. He knew what deep losses could do to a person. Closing your heart off kept you from getting too close and feeling too much. It was easier.

But it was no way to live.

Plus the tangled-up emotion in his chest had little to do with friendship feelings. Tonight he'd really felt at home on the couch beside her, with his feet up on the coffee table. He'd enjoyed the simplicity of sitting at her side, and it had felt right. He'd like to spend a lot more evenings just like that. But not as just her friend.

As the highway unrolled before the reach of the Jeep's headlight, Mitch thought how life resembled his limited view. You just couldn't see what was up ahead. Life came with risks and love did, too. You had to give with your whole heart, but you were really just driving in the dark. The turns and obstacles ahead were a mystery, veiled in the night, and you just couldn't know how things would work out.

All you could do was to walk in faith and not hold back.

Chapter Seven

Doom.

Kelly looked up from her textbook and rubbed her tired eyes. The living room came slowly into focus. Two hours of struggling with the mysteries of algebra, mysteries which she had purposefully forgotten over the years, and the truth, as solid as ever, stared her right in the face. The final regular test of the summer quarter was getting closer and she wasn't going to pull an A. She'd be lucky to get a C the way she was going, and that would pull down her entire average.

Definitely doom.

Mitch's kindly spoken words echoed through her mind and right into her heart. *If I hear you had trouble and you didn't ask me for help, I'm gonna be pretty mad at you.*

Since it was a bright late-Monday afternoon, and Mitch was probably out pick-axing his way up a glacier, she opted for an e-mail instead of calling.

It took just a second to type up an outgoing message to the address he'd given her, as it was only one word: Help! She signed off, including her cell number since she was scheduled to babysit tonight.

The twists God put in a man's path were an amazing thing, Mitch thought as he dialed Kelly's cell number. It had to be no coincidence that he loved math—always had—and that he was in the position to offer her the one thing she'd accept from him— help for her upcoming test. Proof that he was on the right path.

After the third ring, her voice filled the line, dulcet and low as a whisper. "Mitch?"

"Hey, I got your SOS. I would have called you sooner, but we just got in."

"You've been out all day? It's nine o'clock."

"I don't work banker's hours. I'm just lucky I don't have to sleep on the ground tonight. Mountainsides are generally rocky. Not so comfortable. Where are you?"

"Babysitting. Actually, the kids are asleep and so I'm studying, but it's a disaster."

"You've got the right man." He intended to show her that. "What's the problem?"

"If only it were that uncomplicated. I have a test in a week, the last one before finals and it's a big part of my grade. I'm not getting what to do with quadratic equations. It's eluding me."

"Sounds like you're in need of a tutor."

"I am. What are your rates?"

"Barbecue a couple of hot dogs on your hibachi and we'll call it even."

"That's what I had planned for Saturday's dinner."

"I'll come early, we'll get your math crisis figured out before dinner. Sound like a deal?"

"A very good one. How was the ice-climbing?"

"Cold." His chuckle was cut short. There was some noise going on in the background. "Oh, I've gotta go. We've got a surprise field exercise."

"It's almost ten at night."

"Welcome to my world. I'll be at your place, uh, around four-thirty. See ya." The line disconnected.

Kelly sat alone in Amy's living room and stared at the phone, his voice, his words echoing in her head. *Why does he affect me so strongly, Lord?*

No answer came. The brightness Mitch brought to her spirit faded in slow increments with each breath.

And only shadows remained.

Mitch. She couldn't help thinking of him throughout the week. Things would happen that brought him to the forefront of her mind. Driving to work and seeing the highest snowcapped peaks of the Rockies rimming the northwestern horizon, and those glaciers glinting in the hot late-August sun made her wonder if Mitch was out on a snowy peak like those, climbing to his heart's content.

Every time she cracked open her math book or sat in the auditorium class: while she wasn't looking forward to facing a tutoring session, she was glad about her tutor.

Who would have guessed all those years ago that the shy, out-of-place foster girl and the smart, awkward math geek from a middle-class life would wind up being friends? Or that he would be helping her once again?

God worked in funny ways. But she wasn't going to question it. She knew the Lord's hand had been gently guiding them together. Why else would her heart come back to life a little? Why else was she starting to feel a brightness inside her, after Joe's loss had taken it all?

During her shift at the bookstore today, both Katherine and Spence had asked her how things were going with the soldier. Really, they had it all wrong, but when each had asked about him, she started thinking about him all over again. How funny he could be, and how his chuckle rolled like warm joy, low and deep, just the way a friend's laugh should be.

The best part was that she was going to see him in a few minutes. She was running a little early, so she'd have time to get some iced tea made before he came. In a hurry, she whipped into one of the several parking spots in front of her staircase.

Her soul stirred. Strange. She squinted through the windshield to the top landing above. And there, through the shield of poplars swaying in the wind was a silhouette, tall and dependable and waiting for her. Her shining knight—er, tutor.

Like the sunshine streaming through the flickering leaves, her day brightened. She hopped out of the car, bringing her backpack and keys with her. "Hey, stranger. You're early."

"Better than being late." He braced his hands on the rail and leaned, gazing down at her. His smile was wide and friendly, and she knew his eyes were too, behind those aviator sunglasses he wore. He was dressed in jeans again, and a navy-blue T-shirt. "I've only been waiting a few minutes. Are you ready to be put through your paces?"

"Ugh. I knew I was going to regret this. I've been putting off even dealing with anything mathematical all week. It's going to be torture, isn't it?"

"Well, I am a marine. We show no mercy."

"Just my luck." She climbed upward, feeling as light as air. "Lexie wanted me to ask. What movie did you bring?"

"No way. Homework first. Then we'll talk movies."

"Whew, you are demanding." She was close enough to see that there was a military logo on the chest of his T-shirt, and the deep-navy color made his eyes a dark, fathomless green.

Not that she was noticing. "Hey, when you had to get off the phone when we were talking last week— did everything turn out okay?"

"Our CO—commanding officer—thought it would be funny to order us out on a midnight climb."

"In the dark?"

"Well, when you're doing what I do, they don't want you seen. It kind of interferes with the stealthy part of the job. We do a lot of training stuff at night because we do a lot of our missions through the night."

"Missions. That's like what, hanging off cliffs and crossing glaciers? Do you know what?" She unlocked her front door. "I'm starting to suspect that you aren't a normal soldier."

"I told you. I'm like a scout. I do reconnaissance."

"*Like* a scout." Yeah, that was so revealing—not. She opened the door and led the way to the kitchen. "Okay, you keep saying that. You're *like* a scout, but what do you do, exactly? You climb mountains, scuba dive, do amphibious stuff. You're not like Special Forces, are you?"

She feared she knew the answer already.

He shrugged one muscled shoulder, as if it were no big deal. "I'm a Force Recon marine."

Oh, the humble thing was so appealing. Kelly tried to keep her heart still as she took out two cans of soda from the fridge and handed him one. "I don't know what that is. Explain, please."

"Thanks." He popped the top of the can. "We're the elite of the elite. Force Recon is basically the on-the-ground eyes. We patrol enemy territory and act as scouts so our guys know what they're getting into."

"Enemy territory? Like you scout out enemy soldiers?" She took a sip of the icy bubbling cola. It kept her from saying that he looked pretty sane for a crazy person. She tried to imagine how dangerous that had to be. "You need to ice-climb *just* to find out the other side's position? No, you do more than scout, don't you?"

"Yeah. We're pretty big and bad." He shrugged that shoulder again. Apparently that was all he was saying. "Ready to get to it?"

"Math? Sure." Her backpack was still hanging from her shoulder. "We can stay in here, where the air conditioning is, I can turn it up. Sorry." She headed toward the thermostat and adjusted the dial. "Or we can sit outside. Oh, and there's a park a few blocks down."

"The deck is good. I don't want to get too far away from the food."

"I get the hint. Hungry?"

"I could be."

"That's just a hungry man's way of being polite." She grabbed a bag of chips and handed it to him. "Do you like French onion or ranch?"

"Yes."

"I should've known." She grabbed both dip tubs from the fridge and followed him out onto the deck. "Appetizers."

"There's no better." He opened the bag. "Are you ready?"

She tugged her math book out of her pack. It had been a long time since she'd been this happy at heart, especially when it came to algebra.

Mitch's friendship was turning out to be a true blessing in her life.

As Mitch knelt on the deck boards to turn the franks grilling on the hibachi, he could see Kelly's reflection in the large window. She was leaning forward over her plate to scoop her chip through the dip. Her face was turned in profile as she talked with her roommate.

When it came to Kelly, there couldn't be a prettier woman on earth. Not in his opinion. Her golden hair was down today, rippling in the warm breeze and caressing the creamy curves of her face. She wore a sleeveless blouse the exact blue of her eyes, and a black pair of walking shorts and matching shoes. She looked casual and wholesome and womanly all at once.

It really wasn't fair that he was at such a disadvantage.

I hope You know where You're leading me, Lord, because I'm in over my head. He cared for her more than he felt safe admitting, even to himself. He tonged the hot dogs from the grill and onto a plate. "Seconds?"

"It's nice having such first-rate service, thanks." Kelly smiled up at him as she swiped mustard on a bun. "You have great grill skills."

"I've put in a lot of hard practice at the barbecue."

He slid a beef frank onto Lexie's plate before he added the last two to his. Across the table, Kelly was pushing the relish and mustard in his direction. Her fingers were long, slender and delicate, like the rest of her. Her short nails were painted a light pink.

Lexie shoved the tub of deli potato salad closer. "So, Mitch, tell us exactly why you aren't married."

"Because I spend pretty much most of my time on a mission or on standby prepared to head out. It doesn't leave a lot of time for finding a nice lady to marry." He cast a glance sideways at Kelly. "This free time I have—real weekends—is a luxury."

Lexie persisted. "Yeah, but you'd like to get married one day, right?"

"Sure. I just haven't slowed down enough to let a woman catch me and shackle me into matrimony. Yet."

"Shackle?" Kelly questioned with the cute little crinkle at the bridge of her nose.

"That's a totally typical man's answer." Lexie didn't seem too happy with him.

He shrugged, running a line of mustard along both hot dogs. "Apparently a guy should never joke about the seriousness of marriage in front of women."

"Ya think?" Lexie frowned at him, but her eyes said something different. Like she was on to him.

"Let me try again." He set down the mustard bottle so he could concentrate. He didn't want to get it wrong this time. "I'd like to get married one day. I'm taking my time because I want to find the real thing."

"Real love." Lexie nodded her tentative approval. "Don't we all want to find that?"

I think I already have, he thought. All he had to do was to look at Kelly and his heart did funny things, leaving him feeling exposed and vulnerable.

That just couldn't be good. "Is this how you two spend every Saturday evening?"

"Just about," Kelly answered between dainty bites. "Unless I have a babysitting job."

"But mostly it's a budget meal and a rented movie," Lexie concluded.

"The reality of putting yourself through college." Kelly didn't seem to mind. "On the Saturdays after payday, we splurge and order a pizza."

"You live large. I'm guilty of the same kind of lifestyle." Mitch stole more chips from the bag in the center of the table.

"We're flush. Lexie, remember last January? We were both flat broke from paying tuition, I'd lost my retail job due to layoffs after Christmas, and we couldn't scrape enough money together between the two of us for rent."

"My dad's check was lost in the mail, it really was, and he was out of the country," Lexie explained, "so we were, like, digging out the pennies from the bottoms of our book bags and purses."

"And on the floor of the car," Kelly added. "Sure, it's funny now, but let's just say there was a big sale on cases of those cups of instant noodles at the discount grocery. It's practically all we ate for three weeks."

"So," Mitch guessed, "you're telling me not to take you out for noodles?"

"Exactly." She laughed. "I'm definitely noodled out."

Her laughter lightened his world. His voice didn't sound like his own as he made a suggestion. "I saw that a couple of good movies were playing down at the old theater. I thought I'd treat you girls to pop-corn and a movie. Interested?"

Kelly's gaze met his, and, like a spark to kindling, he felt the impact.

"That would be very nice," she said and her smile moved like sunlight through him.

He had to admit that he cared for her. It wasn't a conscious decision and there wasn't much he could do about it.

With the warm still air and star-studded ebony sky, the August evening felt like a dream. Or, Kelly conceded, maybe it was the man she was walking with. Something about being with Mitch made her world better.

"Are you sure we shouldn't have waited for your roommate?" Mitch asked. "It's dark and she shouldn't be walking alone."

"I have a feeling that guy she ran into at the con-cession stand has been wanting to date her for a long time. I bet he'll give her a ride home." It was nice of him to be concerned, though, Kelly thought. See? It just went to show what a thoughtful guy he was. "What you did this evening, helping me figure out my math, is a big deal to me. You may have saved my grade point average."

"Well, not yet. The test is tomorrow."

"But now I've nailed every practice test question the prof handed out. I couldn't do one of them before you came today."

"Ah, you could too. You were just getting psyched out about it. I didn't do much."

"It's a lot to me."

"I'm glad I could help." Mitch rewarded her with his charming, lopsided grin, the one that made her spirit light up.

She couldn't remember a nicer thing, simply walking like this at his side. Maybe it's the gorgeous night, she reasoned, the hush of their footsteps on the sidewalk in perfect synchronicity and the quarter-moon peering over the city so that they walked in its platinum glow.

Or, maybe it was the man—wait, correct that— *friend* at her side.

Companionable silence mantled them as they walked down quiet streets. The bright lights of some of the college dorm windows were visible through the trees lining the sidewalk, and, as they turned the corner and crossed the road, the curtained windows of homes stretched for blocks.

Mitch broke the stillness. "I've got only two more weekends left before they drag me back to my base."

"Two more?" She'd known that, of course, but to hear the words out loud hit like a punch.

"Dad and I are going up into the national park next Friday to spend the night. I want to do that before I head out. With this thing going on in the Middle East, I'm gonna be hard core, and I don't know…I might not make it back until I'm discharged eighteen months from now."

She'd known that, so why did it feel as if she were choking on disappointment?

"It'll mean a lot to Dad, and to me, too. But I've got Sunday afternoon free. You're gonna need to take a study break, right?"

She cleared the emotion from her throat, but her voice sounded thick anyway. "Are you kidding? Finals start in a week. I'll be half-comatose. I'll need a serious study break."

"Something fun."

"What does a guy who hangs off of mountains for a living do for *fun?*"

"There's hang gliding."

"Are you serious? I can't do heights."

"How about BASE jumping?"

"*What?* I'd have to be insane, and I'm not there yet."

"Ice-climbing is out?"

"Don't go there, I'm warning you." Although she sounded almost stern, the hint of a dimple at the corners of her mouth showed, even when she was doing her best to keep from grinning.

"All right. How about this: if you get an A on your test, I pick. You get a B or less, then you can pick what we do."

"I'm only agreeing to this because I don't think there's any way that I'll actually pull an A. The only problem is that I have a babysitting gig at six."

Mitch realized they'd stopped in the shadow of her building. There was his Jeep parked a few car lengths up the curb. Disappointment set in. He didn't like the idea of having to leave her. "We'll have you to your babysitting thing on time."

"How about I'll meet you at the city park around noon, and I'll bring my graded test. We'll take it from there."

"The west entrance." He jammed his hand into his jeans pocket and pulled out his keys. Sorting through the ring gave him something to focus on when he really wanted to do nothing more than brush his lips with hers, gently kiss her soft, rosebud mouth so she would know how he felt.

But she wasn't ready for that. She wasn't ready for more.

Yet.

He didn't blame her. He could relate. This was a scary, unknown path. Especially to a marine who was trained to be swift, silent and deadly, but when it came to *this*—matters of the heart—he wasn't so capable.

He walked backward so he could keep her in his sight. "Thanks for a good evening."

"I should be thanking you. Safe journeys, Mitch."

"Night." He could walk away, but he couldn't stop his tenderness for her that burned like a rocket's glare in the dead of night.

He didn't know where this was leading. He only knew that God was leading him.

He would trust in that.

Chapter Eight

"Are you having fun yet?"

Fun? Kelly studied Mitch over the rim of the giant inner tube she held on to for dear life, although the cool lapping eddy of the river's edge only came to her knees. Fun? That settled it, he was definitely certifiable.

The trouble was, he looked anything but. In running shorts and a military-green tank top, he radiated complete ease and self-assurance as he waded ahead of her into the deeper pull of the current.

I'd have to be crazy to follow him.

She took another step along the rocky river bottom—putting her sanity in serious question.

She squinted through the blinding sunlight bouncing off the wide river's surface at the intrepid man who obviously had no common sense. "This *can't* be your idea of fun."

"You'd better believe it." He stopped waist-deep in the mountain-fed river and took hold of her inner

tube. "That's some death grip you got there. Relax.
I won't let anything happen to you."

"Promises, promises." She cast her gaze down
river, contemplating all the ways she could drown.

"Don't tell me you're afraid of water, too."

"Okay, I won't tell you." She bit her bottom lip to
keep in the squeak of fear that erupted the moment
he gave an effortless jerk on her inner tube and kept
pulling. Her feet lifted off the rocky riverbed as he
drew her through the eddies and directly into the
teeth of the current. The force of it seemed to bite
like a dog, held on and tried to drag her away. Not
the best sensation.

Help? She couldn't seem to make that word come
out of her terror-struck mouth. She wasn't aware how
it happened, but he was at her side and his steely arm
drew her toward him.

Their inner tubes bumped together and she jostled
to a stop against him. There she was, in the shelter of
his arms, up to her chin in water, protected from the
river's tenacious current and shaded from the blinding sun. Safe at his side, her fear trickled away into
nothing at all.

Her feet found a firm purchase on the rocks below
and a different fear coursed through her as he ca-
sually drew her closer still. Somehow she found
enough air to breathe in order to speak. "I thought
we were going wading or something."

"That'll teach you to jump to conclusions."

"No, it was more like wishful thinking. Clinging
to false hopes."

"You do know how to swim, right?" Mitch could feel the way she trembled. Tenderness flowed through him with a force that was greater than the river, greater than anything he'd ever known before.

The emotion sharpened until it ached in his throat. She was so little and fragile and dainty in his arms, and that well of tenderness just kept on brimming. He wished he could hold her close and protect her. Forever.

The question was, would she let him?

He tugged her a little closer, but she seemed to resist. That was his answer, apparently. Okay, he'd work with that.

"I know enough to dog paddle basically." There was that cute furrow again between her eyes. The one he wanted to kiss until her worry went away. He doubted that would make her calmer right now. In time, he thought, although it was tough not being able to take this up a level.

Was it his imagination, or did she cling to him more tightly? His care for her was like nothing he'd ever known before. He longed to be with her in the way mountaintops needed snow, rivers needed the sea. The way night needed the dawn. To feel whole. With a perfect purpose.

Ever since he'd left for boot camp, he'd found a great purpose to his life. One he felt qualified and called to do. But right now, being with Kelly, his whole heart crumpled and fell, changing him forever.

"Don't worry. I'll be right with you," he promised. "I'm qualified in water stuff."

"Water stuff? That makes me feel so much better. *Not.*"

"It should. I'm trained in all sorts of amphibious things. You're in good hands. Ready?"

No, she was *so* not ready. Kelly gave a squeak of fear as she was whisked up onto the seemingly enormous inner tube, which he held safely for her. As aggressively as the current tried, it could not tear her away from Mitch's grip.

This was a very bad idea. Panic roared through her with a quaking iciness, stealing the hot burn from the sun on her face and arms, and drowning out the rush of the river. It wasn't the river that was scaring her now. *That* fear, as great as it was, was nothing compared to the panic threatening to take her over. It was Mitch. Her feelings for him were so strong.

He made it all worse with the gentle brush of heat as he leaned to whisper in her ear. "No worries. I'll keep you safe. Count on me."

It would be so totally tempting to care for him in a way that went beyond friendship, Kelly thought as she clutched the side of the rubber inner tube. Mitch looked like everything trustworthy in the world—he was strong of character and spirit. As a friend, he made her laugh, but he did more than that. He lit up her world.

What could she do about that? She'd stop feeling this way, that's what. She'd hold on tight to her common sense, that's what. At least her panic was in perspective. She studied the roll and hiss of the

wide, fast-moving river. Whatever danger it held for her was nothing like the peril of letting herself care too much for this man.

"Just hold on, whatever happens," he advised.

As if any force on earth could possibly be stronger than her grip! If she could lower the panic level enough to speak, she'd tell him that.

"And don't forget to enjoy the ride." He looked way too confident, as if there wasn't a bit of danger.

Help, he was nuts. "I'm not sure about this, Mitch," she choked out. Translation: Let me off.

"That's only because you've never ridden rapids before."

"There's a reason for that."

"Sure, but you'll have the best time, and once you do, you'll want to do it over and over again."

"I seriously doubt I'll suddenly turn that loony."

She wanted to gaze at the shore with longing—if only she could see it. But her stubborn eyes wouldn't look past Mitch. She couldn't see anything but the solid granite lines of his face, the trustworthy honor that burned steadily in his hazel eyes and the unyielding strength as he held her safely against the river's might. His chuckle shot through her like winter thunder.

Every instinct within her shrieked at her to run to higher ground, quick, before he let go, before she was dashed on the rapids that lay ahead like a hungry predator.

But it was too late. Before she could protest, he was pushing her and her inner tube more deeply

into the river, toward the hungry, gurgling, dangerous current. The rocky beach floated farther away,
and safety with it. The undercurrent grew ferocious,
sucking at her feet, which were dangling off the end
of the tube. The river's gurgle became a menacing
low-throated growl.

Okay, time to get off now.

"M-Mitch?" She couldn't believe it. He'd released
his hold on her inner tube. He was letting her go.

While the current sped her away from him,
she watched him helplessly. Water sluiced off his
sun-browned skin as he hopped onto his tube. He
stretched out on the inflated tube with easy confidence, as if nothing rattled him, nothing troubled
him, as if he could do anything.

Her feelings for him were absolutely without a
doubt way too strong. She clutched the slippery sides
of the tube, fighting down panic on many levels, and
floated into the jet stream of the current. She sped
along so fast that the world whirred by in a blur of
green cottonwoods and amber wild grasses dry from
the midsummer sun, the green grass of the city park
and the clean pure blue of the river.

Her feelings were speeding along too, out of control, just like this inner tube she couldn't stop if she
tried—no brakes. The rapids were imminent, she
could clearly see the upcoming white crests of water
splashing over and around black protrusions of big
river rocks. She was going to hit them.

Oh, Lord, don't let me hit them.

God didn't seem to answer—how could He hear

her over the roar of the river? And suddenly there was a bump against the back of her inner tube. Mitch had caught up with her. He'd come to save her.

"Fun, right?" His wide, happy smile was a grin of a man who lacked all common sense. "You ain't seen nothing yet. Hold on!"

Hold on? To what? He was nuts. Absolutely nuts.

Her fingers squeaked along the rubber tubing as she tried to get a better grip. The river bucked up like a wild bronco and then bowed back down and up again, whirling her backwards and tossing her up into the air like the worst carnival ride. Suddenly she was spinning toward a fast-approaching hunk of granite that looked very capable of breaking her bones if she rammed into it.

But at the last minute, the white-frothing water steered her to the side of the boulder and with a swoosh rolled her around another. Somewhere behind her Mitch was whooping like a kid on a fair ride, but she couldn't see anything except the swirling water turning to bubbling foam. The rapids tossed her up and down without end, as if trying to shake her bones from her body.

With a last surge of effort, the river reared a final time, tossing her upward with such force that she soared into the hot summer air. Wow, it was like flying. The black ring of rubber shot from beneath her and out of sight and she was falling, gravity-bound, watching the swirling water rising up to meet her in a cool splash of wetness. It was like landing in happiness, then she was sinking deep.

A steely hand caught her forearm and stopped her descent. Mitch's hand, Mitch's touch, his protection as she whooshed to the surface, her pulse pounding with joy. Water sluiced down her face and she drew in a mouthful of air, laughing, as Mitch held her steady, treading water.

"You're right. That was fun." She swiped a wet hank of hair out of her eyes to see him more clearly.

Maybe for the first time. His short dark hair was plastered to his head and seemed to accent the strong high blades of his cheekbones, his straight nose and granite jaw.

But as he gathered her in his arms and helped her ashore, where her inner tube drifted, trapped against the bank, it was his touch that affected her. The shadows within her faded, and there was only light.

"How about another run?" Mitch asked, humor glinting in his hazel eyes because he already knew the answer.

Okay, so he'd been right. "I'll beat you there." She hooked her inner tube and started running along the grassy shore.

Hours later, Mitch took another bite of his hand-dipped ice-cream cone. Walking through the grassy public park with Kelly was pretty nice. "This has to be one of the best things on earth."

"This? An ice-cream cone?" The lowering slant of the sunlight brushed her with bronze. She tipped her

A Soldier for Christmas

head back, scattering the long, damp locks of golden hair. "It *is* good, but it's just an ice-cream cone."

"Are you kidding? This chocolate crust is real dark chocolate. The cone is bakery quality, it doesn't come out of a box. You can't get this just anywhere."

"It's good, sure." She ate her cone by peeling off the thick chocolate layer first, eating it piece by piece. "But there are probably thousands of places that sell something like this or better."

"See, you take it for granted." He resisted the urge to touch the wayward locks whipping in the wind across her face, to feel the silken strands against his palm. "That's because you can pick up an ice-cream cone all the time. When I'm deployed, I don't get things like this."

"And that makes it one of the best things on earth?" Kelly picked another curve of chocolate off the top of her cone. She was smirking, as if he greatly amused her.

"It's probably not one of the *very* best things, but it goes on my list anyway."

"What list?"

"The one I keep in my head. For nights when I'm with my team and we're hunkered down on some remote mountain in a blizzard, wet to the skin and half-frozen. There's no fire because we don't want the smoke and the flames. No tent, no dry clothes, nothing but a meal in a can. That's when I haul out my list and try to remember all the good things, so it doesn't seem as bad."

"Remembering ice cream is going to make you feel better in a blizzard?"

"Okay, right. I'll save that for the desert list. When it's 123 degrees in the shade, except there is no shade, then I'll remember this afternoon. How the river was cooling—not too cold, just right. The way you laughed when I pulled you up after the rapids. How this feels right now, eating ice cream and walking with you."

"It's the ice cream you'll remember. Not me." She blushed prettily.

Yep, he was hooked. Something more powerful than tenderness filled him up until it felt impossible to breathe. "Oh, I think there's a fair-to-middling chance I'll remember you."

Like he could ever forget.

He caught a dripping edge of his ice cream, but the rich crunchy outside and the melting chocolate center wasn't what filled his senses. "You could write to me, when I'm away. Right?"

"Write to you? Well, I suppose I *could* be persuaded."

"Okay, what'll it take? How about a burger with the works at that stand over there?"

"We just ate ice cream."

"But it's nearly five o'clock. I believe in eating dessert first."

"I believe in eating dessert any time you can." Kelly managed to keep her tone light, although her heart wasn't—not at all. She didn't want to think of him leaving.

"I'm going to miss—" She couldn't quite say the words.

"Yeah, me too." Without words, he understood.

Without words, they walked together, side by side. When he took her hand in his, it was all she could do to hold closed the locks on her already adoring heart.

Could it be true? Was the baby finally asleep?

With the infant snuggled in her arms, Kelly eased the rocking chair to a stop and studied Shannon's sweet cherub's face. Her eyes were closed, her rose-bud mouth relaxed, lost in dreams. Her warm weight felt utterly limp as she breathed in a slow, sweet rhythm.

It was amazing someone so small could cry so loud and long, but how could Kelly mind? Holding the little one and rocking her until she calmed was a precious thing. After all, teething, even with all the ways to soothe tender gums, was painful business.

As she carefully rose from the comfy chair, she watched to make sure that the baby didn't stir. With love, she eased Shannon into her snug crib, adorned with the cutest patterned sheets, and dodged the rainbow-colored mobile dangling overhead.

It would be so easy to start dreaming, Kelly thought, standing over the crib, not quite able to take a step away. Already her heart was forming a wish she could not give life to. And it was Mitch's fault for being so wonderful, so everything a girl like her could ever want.

At least she had good control over her heart. The last time she'd made fairy-tale wishes for true love Joe had been taken from her. She'd learned her lesson the hard way too many times. Fairy tales weren't real.

Taking care not to make a sound, she stepped back until she reached the doorway. So far so good. Since the baby didn't stir, Kelly continued on, padding quietly down the hall, past the older child's bedroom door, closed tight while he slept.

She made her way to the kitchen, and she couldn't help the happiness rising up inside her. What a wonderful day she'd had. Not only had she aced her test, thanks to a few extremely important pointers from Mitch last week, but she'd had the best time with him.

Her spirit still felt uplifted as she ran hot soapy water in the sink and started washing up the supper dishes. The faint aroma of frozen pepperoni pizza lingered in the air as she scrubbed the stubborn baked-on cheese off the cookie sheet.

She was rinsing the soap off when a faint electronic tune sounded in the far corner of the room, from her half-unzipped backpack slung over one of the kitchen chairs. Who would be calling her this late? It was after ten. Drying her hands as she went, she snatched her cell phone out of the pack's front pocket.

The ID screen only said Out of Area. Hoping it wasn't her mother trying to get hold of her, she answered tentatively. "Hello?"

"I know it's late." Mitch's baritone sounded short and strained. "I figured you'd still be babysitting."

"Yep, for probably another thirty minutes. You know, I'm still smiling. I had the best day."

"I know you did. Your eyes were shining."

"At first I thought I'd drown, what with all the near-death experiences."

"You didn't even come close to drowning. I wouldn't have let anything happen to you."

"I know. I had complete confidence in you. Otherwise I would have never let you drag me out into the middle of that river in the first place."

Yep, taking a chest full of shrapnel must feel just like this, Mitch thought. Deep, sharp cuts that exposed you clear to the heart. "We have new orders. We're leaving. I wanted to say goodbye."

"Wh-what? I thought you had another two weeks here."

The raw places in his chest seemed to throb, as fresh wounds did when air touched them. "Yeah. Orders change all the time. Believe me, this is not the way I want it, but in thirty minutes, I'll be on a bird out of here."

"Just like that?" In the background there was a faint scraping sound, like a wooden chair against linoleum. He pictured her clearly sitting down in that graceful way she moved and a crinkle digging in above her nose, the one he liked so much. Her voice became thin and concerned. "It's just so sudden. Is everything all right?"

"We lost a team and we're being brought in to replace them."

"That doesn't sound good. Y-you'll be coming back, r-right?"

He took a deep breath. *Please, Lord, help her to understand this.* He knew she had to be remembering how she'd lost Joe. "Believe me, I fully intend to come back. I've been doing this for a long time. I'm still here."

"But what you do sounds dangerous."

"I can't lie and say it isn't." He wanted to say this right, for Kelly's sake, ignoring the noise and bustle of his team packing up, all business. He was short on time. "We're well-trained and well-equipped. I know how to take care of myself and my team. You don't need to worry about me."

"Maybe I will anyway."

"No way. Put that energy toward something useful. Like acing your math final."

She didn't say anything.

That troubled him. She'd had a lot of people move in and out of her life. She still didn't trust him enough with those stories, but he could guess at what they were based on with what she'd already told him. In and out of foster care. Burying her fiancé. She'd known too much loss.

How did he make her see that he didn't plan on contributing to it? He didn't know. "No one can look ahead and see what's to come, but that's why we have faith, right?"

"Right. Faith is believing in things not seen. In

trusting that the Lord will work things out for the good of His faithful."

"Exactly. So have a little faith, okay? In God. And it wouldn't hurt to have some in me, too."

"I already do." Her heart felt heavier with each breath. Her chest tighter. "Y-you have my e-mail address. If you get lonely over there, you're always welcome to drop me a note."

"I get awfully busy. I—" There was a lot of sound in the background. He came back on the line. "I've got to go. I just wish—"

Oh, she, too, wished that he didn't have to go. "Be safe, Mitch."

"I will. Goodbye, Kelly."

I can't take one more goodbye, Lord. There was no way she could make herself say more to him, so she disconnected and sat in the silence and shadows.

By the time the plane had leveled out, the city of Bozeman was nothing but tiny pinpricks of light tossed in the velvety night. Mitch pressed forward against the cold glass window, trying to keep the city in view. Kelly was down there somewhere.

I needed more time with her, Lord. It was tough to wrestle down his frustration. While he believed the Lord caused things to happen for a reason, what good could come of leaving her now?

I didn't have enough time to win her heart. It was like starting something he'd never have the chance of finishing. Like a loose end, unraveling. In another two weeks, maybe it would have been a different story. Now, he figured he might never know.

The city lights faded to black. The glacier crests of the Rockies below shone luminescent in the moonlight. Emptiness filled him like the wide endless stretch of the night. The gnawing feeling he'd left everything vital behind ate at him.

Kelly would be done with her babysitting job by now. She'd probably be heading home. She'd disconnected without saying goodbye.

That couldn't be a good sign. Not a good one, at all.

So many regrets. He disliked every single one of them.

Images of their afternoon together stuck in his mind. How she'd dazzled him when he'd pulled her up out of the water. He could still hear her laughter. How tender she'd made him feel. How right she'd been in his arms. The vanilla scent of her shampoo.

How could it be that the day wasn't yet over and he already missed her?

This might have been God's leading, but Mitch also knew with absolute certainty that she was his heart's choice.

In the well-lit apartment parking lot, Kelly locked her car door and glanced around the dark vehicles to make sure she was safe. The only movement was the shadows of the trees when the breeze rustled them. She sorted through the keys on the ring as she walked up the sidewalk. High overhead an airplane rumbled. It was a passenger jet from the local airport, not a military plane, but she thought of Mitch heading toward places unknown. Toward dangers unknown. And that made her feel as vulnerable as an exposed nerve.

There was no comfort in the hot, still night as she unlocked the front door and stepped into the darkness. Cool air blew over her as she crept into the kitchen, careful not to make a noise. Lexie was probably asleep by now, she thought as she opened the fridge and pulled out an orange soda.

But there was no comfort from the sugary drink. While the bubbles hissed and popped in the stillness, she curled up in the overstuffed chair in the living room where the moonlight and the glow from the streetlights fell through the window and onto her.

Mitch's words came back to her, rubbing on the exposed nerves in her heart. *I get awfully busy. I—I've got to go.*

In other words, she shouldn't count on him writing to her. She remembered his saying it was rare for him to have much free time. So, he was going to be way too busy to keep in touch. And, in time, too busy to remember her.

And if that made her sad, it wasn't like she was going to admit it. This was just as well—and how things were meant to be. The way she wanted it. She was keeping herself here on the riverbank of life. And she was afraid that if she reached out for those good, rare blessings she wanted, they would be whisked from her grasp.

Just like always.

Just like Joe had been.

Her devotional was in her backpack, and she dug it out. She couldn't remember the morning's passage—it had been such a long day. She felt a craving for the Scripture and flipped to the morning's text.

I teach you what is for your good, and lead you on the way you should go.

She gazed out at the night stars. Mitch was out there somewhere.

Keep him safe, Lord. He's a good man. Please give him a piece of the happiness You have in store for me.

It was all she had to give him. Mitch had his life, she had hers. That was the way it was. But she would always hold close the memories of their friendship. She would always treasure the chance to have gotten to know such a good man.

Chapter Nine

Kelly sat in a quiet corner of the campus cafeteria in the wash of the early-fall morning sunlight. Outside the sparkling windows other students hurried to their classes. She took a sip of coffee and turned the page of her sociology book.

Deep in the pocket of her backpack, her cell phone began to ring. Probably Amy calling to confirm—or to cancel—babysitting for a few nights this week. Kelly flipped open her phone. It wasn't Amy. She didn't recognize the number, but it wasn't a local one.

She answered it, and popping static filled her ear. "Hello?"

"Can you hear me okay?" asked a deep, familiar baritone that sounded very far away.

No, it couldn't be. "Mitch? Is that you?"

"The one and only. I'm just glad you remember me. It's been a while since I've talked to you."

How did she tell him that the days of September

had slipped away like water down a drain, but he had been in her prayers every one of them. "You sound like you're calling from the moon."

"Just about. I feel like I'm in another world. There are no ice-cream cones here."

Oh, he sounded so good—so good and alive and strong…just like Mitch. She closed her eyes, and there he was in her mind's eye that day on the river. Standing waist-deep in water and grinning at her with a challenge. So larger than life and vital, looking as if nothing could hurt him. Of course, she knew that he was as vulnerable as anyone. "I can't believe it. I thought I'd never hear from you again."

"No way. You just try and get rid of me. I thought we were…friends."

"We are." The light in her heart brightened.

"I've got about ten minutes on this card. It has to be early there."

"It's twenty past seven in the morning, but I'm already on campus. Sitting in the cafeteria and trying to get some reading done before class. It's good to hear you. I've been—" Missing you. "—worried about you."

"Hey, I miss you. The guys I hang with aren't nearly as pleasing to the eye. How did the math final go?"

"I pulled an A. Thanks to you, but you don't want to hear about my classes."

"Sure I do. I put you in prayer every night. Even when I'm out with my team doing things I can't tell you about, in places I can't tell you about either. Let's just say you're on my list, Kelly."

"L-list?"

Mitch's chest hitched painfully at the uncertainty in her voice. Nearly four weeks had passed since he'd left, and yet everything came back in a single heartbeat. The way her honey-blond hair gleamed. The dark-blue strands in her jeweled eyes. How her smile lit up his world.

She was the one. Thousands of miles away and continents apart, mighty affection crashed through him like a tsunami.

Whatever he did, he couldn't let her know. Not yet. The last thing he wanted to do was to scare her. He cleared his throat. "The list of the best things, to get me through. You know: ice-cream cones, riding the rapids, walking in the sunshine with a good friend."

"Right. That list." She sounded relieved, relaxed.

He was glad about that. They were friends now, but in time, he thought they could be more.

Her gentle alto warmed. "You're on my list, too."

"That means a lot. You can't guess how much." He didn't know how to tell her how tough the past weeks had been. It was a different planet where he was, or it seemed that way, where the phone bank was a luxury, and the fact that he'd had a lukewarm shower and hot chow for the first time in three weeks felt like a blessing. So were phone cards. His time was ticking away, and he hated that.

"When you called me before you left last month, you mentioned a team that was l-lost."

He squeezed his eyes shut, briefly, to hold everything in. "Yep. No one died. They were lucky, but there were serious casualties."

"Anyone you knew?"

"Yep. All of 'em. Don't worry. Those guys in 3rd Recon aren't as superior as my platoon."

She heard the catch in his voice. "I suppose you're invincible, huh, Mr. Action Figure?"

"Nope, just very careful. I intend to make it back home. You liked floating the rapids so much, I thought I might make good on my threat to take you mountain-climbing."

"I'm going to hold you to that threat."

His voice rumbled with reassurance. "Then we've got a deal. I'll be here in camp for a bit. They have us training pretty hard, but I'll be able to e-mail."

The line was crackling worse. "Mitch, I can barely hear you."

"Time's up. I've got to—"

There was a click and then nothing.

Be safe, she added silently as she disconnected.

The noise of the cafeteria was increasing around her as more students filed in for a quick breakfast. The tables nearby filled with students who gathered in groups to talk or sit quietly alone with their books and their coffee.

How come Mitch had such a hold on her heart? It took all her effort to turn her attention back to the work before her. She kept going over their conversation, over the sound of his voice. She kept picturing him, so handsome and capable in his camouflage clothing. Her heart gave a tug of admiration.

Careful, Kelly. No dreaming allowed.

Her phone rang again. Foolish seeds of hope sparked inside her, but it was Amy's number on the ID screen. Life went on as it should—with school, work and babysitting.

She knew better than to hope for more, but she sure wanted to.

Mitch hung up the phone. The hootch around him buzzed with pieces of conversations between other soldiers and loved ones at home, making him feel more alone than ever. Kelly was just so far away.

He tried to picture her in a campus cafeteria, probably lots of tables and chairs, noisy talking and the clatter of flatwear and dishes. She'd said she was reading, but was she studying? Or reading her devotional? He should have asked more questions to fill in the missing pieces.

She'd probably bought a cup of coffee, but anything else? A muffin? A breakfast sandwich? What was she wearing? It could get pretty cool in Bozeman—probably a pair of jeans and one of those feminine cotton blouses she was always wearing. Maybe with a sweater. Was her hair pulled back in a ponytail with those little silken wisps curling around her face, or was it unbound, falling in a long sleek wave past her shoulders?

Not enough time. Not time on the phone and nowhere near enough time with her in Montana. When a man got down to it, there was never enough, not in a life, and he hated this feeling of regret. Of leaving things unfinished. His life had always been tidy, he liked things that way. It's what made him a good Force Recon marine. But the loose ends he'd left when he'd said goodbye to Kelly were ones he feared would unravel with distance.

There's not much I can do from here, he thought. His way of life was rugged and solitary, and there was no room for much else but his work. It would be simple just to let this go, whatever it was building between him and Kelly. That would be the safest route. That way he wasn't putting anything on the line. But he didn't want to move on from her, not deep down.

As uncertain as the path ahead was, he was committed. He was going to risk it all. She was far away, but he would do what he could.

He'd write her and he'd keep writing her until this tour was over and he was back on American soil.

While the noodles from her box of macaroni and cheese were boiling, Kelly set up her laptop on the dinette table in the eating nook and went online.

Should she be checking her e-mail? No. She had a ton of reading to do, but could she concentrate?

No way. Her conversation with Mitch had been on her mind all day. Of course.

Hearing his voice had done her heart good. Her day had been brighter as she hurried across campus from one class to another, took notes, grabbed a bite to eat on her way to her afternoon shift at the bookstore. Knowing that he hadn't forgotten her, that he still wanted to be friends, meant more than she wanted to admit to herself or to anyone.

She popped up from the table to give the noodles a stir—they were bubbling merrily on medium high—and then returned to study her screen. There was a new e-mail. Already? She couldn't believe her eyes. Her computer screen still looked the same—it wasn't her imagination. There really was an e-mail from Mitch. She opened it and started reading.

Kelly,

No hand-dipped cones here. Chow hall pizza isn't half bad, except there are no cheesy sticks. But no complaining there. It's a step up from the meals in a can I get when we're out. Base camp is basically a lot of tents, but we've got heat most of the time. I'm glad I got hold of you this morning. Good to hear a friendly voice from home. How did your classes go today? The next time you order pizza, eat a slice for me.
Mitch

The stove timer beeped a rhythmic electronic warning, dragging her away from Mitch's note. Already she felt happy as she drained the pasta, measured out the margarine and milk and stirred in the powdered cheese packet. Adding a generous sprinkling of pepper, she stirred until the cheese was warm and melted and dumped it onto a plate. On her way back to the laptop she grabbed a fork and sat down.

After a quick blessing over her food, she reread Mitch's e-mail, wondering what on earth to say back. He would probably be bored by her life; after all, he got to do all kinds of exciting things in a day. Her life was almost as boring as you could get.

She tried to picture living in a large camp of tents, but she could only imagine reruns of a seventies TV show that she'd watched over the years. Maybe it was something like that, sleep in one tent, shower in another, eat in another. If he'd mentioned the blessing of having heat that worked, then he had to be somewhere very cold.

She had no clue what to write. As she munched on her mac and cheese, she gazed out the window at the turning poplar leaves and the sunset blazing purple and magenta across the dome of the darkening sky. What would she say if he was standing in front of her?

Her heart stirred, and she started to type.

Mitch,
    You don't know what it means to me that we can keep our friendship going when you're so far away. I get pretty wrapped up with studying—don't be shocked—I'm a little bit of a study-aholic, to use Lexie's term. Between trying

to keep my A average and work enough hours to meet my monthly bills, I have about two hours left over in a week for a social life—which is mostly attending a weekly Bible study.

Lexie has been a blessing for a roommate because she tends to drag me places with her, like on Sunday afternoon. We went to the Museum of the Rockies with a couple of her friends and looked at fossils and Native American artifacts.

You're laughing, aren't you? Because that is so not a social life by most people's definition. The college group at church is having a singles' get-together at the town ice cream parlor next Friday night. Lexie has already told me she's meeting me after my shift at the bookstore and dragging me there. Should be fun.

Not only will I have a slice of pizza for you, but I'll make the sacrifice of eating a hand-dipped chocolate ice-cream cone for you, too. I'll suffer, sure, but friendship is worth it.

Blessings to you, and stay safe.

Kelly

P.S. What kind of meals come in a can?

As she polished off her meal, Kelly reread the e-mail, corrected spelling and sent it. It wasn't as if he'd have time to e-mail her for a while, but it felt good to write to him.

Maybe God had placed Mitch on her path because He knew how solitary her life had been since she'd buried Joe. Maybe He knew that Mitch needed a friend too, being so far from home and in danger.

She took comfort in that.

"Hey, I'm off to the library." Lexie burst out of her bedroom in a flurry. "Where did I put my card? I'm losing my mind. That's what I get for majoring in psychology. They say you gravitate toward what you need most, which is apparently therapy for me. Oh, now where did my keys go?"

"Over here." Kelly blinked to bring her eyes into focus, she'd been reading solidly for the past two hours. Night had fallen and the heat had kicked on. The weather was getting colder. She thought of Mitch and hoped that wherever he was, he was keeping warm. She grabbed the ring of keys on the coffee table by her mug of herbal tea and gave them a toss.

Lexie caught them. "Thanks. Oh, and I'd better leave the rent check with you now, or I'll totally forget tomorrow. I've got it written out and everything." She pulled a check out of her pocket and dropped it on the counter. "I'll be back late. Anything you need while I'm out? Okay, I'm gone. See ya!"

Alone once again, Kelly tried to sink into her reading, but no such luck. In theory, her mind should be occupied enough with her studies to completely shove out every last thought of Mitch Dalton.

The practical aspect was a little different. Since she was never going to be able to concentrate properly unless she checked, she popped online while she microwaved another cup of apple cinnamon tea. Like he'd had time to answer her. No, not when she hadn't heard from him in a month. He'd already called, he'd already e-mailed.

She was not going to analyze the fact that she was hoping he'd answered. Apparently, Lexie wasn't the only one in need of therapy.

What she was not going to do was to check. She was going to go on to the library's Web site and do a little preliminary research for her next paper. Then, when she was done, she'd check her e-mail account.

The computer made an electronic bleep. An instant message popped on the screen from Mitchell Dalton. Kelly, got time to type at me?

The light inside her brightened another notch. She started to type.

For you, Mr. Action Figure, sure. I didn't know your extensive scouting skills included the ability to instant message.

She hit Send and waited. In a few moments, his answer popped on the screen.

I know a lot of stuff. So, what's this about a singles' meeting?

Now why would he ask that? she wondered. He was probably interested in the ice cream. She typed, You know the creamery shop downtown?

He answered in an instant. They have the best banana splits.

They do, she agreed. I usually get the chocolate fudge sundae, the one they sprinkle peanuts on top.

His answer shot back, You're killing me. I just had an unrecognizable casserole. It tasted like tuna and creamed potatoes.

Yum, she replied. It puts my mac and cheese to shame.

She left the message to post while she grabbed her steaming cup of water from the microwave. When she returned to the table, Mitch's answer was waiting for her.

You didn't elaborate on the singles' thing. You said you didn't date.

She shook her head in disbelief. Mitch had been blatantly clear about only wanting a friendship with her, as she'd been with him. She typed, It's not a date. It's a church group function.

A singles' function. His reply was almost instant.

I go for the ice cream and fellowship. I don't think I'll ever date again, she wrote.

Why not?

She stared at his question. The fragments of her past began to whisper behind the locked places in her heart. She wanted to silence those whispers, but her fingers were typing the words before she thought them.

Because I've stopped believing that good things are meant for me. She hit Send and waited, watching the cursor blink and feeling the beat of panic pulse through her. That was way too honest, but it was too late to take back the words.

Mitch's answer came immediately. I don't believe that. Not for a single nanosecond.

Old wounds ached like a sore tooth as she steeled her heart and wrote the plain truth. Life isn't a fairy tale—at least my life isn't. End of discussion. You never answered the question in the e-mail I sent. What kind of meals do you get in a can?

Nice try, came his answer, but I'm not gonna let you change the subject like that. What happened with Joe?

Her hands shook as she typed an answer. Two Saturdays ago I went to put flowers on Joe's grave. He's been gone three years now.

Maybe that was being way too honest—for herself and for poor Mitch who was just wanting to hear about the ice cream shop back home.

Then came his unexpected reply. I'm sorry. I know how painful it is to lose someone you care about. If it happens often enough, there comes a time when you can't stand to let anyone else too close. Not one more time.

He knew. Kelly squeezed her eyes shut to hold the emotions inside. How did she answer him? Anything honest she could say would hurt too much.

More words appeared on the screen. I've lost a few buddies over the years. Men I respected and thought of as my brothers. It's never easy to understand why. You had to have been devastated.

Yes, she typed and then stopped. Emotions she'd frozen in place and tucked away seemed to melt like icicles, and the drip of fresh pain made her want to push Mitch away and keep pushing.

The pieces of the truth she'd buried, that she hadn't shared with anyone, lay exposed.

She typed, I was devastated, but some wishes aren't meant to come true. You don't want to hear about that.

He answered, Sure I do.

Just find the words, Kelly. She dug down deep, and found the strength. Prayed for the ability to keep the tears out of her eyes and the sorrow from her heart. She should just tell Mitch, and then he would quit bringing it up. Besides, maybe it would be better for her to release the pain, write it down instead of saying the words out loud.

She began to type. Joe was working as a firefighter. You know the terrible forest fires we had in the national forests a few summers ago?

Yep, they made the national news. Even I read about them. Didn't a couple of fire fighters die over there? One of them was Joe?

She took a gulp of air as Mitch's question scraped against her exposed, open wounds. Yes, she answered. An unexpected high wind kicked up and trapped him and two other members of his team. This happened eight days before we were to be married.

She hung her head. She couldn't type another word. When she was finally steady enough to wipe at her burning eyes and face the screen, Mitch's answer was there, waiting patiently for her. You must have thought you'd finally had a real home. You lost everything with Joe. I'm sorry for that.

It wasn't meant to be, she typed and hit Send, feeling the shadows in the corners press against the light, against her.

She'd fallen so in love with the idea of being married and of being welcomed into such a warm and loving family. The little girl who'd always felt alone and adrift had finally come home to a husband and a kind extended family. It was her most heartfelt dream.

And to stand in the church sanctuary silent with hope and promises, and to plan, instead of a wedding, a funeral. To tuck away the dreamy wedding gown of silk and lace that Joe's sister had sewn for her and realize that this is how it would always be.

Mitch's answer flashed onto the screen. You're not alone.

How was it that he could know the words she most needed? She felt alone, at heart, at spirit, down to the soul. She knew God cared, that He watched over her, but not even her unerring faith could chase away the loneliness that clung with hungry talons and would not let go.

More of Mitch's reply scrolled across the screen. "Yet it was our weaknesses he carried; it was our sorrows that weighed him down."

She recognized the passage from Isaiah. Those words were a comfort that helped to chase away the memories lying as vulnerable as an exposed root: memories of the little girl she'd been, the child with no stability or security, always wishing for someone to love her, just wanting to fit in, to belong to a real family.

The aftereffects of those memories left a bitter, cutting residue and her throat burned with unfelt emotions. She tried so hard to swallow them down, but they remained like a sticky mass, a tangle of feelings that she could not sort out. It took all of her effort to will the fragments of her past, of her memories, back into the locked room in her soul.

They typed at each other for another twenty minutes before he had to go. With training exercises awaiting him, he signed off, his heart heavy. He could feel the fragments of her broken dreams as sorely as if they were his own.

He missed her with a force so strong, he didn't want to examine it. But as he headed out into the bitter cold, and into the remote base camp of tents, not even the miles between them could break the connection he'd felt with Kelly.

His twisted-tight emotions roiling inside him began to unravel, thread by thread. He wanted to protect her. He wanted to comfort her. He wanted to make sure she was never alone. That she never hurt like that again. Overwhelming tenderness detonated like a cluster bomb, and he gritted his teeth as the explosion hit. There was no hiding from it. No denying it.

This love for her was as steady as an ocean's current. As steadfast as the northern star. And twice as enduring.

It remained through the day of exercises and all through the night and into each long absorbing day of hard work.

It did not relent.

Chapter Ten

With the light of a new morning, Kelly had nothing but regrets. She'd stirred up feelings that she hadn't intended to. What troubled her most of all was that she trusted Mitch enough to tell him.

It had been easier, sure, since he was so far away, and she hadn't had to actually say the words out loud. But talking about her loss of Joe was one thing. Feeling Mitch's understanding was another.

He was beyond wonderful for having listened to her so politely, when he'd probably expected a much lighter electronic conversation. He'd been way too close, ironically, seeing as he was half a world away. Without seeing her, without so much as hearing her voice, he'd been able to crack her careful defenses. Defenses she hadn't realized were breachable until he'd walked into her life.

There was an e-mail from Mitch.

Kelly,

Glad you let me steal time out of your studies last night. I didn't really know Joe back in high school. You know he was a year older and ran with a different crowd, but he was a good guy. I am sorry for the grief you've gone through. We lost a team member this past year, he and I met at boot and we were buds. It was like losing a brother. Nothing is quite the same again—it isn't meant to be.

Hang in there. Write me when you get a chance. They keep you pretty busy here, but when you stop moving, you miss home and everyone there. I'm glad we're friends.
Mitch

Kelly took a sip of her coffee, warmed through by his words. Relieved, too. She put aside her cup and started to type.

Mitch,

Talking with you was the best possible study break. I was worried I'd been too personal last night. I'm used to keeping the real painful stuff private. It's just easier to deal with that way. The psychology classes I've taken say otherwise, but it works for me.

I know you've known loss, too. I am sorry about your friend. I imagine, when you eat, sleep, work and train together, that builds an immeasurably strong friendship.

I'm running late this morning, I should *not* be online but I was glad to see a note from you in my inbox and wanted to say thanks for listening. I'm pretty glad we're friends, too. I've got to go or I'm going to be stuck in the traditional 7:45 a.m. campus traffic jam.

Plus, then I'll get the farthest out parking spot and have a stitch in my side if I have to run to get to class on time. I have a policy on running, jogging or any kind of exercise—I am firmly against it.

Have a great day and stay safe.
Blessings, Kelly

Dear Kelly,

What? A no-exercise policy? That would never work for me. I have more of an exercise-only policy. I've been on the go since 0500 and it's after 2000. One hundred percent of my workday is physical. Did you make it to class on time? Inquiring minds wanna know.
Mitch

Dear Mitch,

I have a strict no-tardy policy to go along with my no-skipping-class policy. I'm sadly scholastically minded. I often sit in the front row, take copious notes and then study my notes that evening.

Scary, I know. I'm lucky my roommate still talks to me. She says I'm way too intense so that's why she hauls me to social events. There's an on-campus thing, Shakespeare in the Grass, that the drama department does, weather permitting. We're going to see *The Tempest* and then hit the pizza buffet. The play is free and there's a great student discount at the pizza place. So it's a night out that fits a student's budget perfectly. Keeping you in prayer, Kelly

Hi there, Kelly,

Ice cream and pizza in the same week? See, I'm fishing for information. How did the singles' thing turn out?
Mitch

Dear Mitch,

I had a banana split with extra fudge sauce in your honor. Lexie and I got together with our friends Jessica and Rose. Sadly, the same guys keep coming to these events and no one is actually apparently going to date them, so the singles' thing is a misnomer. Plus, I am, like, three years older than any guy there, since I'm working my way through school so slowly. Jessica and

Rose are coming to the play tomorrow, and because these guys overheard us talking, now the entire singles' group is coming. Stay tuned. I'll let you know if this blond perfect-looking dude that really likes Lexie actually talks her into dating. Lexie has a strict no-dating policy too. She thinks guys are untrustworthy.
Sincerely, Kelly

Dearest Kelly,
    Hey, I'm trustworthy.
Mitch, the most trustworthy guy ever.

Mitch,
    I never said you weren't. Lexie actually gave you two thumbs up, a rare review. I think you won her over with the cheesy sticks.
Blessings, Kelly

Hey, Kelly,
    What can I say? Buying cheesy sticks is always the sign of a quality individual. I'm kidding, but there's no way you can tell from here. I've never seen a Shakespeare play. My impression is a stuffy production where guys wear tights. Doesn't sound dignified to me. I prefer something with a lot more action. Hey, is watching Shakespeare better outside or something?
Mitch, the uncultured

Mitch,

You might be able to scale a glacier on a mountain peak or know how to scuba dive and you've probably done that sliding-down-the-rope thing from helicopters, but you don't know excitement until you've experienced Shakespeare. There's a lot of action. If you're ever in this neck of the woods again, and school is in session, I'll drag you to one.

The play we went to this evening starts with a ship that wrecks at sea in a storm, and right when it was supposed to be raining in the play, it really did start to rain. There were cold storm gusts while the characters were getting blown around by the storm in the play. It was really cool, actually, but we were drenched. Lightning started up, and they had to call the production off due to the real tempest. We (the girls) hit the pizza place, stuffed ourselves with pizza and cheesy sticks and talked girl talk until about nine.

How did you spend your Saturday night?
Grace and peace, Kelly

Dearest Kelly,

Cleaning my gun. Then we had a rousing match of chess. I won every match except the championship of the night. It was a close call, but I fell in a brilliant move by Luke after an hour of battle. At least I went down with honor.

Cheesy sticks and pizza? I need details.
Take good care okay? Mitch

Dear Mitch,

We had our pick of every variety of pizza. I make it a policy to have a slice of each kind—the works, the meat supreme, the veggie, the Hawaiian, pepperoni, sausage and pepperoni. You name it. All but the cheese. The owner always boxes up the leftover pizza when the buffet ends and distributes it to the students. He's an alumni and says he gets the student budget thing.

This is why we had cold pizza for breakfast. I went for the straight pepperoni but Lexie prefers the pepperoni and sausage mix for a higher protein breakfast. And guess what we had for lunch after church? You guessed it. Pizza. Enough calories to see me through a long afternoon study session. Do you get Sundays off?
I'm still keeping you in prayer, Kelly

Kelly,

Only in the sense that we're fragged for a mission so this afternoon is prep. I'll be out of range for a while, but I'll e-mail you when I get back. It's rumored we may do that sliding-down-the-rope thing from a helicopter that you mentioned before.
Thanks for your prayers, Mitch

Dearest Mitch,

I know, I have an amazing lack of military vernacular. Keep your head down. Isn't that what they always say in those old war movies? Stay safe.

Sending even more prayers, Kelly

Dearest Kelly,

Count on it. You're in my prayers too.

Mitch

Why did stat class always give her a headache? Because math was involved, that's why.

Kelly rubbed her forehead as she followed the stream of students searching for lunch. Noise from the lounge drifted into the busy corridor and Kelly picked up the concerned voice of a newscaster.

"Today, three marines were injured, when—"

The noise surged around her and drowned out the televised report.

She cut through the student traffic flow to the doorway of the lounge, where students sat with their lunch or books, listening to a cable news network. On the screen in the corner, she could make out a picture of a burning car in a desert-city street before the scene flashed on to other international news.

Mitch was in the mountains and not in the desert, so that news report wasn't in any way about him. But that didn't stop her fear or her worry for him. That was reasonable—he might think he was invincible, but he was wrong. He was not made of titanium.

The roar of the passing students drew her away from the lounge. She wanted to be able to find a table and the longer she stood in the hallway, the less likely that was going to be. She joined the herd moving toward the turnstiles at the cafeteria. The buzz of conversation, the clatter of trays and crunch of the ice machine echoed around her. It had been nearly five hours since Mitch's e-mail, and you'd think she'd stop thinking about him by now, but no.

There he was, front and center. What did she do about that? She cared about him, of course she did. He was a friend. A friend, nothing more, right?

As she grabbed a tray and maneuvered through the crowd toward the beverage dispensers, Mitch remained in her thoughts along with the strength of emotion she'd felt when they were online together. She missed him. It was that simple.

Not only had Mitch slipped beneath her defenses as if they were made of water, but he'd made her care about him. He'd made such an impression, he'd been such a good friend, that she missed having him present in her life.

It was certainly okay to care about a friend, so she shouldn't let it bother her that he was a male friend, right?

She grabbed a large cup and headed to the ice machine. She waited for the guy in front of her to finish. Her chest felt so torn apart, it hurt to breathe. Over the rattle of the ice and the sluice of lemonade into her cup, she tried to stop thinking. Tried to stop feeling.

She grabbed a container of strawberry yogurt and headed for the checkout lines. She chose the shortest one, but it was still a wait. As she inched toward the cashier, she didn't see an available table anywhere. Maybe she'd head outside and find a place in the shade, enjoy the last of the sunshine before it became too freezing to sit outside at all. Maybe she could get a start on her assigned reading. She had a huge paper due soon. *That* was what she should be thinking about—not a man God couldn't mean for her to have.

Mitch was far away preparing for a mission. She had no idea what that would be like, but it couldn't be easy or safe. She remembered how he'd mentioned tough nights sleeping in the elements, or creeping through enemy territory not knowing what waited ahead. How he'd said he needed a friend.

Well, that was what he was going to get.

Focus, man. Mitch crept forward with his team, silent and vigilant, weapon in hand. He heard something.

The clear thin air seemed to make the predawn shadows look like liquid silver hugging the eastern side of the jagged mountain range. Bitter wind sliced across his face as he clenched his right fist and held it close to his chest. The team froze, sinking into the brush. His team members kneeled, facing outward, their backs to one another, defensive.

No sound. Nothing. That was troubling. He waited through long minutes until he heard it again. Mitch exhaled completely before speaking so his whisper would carry no real sound. "Someone's coming."

Every sense alert, reading the shadows, becoming part of the hillside, he waited. Mitch was confident whoever it was would pass on by without noticing his team. With any luck, they might get some scoop on the insurgent force in the area.

Low on the horizon the stars began to wink out as pale-gray light made the landscape stand out in black relief. The inky shadows turned from black to leaden gray, and dark purple brushed the high nearby peaks. Dawn was coming. They waited.

For one brief instant, a single thought pierced his concentration. Kelly. Half a world away, she was sound asleep, safe in her apartment.

The last stars faded as dawn came in its quiet glory. The light did not touch him as he remained motionless in the bitter cold, still waiting.

The cold autumn night temperatures nipped at Kelly's fingers as she fitted the deadbolt key into the door. Her ears were freezing, too, as she hadn't bothered with a hat or mittens for the short trek from the car to the apartment. Not her most brilliant move. What could she say? It had been a seriously busy week.

Shivering, Kelly let the storm blow her inside, fallen leaves raining down behind her as she closed and relocked the door. The air was chilly here too, although definitely not as cold as outside. She shrugged out of her coat.

"Sorry, I turned the heat on as soon as I got home," Lexie called from the kitchen. "But as I only got in about five minutes ago, it's still sixty-three degrees in here."

"What is that incredibly amazing aroma?"

"The upscale hot chocolate I love but can't really afford. My mom sent a care package today. Do you want chocolate raspberry, chocolate mint or chocolate hazelnut?"

"The raspberry one, please." Kelly dumped her backpack in the living room, where an opened cardboard box sat in the middle of the coffee table. All kinds of good things were exposed. "Your mom went all out."

"She wanted us to have good study food for midterms coming up. We'll be snacking off that for weeks. Hey, about an hour ago someone called for you." Lexie hit the timer on the microwave. "A certain handsome soldier."

"Mitch? He said he'd e-mail, not call. He's okay, right? He wasn't calling because he was hurt or anything?" She was talking way too fast. "I can't believe I missed his call. Why didn't he try me on my cell?"

"Oh no, he sounded perfectly macho and fine to me." Lexie leaned against the counter and smirked. "He was awfully eager to talk to you. In fact, when I told him you were working until eight, he said he'd call back between eight-thirty and nine. And guess what time it is right now?"

Kelly's gaze flew to the wall clock. "Eight twenty-nine."

He was going to call! Excitement at being able to talk to him had her heading to her room. "If it rings, I'll answer the extension in here."

"I'm glad you and he are *just* friends."

Was that a hint of teasing she heard in Lexie's voice? But the electronic jangle of the phone made her forget Lexie's comment as she dashed the rest of the way down the hallway and into her room. She dove into her reading chair, snatched the receiver from its cradle and realized even as she said it, she was betraying her feelings way too much. "Mitch?"

"Yeah, it's me." His chuckle rumbled, wonderfully masculine and familiar, one of her very favorite sounds. "I'm glad I caught you. I thought for sure Lexie would answer and tell me that I didn't have to call at exactly eight twenty-nine."

Maybe she wasn't the only one who'd missed their friendship. That was nice, wasn't it? She leaned far enough, and stretched the cord so that she could nudge the door closed. "So, you're back all in one piece? No worse for the wear?"

"Well, I don't know about that. There isn't such a thing as a piece-of-cake mission, not on Force Recon, but it went like clockwork. Lasted longer than we thought. It's snowing where I am and hard enough that we're pulling snow-shoveling duty. I'm gonna need snowshoes just to get to the chow tent tonight."

"We haven't had a single flake here yet. What can you tell me about what you've been up to?"

"Not much, seeing as how it's classified, but I can say that I continue to win the best-cup-of-C-4-coffee honor in the team, twelve missions running. Luke thought he came close this time, but there's a talent to it he lacks."

"You're just naturally gifted, huh?" That made him laugh, warmed her heart, right down to her soul. "First I have to ask. What is C-4 coffee?"

"It sounds like extra-explosive caffeine, doesn't it? Nah, we can't have a fire to cook on, the smoke would definitely give us away, thereby ruining the stealth aspect of our mission. So we light teaspoon hunks of C-4 on fire and cook over the flame. It takes a lot of practice to make that perfect cup of morning coffee."

"You're kidding me, aren't you? You can't cook with explosives. Can you? It doesn't sound sane."

"Now I never said I was sane." That made him laugh. "I'm telling you the truth. It's how we heat our cans out of our MREs, Meals Ready to Eat. It makes whatever is inside the can—no one can tell for sure—taste almost edible. But when you're hungry enough, you don't really care."

"That's why you were so interested in my pizza when we were instant messaging."

"There's a lot of things I miss when I'm over here." Pizza was the least of those things. She'd gone right to the top of his most-missed list. After spending the last two months hunting down terrorists, a physically and mentally tough duty, being able to hear the goodness of her voice was a true luxury. "I'm already running out of things for my warm-thoughts list."

"That sounds serious."

"Yep, I don't want to be forced to head out on my next mission with a diminished list."

"Wow, that would border on a crisis." The smile was in her voice.

Mitch's chest twisted tight. "Help me out, would ya? You could send me suggestions in e-mail. That way I could fortify my puny list with all kinds of real-life details."

"Trust me, my real life isn't all that splendid."

"Hey, I think so. Besides, I had a long list prepared, and I've gone through it already."

"It must be pretty rough and pretty cold where you are right now. You know I'd be happy to do anything I can for you. Be-because you're such a good friend."

He loved that hitch of emotion in her voice. Yeah, he thought, he had the same problem. He was starting to care way too much for safety's sake. And that was all right with him.

"Friends ought to help each other when they can." Her heart was in her voice.

He liked that. "I'd like to hear about all the good things in your life that shouldn't be taken for granted. For instance, the heat in your apartment."

"It's a lovely thing. You turn on the thermostat and the place warms right up. So, are you sure you want to hear about all the warm blessings in my life? I'll probably bore you."

"Not a chance." Caring like this was nice, but it was also a little like watching a grenade roll toward him, closer and closer, about to go off and there was nowhere to escape. All he could do was brace himself for it to blow.

"Then I'll send you an e-mail every day and tell you about the good things in my life, if you do the same."

"I'll be scarce, but when I'm in, I'll send you my daily compilation. How's that?"

"Perfect."

Yep, that pretty much described how he felt, too.

As they talked through the two hours of his calling card, he couldn't help feeling they became closer with each passing minute. It was nice. Real nice.

Chapter Eleven

It was seriously late, nearly midnight on a Friday night, and they'd been slammed at the bookstore, and closed up nearly an hour later than usual. But Kelly wasn't about to renege on her promise to Mitch.

As her laptop dialed in, she tiptoed around the kitchen and grabbed an orange soda from the fridge and a bag of iced animal cookies Lexie's mom had sent. There was a sticky note on the bag that read, "Kel, eat these please, before I go up another pant size."

Misery loves company, apparently, or at least the diet-challenged. While she munched on an iced elephant, she checked her inbox. There was an e-mail from Mitch.

Dearest Kelly,

Hiya. Here's my list from today. One. Never take a small snowfall for granted. When twelve inches falls in a twelve-hour period, you learn what else to never take for granted.

Two. Your back remaining pain-free and limber.

Three. Food you recognize. They said it was taco-seasoned hamburger, but we were skeptical, as the refried beans looked the same.

Four. Never take for granted sleeping through the night.

What's your list?
Keeping you in prayer, Mitch

That man sure could make her smile. Kelly sipped her soda and sat at the table, trying to stop the memories of their talk last night. He'd had her laughing for nearly an hour solid. He'd said nothing notable, he was simply being Mitch, and she loved his sense of humor.

He made her feel as if she'd been filled with stardust. Even now it was a wonder she didn't glow like the Milky Way.

She started typing.

Mitch,

First on my list. Iced animal cookies. Not great for your warm-things list, but they go perfectly with any hot drink. Coffee. Tea. Cocoa.

Second. Sunshine on your face. It was a perfect late-autumn day today. You know how the mid-afternoon sun gets toasty warm, even though there's a chill in the wind? The air smells woody and morning frost smelled like winter. And all day long there's the crisp crackly frost on the ground.

How am I doing?

Third. The quiet right before midnight. When you've had a long hard day, and you sit in the shadows and let the peace settle around you. There's a half moon mid-zenith, shining as orange-yellow as a harvest moon. It makes the glacier caps on the mountains shimmer like opals. It's the perfect time for praying. It feels as if the angels are leaning over, listening extra hard.

Tonight, when I say my prayers, I'll put you in them. Be safe.

Your friend, Kelly

Kelly hit Send. And because it *did* feel as if the angels were waiting, she bowed her head and prayed from her heart.

While racking a round into the chamber of his weapon in the base camp's firing pit, Mitch felt a strange tug in his chest. Not like a kick of adrenaline, but this was a slow steady burn like a star winking to life in a twilight sky.

A snowflake brushed his cheek and as he cradled the familiar weight of the MP-5 in both hands, he knew that back home, Kelly was awake and thinking of him.

This relationship thing was still like driving in the dark, but at least he wasn't alone.

Dear Mitch,

Hi. The list of good things continues: Fellowship. The college group at church. We're too old for youth group and too young for the women's groups, the women there are married, and if not, then they are at least adults with real lives. College is that sort of in-between place. So we stick together, firmly bound by worries over our studies, grades, professors and what-are-we-going-to-do-when-we-grow-up kind of things. We had volunteered to help with the autumn harvest festival, which we have for the kids' Sunday-school groups on Halloween, so the kids have a good place to go for that evening. Our group is making the candy bags.

So, picture about twenty college kids sitting around the multi-purpose room talking and stuffing gallon-sized zipper bags with miniature packages of M&Ms and little Snickers and, my personal favorite, Whoppers. Sadly, some of the candy never made it into the bags. Needless to say, we were all extremely sugar-buzzed by suppertime and had to go out and buy more candy to replace what we'd consumed.

I'll keep you in prayer. Stay safe.
Kelly

Dear Kelly,

Hey, I love Snickers and candy corn. I once ate an entire pound bag of them, and Mom had the biggest conniption. I was six, and after zipping around the house full-speed for thirty minutes, I got seriously sick. I learned my lesson. Sadly, I had many such lessons to learn as a little kid.
Mitch

Dear Mitch,

You? I find that hard to believe.
Blessings, Kelly

My Dear Kelly,

Believe it. The most memorable lesson was the coronary I gave my mom when I was four. I climbed the rock wall of the living-room fireplace to the top—all two stories. My little sweaty handprint is still on the cathedral ceiling. I can still hear Mom, over twenty years later, scolding, "Mitchell James Dalton, *what are you doing*? You get down here right this minute!"
Sending prayers, Mitchell James Dalton

Dear Mitchell James Dalton,

So, you're telling me you were trouble right from the start? And your poor mom. She didn't deserve that.
Kelly

Dearest Kelly,

That's what she says, too. But I always tell her the apple doesn't fall far from the tree.
Mitch

Shivering from the morning cold, Kelly slid into her usual chair in the middle of the auditorium class-room, balanced her to-go cup of coffee on the desktop and lowered her backpack to the floor at her feet.

A glance at the clock over the door told her she had fifteen minutes before class started. Perfect! She'd had such a great time e-mailing back and forth with Mitch over the last few weeks, that she'd been collecting ideas for her list on the walk to campus.

She set her laptop on the desk and started a letter to send later, when she was on break at work.

My Dear Friend Mitch,

Eggnog lattes. I had the very first one of the season from the coffee shop at the corner of campus. Sweet creamy eggnog meets hot soothing coffee. Whoever invented this drink is a certifiable genius. It's perfect on a crisp November morning to warm you clear through, which leads me to the next thing on my list.

Frosty wintry mornings, the kind where white frost has settled everywhere and on every-thing—tree branches, crisp fallen leaves, car windshields, and it glitters when the sun hits it. Little waves of evaporation rise up from the early-morning streets, and the blades of grass crunch beneath your shoes. The cold burns your face and your breath rises in cloud-like puffs. There's a peaceful joy to walking to your first class on a morning like this—with an eggnog latte.

Kelly paused over the keyboard. It was an odd thing, how different she felt whenever she was thinking about Mitch, or writing to him, or simply hearing his voice. The shadows and difficult memories she hid behind lock and key faded away, and her heart felt whole.

A movement over the top of the screen caught her attention. It was Lexie, on her way to her class down the hall. She dropped into the empty seat next to Kelly. "Hey, roomie. You look studious. Oh, a letter to that soldier of yours. Nice."

"He's not mine. You know that."

"Sure. Just friends. I get it." Lexie rolled her eyes, good-naturedly. "Hey, I saw the note you left on the message board. I'm in. What time do you want a shopping buddy? And what are we shopping for?"

"Your mom's care package inspired me. I want to send something like that to Mitch."

"Great idea. Where is he stationed, do you know?"

"He only said it was a remote base camp, but I think the location is classified."

"Cool. I've never known anyone before who was

classified. Ooh, I'll think of a list of stuff while I'm trying not to fall asleep in class. Which I've gotta get to. Adios." She rose, hoisting her backpack onto her shoulder. "How about in front of the library, around eleven?"

"See ya there." One glance at the clock and the students streaming through the doorway told her that she didn't have time to write anymore.

But she was going to start a list of her own, too. He was going to get the most fun care package ever. She hated to think of all the hardships he lived with every day. By choice and by duty, she understood that, but still. It was a sacrifice to be so far from home, and she owed him a little happiness in return for what his friendship had given her.

Just when she'd thought her heart would be as if in shadows forever, Mitch had come along and unknowingly made her feel joy again.

Yep, wherever he was, whatever he was doing, she owed him. Big-time.

The medevac's *whop-whop* faded into the silence of the high-mountain Afghan night and Mitch gave one last thought homeward as he moved out with his now three-man team. Luke had been shot during their ambush.

Not good. His team hadn't been standing still for more than a couple of minutes while they'd loaded up Luke, but already they were all shivering.

"Pick up the pace." They had to put in as much distance as they could as quickly as they could, because the helicopter was like a flashing neon sign to the terrorists, hey, look over here.

At least the storm blowing in would eventually cover their tracks. They had a long hard walk through thigh-deep snow. There was nothing like a fast hike with their packs on their backs to get the blood pumping again.

Kelly. There she was, like a steady candle's flame burning intractably against the dark. Right in his heart, and that light did not fade even as his every thought and his entire focus was on staying alive and completing his mission.

By the time this was over, he was going to forget what warm felt like. But he knew that light would still be burning.

The first frozen pellets of snow tapped off his shoulders. Yeah, it was gonna be a tough night.

With fifteen minutes to spare, Kelly pulled into a spot in the employees' parking behind the store and slid to a careful stop. Gray skies spat freezing drizzle, and a fine coating of ice gleamed on everything.

But did she care? Nope. Her boots skidded as she stood, but she managed to keep her balance as she grabbed her backpack and the huge shopping bag full of Mitch's stuff from behind the seat. It was heavy—she and Lexie had totally blown her budget—but she couldn't wait for him to see all this.

Happiness filled her up and she hardly noticed the drip of ice against the back of her neck as she struggled past the door and into the warmth of the building.

"I'm glad you made it in one piece. It's horrible out there." Katherine looked up from her book, propped open on the lunchroom table before her. She looked elegant, as always, in a slim black blouse and skirt, and her eyes lit up with interest over the bag. "Hey, you've been shopping. Did you get anything good?"

"Lots of stuff, but not for me." She dumped her pack on the floor by the employee closet and set the bag on a corner of the table. "Would you mind if I used one of the empty boxes from yesterday's shipment? I'm sending this to a friend."

"Sure. This wouldn't happen to be for your marine, would it?"

"Oh, he's not my marine." Just saying that aloud made her feel…strange.

"You mean you aren't staying in touch with him?" Katherine peeked into the bag. "We're talking about that drop-dead gorgeous guy with the shoulders of steel, right?"

"That would be the one. We're e-mailing now and then. And he called me."

"Good." Katherine seemed sedate as she rifled through the bag, but there was a subtle glint in her eye.

Kelly didn't miss it or the meaning behind it as she removed her coat. "He's just a friend."

"Right. Of course he is." Katherine didn't look convinced. "Where is he stationed?"

"He's overseas at a base camp. I'm guessing in Afghanistan or somewhere close to there. He said he couldn't say. He's on something called Force Recon."

"Oh, I know what that is. I used to be engaged to a guy whose brother was a Force Recon marine. Those are the real stealthy guys. I know Trevor did everything from deep-ground reconnaissance to counterterrorism. The training is more extensive than for the SEALS, I think. That's like, wow."

Kelly was starting to have the same opinion about the man. "That would be Mitch."

Katherine marked her page and put her book aside. "You know, we don't have a single customer. The weather is keeping everyone away. Why don't we start going through the store? I'm sure there a few things we can find that your marine would like. Some of the Christmas shipments have started to come in, and there's a lot of fun stuff. C'mon."

"He's not my marine." Why did the pieces of her lost dreams seem to ache when she said that? But Katherine apparently wasn't listening, she'd already swept out of the room.

Katherine was right, there was a lot of good stuff. As they sorted through the boxes waiting to be inventoried and shelved, Kelly couldn't get her mind off her boss's words. *Your marine,* she'd called Mitch.

It was really strange, because Lexie had called him *that soldier of yours* earlier this morning. It was like a clue from heaven—except that was totally not possible. No way. It wasn't what she wanted; it wasn't what Mitch wanted. Not rationally, anyway.

But, in truth, her heart longed for more than friendship. The little girl inside her, always alone and wanting to belong, longed, too.

If only there was a way he *could* be my marine, she thought. It was a wish that came from her heart, where she could not afford to start wishing. Only pain came from that.

She'd lost enough. Mitch was her friend. When he was done with his tour of duty and stationed in California, which he called home, he wouldn't be needing a friend. He wouldn't be needing her.

It was best to be practical. It was the only way to protect her heart. She was alone.

And that was how it was meant to be.

But as she sorted through the new stock, which would be perfect for stocking stuffers or a care package, she couldn't help the smallest hope in her heart that wherever he was, he was safe. And, did she dare hope that he was remembering her?

If he'd had a more miserable night, Mitch didn't want to think about it. His turn at watch was over and as he huddled into his sleeping bag and stared at the tarp tied overhead to keep off the falling snow, he shivered hard. Now, if he could only warm up enough to fall asleep, he'd be happy.

Not so easy. The frigid chill from the permafrost he'd bedded down on seeped through the bottom layer of the sleeping bag. He let his mind wander to that summer afternoon with Kelly. It had been hot that day, so hot it warmed to the bones. He tried to remember how that felt, the warm lush green grass, the sunshine so hot and bright it sizzled across the river water onto his skin, but he couldn't visualize it. The images remained in the background, kind of fuzzy and distant.

What he remembered, as clearly as if he were in Montana right now, was Kelly. The rippling sound of her laughter when he'd scooped her out of the river. How good it had felt to have her at his side as they'd walked through the park. She'd looked pretty as could be in the university T-shirt and denim cut-offs she'd worn, and her sneakers had squeaked in the grass, still damp from the river.

He remembered how the sunlight had brushed her with bronze, making her blond hair blow loose ripples and shine like gold. How she'd eaten her dipped cone by peeling off the thick chocolate layer first, eating it in dainty bites.

He tried to imagine her right now, using what she'd told him about her life. Her morning classes would be over. She'd probably be starting her shift at the bookstore. Maybe she'd have an eggnog latte to keep her warm, and she'd be ringing up sales in the store, chatting with the regular customers, or bowed over one of her schoolbooks during the lulls.

While he thought of her, the misery of the frigid cold and the hard day's exhaustion released its hold on him and he slept.

Chapter Twelve

The low squeak of a door startled Kelly out of her thoughts. She looked up from the final printed draft of her research paper. She'd been concentrating so hard, she was surprised to see the gray light of dawn sneaking around the closed blinds and her room-mate stumbling in her robe and slippers toward the bathroom.

"How long have you been up?" Lexie asked on a big yawn.

"Since five. I keeled over about one and thought I'd get up early and get this proofed and printed before I left this morning. Ha." At least, it had seemed reasonable in the wee hours of the morn-ing, but in the light of day, not so much. "Not as easy as I thought."

"Tough. I'll be you next week. I've *got* to start the paper that's due." Lexie wandered into the bathroom, yawning.

It was contagious. Kelly stifled a yawn as she

spotted a typo and turned to the computer to correct it. The printer she'd set up on the corner of the table whirred and spat out the corrected page. She forged ahead with her reading.

Time kept ticking past and when finally she was satisfied with her printed copy, Lexie was out of the bathroom, hair wrapped in a towel and grabbing a container of yogurt from the fridge. "Kelly, you need any help?"

"No. Ta-da! I'm done." With not a second to spare. She had just enough time to grab a quick shower, pack up and race out the door.

It didn't occur to her until she was bundled up and scraping the thick sheet of ice off her windshield, that she'd forgotten to check her e-mail. Well, it was too late now. She'd faithfully sent an e-mail every day, and she hadn't gotten a response since she'd shipped off the package last week. She'd spent the last six days trying not to think of him. And she'd failed.

And now here she was thinking of him again and feeling confused and turned upside down and vulnerable all at once.

She missed him. As a friend, right?

But, as she circled around to the rear window and began to chip away at the stubborn sheet of ice, she was no longer sure.

No answer.

Mitch swiped his hand over his face. Disappointment hit him like a brick. He'd thought for sure there would be another day's e-mail, sent like all the others. But for some reason she'd skipped the last two days, and now this morning.

Why? *Lord, I'm too far away. You gotta help me here, I'm begging. Don't let her start drifting away.* Considering his current altitude, he was closer to heaven, but Mitch didn't get a sense that God was hearing him any better for it.

He felt lost as he sent his e-mail. Kelly and her world of brightness and sweetness, of eggnog lattes and studying and college-life groups no longer seemed real at all. One of his best friends had been evacuated to a hospital, and while they'd succeeded in their ambush, they had paid a price.

He'd reread her e-mails, he'd saved every one, listing all the good things in her daily life. But even reading her words didn't make him feel as connected to her as he once had. He wanted to hear her voice. He needed to hear it. But, when he counted ahead to calculate her time, it was about eight o'clock in the morning. She'd probably be seated in her first class, bright-eyed and ready to take copious notes.

He bit back the frustration. He'd try her later, after he hit the rack and got some much-needed sleep. Maybe she would have found his e-mail by then and responded.

"I guess our Christmas rush has officially started." Katherine sounded exhausted as she locked up her till. "I'm going to take my lunch now that we seem to have quieted down for a moment. I'll be in the back. Page me if you get overrun, okay?"

"Are you kidding? It's two o'clock and you've been running since well before I got here." Kelly looked up from where she knelt before the point of purchase displays near the front counter. "You just go put your feet up, get something to eat and relax. You deserve it. Whatever happens up here, I can handle it for a bit. Ava should be coming in any time to help out."

"Yeah. Send that sister of mine back when she gets here, all right?" Katherine grabbed her book from beneath the counter and tapped away in her heels.

Kelly kept stocking. While the sound system played instrumental hymns, she replenished the bookmark display, moving just as fast as she could. The coupons Spence had printed in several of the local church papers had brought in more business than they'd expected. And she still had the card section to get back up to snuff before the next wave of customers hit.

It looked as though there wouldn't be much of a chance to study from here on out. Or, she thought sadly, a chance to log onto her account, using her laptop in the break room, to check her e-mail. Not that Mitch was likely to answer. He was probably busy climbing mountains, rappelling from helicopters, practicing his marksmanship and saving the world. He had important things to do, and she was only a friend. Like a pen pal. Which is exactly what she'd wanted all along. So exactly why did that hurt?

Why was she swallowing down a wave of disappointment?

Whatever happened, she could not give in to
hoping. Not even a little. So she sent a gentle *friendly*
prayer his way.

She would simply have to accept that it was
only natural that he would start to drift away. Their
friendship was only temporary. He was partway
through his tour of duty. By sometime in December, he would be back at his home base in California
and he wouldn't need a pen pal after that.

No. She had to simply deal with the fact that as
much as she respected Mitch and as much as she
liked him, he wasn't hers to keep. As a friend or
otherwise. Their lives had gone separate ways and
that's how it was meant to be.

She'd known that all along. Mitch would be just
another person in her life she would have to say
good-bye to. But if she was smart, she could keep
him from getting too close. That way, she could
be sure that when he did say goodbye for good, he
wouldn't be taking a piece of her heart.

It sounded logical, like a good plan. Except the
thought of losing Mitch—even as a friend—cracked
her heart a little more deeply.

Too late, she thought as she stood, taking the
empty boxes with her.

Mitch was glad to be back at camp. He wasn't
glad that it was 0500 and he was freezing, but he
tried checking e-mail anyway.

No go. No phones with the current storm. They were under whiteout conditions. When they'd be up was anyone's guess. He might as well be based out in the northern tundra for all the good these gadgets were doing him.

Frustration ate at him like the gnawing cold. The heater had conked out again and couldn't keep up with the subzero temps. And he couldn't keep up with his growing frustration.

"C'mon, Dalton." Pierce poked his head in. "We've got PT in five."

"Yeah, I know."

Mitch stood, biting down his frustration. Physical training was just what he needed. It would give him something to focus on. He'd be able to shove out these tangled emotions and struggle with something that was concrete and easier to overcome. He would push harder and harder until every problem and every feeling faded into nothing.

At least, that was the theory. But as he turned his thoughts to the workday ahead, he suspected that all the ways he missed Kelly would remain.

No matter what.

Kelly stumbled through her front door a few minutes after eight-thirty. Her veins were still pulsing adrenaline from her icy drive home. "I can't believe I made it in one piece."

"Whew, I'm glad to see you." Lexie looked up from the couch, where a thick text was open on her lap. The TV droned, volume low, in the background.

She capped her highlighter. "There was an emergency broadcast on the road conditions. I'm glad they sent you home early."

"Spence closed the store when we lost power, half the town is out, but it took me forty minutes to drive three miles." She hung up her coat and carted her backpack and computer case into the warm kitchen.

Finally, she thought as she unzipped her laptop. She'd pop online, send her daily list and maybe there'd be a letter from Mitch. And if there wasn't... well, she refused to be disappointed.

But before she could find the phone cord to plug into her computer, the lights blinked. The TV silenced. Darkness washed over them.

"No fears," Lexie said from the pitch-black living room. "I've got a flashlight here *some*where."

There was rustling, the sound of something hitting the floor, and a round beam of light came to life, highlighting Lexie's smile. "I was prepared. With the ice storm and winds, I figured we had a good chance of losing power."

"I can still dial in if there's a dial tone." She checked the line. Yes! It was working. She connected the phone cord and dialed in quickly, before she lost that, too.

"I'll light candles," Lexie said as she rescued the remote control from the floor. "You check for love letters from Mitch."

"They aren't love letters, trust me. Why does everyone have the same misconception?" Kelly knew it irritated her for only one reason—a tiny part of her was wishing for love. And how crazy was that? Insane. Certifiable. She knew better, too. Whatever it took, she would *only* allow friendship-type thoughts and feelings about Mitch.

And that was that.

There was an e-mail from Mitch waiting for her. She couldn't believe it. She had to blink twice just to make sure. His name really was there. He was safe, and he hadn't forgotten her *yet*.

She could hardly breathe past the joy filling her as she downloaded the document before the phone went out too. Lexie circled around the counter and set a pillar candle on the table. Kelly looked up. "I should get up and help you."

Lexie grinned knowingly. "You should answer Mitch. I take it he wrote?"

"Yeah," she cleared her throat, trying to sound blasé. "I guess he had time to write or something."

Lexie lit a match and set it to the wick. Just as blasé, she said, "Then I guess you should answer him or something."

"Maybe." Kelly didn't want to admit it, but everything within her yearned for the sight of his words.

This was more than simple friendship, a tiny voice at the back of her mind warned her, but she refused to listen. She was already opening the document, devouring his letter.

Dearest Kelly,

I know, I'm finally getting back to you. Hey,

your lists are great. You don't know what it means to come in after being out for over a week, and have so many e-mails waiting for me. Here's my list of things:

1. I'll never take a Saturday afternoon relaxing on the couch for granted. I especially miss this luxury after hiking with my team ten clicks with a fifty-pound pack on my back in a high-mountain blizzard.

2. Not having to watch your best buddy get shot.

3. Being warm enough to feel your hands and feet at all times.

4. Going to sleep without having first to set up claymore mines and sensors. Each man takes turns at keeping watch, but deep sleep is impossible. You're always listening for the sound of one of the mines going off, meaning your armed enemy is close while you're still in your sleeping bag.

5. Sleeping in a warm place instead of being too cold to fall asleep.

6. Life is uncertain. Never take your friends for granted.

I'll give you a call as soon as I can.
In prayer, Mitch

Wow. Kelly's jaw dropped. She couldn't imagine what Mitch had been through. She reread his words and felt sorrow for his suffering.

"What's wrong?" Lexie turned from lighting a pillar candle on the counter. Light flickered eerily as she hurried over. "Mitch is okay, isn't he?"

"I guess." What did okay mean? She didn't know. "Read this and tell me what you think."

"Mitch won't mind?"

"No, we're really just friends, and he's writing nothing that's private." At least, she didn't think so. Mostly, she couldn't quite believe what her eyes told her, and her heart didn't want to feel. She'd seen enough war movies to be able to fill in the blanks in all that he hadn't said with images of her own. "What do you think?" she asked when Lexie finished reading over her shoulder.

"I'll tell you when my jaw stops dropping. What does Mitch do, anyway? Is he Special Forces?"

"Yeah." Kelly didn't want to get online to answer him. What if he tried calling? He'd get a busy signal. "I hope his friend is all right."

"Me, too. That puts my day in perspective." Lexie pulled out a chair and sat down. "I'm really glad you sent him that care package. He probably hasn't gotten it yet?"

"Doesn't sound like it." Kelly shrugged, wishing she could do more. So much more. Then she realized it was late where he was. In the wee hours of the morning in his part of the world. He wouldn't be calling, so she tried to get back online, but the modem couldn't get a dial tone.

Just as well. She was no longer a child to believe

in fairy tales, but it was nice to know there were good guys in the real world. Very nice.

She shut down her computer and got right to her studies, but her thoughts kept drifting to him. To the radiance he brought to her soul, like starlight on a frosty winter's night.

Mitch shivered in the freezing cold tent and hooked the receiver between his ear and shoulder. While he dialed the last digits of Kelly's home number, he knew chances were good that she wasn't home. She had probably headed straight to work after her morning classes.

As he listened to the first ring and then the second, he figured he'd at least leave a message on her answering machine. He wouldn't try her cell, not when she'd probably be at work.

Sure enough, a recorded message answered. "This is Kelly," came her voice as sweet as the dawn. "And Lexie," Lexie added. "We're away right now," and Kelly's soft alto piped in, "so please leave a message!"

He waited for the beep. "Hey, Kelly, it's Mitch. I'm bummed that I missed ya. I'll try back."

He hung up, the numbers on his watch showing it was four minutes past four in the morning. He'd gotten up early just to try calling her.

Well, there was nothing to do but to keep at it. He wouldn't stop calling until he reached her. Until he could hear her voice, all heart and goodness, because he needed some of that.

He needed her.

* * *

In the silence of Amy's living room, Kelly snapped her book shut, the sound as startling as a gunshot in the sleeping house. The kids were asleep. The scents of crayons and SpaghettiOs lingered pleasantly in the air. With the fire crackling in the hearth, she should feel peaceful. It was a perfect studying climate. But could she concentrate? No.

Lexie had called about an hour ago, while she was clearing supper dishes from the table, to tell her that Mitch had called and left a message. Ever since, she'd been keeping her silent cell phone close just in case Mitch tried again.

She resisted the urge to hop online and check her e-mail account. That would make it obvious, even to herself, how eager she was to hear from Mitch. And if she was going to hold tight to her stance and to her vow to keep her feet on the ground when it came to Mitch, then she couldn't go around acting as if she wanted to fall in love with him, right?

Right.

The living-room walls felt as if they were pressing in on her until she couldn't draw a single breath. She wanted to blame it on studying too hard, but she *always* studied hard. That was no excuse. The real explanation was something she didn't want to think about.

And somehow, she had to make sure she stopped thinking about Mitch and kept every thought of him from her mind. Maybe it was better that he hadn't called. Maybe this was a sign, this pattern of missed communications. Maybe, she thought desperately and with hope, it was a sign from above reminding her she was looking down the wrong fork in the road.

Her cell phone rang. Surely that wasn't a sign, either. She checked the screen—an out of area number. Mitch, her heart hoped wildly before her common sense kicked in and she let it ring a second time. Then a third.

Now she was *definitely* in need of therapy. First she couldn't wait for him to call and now that he probably was, she didn't want to answer the phone. For some reason it felt like a monumental decision as she pressed the button to accept the call, which made no sense at all. At the back of her mind, she worried this could be her mom calling, too. "Hello?"

"K-Kelly." Above the crackle of static in the long-distance line, she heard his voice.

"Mitch." His name was on her lips, as if straight from her heart, and her voice betrayed her. Joy blazed within her. She hadn't realized until this moment how much she'd missed him. How much she'd worried over him. His voice might be her most favorite sound on earth. "I can't believe it. It's really you."

"No imposter this time. You're a difficult lady to get a hold of lately."

"Not as difficult as you are, mister. Are you okay?"

"Right as rain, or maybe I should say snow this time of year. Are you all right? When you answered, you sounded like were hesitant to talk to me. You're not at work, are you? It's okay that I'm calling?"

Please, let it be okay. Mitch gripped the phone tightly.

"Y-yeah, it's absolutely okay, I'm just babysitting. It's just that your number came through as 'out of area' and with an area code I didn't recognize. I was afraid it was my mom using a calling card from jail."

"She does that a lot?"

"No, I'm just always cautious. But you didn't call to hear about that. How is your friend doing?" There was her heart, unmistakable in the warm tones of her voice.

Man, it was good to hear. His chest twisted tight, so strong it was a physical pain that came from missing her. "Haven't heard about Luke yet. He's been flown to a hospital in Germany."

"He must have been hurt pretty badly."

"Y-yeah." He cleared his throat. He'd save thinking about what had happened, seeing his friend shot and defending him while their corpsman worked frantically to save his life, along with the rest of them. Their ambush on the enemy had been a success, and their mission was completed—but at a personal cost. As always. "All we can do is wait. And pray."

"I've been keeping him in my prayers, and Lexie has, too. I let her read your e-mail. Was that all right?"

"Sure."

Emotions tangled emotions like a knotted rope

yanked hard, because he had her on the phone, he was listening to the sound of her lovely voice and yet she felt so far away. He closed his eyes, shutting out the officers' hootch and the clatter of the heater working hard in the mountain cold. He fought to bring a picture of her into his mind.

What he saw was her that first day in the bookstore, when she'd been awash in the bright, cheerful light of summer. Her hair had glinted like pure gold and fallen in a soft swoop around her lovely face. Her rosy complexion looked as satin-soft as a rose's petal.

His throat ached as he remembered how dainty and sweet she'd looked in a pale-pink sleeveless blouse. But what he wanted was to see her now. To picture her in the solemn shadows of a November's night, when darkness came early in Montana. He could not picture her. Frustration ate at him.

Kelly's voice interrupted the static on the line. "Lexie said it best. She said that your e-mail put her life in perspective, and I felt the same way. The lists I sent, about all the little unimportant things in my day, probably didn't help you much. It probably seemed trite and disrespectful—"

"No, you couldn't be more wrong." No Kevlar vest could protect him from pain like this. Just the thought of her not writing could nearly do him in. "You have no idea how much I appreciate your lists. So, what's this about your mom?"

"Like I said, you didn't call to hear about my mother."

"I called to hear about you."

There he went, trying to get beneath the appearance of things and into a deeper part of her life where she didn't want him to go. "My mom is out of my life. End of story. Some people say that's harsh, that she deserves a second chance, but the truth is that she's on her six-billionth chance, and I just can't take any more. How is your mom doing?"

"Nice change of subject." He didn't sound upset by it, he sounded amused. "Funny you should mention her. I got a pretty interesting e-mail from her. She wanted to know how long I've been seeing you."

"No, that's not true. She couldn't possibly have thought that. I found her number in the phone book a while back—"

"And why would you do that?"

"Well, it's a surprise. Let's just say I wanted to send you something. As one friend to another, of course."

"Sure." He chuckled, as if he understood perfectly. "I bet Mom didn't see it that way. It's just wishful thinking on her part. It's not me she cares about, she said she wanted a daughter-in-law to spoil. She's never forgiven me for being a difficult kid."

"I know that isn't true. When I told her who I was and that I knew you, she went on and on about what a great man she thinks you are."

"Oh, no," he groaned. "She didn't. Really? Now I have to disown her. I can't have a mom embarrassing me like that."

She heard straight through his facade to his big heart beneath. He came from a family like this one, she thought, as she looked around the loving home Amy had made here with her husband and kids. Happiness settled in the air like stardust through the windows. A hundred pictures hung on the wall or were mounted in fat photo albums or were over-stuffed in a drawer, waiting for framing. Homemade cookies were fresh in a cookie jar on the table, and love and caring seemed to gleam like moonlight on the polished wood.

Did Mitch know how lucky he was? She thought he did. She hoped he did. "I talked to your mom for less than five minutes, but she seemed like a really lovely lady."

"That would be Mom."

Yes, she thought, he knew. She could hear it in his words. "I'm guessing that when you were grow-ing up, she baked your favorite cookies before you had the chance to ask for them. It sounds like she is still your biggest fan."

"Yeah, everyone needs that in their life. I am blessed with my parents, I know I am. I take it that your mom wasn't the kind of mother who ever baked cookies."

"No." The wounds within her began to reopen, whispers of memories that she *had* to silence.

"Or ever baked a birthday cake?"

"Good guess." She steeled her defenses. She could not let him in any deeper. "My birthday is coming up, and between that and the holidays, she often tries to contact me."

"How much longer does she have on her sentence?"

"I honestly don't know. I expect she'll be out by the end of the year." That's all she wanted to say to him. One more word and she would have opened up too far. "Speaking of time, you should be about halfway through your tour, right?"

"Will she look you up?"

"I hope she doesn't." She squeezed her eyes shut, but that didn't diminish the ugly voices of her past, murmuring in her mother's voice. How she wasn't good enough. Like mother, like daughter. How did she silence those memories? "The last time she got out of prison, she showed up pretending to have missed me, but she stole money out of my backpack when I went to make her some coffee. I'd just gotten paid and that cash was my grocery money for two weeks. I didn't have anything to fall back on."

"I'm sorry, Kelly. You've come a long way on your own."

"I'm not alone."

She touched him deeply, Mitch realized, beyond his comfort level and deeper still, where he'd never felt anything like this before. A fierce steely need to protect her anchored him, and he hated the miles that separated them. "When *is* your birthday?"

"In December."

"What day in December?"

"The second."

Okay, he knew what to do. As he checked his watch, time was ticking away, and he was looking at a hard afternoon of training ahead. But he couldn't hang up yet. He couldn't say goodbye. There was so much he wanted to say, but he was afraid of scaring her off. Afraid of moving too fast. He still didn't know where she stood, if she was moving away from him, or if he could pull her closer.

"Oh, I think I hear the baby." Her heart was showing again. "Let me just whisper, because I don't want to disturb her if she'll fall back to sleep."

He could picture her walking with care down a hallway, to check on a sleeping baby. "Who are you babysitting for tonight?"

"One of the McKaslin cousins, Amy. I've been babysitting for her since Westin, her oldest boy, was three." She paused. "Oh, it looks like little Shannon just needs some comfort. Hello, sweetie. Want me to rub your back? Oh, she's going back to sleep. I was dating Joe then."

"After all this time, they must be like family."

"Family of the heart, that's for sure. Is that what your team members are to you?"

There it was, the depth of her heart in her voice. He felt the distance and the miles melt away. It was a little like being lost in the dark, and she was a beacon lighting the way.

"Like brothers," he confessed. "We spend most of our time together. Sadly, I've got to go before they start without me. But before I do, what are you doing for Thanksgiving?"

"Oh, you're worried that I'll be alone, aren't you? Well, I've turned down Lexie's offer, and Katherine and Spence's offer and Amy's offer to join them for the holiday. I'm going to volunteer again at the free dinner that the local church charities host, and then I'm taking a meal out to my aunt at the hospital."

"I was going to have my mom invite you, if you weren't doing anything."

"That's really nice. But I'm fine. Thanks. What are you doing?"

"I'll be lucky to be here. There's a rumor we're actually getting real turkeys, but I'll have to see it to believe it. I have to go."

Kelly couldn't believe how hard it was to say goodbye. "You'll call again?"

"Count on it." There was a click and he was gone.

Oh, that man could make her feel—make her come alive—like nobody ever had. And wasn't that the problem?

It was as if he was able to see her bare to the soul, where there were no longer any shields, anything safe to hide behind. That left only the truth—of who she'd been and who she was now—and how much she longed to love again.

Longed to love him.

In the quiet of the living room she slipped her phone back into her pack. And thought of Mitch, so far away. Her heart tugged, impossibly, with emotion she could not let in. *Please, Father, watch over him, keep him safe.*

The rain battered the black windows with renewed fury and the ghosts of the past, of the truths she'd spoken of tonight, seemed to whirl in the air around her. The heavens opened as rain hailed against the roof, pounding like a thousand bullets.

She hurried down the hall to check again on the baby, but Shannon was still lost in sweet dreams, safe and soundly asleep. Looking like the precious gift she was.

What a dream it would be to have one of her own, and a life like this. Kelly couldn't help hoping, just a little, and it made the loneliness ache. Careful not to disturb the little one, she tiptoed out of the room and wandered back to her school books, which were waiting for her.

Okay, time to buckle down and concentrate on the attainable dreams in her life. She settled down to study, but every neuron in her head seemed focused on Mitch. On the big, mighty, wonderful, kind man he was.

If she closed her eyes and made a wish, it would look just like him. And wasn't that the danger? Dreams weren't meant for her. She knew that for absolute certain. But it was there, anyway. She'd fought so hard not to let a single hope take root, and it had—for a moment—but she'd dared to let in the smallest wish.

And wasn't that the problem? You started small, with the purest, tiniest wish—and before you knew it, that wish bloomed into a full-fledged, all-of-your-heart dream.

I so want him to love me.

There came the wish, the smallest hope, alive inside her. She screwed her eyes shut against the hot blinding tears that rose. The memory of the day at the river, when Mitch had pulled her against him, protecting her from the current...she wished she had laid her cheek against his chest so she would have known how it felt to be held like that by him. She longed for his tenderness as the stars longed for the night.

And it was impossible. She was in someone else's living room, with the cold November night pressing in around her and she was alone.

Always, endlessly, alone with a dream that could not possibly come true.

Chapter Thirteen

Dear Mitch,

I haven't heard from you since last week when you called. I'm keeping you and your friend Luke in my prayers. And sending warm thoughts your way. The first snow of the season fell today—late for Bozeman—but no one is complaining. Here's a list of good things in my day.

One-dollar movie night at the Garland. We watched *Pride and Prejudice* and ate a vat of fake buttered popcorn. (Lexie says hi.)

Sadly, that was the only good thing in my day. Sending my very best wishes, Kelly

My Dear Kelly,

What do you mean you only had one good thing in your day? Maybe you should add the bad things, too, because I'm not getting an accurate picture here.

Good things in my day: Word is that Luke is

gonna pull through. I'm back from stealthing around, but we're going right out on another mission. We had recognizable chow today—at least, we *think* it was chicken.
Sending my prayers, Mitch

Dear Mitch,
    I'm so glad for your friend.
    The best thing about today was that I recognized everything I ate.
    The worst thing about today was that a call came in from the county jail, which Lexie rejected (I wasn't home at the time).
    Wherever you are, I hope you're safe and, if not warm, then not too cold.
Keeping you in prayer, Kelly

Dearest Kelly,
    I'm sorry about your mom. If I don't get back in time, Happy Thanksgiving. Eat some pie for me.
Always, Mitch

Over the next week, a certain theme had started to emerge in her morning devotional and it was really starting to annoy her. Kelly wished she could take the passage to heart.

I will turn their mourning into gladness; I will give them comfort and joy instead of sorrow.

This was not helping her stay realistic with her expectations in life.

In the morning quiet of her apartment, she rubbed the pad of her forefinger over the text in her devotional. That is *so* not my life, she thought.

She had to prepare herself for the inevitable, Mitch moving away. And maybe this was it? She'd had no word from him, nothing. The logical side of her brain said that he was busy, that was the nature of his work, to be away from his base camp for days, or for more than a week at a time.

But the totally nonrational side of her knew that goodbyes were inevitable. She was not going to give in to the temptation to believe otherwise. With a thump, she closed the devotional and set it aside. She concentrated on her second cup of coffee on this leisurely holiday morning.

She had the apartment to herself. Lexie had driven home to have Thanksgiving with her parents, and the bookstore was closed today, of course. It was a rare thing to have nothing to do and nowhere to go for an entire morning. She intended to enjoy it while she could.

The trouble was that loneliness seemed to creep into the corners of the apartment like the cold air from outside. Why did her mind automatically switch to thoughts of Mitch? Of the warm, cozy rumble of his baritone, of the comforting brush of his heart against hers when she talked about her past, and of the way his chuckle, so kind and good-natured, chased away the shadows.

She was letting a wish for Mitch's love and a happy life with him take root in her soul. That was wrong, wrong, wrong. The realization sent fear zinging through her veins. What was she going to do about that? It was simple. Don't think about him. Don't go there. That was the only solution.

She took another sip of her coffee. Where did her thoughts go? To the devotional open on the table in front of her—no, of course not. Her thoughts were thousands of miles away with Mitch, wondering if he'd gotten the rumored turkey for his Thanksgiving Day dinner.

You absolutely have to stop thinking about him, Kelly. She sighed, frustrated at herself. This man was already too far into her heart for safety's sake.

Maybe she'd just get online and send him a happy holidays wish. Then she'd be able to get her mind off him, right? It was worth a try.

While her laptop dialed in, she poured another cup of coffee. But the memory of their last talk remained. How close he'd felt, how carefully he'd listened, how he'd somehow made the past less painful, the shadows less dark. That made no sense whatsoever.

An electronic beep from her laptop interrupted her thoughts. She brought her cup with her to the table, attention on the screen, her pulse skipping, because what if that was Mitch?

There, on the instant message screen, was an electronic note from Mitchell Dalton.

Kelly
   Happy Thanksgiving. And thanks. That was some care package you sent.
Mitch

   Happiness filled her up and buoyed her spirit. She dropped into her chair, already typing.

Mitch
   You got it? Great. I thought it might have been sent to Mars by mistake.
Kelly

Kelly
   I think I saw Mars stamped on the package. I had to beat off the rest of the guys. Apparently candy corns are a great hit with Force Recon marines. Second only to the candy made in the shape of garbage cans.
Mitch

Mitch
   I personally love the bottle-cap ones. Lexie went with me, and we hit every candy counter around the university. I hope you don't get too sugar-buzzed. Katherine contributed the candy canes and the tin of chocolate sugar crunch cookies.
Kelly

Kelly

Thank her for me, would you? I'm vibrating from eating all the candy corns. Apparently I didn't learn my lesson when I was six. Hey, are you gonna be home for a while?

Mitch

Mitch

I'm here for a few more hours. I'm not needed at the church's kitchen until ten-thirty.

Kelly

Kelly

Then log off and I'll give you a buzz. Deal?

Mitch

Deal. She hit Send and signed off. She was way too happy that he was calling her. But did she try to hold back her heart? No. She didn't have time to try, because the phone rang and she snatched it up before it could ring twice. "Mitch?"

"It's me." Yep, he was hooked, Mitch thought, the instant he heard her voice. He felt every inch of the distance that separated them as he leaned back in the metal chair. "Why the church kitchen? Most folks just want to take it easy, not have to work on Thanksgiving."

"I started the year Joe died, when there was an announcement in the church newsletter asking for volunteers. It sounded better than spending the day with Joe's family or alone with wishes of what could have been. I liked it, actually, so I've done it ever since."

He wasn't surprised. Classic Kelly, he thought, kindness and sincerity and the greater good. That was just another reason why he was falling in love with her. "Your mom hasn't called again?"

"No, thank goodness. I expect she'll try." Her voice went thin. "I try not to think of her, except when I have to. Did you get a nice dinner?"

"We had meat that was supposed to be the rumored turkey. When we slathered it with the pasty gravy, who could tell? It might have been turkey. I'm happy enough with that. You're a long way away. Tell me what you've been up to. What haven't you put in your e-mails?"

"Like with school?"

"Yeah, school, work, social life."

"What social life? Finals are coming up, so I have a close personal relationship with my textbooks. I'm seeing them exclusively."

"Ah. Still not dating, huh?"

She sounded choked. "You like to get right to the point, don't you? I've given up on dating forever."

"There's some poor man somewhere who is probably pretty broken up to hear that."

"I don't think so. In fact, I'm pretty sure there isn't. There can't be."

A spear of sorrow arrowed through him, it was her pain, he realized, and his pain for her. "Why not?"

"It's not meant to be. You said your friend Luke was doing better?"

"Yeah." He understood why she'd changed the subject. He'd gotten too close. He'd noticed that pattern before. She wanted to keep him at a friendly distance, where she felt safe.

Well, fine, but he was going to push that, if not now, then later, because she would always be safe with him.

But he was coming home in about three weeks' time. He had to know where she stood. The last thing he wanted between them was regret.

"Luke's still recovering. He got hurt pretty bad. Are you thinkin' that I might be next?"

"It crossed my mind."

"Don't let it worry you. I won't be. Besides, just living is risky business."

"Yeah, but we're friends. That gives me the prerogative to worry about you."

"Then I'll worry about you and we'll be even."

"What risky things do I do? Oh, I know. You're going to say that I drive."

"Yep, you get in a car every day. That's risky stuff, too." He hated the distance between them, the miles that kept him from reaching out to her and pulling her into his arms and holding her until she believed. Until she could see he had no plans to break her heart. "Is that why you aren't dating? You're afraid of caring about someone and losing them again?"

"Something like that." Her voice sounded sturdy, strong.

But he could feel the waver of emotion; he could feel how vulnerable she was. "The package you sent, it meant a lot."

"Good, because I wanted it to. You helped me when I really needed it." Her tone was friendly, but her heart betrayed her.

At least, he wanted to think it was her heart he felt, even half a world away. "Are you talking about the little bit of help I gave you on quadratic equations?"

"It made the difference between an A and a B. I know that doesn't sound like very much, but it does to me. I have a four-point grade average, and I'd like it to stay that way, since I'm looking at graduate school next year."

No, this was more than a thank-you. He looked down at the good-sized cardboard box stuffed with candy. Candy shaped like garbage cans, like popbottle tops, fruit and people. There was taffy and bubble gum and jawbreakers in every color, gummy bears and gummy worms and long red ropes of still soft and still mealy licorice.

And not only candy, but animal cookies and cheese snacks and gum and the latest military suspense he'd been wanting, cupcakes and Twinkies and packages of beef jerky. At the bottom of the box was an MSU T-shirt, extra-large. She'd sent books of word jumbles and crossword puzzles and a travelsized chess set.

Not an ordinary care package. He knew, because his mom sent them all the time. Shoeboxes stuffed with homemade brownies, not boxes full of all kinds of stuff that took time and thought to put together. Kelly might say they were friends, but her actions and the emotion in her words said more.

Good to know, since he was walking without cover. Heaven knew he was feeling out of his depth. He was a Force Recon marine, he knew how to be patient, when to wait and when to take a step forward. "You want to go to graduate school there in Bozeman, or are you looking to go somewhere else?"

"I'd like to stay here. I have to be accepted to the program first."

"You will. I believe in you, Kelly."

What on earth could she say to that? Kelly squeezed her eyes shut. Did he have to say those words as if with all the tenderness in his big heart? He made her feel like a new, twinkling star; he also stirred up pain. Like a powerful river's current, scudding along the bottom of the river bed, scraping up raw places and exposing them, the places within her that longed to love again.

But Mitch was right. It hurt too much to let someone in—especially him. What she had to do was stop this, before she'd taken another step on a path leading to where she didn't want to go. How could she let him into her heart any farther? It already hurt too much.

"Mitch, I don't think—" She bit her lips, torn

apart by pain. By fear. "I value our *friend*ship, but—" *That's all I can do,* she thought.

"I value you pretty highly, too."

The certainty in his voice frightened her as much as the tenderness in his words. It was a tenderness she could feel as if his emotions were coming right through the long-distance line, too, and into her heart.

I could love him so much. If *things were different. If I were different.*

How did she tell him that?

There was a rustle, as if he'd dropped the phone, and in the background it sounded like men were shouting. "I gotta go." It was all he said before he hung up, leaving her with an empty line.

What had happened? Was he okay? She tried to banish all the images of war she'd seen on televised news reports and told herself maybe it was a high wind, knocking out the phone connection. It didn't mean something horrible had happened.

She tasted fear as she hung up the phone. Her fingers trembled as she pulled the cup of lukewarm coffee into her hands. Fear for him double-beat through her veins and into her soul.

Please, keep him safe, Lord. It was the only thing she could do for him, so she prayed.

She could not stop the sick cold dread that had followed her all through her day and crept into her like the night's chill. Shivering from the bitter winds and covered with snow, Kelly gratefully turned the deadbolt on her apartment door behind her. The roads had been terribly icy, but she'd made it home safely in one piece.

Her day had been a busy one, but Mitch had stayed in the forefront of her thoughts, where he was still as she shrugged off her coat and hung it over the back of a chair to dry.

She pulled her cell from the pocket. No calls. She knew it hadn't rung, but she had to check anyway. It was another sign that she already cared dangerously too much for this man.

As she turned up the thermostat, she noticed the time. Eight fifty-three. No way was she going to be able to wind down enough to sleep anytime soon. Her mind was spinning with all the horrible possibilities she wouldn't quite let herself imagine—and her stomach was one nauseated knot, as it had been all day.

I'm afraid for him. She couldn't deny it. She'd sent so many prayers skyward, surely every angel in heaven had heard them by now. She dropped her stuff on the floor and sank onto the edge of the couch. What was she going to do? She ached with regret. With all the ways she would never be able to care for this man.

With all the ways she wanted to.

In the silence of the night-dark apartment she fought to keep the past from coming alive. From seeing Joe's coffin, polished black in the funeral home, feeling the shattered pieces of her heart like broken glass shards, impossible to put back together.

Her mother's words resonated in her head. "I told you. Didn't I tell you?"

She choked down the rest, forcing the images and sounds and feelings back down behind lock and key. If only she could wipe them away like an eraser over a chalkboard. Life wasn't like that.

To help chase away the shadows and the silence, she clicked on the TV and surfed, looking for something that caught her attention. But what she really wanted was for the phone to ring and Mitch's voice to be on the other end of the line.

She paused over the cable news channels for anything that would possibly concern him, but there was nothing there, and she really didn't expect there to be. He's fine, he's said over and over how well-trained he is. And, she thought, he certainly is a capable man, but that didn't break apart the concern that sat like an iceberg in the middle of her chest.

She didn't need one more sign. Look at how much she was hurting for him. Over him. This is too much, she told herself and buried her face in her hands. She wanted him to be safe with all of her might, but one thing was clear.

She was overinvolved. She cared too much. She *had* to stop ignoring the truth.

I'm in love with him. She was starting to dream, to let hope for a happy life with Mitch begin to grow. And wasn't that the worst mistake ever?

The snowstorm raged and thunder cannoned overhead. She sat unmoving while the darkness at the

edge of the lamplight's reach deepened like despair.
The phone rang once. Twice.

She leaned far enough over the arm of the couch
to read the caller ID on the living-room extension.
Out of Area. The same area code Mitch had called
from earlier in the day.

Good, he was safe, thank God, that's all she
needed to know.

She let it ring.

Chapter Fourteen

It's probably the intensive study week right before finals—that's why Kelly hadn't e-mailed him. Mitch rubbed his hands together in the cold hootch. The heaters had conked out again—they couldn't keep up with the cold. Maybe he'd send another e-mail, just so he would feel as if he'd done something instead of letting her slip away.

He started typing.

My Dear Kelly,

Sorry again that I had to cut our talk short. I know you're busy getting ready for finals, but here's another list. It's the good things I wish for you.

Easy finals that you breeze right through. Ice-free roads wherever you travel. Eggnog lattes steaming hot, every time you need one. I hope you get plenty of time to relax, take time for friends and that you have no regrets.

I'll be out, but I'll keep you in my prayers.
Love and fellowship, Mitch

And, he thought, he'd keep her in his heart. It
wasn't enough, he thought as he sent the letter whiz-
zing through cyberspace, but it was *all* he could do.

He'd leave the rest in God's hands.

"Did that poor man call *again?*" There was no
mistaking the disapproval in Lexie's voice as she
drizzled melted butter over the two heaping bowls of
popcorn. "I say the gender is entirely untrustworthy,
but there's always an exception to every rule, and I
think Mitch is that rare exception. You should date
him."

"No way. Especially not him." She didn't mention that she had his latest e-mail on her screen. That
she'd gotten online to do some research at the library
and what did she do? Check her e-mail just to see his
name listed in her inbox.

What did that say? That she'd fallen hard for him.
And that was one truth she could hardly admit to,
and it was a truth she had to change.

She studied the half dozen e-mails he'd sent, one
for every day that had passed since they'd spoken.
The first apologizing for hanging up on her, that
there had been some kind of attempt to attack their
base camp, the second came posted near midnight
his time, that they'd successfully tracked down the
insurgents, and everyone in camp was safe. And

of the remaining four e-mails, each was more concerned than the last. He was reaching out to her.

How did she tell him to stop reaching? To stop pushing? He wanted friendship. And she wanted... well, it was better not to put *that* into words.

"Why especially him?" Lexie wanted to know as she reached for the salt shaker.

"Because that man is a dream."

"Yeah. Duh. He ought to be your dream and you're going to lose this chance with him."

"A chance at what? He's stationed in California. He's just a friend. Here, let me read this." She pointed at the screen for emphasis. "'That you take time for friends.' He wrote that because I'm not emailing him back. He thinks I'm busy. So, we're friends. See? Just friends."

Lexie slipped one of the bowls on the table next to the laptop. She studied the screen doubtfully. "I saw the way he looked at you, and it has *nothing* to do with friendship."

"Exactly what does that mean?"

"Hey, don't get angry at the messenger." Lexie scooped the other bowl from the counter and filled her hand with the fluffy popped corn. "Mitch looks at you like you're a morning star he'd plucked from the sky to dream on. Write him or call him. I mean it, Kelly. He's one of the good guys."

Wasn't that the problem? And why was she so mad at him all of a sudden? Mad that he was so wonderful and perfect, that if he had been anything less than that, she wouldn't be hurting like this. She wouldn't be torn between the past and the present, between the lonely road she'd chosen and everything she was afraid of.

He wasn't hers to keep, but there was love in her heart for him anyway.

"Well, think about it." Lexie settled down on the couch and turned her attention to her schoolbooks.

I don't have to think about it. She knew exactly what had to be done. She hadn't realized how far he'd crept into her heart, but fearing for him showed her exactly how much she cared. She couldn't go back and pretend the interrupted phone call hadn't happened. She couldn't deny how deeply she'd been afraid for him or the breadth of her caring.

But neither could she take one more step on this path. She was in love with him. She didn't *want* to be in love with him because it was going to lead to heartache.

Be sensible, Kelly. She steeled her heart and gathered her defenses. She clicked closed the e-mail screen and typed in the library's address. She had priorities. She had her own goals, goals that would still be within her reach when Mitch was back safely from his tour and in California, where he belonged.

And if that broke her heart, it was only the truth. She'd learned the hard way never to dream.

Being really cold wasn't half-bad, once you got used to it. Mitch gulped down the dregs at the bottom of his C-4 cup of coffee and considered his current problem. He hunkered into his sleeping bag and considered his options.

He had second watch, so there was no sense to going to sleep for an hour, and with so much on his mind and the subzero temps in the small cavelet they'd found for the night, it would take him that long just to shiver himself warm enough to fall asleep.

His real problem was what to do about Kelly. He knew he wouldn't find an e-mail waiting for him when he got back to camp. Had he scared her off with his talk of dating and the future? Well, he'd just wanted to know where he stood and how he could make this work. Surely the good Lord hadn't brought him this far only for heartache.

Next to him Pierce was snoring, sound asleep. The next bag over Mark was writing to his wife. That's what he was thinking of doing too, except he was pretty sure Kelly hadn't written him back. She was moving away from him. He could feel it in his heart, like a light dimming.

Right now, there was nothing he could do about it. Not one thing. He only knew that he wouldn't be able to call her on her birthday like he'd wanted. It would be days before he had the chance to call, and who knew what mission after that? He was losing her.

Or was it already too late?

Lord, I need help on this one. Please. There came no answer in the frigid night.

* * *

In the pleasant warmth of the bookstore, with Christmas decorations cheering up the floor and customers shopping to the sound of holiday carols in the background, Kelly *should* have had enough on her mind with ringing up sales, gift-wrapping and helping shoppers.

In theory, she shouldn't have a free brain cell to spare, but she obviously did. And what was she doing with it? Going over her notes in her memory because her first final was cumulative and would be here before she knew it? No, she was thinking of Mitch's last e-mail. The one she'd sworn not to read, and then gone right ahead and read it.

Apparently she needed to ask for more willpower in her prayers tonight.

Kindly Mrs. Finch, her very favorite customer, ambled up to the cash wrap and slid a beautifully illustrated Bible on the counter. "Thank you so very much, young lady, for this wonderful suggestion. It's perfect. My great-granddaughter will treasure it."

"I'm sure she'll treasure you more, Opal. Would you like me to gift wrap this for you?"

"That would be wonderful, dear. I would like the paper with the golden angels."

"It will look really nice, I promise. And there's a coupon on this, so I'll ring it up at the lower price."

"That's good of you. I surely do appreciate the savings."

Kelly grabbed an in-house charge form and a pen. "This will just take a moment to wrap. You could get a cup of hot apple cider and wait in the reading area. That way you can put your feet up and relax."

"I'll do that, then." Opal's smile was as pure as always. "You and I haven't taken time to catch up. You must be working hard at your college studies."

"You know I am." Kelly rang up the sale and presented Opal with her copy of the charge slip. "Finals are coming up. You and I need to compare notes about the devotional."

"Oh, my!" Opal lit up as she slipped the charge slip into her cavernous purse. "It uplifts my spirits every day. Did you get a chance to read today's yet? 'My purpose is that they may be encouraged in heart and united in love.'"

"I did." Kelly was doing her very best not to dwell on it as she found a gift box on one of the lower shelves beneath the register. Time to change the subject. "Your great-granddaughter is hoping to get into MSU, right?"

"Now, don't change the subject, dear. I want to hear all about that handsome soldier who was so sweet on you." Opal looked delighted. "Spence mentioned him the last time I was in. Is he still serving overseas?"

"Yes, he is, and he's not sweet on me. Spence needs a talking-to." There was no venom behind her words; how could she fault Joe's cousin who was always looking out for her? He meant well. He simply didn't understand. "Mitch is only a friend."

"I'm sorry to hear that. He was such a strapping young man." Opal smiled knowingly as she turned away, adding over her shoulder, "Remember, there's more to life than studying. But don't take my advice. Turn to Scripture, dear."

This morning's devotional text popped into her mind. "My purpose is that they may be encouraged in heart and united in love."

Why did that feel so much like *not* a coincidence? Maybe because it couldn't be a sign. She refused to mistake it for one. No matter what. She would not be fooled again.

As she placed a torn-off sheet of the fragile golden-foil angel wrapping paper on the counter, the bell above the door announced another customer. Kelly recognized Holly from the jewelry shop a few blocks down, a close friend of Katherine's. "Hi, Holly, Katherine's in her office. Go right in."

"Actually, I'm here to see you." Holly set the small tasteful gift bag she was carrying on the counter. "This is from Mitch. Happy birthday."

"What?" Kelly stared at the bag, small and dainty. Only one thing could fit in a bag that small—the lovely jewelry that Holly made. "From Mitch?"

"He contacted me from his base. He'd had me hold this for him ever since you two were in my shop last summer." Holly slipped around the corner. "He must really be fond of you."

Mitch. She could only stare, stunned, at his thoughtfulness. He'd remembered her birthday. He'd remembered—no, he'd known at the time how much she'd admired the beautiful jewelry. Surely he hadn't bought the pearl angel she'd liked. No, he hadn't done that. He couldn't have. Because then that would mean *way too much*.

"Open it," Katherine said from her doorway, with a secret smile that said she'd known about this for some time. She disappeared into her office with Holly, but they left the door ajar.

Kelly's hands were shaking. A customer was approaching, shopping basket brimming, and she set the bag on the back counter. She resisted the temptation to glance inside because it would only make the locks around her heart buckle a tiny bit more.

"I'll get this." Spence stepped in with his no-nonsense attitude and stern manner, but there was a hint of a smile at the corners of his mouth as he took over her till. "You go take a break."

"Not until I get Mrs. Finch's Bible gift-wrapped." She stubbornly turned to her work, the gift bag glinting with foil threads of silver and gold.

Mitch. How was she going to keep hold of her senses now? His thoughtfulness touched her in the worst possible places. Her love for him remained, dazzling and enduring even as she fought it.

"Open the gift," Spence told her between ringing up sales. "It's your birthday. It shouldn't be a day of all work and no celebration."

"But that's why I'm here." She folded the last corner on Mrs. Finch's gift and taped it down neatly. "I'll open it later, when we're not so busy."

"What am I going to do with you?" Stern, Spence shook his head and frowned at her, but the concern in his eyes betrayed him.

She didn't know what she was going to do with herself either. She could not let herself start believing in fairy tales and happily ever afters. She was not Cinderella. She would not take a single step off her chosen path, the safe one God had graciously given her to walk. See what heartache came from dreaming? From wishing, just a little?

She secured a generous length of ribbon and made an extravagant bow on Mrs. Finch's package, slipped it into a shopping bag with a few coupons and complimentary sugar-free candy canes, and delivered it to Opal, who was enjoying a cup of apple cider and was pleased with the wrapping.

The store was busy with holiday shoppers, moms toting their babies or pushing strollers, families bursting with secrets as they browsed the store. It was like looking at the pieces of her broken hopes, seeing the happiness around her. The first year losing Joe had broken her to the core, and she had finally, two years after that, come to a numb acceptance.

Deep in her heart, in the secret quiet places only God knew, was the little girl's wish for a real family, a place to belong and someone to cherish with all of her heart. She used to believe God's promise that there would be good in her life. And love, which was the greatest of all.

But here she was, twenty-five today, with plenty of blessings and a calling to do good in this world, and what was she doing? Wishing for more than she deserved. And she knew it. Why? Because at the back of her mind she was waiting for the other shoe to fall. It was her birthday. That could only mean one thing.

"I want to see this gift," Katherine told her, after seeing Holly to the door. "Go into my office if you want some privacy first, but Kelly, this is a big deal."

"No, it's a birthday gift, something thoughtful, but it doesn't mean—"

"It does. You're still in contact with him, right?"

Kelly felt the twist of pain but she swallowed it down. Mitch. Each passing day she'd thought of him. Each day she'd resisted checking her e-mail. How did she explain? She didn't understand it herself. "I'm not dating him. You know that we're just friends."

"That's how it starts, you know."

"How what starts?"

"The real thing. True love. Happily ever after. It starts with being best friends. At least, that's what they tell me. I know, I know, you're going to start arguing with me, and that's okay. As long as you remember that as much as we all wished you could have married Joe and you'll always be a member of our family at heart, you need to move on. Find the blessings God has in store for you."

"Oh, Katherine, please don't break my heart like that." There was the past, the dreaded past, rising up like a tidal wave threatening to pull her into an ocean of feelings she did not want to face. She swallowed past the hopelessness. "Believe me, I have so much in my life to be thankful for. I have enough."

"I know the hard way—it's not enough. Life isn't quite as sweet or as meaningful without someone to love deeply."

Kelly couldn't speak past the emotions in her throat. In her heart. Weighing down her soul. She was hardly aware of Katherine steering her, along with Mitch's gift, into the cozy comfort of the corner office.

What did she do? If she didn't look inside the gift bag, then she wouldn't have to face the truth she'd been afraid of all along. She loved Mitch. He might feel more than friendship for her. Nothing could terrify her more.

Her chest clogged tight, as if buried under the weight of her broken dreams. She couldn't take one more loss. One more goodbye. *I will not step off this path.*

She swiped hot tears from her eyes, feeling as if her spirit was ripping down to the quick. It was fear that filled the cracked places and the wounded places inside her. Terror of being hurt like that again because she'd believed in the impossible.

I cannot believe in this. In what she could never have. Her finger shook as she pulled the small box from the bag. She already knew what she would find as she cradled the jeweler's box in the palm of her hand, but her pulse stalled at the gleam of pearl, and the shimmer of delicate gold that made up the halo and wings of an angel.

A small gift card said, "Here's a guardian angel to watch over you until I get back and can do the job."

Mitch. Did he have any idea what he was doing to her? She was breaking apart, the safeguards she'd built around herself crumbling like clay, exposing the raw, most vulnerable places that longed to believe. The heart of the girl she used to be when she believed in fairy tales and in dreams coming true.

When she'd believed God would find a way one day to give her real love and a place to belong.

Maybe this is your chance. The hope came in the quiet between heartbeats. It came from the deepest parts of her soul. Hope burned like banked embers breathing back to life.

I so want to love this man. What was she going to do? And even if he loved her in return...

No, don't go there. She closed the door on that thought and locked it away. No more wishes. Not one single hope. She replaced the lid on the box, and slipped the box into the gift bag.

If only she could put away the feelings in her heart as easily.

Lord, help take this wish from my heart. Please.

There was no answer. Only the constant slanting fall of the snowflakes outside the window and the faint musical rendition of "Silent Night" from the store's stereo system.

She'd never felt more alone.

Chapter Fifteen

The parking-lot lights beamed a safe path from the pizza parlor all the way to their parked cars. Since her arms were full with the pizza box of leftovers and bags of gifts from her party, Kelly held the door with her shoulder for her friends.

Lexie caught the door handle and helped her, juggling the remains of a cake. "What do you say we hit the ice creamery? We could carpool over. The roads look icy. I've got four-wheel drive."

"Sounds good to me." Jessica commented as she filed outside, zipping her parka snug. "I don't have to hurry home. How about you, Rose?"

"Count me in." Rose brought up the rear, pulling on her mittens.

It had been fairly easy not to have to think about Mitch's gift, which was tucked safely in her backpack's front pocket. But now, with the icy snowflakes brushing her cheeks and the momentary quiet as they all negotiated the icy parking lot without falling, Kelly had a split second where Mitch crowded her mind.

Maybe it was because the greasy, pepperoni tang of warm pizza drifted up through the lid of the pizza box she carried, reminding her of the bright summer night he'd shown up with pizza in hand and had affably watched the romantic comedy Lexie had picked up at the video store.

Just the remembered feeling of being in his presence that day made peace trickle all the way down to her soul. That peace remained through the hour spent at the ice cream shop and into the quiet of her bedroom where she studied, huddled in her flannel pajamas and fleece slippers, while the baseboard heater tried to keep up with the cold seeping in through the window and walls.

Why was she hurting like this? Everything within her ached like a snapped bone, and she couldn't concentrate at all on her studies. As pointless as it was, she took Mitch's gift from her backpack and opened the small box. In the bright reading lamp, the delicate angel's lacey wings and lustrous pearl gown gleamed like a promise.

This was no minor trinket and not a simple gift. This had come from his heart. She rubbed her fingers over the black inked words, written in a delicate script, probably Holly's, but she knew they were Mitch's words. "Here's a guardian angel to watch over you until I get back and can do the job."

Katherine's words from today troubled her. *The*

real thing. True love. Happily ever after. It starts with being best friends.

She forced the fears and the whispers from the past aside.

Is there a way, Lord? Could Mitch really be meant for me? Every cell of her being hurt with the wish. In the deepest places within her soul, she wanted to believe. But was it possible?

Losing Joe still had a hold on her. How did she find enough faith to believe that the future could be different? That there were good things waiting for her, good things that wouldn't be jerked from her the minute she reached for them?

The phone rang. When she checked the caller ID, it was Out of Area, from an area code she didn't recognize. It was her birthday, and that was often a day her mom tried to contact her, but what if it was Mitch calling?

"I bet it's Mitch," Lexie called from her room.

I bet it is, too. It would be just like him to call to-night. She lifted the receiver, longing for the warmth of his baritone and a connection to him, and terrified of it at the same time. "Hello?"

There was no crackle on the line, no overseas static. The hesitation was all wrong. She knew who it was before she heard her mother say her name. "Kelly? Is that really my sweet baby?"

I should have had Lexie answer it, Kelly realized, too late. The voices from her past rose up, and there were no defenses strong enough to stop them. Memories she'd held down for so long crashed like a tidal wave, making the past so immediate and vivid she could taste the hollowness and desolation. She knew this was part of her mom's pattern—she'd try to make up and then the pleas for money would start. Then the stealing.

"Mom," she managed to choke out. "You're not supposed to call me. The court said you can't."

"But you're my own little girl."

How many times had she heard that phrase? When she'd been six years old, holding her mom's hair when she was sick from being drunk. When she was ten years old and her mother was high on drugs. When she was twelve years old and they had lost their apartment and were standing in line at a shelter.

Stop it. She squeezed her eyes shut, gritting her teeth, but the images just kept coming. Her mom's anger when Kelly had wanted to live with her aunt Louise. The calls and every attempt to visit whenever Kelly had her life finally leveling out. Her mom arriving uninvited at Joe's funeral and whispering, after the service, "It's just as well he's gone. You might as well learn it now. No one's gonna love you enough to last, girl. You're too much like me."

For once, Kelly broke the pattern and hung up the phone. It was as if all the footholds she'd built to hold up her life buckled and came crashing down. What if her mother was right? That's exactly how it felt. What if every time her life became stable, all it took was her past to knock it down? What if the foundations of her life, her beginnings in life, were not strong enough to support a good future? Whatever the case, Kelly couldn't allow her mother back in her life until the woman made a significant effort to heal.

As time ticked by she placed the jeweler's box into her backpack. After a while, the dark shadows did not seem so bleak. The memories of the girl she'd been, heart wide open waiting to belong, faded away.

She didn't know how long it was until the phone rang again, and Lexie hurried through the doorway. "We'll just turn off the ringer. Is there anything I can do?"

Kelly shook her head.

"I'll make you some tea. My mom says honey and chamomile tea makes anything a little bit better." Lexie disappeared.

Kelly reached for her Bible. She knew that the Lord worked all things for the good of His faithful. Sometimes it was all she could do to believe, but she held on to her faith with both white-knuckled hands and did not let go.

In the bleak gray of the rugged eastern Afghanistan landscape, Mitch huddled with his team. The spot they'd chosen was well-hidden from the road below, and it offered good protection from the cruel wind whipping down from the glaciered peaks. Hunkered down, they should be undetectable, but he stayed on high alert.

Pierce leaned close, speaking in a voice lower

than a whisper. "Not a lot of activity. Doesn't feel right, though."

"Nope. Like we're in the crosshairs." It wasn't a good sign when the hunters felt hunted. He scanned the lower, opposing slope with his gun scope.

Nothing. Maybe it would stay that way. A few more hours, they would radio command, and come dark, extraction. He'd be on a bird out of here.

And then he felt it, as if a steady light in his heart winked out. It was Kelly. She was gone, just like that, and he knew that he'd lost her love. That she had let go of him.

And there was nothing he could do about it.

Hopeless, Kelly opened the window blinds so she could feel the gray light of dawn fall across her face. Exhaustion settled around her like the freezing fog outside, cloaking her, keeping her numb. Her heart beat dully, without feeling, like the deadness that follows a great shock.

Or a great loss.

How can I do this? How can I find the words to tell Mitch goodbye? Rising tears burned in her throat.

Outside the window, freezing fog shrouded the treetops and veiled the sky and mountains from view. Snow mantled the world, clung to the barren poplar limbs, covered the sidewalks and street and rooftops below, and frosted the view like icing on a cake. The gray cold seeped into her soul.

Being alone was the truth of her life. A truth she'd

learned to accept the hard way. She didn't want any more lessons teaching her that. The ones she'd had so far had been painful enough. She couldn't go through that loss one more time.

You have to let him go, Kelly. She felt the past whisper. Felt the pain of Joe's loss rising up through the numbness. The wounds within her began to reopen, whispers of memories that she could no longer silence. Joe, who'd come from the black-sheep branch of the McKaslin family, who'd grown up with his dad in and out of jail, who'd understood. How her greatest fear in life was that her mother was right.

How would Mitch understand?

What if God had already worked a miracle in her life, bringing her on this path instead of into a desperate life like her mother's? What if this was the great good meant for her and there would be nothing more?

Down deep, she knew, if she took one step off this path and risked her heart again, everything would crumble. She'd had that lesson over and over again. Fear clawed through her, sharp-taloned and relentless.

I don't need to hurt like that one more time.

Letting him go was the sensible thing to do. It was the right thing to do, the safest decision. Just do it, Kelly. Stop procrastinating. Do the right thing.

She stared at her computer screen, alone in the apartment, heartsick. How was she going to say goodbye? She had no heart left to feel with. No faith left over to try to believe. Even if he was her dream come true. Even if he was everything wonderful and noble and good she'd ever believed in. Summer felt so far away, with the bright green world and bold sunshine and the rumble of Mitch's laughter as he'd hauled her out of the cool river.

That's how it starts, Katherine's words came back to her. *The real thing. True love. It starts with being best friends.*

She buried her face in her hand and remained perfectly still, letting the past settle down, hoping the memories would release her, but they didn't. There was no solace, no comfort as the heater clicked on, whirring under the curtains, which swayed and billowed. The pain and emptiness of her past was nothing compared to the anguish of this moment without Mitch. And of all the moments to come without him.

She covered her mouth, stopping the sob from escaping. Nothing could stop the grief shattering her soul.

I'm so sorry, Mitch. She was a realist these days, and not a dreamer. She would keep both feet on the ground. Mitch was not hers to keep. Not now. Not ever.

All the prayers in the world wouldn't change it.

Her vision blurred as she placed her trembling fingertips above the keys. Just when she thought she couldn't take another goodbye, here she was, typing that dreaded word that cut like a blade through her soul.

Battle-weary and heartsick, Mitch wasn't at all surprised to see a single e-mail from Kelly waiting for him. He was exhausted, the images on the screen blurred. He scrubbed his eyes and tried to focus.

This could not be good news. He could feel it in his gut, the same way he'd known in the bush deep in enemy territory that things were about to go south.

Retreat would be safer.

He opened the e-mail and felt as he had on the side of the mountain, as if he were caught in a rifle's scope.

Dear Mitch
First of all, I hope you are safe and well. I care about you and I always will, and I want good things for you and your life.

He rubbed his beard, greasy from face paint, and tried to calm the shock settling in his chest. He'd known this was waiting for him. That wasn't what surprised him. It was that she was really doing it, that there was no way to undo this. He was half a world away and it might as well be the whole universe separating them. She was ending it. No, he corrected, feeling the void in his heart. She already had.

I'll always be glad you walked into the bookstore that bright summer day. You have no idea how much I will treasure this time I've spent being your friend, but I have to say goodbye. Although I was touched by it, I can't accept your

gift. Finals start next week, and I'm going to be too busy to e-mail, and by the time they're done, you'll be home in California and you'll have no more need for a pen pal, I'm sure, so I'll just say goodbye.
Kelly

Goodbye. He stopped breathing at her words. It took a moment to sink in. She was returning the gift. Pretending all that had ever been between them was a pen-pal thing.

His heart broke, piece by piece, cracking all the way down to his soul. How could she end it like this?

"Dalton." It was Scott, the corpsman, lumbering into the hootch looking as haggard as Mitch felt. "I gotta take a look at your arm."

"It's nothing. Just a little shrapnel."

"After you hit the shower and chow, stop by and let me look at it. You'll need stitches."

"Nah. I'm good." It wasn't the jagged gash or the hunk of metal he'd pulled out of it that was his problem.

"You'd better come, or I'll hunt you down," Scott called over his shoulder on his way out.

The hootch was empty this time of day, and the sounds of other teams training outside faded into the background. Mitch rubbed his forehead with the heel of his hand. How was he going to fix this? Was it possible? It had to be. *Right, Lord?*

No answer. He'd halfway expected one, he

thought as he thumbed a calling card from his pocket. How could he have lost so much in a single day? He hauled his overtired body out of the metal chair. It was 0400 in her part of the world. He'd call her after he showered and put some food in his gut. Maybe by then he would have mastered this pain. Maybe by then he would have figured out a way to fix this.

He knew one thing for sure. He would not give up, he would not give in, and he would not go down. Nothing in his life had ever mattered like this. Kelly was his heart's choice.

No matter what.

He prayed to God that he could still be her choice, too.

In the cocoon of the university's library, Kelly chose an empty table next to the stacks. All around her other students were busy studying, reading or researching. She had a few more facts to look up for her term paper, which was due tomorrow. As she unzipped her laptop case, she noticed an ROTC student in his uniform seated two tables over.

Mitch. Her life had been just fine until he'd first walked into the bookstore. From that moment, her life had changed. She hadn't realized it, but coming to know him and fall in love with him had filled a place in her soul she hadn't known was empty. A place that had never been filled before.

It was empty now, like her life. How had he come to mean so much to her? Mitch had become a part of her day. She hadn't realized all the time she'd spent thinking about him, or finding fun things to tell him in e-mails, or looking forward to checking her inbox and seeing his name there.

Every time she'd turned on the TV, she'd checked the news channels. When she saw the reports and footage of the devastation left by car bombings, or reports of the latest military conflict far from home, she knew that Mitch was out there with his men and his weapons and his skills doing his best to protect freedom.

And his gift...the image of his words were etched in her mind. He wanted the job of watching over her.

How had it come to this? How had she let it?

Forget his strength and tenderness. Forget the joy he'd brought to her life. Forget the emotional connection he'd made to her heart.

Forgetting wasn't so easy. Longing filled her, an unstoppable love for Mitch. With every breath she took, it was as if more love filled her up. More affection for him. She couldn't stop it. She wasn't strong enough to stop it.

Take this love for him from my heart, Lord. Please.

There was no answer. Just the one in her heart growing stronger and more true. Right along with the dreams she knew better than to let herself start believing.

In the purposeful activity of the staging area, Mitch shivered in the open air, despite the adrenaline kicking through his veins. He was packed and good to go, except for this one last thing. Impatient, he waited for the satellite phone to connect.

So far away, the line began to ring in Kelly's apartment. He counted the rings above the drone of the prepping helicopters. Two. Three. Four.

C'mon, Kelly, pick up. Gritting his teeth, he waited, his heart dark and empty. Four rings. Five.

He bowed his head. *Please let her answer, Lord. I'm out of time here.*

Six rings. Then an electronic beep. He hung on, he needed to talk to her. He needed this fixed before he went out. Then he heard it, her voice. Her sweet soft voice.

"Please leave a message," was all she said. The gentle sound was like a guiding light in a dark storm, and eased some of the pain down deep.

He scrubbed his hand over his face. Leaving a message was the last thing he wanted. "Kelly, if you're there. Pick up."

Nothing. He knew she was there. Rent down to the soul, he did the only thing left. He told her the truth.

"I'm headed out on a pretty serious mission. I don't know when I'll be back. I just…want to know what I did wrong."

He waited, *feeling* her on the other end, listening to him. He knew what the losses she had suffered could do to a person. He was guilty of some of that himself—closing your heart off and staying distant to keep from getting too close and feeling too much. It was easier.

But it was no way to live. Maybe God had led him to Kelly, because she needed more.

And, Mitch was man enough to admit, he needed more, too.

He cleared the raw emotion from his throat. "You are an awesome blessing in my life, and I—" Love you more than I thought possible, he didn't say, he held back the truth, the frightening truth because he could feel her rejection ready to fall like a thrown grenade.

"Don't forget me." It was all he could say before his throat closed. He loved her. No matter what. And that love, even if she could not return it, remained, not fading, and not budging.

I'll be back, he promised as he handed back the phone, grabbed his MP-5, ready to roll.

Lord, please keep her heart open to me, he prayed. But a cold fear began to gnaw at him. What if there was no way to fix this? What if it was too late?

His future stretched out before him without her, without light. Like the sun going down on his life.

Safe in the warmth of her apartment, Kelly turned away from the answering machine, pressed her face in her hands and fought the bleak, heartbreaking grief. The last hope within her had died.

Letting him go wasn't easy. It *was* the best thing. The safest decision for them both.

But it didn't feel that way. Neither determination, nor distance, nor her own fears could halt the love she felt for him. She feared nothing could.

At least it was over, she thought with relief. She had her path in life, and Mitch had his.

Chapter Sixteen

It was Christmas Eve, and Kelly was thankful she had volunteered to work at the bookstore until closing. It kept her from thinking, and since her thoughts always wandered to Mitch, it was a good thing to keep busy. It was easier to ignore her shattered heart that way.

As she carefully removed the porcelain figurine from the front window display she had a perfect view of the dark parking lot as an SUV pulled off the street and maneuvered through the snow.

Although the snowfall obscured all but the headlights from her sight, the vehicle parked right in front, beneath the filtered glow of the tall security lights. The driver's door open and a booted foot hit the ground. Her pulse jerked to a stop.

That was a military boot, just like Mitch wore. No, it can't be him. She froze, the warmth of the store, the caroling of the sound systems, the frantic bustle of last-minute shoppers faded into nothing.

There was only the sight of the soldier dressed in camouflage climbing from his vehicle. One look at his wide shoulders and joy speared through her soul.

Mitch. The cry came from the deepest part of her being. In the exact same split second her eyes registered that the man wasn't as tall or as powerfully muscled, and, as he cut through the light crossing in front of the vehicle, he wasn't Mitch.

Disappointment left her arctic cold. The pain of it left her light-headed, but she could not look away from the soldier, who opened the passenger door and helped a woman from the front seat.

Kelly could only stare, captivated, by the sight of the soldier and his wife as they gazed into one another's eyes for a brief moment—a moment that seemed to stretch timelessly—before he turned to lift a baby in a carrier from the back seat. The loving family was straight out of her most secret dreams.

It was like looking at what might have been, what could have been.

What still might be, her heart whispered so strongly.

It can never be, she thought firmly. Hadn't she put all her foolish wishes to rest?

The couple approached the front door, and the soldier released his wife's hand to open it for her. They smiled loving, quiet smiles to one another, clearly bonded in love.

Broken pieces of her dreams were all around her, but she managed to smile at the couple who entered the store and walked past her, hands linked, talking low and warmly to one another.

See how I don't want that at all? She thought as she took a sheet of bubble wrap and carefully covered the exquisite shepherd with it. Okay, she was just saying that to protect herself. To try to make it true. It was basic psychology. You simply couldn't lose anyone you loved truly, if you refused to love anyone that much.

By the time she'd boxed the figurine, wrapped it and added the purchase to Opal Finch's charge account, Katherine was ringing up the soldier and his wife, who had purchased a blown-glass angel, a last-minute gift.

It took all her strength, but she couldn't stop a great sense of loss from wrapping around her. Wasn't she supposed to be forgetting Mitch? Moving on with her life? She'd prayed and prayed for God to take this love from her heart, but it remained, stubborn and strong no matter what she did to try to get rid of it.

She delivered the gift to Opal, waiting in the reading area where refreshments and Christmas cookies were set out on red-clothed tables. Opal glanced up from chatting with her daughter, and her smile shone warmly. "You are a lifesaver, dear girl. I was at my wit's end when I learned Margie's mother-in-law was coming to town after all."

"I'm glad I could help." Kelly handed the bagged package to Opal's youngest daughter, a lovely middle-age woman with Opal's same smile and gracious manner. "If there's anything else you need, you just let me know. I hope you both have a Merry Christmas."

"I wish you Merry Christmas, too, dear." Opal looked lovely and content as she sipped from her cup of holiday blend tea. "Margie and I have done all our running for the day, and it's a comfort to sit right here and enjoy the decorations. Will I see you at the candlelight service tonight?"

Kelly fetched the teapot, still hot in its cozy, and removed the insulated cover. She leaned to fill Opal's cup. "I'll be there."

"Wonderful. Why, you'll just have to meet my new great-grandbaby. She's just three weeks old, but good as an angel. You make sure and come find us."

"I promise," she vowed as she filled Margie's cup.

If Kelly was given a wish to be fulfilled by the angels on this cold Christmas Eve night, it would be to have a life like Opal's. To be content in her golden years with family she took joy in, and a life behind her in which each and every day had been filled with love, as would all her days to come. Loving Mitch, of course.

Too bad she wasn't the kind of girl who believed in wishes and dreams.

Although how she wanted to.

"Kelly, did you read from your devotional this morning?" Opal asked over the rim of her teacup. "'With the Lord, nothing is impossible.'"

Kelly replaced the teapot on the table. How did

she answer that? Some thing *were* impossible, she knew that for certain. "I did read the passage."

"I'm holding out hope for you." Opal's eyes twinkled. "It's the season for miracles, you know."

"I know, and there's more to life than studying. I can't argue with that." Mitch. Why did she think of him and miracles in the same breath?

The store's frantic Christmas Eve rush had thinned ten minutes before closing time. As she pitched in to help Katherine catch up on the gift-wrapping at the front counter, she tried to get her thoughts in the right place. No more thinking of Mitch. End of story.

As she folded and taped the last corner of Mr. Brisbane's gift, Katherine surprised her by withdrawing a small package from her blazer pocket, wrapped in simple gold tissue paper. "I know we're exchanging presents when you come over to dinner tomorrow, but I want you to have this. It will look perfect on your Christmas tree."

Kelly studied the small gift that fitted in the palm of her hand. "Thanks, Katherine. Should I open it now?"

"No, this is definitely something you should open alone. Why don't you do that now? Go. I wanted to let you go earlier, paid of course, as a treat, but who knew we were going to be so busy?"

"I have no one waiting for me at home. I can stay and help you close."

"I'm not doing anything but unplugging the coffeepot, counting down the tills and setting the alarm.

That's it. So, go on." Katherine took the gift from Kelly's hand, snapped a gift bag open and dropped it in, and clipped around the long counter. "Go home, Kelly. Merry Christmas."

"Merry Christmas, Katherine." She so loved working for the McKaslins. There was no way she would ever feel lonely in her life, not when she had the blessing of truly nice people in it. There was little to do but to wave goodbye to Opal and her daughter, grab her coat and backpack and trudge out the back door.

Snow fell in a thick veil, scouring her as she fought her way to her car. Her poor ten-year-old sedan was buried in snow, and by the time she'd swept off the windows and scraped the crusty layer of ice off the glass, her curiosity was getting the best of her. What had Katherine given her?

Huddled in her cold seat, with the defrosters on high fighting at the foggy windshield, she folded back the tissue paper and there, in a bed of gold, lit by the glow of the dash lights, was a small tin soldier. An ornament for her tree.

Her heart broke into a million pieces, and how could that be? It was already broken. Tears struggled to the surface, no matter how hard she blinked to stop them.

I love him so much, she thought, not knowing if she was wishing or, more, if she were praying. She'd lost too many people she'd loved. That was her life, it was not going to change. It was impossible. Right?

Mitch was an elite soldier. Talk about a risky profession. And it wasn't only the fear of him being killed in combat, but the fact that he belonged in California, and that she was safer with him far away.

This was the path God had made for her, and she clung to it with everything she had. It felt as if the ground was crumbling beneath her feet and she was holding on to a fraying rope. Watching it unravel. Watching it snap.

Knowing she about to fall.

With the Lord, nothing is impossible. The text seemed to follow her as she put her car in gear and navigated through the storm. Or was it the fear in her own heart? She tried to banish memories of the lost little girl she'd been, stubbornly clinging to the hope for the happy endings, like those she read in books.

She fought against the memories as she negotiated the icy city, but the images of Christmases past rose up, unbidden and unwanted. The Christmas Eves her mom had come home horribly drunk or high, and the Christmas Eves when she hadn't come home at all.

As a little girl, Kelly would sit in the living room of whatever apartment they'd been in that year, with no glow from a Christmas tree and no presents, and wish on the brightest star in the sky, which she'd thought was the real Christmas Star, for her mom to get well. For a place to belong. To grow up like the princess in the fairy tales and find true love, a good handsome prince—just like Mitch—and a happily ever after.

Even now, there was Mitch. In her thoughts. In her heart. In her soul. Snow fell harder as she eased down the street in front of her apartment building. If she saw a tan Jeep covered with snow along the curb, it had to be her imagination. She pulled into the nearly vacant lot—most students had fled campus for home—and shut off the car.

Snow tapped in big determined flakes, blanketing her windshield. She glanced at the ornament, cloaked in night shadows, and felt the truth bubble to the surface. She still felt like that little girl, deep at heart, alone in the dark, afraid of being alone forever. The little girl feared she wasn't good enough to love. And if something good happened to her, then it wouldn't last.

Now she was an adult with the same fears, fears she'd never faced, and never overcome. Maybe pushing everything down wasn't the best way to deal with them, she knew, but it didn't matter now.

Tucking her heart away, she zipped the soldier ornament into her backpack and stepped out into the freezing storm. The snow tapped loudly, filling the eerie emptiness of the parking lot. Her thoughts drifted to Mitch, always to Mitch. Where was he on this holy night? Was he cold or warm? In hostile territory or home with his family? He'd come back from his last mission safely, right?

Wherever he was, she wished him warm, safe thoughts. She would always love him, no matter what, no matter how far away and how separate their paths in life.

A hunched shadow emerged from around the corner of the building, barely visible through the haze of snowfall.

Alarm coiled through her even before she recognized the woman's voice, the sound from her past, the sound of her fears.

"K-Kelly, my sweet baby? Is that you?" Her mother's thin hair sticking out beneath a worn-looking knitted hat was gray, and her face was marked by time and hard wear. She had that false look of caring on her face.

Kelly took a step back, fighting down the shame and the hurt roiling up out of the shadows of memories. She caught a faint scent of cheap whiskey. Of course her mom was drinking. She knew her mother would never change, and that meant the woman had come for sympathy and to try to steal something to support her other habits. It was the past that hurt so much, the memories and the betrayal. "You have to go back to the shelter, Mom. It's not that far."

"But I come all this way. In the cold. Just to see my baby girl."

"No, Mom. You know you're supposed to keep away from me." She felt the weight of the past like an open wound, bleeding and raw. "The court says you have to."

"But I'm clean." She swayed as she limped along the snowy walkway. "I brought you a present. Are you gonna let me come in?"

"I don't want something you stole." The rank scent of cheap alcohol on the wind was stronger, bringing up memories that cut straight to her spirit. "I'm sorry. You have to go now. Go back where you belong."

"That is no way to treat your mother. What is wrong with you? No wonder you're all alone. You think you're so high and mighty, but go ahead. All that praying won't change the truth. You're still the same down deep."

She knew that her mom was drunk and mean, but logic didn't rule the heart. Nor did fears nurtured by a lifetime of being alone. Kelly took another step back, whipped her cell phone out of her pocket. "Mom, you aren't supposed to leave the shelter, I'm sure. So, if you'll be nice, I'll call a cab and pay the fare for you. Or I can call the police. It's up to you."

"Why, you no good little—"

Before her mother could fly at her, a tall, powerfully shouldered man materialized soundlessly out of the shadows. Coming through the thickly falling snow and shadows, he caught Dora Logan by the upper arm, subduing her. "You heard Kelly. You need to get to a shelter, or you'll be dealing with the cops."

Mitch. His baritone boomed with authority. He radiated honorable strength. That attractive capable masculinity. Just like that, he was in her life again. Towering before her, looking like her best and brightest wish, too good to be true. Sweet longing welled up through her soul.

As her mother left, sputtering curse words that faded as she melted into the darkness, Mitch remained, invincible, at her side. For an instant, she felt as if it was summer again, with sunshine on her face and Mitch's presence like a steady light in her heart.

But then she realized he had to have heard her mom's words. Every last one of them. The damage was done. Her head hung, and in the endless stretch of silence between her and Mitch, she couldn't think of a single thing to say to make this better, to erase the echo of her mother's words. Or the truth of them.

She heard the icy flakes tap against her hood as she stumbled toward the steps. Her throat was one giant knot of misery she couldn't speak past, not even to thank him. For, in saving her, he'd learned the terrible truth of who she was and where she came from.

He now knew that beneath the responsible girl and straight-A student and faithful Christian, she was afraid that she wasn't worthy of being loved. That her past was like a wandering black hole sucking up all the goodness that would ever happen in her life.

She started up the snow-covered stairs, shame sputtering through her.

"Kelly, are you all right?"

She shook her head; she wasn't all right. His question was like a knife piercing deep. She hesitated midstep. "Thank you for—" She couldn't look him in the eye so she stared into the storm where her mom had disappeared. Her throat closed up again. What did she do now?

"C'mon, let's get you out of the cold." Mitch padded towards her like a lone alpha wolf.

She didn't have to look to know how shadows darkened the hazel-green of his eyes or to see the wince of sorrow around his mouth. She felt the emotion in his heart as if it were her own. She didn't want to feel so much, to be too close to anyone. Ever again.

But he was coming ever closer, the nearly silent sound of his boots halted directly behind her. She could feel his affection radiating like the wind against her cheek, and when she heard the faint rustle of his jacket she knew, even before the solid weight of his big hand settled on the dip of her shoulder. Peace trickled into her cracked heart like hope, like mercy. And her love for him flared brightly, like a light burning despite the darkness, a love she could not put out.

His touch remained, firmly guiding her as they ascended the steps together. Helpless to stop him, unable to speak, her hopes gone, she swiped the snow from her face and felt tears burn behind her eyes. Whatever she did, she would not cry. Could not.

She had to face this—face him—with as much dignity as she could muster. She was a pro when it came to pushing shame and hurt down into the rooms of her heart and locking the door. She had to do that now.

He was going to withdraw now—she knew it. He'd seen her in a different light—and he would never see her the same way again. The only thing she could do was to expect his coming rejection and his inevitable departure.

Her fingers fumbled stupidly with her key ring.

"Let me." His words were a gentle fan against her cheek as he leaned closer and took the keys from her.

For Mitch, all it took was one touch to her hand and a supernova of certainty blazed through him. He felt whole. It felt right, having her here at his side. Tenderness brightened in degree and volume until his heart could not hold it all.

As he unlocked the door and held it for her, blocking the worst of the wind-driven cold, he had time to think. He could see why Kelly was so persistent at pushing him away. Well, other than Joe, whose leaving had been accidental, he could see a long line of people in Kelly's life who hadn't had the character or the inner fiber to love her enough to stick by her.

It made sense, he thought, as he followed her into the apartment and closed the door against the driving snow, that she'd lost faith. She felt her heart had been broken too much. A long line of experiences of never belonging, of never having anyone to depend on, might lead you to believe that.

But he was the one man who knew how to stand and fight for what—and who—mattered. He saw now why people risked so much for the chance at real love. For the chance to make a marriage work, despite the uncertainty and the failure rate. He would have no life of any value unless he had her at his side. She gave meaning to his life. To him.

The question was, had he come all this way for nothing? He couldn't see an answer either way, yes or no, as she shrugged out of her snow-flocked parka.

He was used to danger, he was well-trained and prepared to handle any adversity in the field. He risked his life every time he went out on a mission. He spent his life training and working and practicing to be good at what he did. But when it came to Kelly, he was walking along a vulnerable path. No flak jacket existed to protect him from heartbreak if she shot him down.

She held out her hand for her keys. "Th-thank you for coming along when you did." Her voice echoed faintly in the hallway, and she didn't meet his gaze. "I-I'm glad you're back safely."

"Good." Mitch placed her keys in her gloved palm. "I need to know that you care for me. And how much."

What did she do with this man and his constant caring? She wanted to lash out, to say whatever it took to push him back, to put safe distance between her heart and his.

She squared her shoulders and faced all six-feet-two-inches of him. If only there was a way to change the deepest places within her, all the cracks and old wounds, so that she was good enough and whole enough to try to hold a dream again. A part of her wanted to tell him the truth, the part of her that loved him beyond all reason and good sense and with every last bit of her soul.

He padded closer, soundlessly, as stealthy as a stalking wolf, until he towered over her, close enough to touch, one hundred percent good man and noble heart. "Maybe it would help if I went first."

"I don't think that will help at all." All it would do was to shatter her a little deeper. She had no more strength, she was not strong enough to keep the walls around her soul from crashing down.

He took a box out of his pocket and cradled it in his palm. "This is why I'm here. To ask you to be my wife."

Yes, her heart answered. She knew it was impossible, she was too afraid to believe. Her soul ached with dreams yet to be made and wished and to come true.

Step away, Kelly. Right now. Her heart did not want to. Her soul felt ripped apart and she couldn't do it. She wanted to pray for the chance to say yes to this man, to wear his wedding ring and take his name and share his life.

There I go, dreaming again. Believing in fairy tales. She was a realist these days and not a dreamer. She would keep both feet on the ground. Mitch was not hers to keep. Not now. Not ever.

All the prayers in the world wouldn't change it.

Wait, her heart told her. *Only* prayer can change it.

He cradled her chin with his free hand, gazing down at her and in his hazel eyes she could see his soul, full of love for and devotion to her.

Both the little girl she'd been and the woman she was ached to know what real love was like—real love that could last. That could shelter her from the storms of life, that would show her a loving man's tenderness and care.

If only she could have this man to love. If only God could see fit to change her path, change her destiny and give her this one chance. *Please, Lord.* Her entire soul shattered with need.

As if Mitch heard her prayers, he slanted his mouth over hers. Her spirit stilled. Her heart paused. He covered her lips with his in a tender caress.

Her soul sighed. His kiss was like a dream. Sweetness filled her. Like the river whirling over the rapids, the power of it burst through her with the purest force—and there was no way to stop it. She breathed in the brightness. She curled her fingers into his snow-damp shirt and held on to this perfect moment. Where there was no emptiness. No shadows. No pain.

Just the rush of true love swirling up from her soul. Filling the emptiness. Pushing out the shadows. Healing every crack and fissure and broken place inside.

"I know you're afraid of loving and losing again," he said as he pulled an engagement ring of pearls and diamonds from the box he held. "But I want you to know that the love I have for you in my heart is infinite. Nothing can end it. Nothing can diminish it. Not hardship, not distance and not death. The truth is, only God knows what is going happen, but I want you to know I'm committed. I want to walk the rest of my life with you. So, will you marry me?"

She rubbed the heel of her hand over her heart, surprised it was whole. Didn't the Bible tell her to hold on until morning? All sorrows ended, all hurts would heal, and joy would come? She had enough faith, after all, to dream. "I love you with all of my soul. Yes, I will marry you."

"I am so glad." He slipped the ring on her trembling finger. "Because my mother is hoping you'll come to church with us tonight. She's vowed to spoil you. As for me," he brought her into his arms and cradled her to his heart, "I'm going to love you forever."

"That's a promise I'm going to make you keep." She saw the future stretch out before her, full of promise, of family, of loving Mitch.

It was a night of miracles, she thought, as she laid her cheek against his granite chest. It had been a rough journey, but God had seen her through. He had brought her here, to Mitch. She was sure now that there would be more miracles to come.

* * * * *

Dear Reader,

Thank you for choosing *A Soldier for Christmas*.
I hope you enjoyed Kelly's story as much as I did
writing it. Kelly fears her past may always have a
hold on her and that's why she's afraid to believe
in the possibility of a happy future. That is until the
right man comes along to show her differently.

Sometimes it is so hard to understand why we have
to go through difficulties or pain in our lives. It is a
comfort to know that God doesn't leave us to deal
with hard times alone, but walks with us through our
sorrow to the other side, where joy is always waiting.
If you are walking through a painful time, please
don't lose hope. The best is yet to come.

Wishing you peace and grace,

Jillian Hart

CLASSICS

#1 CBA Bestselling Author

DEE HENDERSON

brings you two heartwarming stories of love,
redemption and faith

The Marriage Wish

&

God's Gift

Available January 2012 wherever books are sold.

www.LoveInspiredBooks.com

LIC65151